THE LAST GOOD-BYE

Slowly, she pushed up on her elbow, pausing when the mattress creaked. One look confirmed Pete was still sleeping. His head was tipped her way, his mouth slightly open. The little bit of light coming through the slit in the curtains highlighted blond hair falling across his forehead, the shadow of beard on his jaw. Even his long eyelashes, blond at the root, darkening to a warm brown at the tips. She listened to the steady draw of his breath, watched as his bare, muscular chest rose and fell, and felt a little of her heart break all over again.

She was doing the right thing. Leaving now before it was too late. Before he was more embroiled in this whole mess. She now knew Busir was just a hired thug, that this went higher than she'd thought, into the SCA, possibly into INTERPOL. If this was ever going to be over, she had to figure out who was behind it all. What she'd seen and how it all meshed together. She knew where she had to start, and she knew she didn't want Pete tagging along. Not when she was starting to question his involvement from the very beginning. What if she'd been wrong about him?

Trapped miserably between her heart and mind, she closed her eyes, fought back the tears, opened them again and stared down at his features. But even with that debate still raging, she knew, deep in her heart, that he was the one. The love of her life. The happily-ever-after she'd never have. It didn't matter what he'd done or who he'd been before they'd been together. When he'd been hers, he'd been everything she'd ever wanted.

She held her breath as she leaned close to brush her lips softly over his. Just a whisper of a touch. Just one last kiss.

Other *Love Spell* books by Elisabeth Naughton:

STOLEN FURY

STOLEN
HEAT

ELISABETH
NAUGHTON

LOVE SPELL NEW YORK CITY

LOVE SPELL®

August 2009

Published by

Dorchester Publishing Co., Inc.
200 Madison Avenue
New York, NY 10016

ISBN 10: 0-505-52794-4
ISBN 13: 978-0-505-52794-3
E-ISBN: 978-1-4285-0720-3

The name "Love Spell" and its logo are trademarks of Dorchester Publishing Co., Inc.

Printed in the United States of America.

10 9 8 7 6 5 4 3 2 1

Visit us online at www.dorchesterpub.com.

For my mom, Georgiana.
Thank you for always being right where I needed you most.

ACKNOWLEDGMENTS

Big thanks to my agent, Laura Bradford, for her honesty, hard work and advice regarding this book. Thanks also to my editor, Leah Hultenschmidt, and the entire crew at Dorchester for their unflappable attention to detail.

Special thanks as always to my rock, Joan Swan, who makes writing just plain fun. My "girls" . . . Lisa Catto, Becky Hakes, Kendra Elliot & Alice Sharpe for always responding to *"just one more thing."* To Bethany Cunningham Gabbert for her fab legal advice; Rita Van Hee, Tonia Wubbena & Connie Dingeman for dropping everything to read for me; and Tiki Gaugler, who sailed to my rescue in the middle of this book when I needed it most. Thanks also to Karl Wingren and the staff at the Clackamas County Public Safety Training Center for a great day on the range and for answering all my questions.

And finally, to my husband Dan, who puts up with the long hours I spend at the keyboard. *I love you, babe.*

STOLEN
HEAT

CHAPTER ONE

Worthington Fine Auction House
Downtown New York City

All things considered, she looked pretty good for a six-year-old corpse.

Katherine Meyer checked her reflection in the bathroom mirror one last time and smoothed a few wild strands of hair back from her face. The black slacks and matching jacket were perfect, not one thing about them the slightest bit memorable. No one glancing her direction tonight would ever see anything other than the professional assistant she resembled, and that was precisely the way she wanted it. The less attention she drew, the safer everyone would be.

Her stomach rolled as she turned down the long hallway. Her sensible flats clicked along the cement floor. Muffled music from the party out front drifted to her ears. Ahead, a security guard looked up from his post at the end of the corridor and gave her the once-over.

She smiled what she hoped was a confident grin as she approached and flashed the I.D. badge she'd lifted from a Worthington's employee days before. The picture had been digitally altered to match her current disguise—dark brown, bob-style wig, blue color contacts, tortoiseshell glasses. As long as the man in front of her didn't look too closely, she was home free.

"Hold up there."

So much for easy.

The guard stepped from behind the counter, blocking her path, displaying at least six feet, three inches of hulking muscle. He wore the standard blue uniform, had short-cropped dark hair, was big and brawny and the epitome of the straitlaced no-one-gets-by-me-without-a-pass gatekeeper.

Kat took a quick breath and glanced at the name tag on the man's chest—James Johnson—then at his waist where a utility belt held a two-way radio.

No guns. Not that she could see anyway. And as far she was concerned, that was the best news she'd had so far tonight.

"Only authorized personnel past this point," he said in a gruff voice. "I'll need to verify your I.D."

She smiled, unclipped the badge from her jacket and handed it to him with hands she somehow managed to keep from shaking. "Big crowd out there tonight," she said casually.

Breathe, Kat. Just breathe.

His eyes flicked from the badge up to her face. "What's your business in the storage room, Ms. Anderson?"

"I'm working with Marsha Griffin, the liaison between Worthington's and the Odyssey Gallery. Just doing one final walk-through before Ms. Griffin arrives and the auction begins. You know how anal some of these independent gallery owners can be on their big night." She rolled her eyes for effect.

"It's Jim, right?" She reached for the badge before he could study it in depth again. "We met about two months ago when I was doing work with the Met."

His brow wrinkled in confusion, like he was having trouble remembering back.

Perfect. Just what she wanted.

She clipped the badge to her jacket again, gave a small

smile and did her best to look nonchalant. "How's your daughter? Broken arm heal up okay?"

His eyes widened in surprise. It was obvious he was searching his memory for their last conversation. Too bad he wouldn't find it.

"Uh, yeah." He scratched the top of his head. "Sarah gets the cast off on Tuesday. How did you—"

"I bet she's thrilled." Kat took a step around him and headed for the steel door at his back. Distract, dismay, then detour. That was her life motto. Or, at least, her *new* life motto. "Broke my arm when I was seven. Longest six weeks of my life."

She paused at the door, looked over her shoulder and lifted her brow as she waited.

He stared at her a full second, then gave his head a small shake and turned. "Oh, right. Sorry. You'll need to sign in first, Ms. Anderson. It's standard procedure."

"Sure." Kat took the clipboard, signed her alias and waited while he unlocked the door from his station. "Thanks, Jim. I'll only be a few minutes."

She eased into the room and closed the door behind her. Leaning back against the cool metal, she let out a long breath. Her performance had been near Oscar worthy.

She reached up to wipe her brow. Top-notch acting, but sweating buckets. It was a wonder Jim-the-Sentry hadn't noticed. One tiny mistake like that could send her to an early grave.

Or late, considering how you looked at it.

Since, legally, Katherine Meyer had died in a car bomb in Egypt, she couldn't possibly be breaking into one of the most famous auction houses in the world. But here she was. The trick now was simply to stay off everyone's radar. The trick *always* was to stay dead.

She glanced around the storage room. The space was big, at least thirty feet by thirty feet. Long tables were lined up in linear rows and covered in black fabric. Artifacts lay positioned on the tables, and stock cards with printed numbers sat in front of each piece.

She checked her watch. In a few minutes the room would be a flurry of activity, auction house specialists and assistants moving pieces through the adjoining door at her right to the auction room stage. That was why she'd waited to make her move. Chaos was the perfect way to cover her tracks. She had mere moments before her window of opportunity was up, though, and she needed to find *it* before that happened.

Wasting no time, she wove through tables of Egyptian artifacts and tried not to look at the Late Period jewelry, the Middle Kingdom carvings. Inside, though, her blood warmed as the past surrounded her. And with it, the dread that had been dogging her for longer than she could remember.

She pushed the feeling away and kept searching. Panic rose when she neared the back of the room and still couldn't find it. On a deep breath she hoped would calm her pulse, she stopped and turned a slow circle. And that was when a sparkle three tables over caught her eye.

Her hand shook as she crossed the floor quickly and reached for the gold statuette of the crouching pharaoh, no more than three inches long, stuck between a chipped stone relief of Queen Tiy and a sphinx statue. The metal was cool to the touch; the gold chain looped through a small hole in the back, soft against her fingers. It was heavier than she remembered, and while it looked solid, Kat knew without even checking that it was actually hollow.

After all this time, it was here. Just like she'd hoped. He hadn't sold it after all.

With quick fingers she unbuttoned her jacket and took the forgery out of the small front pack she'd attached to her waist. She refused to think about why he was selling the relic now. Refused to acknowledge that whatever sentimental value it might have once had for him was now gone.

Sentimental value? Yeah, right.

Okay, so there was still a little twinge in her heart when she thought of him, but her brain was working these days. And there was no way she'd ever make the same mistakes she'd made back then.

Thank goodness for baggy jackets and guards who didn't pat you down. She said a quick prayer of thanks to St. Jude and Sister Mary Francis, the woman who'd taught her all about hopeless causes, and slipped the artifact into the pouch. After repositioning the forgery on the black drape of fabric, she rebuttoned her jacket, then headed for the exit.

The knob on the door rattled, stopping her feet two steps from freedom. A muffled, angry female voice drifted through the metal, followed by the jangle of keys.

Kat's heart rate jacked up.

They'd figured out she was a fake. Jim-the-Sentry must have called someone when her signature didn't match those on file. It was only a matter of time until they barged in and cuffed her, before her cover was blown and the pendant . . .

She darted a look to her left, spotted the door to the stage and knew it was her only option.

"Come on, come on, come on," she muttered as she punched in the access code on the keypad and prayed it was the right one. If her source was wrong, she was toast.

The light flashed red twice before finally clicking green. The door gave with a pop just as the exterior door to the hall burst open. Kat squeezed through the small opening, turned and shut the metal door with her shoulder without pausing to see who came barreling into the room she'd just exited. She saw a heavy table to her right and muscled it against the door.

Breathing hard from the exertion, she paused to scan

the area. The back of the stage was dark, but voices and music from the party were much louder here. A velvet curtain hung between her and the festivities. She considered her options. She knew from studying the blueprints if she turned left it would take her to the kitchen. To her right she'd have access to the offices and the elaborate hallway system that ran through the building. Her best option if she wanted to disappear.

"There's no one in here," a male voice said from inside the room at her back.

"Dammit!" a female exclaimed. "This door's blocked. Call security. Have them search the stage and the auction room. I want that woman found!"

Kat moved to her right. Just as she reached the hallway opening, a man in a suit blocked her exit.

He was busily studying papers in the file folder he held when she nearly plowed into him. He glanced up with startled green eyes that quickly sharpened and focused. "What are you doing back here? Let me see your I.D."

Shit. So much for options.

She didn't think, simply charged the curtain and her last hope for escape.

To her luck, the auction room itself was empty but for an elderly man placing programs on each of the plush chairs. Kat stumbled across the stage and nearly tripped down the three small steps onto the expensive carpet below. She stiffened her shoulders and tried to look like she belonged as she moved quickly toward the open double doors at the end of the room.

Just then the curtain whipped back and the suit she'd almost run over appeared, looking seriously ticked off. "Stop her!"

Kat didn't hang around to find out what would happen next. She beat feet through the main double doors to the lobby and pulled up short when she saw the massive crowd gathered there. One look told her she wasn't going out the front door, not without causing a scene.

Oh, man. She was quickly running out of options.

Please just let me get out of one more mess.

Darting a look around and seeing her last hope for escape, she wove through the crowd and headed for the kitchen.

Her nerves shot up another level as she unbuttoned her black jacket, slipped it off her shoulders and looped it over her arm. Carefully, she unhooked the front pouch and tucked it in the folds of her coat. A look back confirmed security had finally wised up to what was happening. They stood with the suit at the auction room doors, searching the crowd for her.

She ducked behind a heavyset man nursing a glass of champagne and waited until the kitchen door swung open wide and a waiter appeared carrying a tray of bubbly. And just as she was about to make a beeline for the kitchen and her last shot at freedom, she heard it. A deep, familiar baritone.

She whipped around so fast she nearly took out the man in front of her. Muttering apologies, she slipped into the shadows in the corner of the room and cautiously looked toward the lobby's main entrance, where two couples had just stepped into the room. Her mind screamed, *run!* But it was already too late. The crowd parted, and then he was there. And she couldn't look away even if she'd wanted to.

Just her luck, he was better looking than she'd remembered. His nose was straight, his eyes the same captivating smoky gray, his hair as dark blond and wind-ruffled as she'd always liked.

His body hadn't changed much in the years since she'd seen him last—he was still strong and broad and, she was sure, chiseled beneath that spendy tuxedo like always—

but for some reason he seemed taller than she remembered. Bigger everywhere. Larger than life. More . . . alive than even she'd fantasized.

And though she hated to admit it—even to herself—she'd definitely fantasized over the years. Then berated herself for being a complete and utter fool.

Peter Kauffman. *Her* Pete.

The group around him chatted as he reached for the coat of the woman he was obviously with. She shrugged out of the garment, revealing a slinky, winter white gown, then turned and placed her hand on Pete's chest. With a sultry grin, she eased up on her toes and kissed that jaw Kat had nibbled and licked and tasted a hundred times herself.

No, not hers, Kat realized as she stood there staring. He'd never really been hers, had he?

"Just what the hell do you think you're doing?"

Jolted out of her reverie, Kat jerked around.

"You're supposed to be serving drinks," the man said with a scowl. His name badge identified him as Antonio, the head bartender.

Her brain was complete fuzz, but one thing got through: this yahoo thought she was a waitress.

Conversation behind her quieted. In the silence, she could hear the blood pounding in her ears. Just as she opened her mouth to rattle off a lame excuse, footsteps quickly crossed the marble at her back.

Oh . . . *shit!*

"I'm sorry," she mumbled. "I . . . it won't happen again."

The footsteps drew closer. Kat darted around Antonio, used his body as a shield and sped toward the kitchen door before security cued in on what was happening.

"Hey. Wait a minute."

Kat's eyes widened at the familiar voice at her back. Her legs wobbled as she tried to push her way past guests. She could hear Pete behind her, growing closer. Panic and a sea of bodies closed in around her, choking the air in her lungs. A strand of hair from the stupid wig whipped across her face and stung her eyes. Why wouldn't these people move? Couldn't they tell she needed to get out . . . *now*?

"Can I be of assistance, sir?"

Kat paused long enough to peer back through the crowd, hoping the people around her provided enough cover. And that was when she realized coming here was an even bigger mistake than she'd ever imagined.

Two men stood on the far side of the foyer, past where Pete and Antonio were muttering words she couldn't hear. They had obviously just stepped into the lobby, their shoulders and hair covered with a smattering of snowflakes. One was hidden in shadows, but the other, the one with the buzz cut . . . his was a face Kat would never forget.

Terror clawed at her chest. She knew she needed to run, but she couldn't. For a split second she was back in that tomb, fighting for her life. The man's eyes ran over the crowd, past where she hoped she was shielded by partygoers, searching. And then suddenly those eyes stopped, darted back to her location near the kitchen door and held.

She swallowed hard, tried not to move, but knew she stood out like a beacon in the night. After all this time, after all her disguises and years of hiding, her cover was blown. All because she'd veered off her plan and stumbled into this godforsaken lobby.

She held her breath. Waited. Watched like a deer frozen in the headlights. There was still a chance, though. So long as he didn't . . .

The buzz-cut man's eyes darted across the room to zero in on Pete. Her gaze followed. Pete had rejoined his group, but he didn't look happy anymore. He seemed troubled as he sipped his champagne and glanced around the lobby at the other partygoers.

No, no, no.

Kat looked back toward the main door and, in a fog, watched a sinister smile spread across the buzz-cut man's face.

Shit! She *never* should have come here.

She pushed the kitchen door open as her adrenaline surged. Reached up and rubbed her fingers over the medallion hanging from her neck. And prayed this time no one died because of her.

CHAPTER TWO

"You look like you've seen a ghost."

Peter Kauffman pulled his gaze from the crowd he'd been studying intensely half the night to glance toward his date for the evening, Dr. Maria Gotsi.

No, "date" was too broad a term. "Friend with benefits" was more appropriate, although even that implied a relationship they just didn't have.

He tried to smile so Maria wouldn't know what he was thinking but knew he did a half-assed job by the way she frowned back at him. "Just preoccupied."

"You seem off tonight, Peter," she said in that cultured Greek voice of hers.

Hell yeah, he was off. First because of this auction she'd finally talked him into, then because he was pretty sure he was losing his freakin' mind. No way he could have seen what he *thought* he'd seen.

"I'm just tired. It's been a long day."

Maria smiled and moved closer, slipped her arm through his and rubbed her hip against him. Any other moment, that well-timed contact would have sent electricity straight to his groin, but tonight it didn't even garner a response.

"You should be celebrating, darling," she whispered close to his ear. "The auction was a huge success."

An enormous success, actually. The Odyssey Gallery's collection of Ancient Egyptian Art had netted more than six million dollars, far above what even he'd anticipated. The party in the Worthington's ballroom swirled around him as he stood there, sipping champagne he didn't really want, and though he should have been ecstatic, for some reason, he wasn't.

Maria, already deep in conversation with someone at Pete's left, laughed and tossed her dark hair back, the sound and movement dragging his attention her way. He watched with detached interest as she expertly flirted with the manager of the auction house, then moved on to someone else Pete had no interest in meeting, meticulously working her way around the room and mingling like the pro she was.

The woman had balls, he had to give her that. And she wasn't just another pretty face attached to a sinful body. She was smart, too, the director of one of the top archaeometry laboratories in the world, the backbone of the Art Institute of Athens.

Her eyes slid in his direction, and she smiled that come-get-me grin he knew meant she was ready to go back to his hotel and screw his brains out. A tiny part of him recoiled at the thought.

Before he knew it, he was scanning the crowd again, looking for that waitress he'd seen earlier. The one who'd had those wide, almond-shaped eyes, that strong, straight nose, the high cheekbones and stubborn chin.

Damn. He was doing it again. He'd stopped seeing her face in crowds years ago. So why the hell was it happening now?

More than ready to leave this party behind, he set his empty flute on a nearby table, tucked one hand into the pocket of his slacks and headed in Maria's direction.

Voices tinged with Middle Eastern accents drifted his way as he drew close. Maria's back was to him as he approached the trio, but over her shoulder he got a look at the two dark-skinned gentlemen she was speaking with, and he stiffened. Something in his gut said this was no coincidence.

Definitely time to bail.

He slipped his arm around Maria's waist and leaned close to her ear, hoping to pull her away without a scene. "I'm ready to go."

She pressed a hand against his chest and smiled. "Peter. There you are. I'd like you to meet Aten Minyawi and Hanif Busir. They're in the market for some prime Egyptian pieces."

Yeah, he just bet they were.

He barely spared them a glance and knew without even looking that not an ounce of recognition would show on Busir's face. "I don't deal in Egyptian art anymore. Sorry."

Pete started to tug Maria away, but she halted his movement with a hand on his arm. "Mr. Busir's from Cairo. He runs a museum in the city, and he's always on the lookout for historic pieces that might have been removed from his country without government knowledge or approval. Several of your artifacts tonight intrigued him. In fact, he purchased quite a few and is in the market for more."

God, she was buying their bull hook, line and sinker. But then, Busir was a pro at weaving crap on a stick. As good as Pete had once been.

"Good for him," Pete said. "Everything I have has already been auctioned off. That was the point of tonight, remember? The car's waiting, Maria."

"Peter." She stopped him with a look that read, *what the hell's wrong with you?* "Mr. Minyawi and Mr. Busir are also interested in contracting the Institute for authentication on some of their pieces. I'm sure you can wait a few moments, can't you?"

Nope. Not for anyone from Egypt. Not ever again.

She tugged her elbow from his hand, turned away before he could answer and made some lame-ass excuse about his rude behavior.

Yeah. *Whatever.*

He squared his shoulders and glanced back at the two men while he waited. Minyawi was over six feet, had long dark hair and a full beard. A thin scar ran down one side of his face. He never made eye contact, but something about the way he held himself was familiar to Pete. And that familiarity only flared as Pete watched the man's gaze sweep the crowd as if he were searching for someone. Or waiting for some*thing* to happen.

Not good.

Pete's gaze drifted to Busir, a good two inches shorter than Minyawi, but wider and more muscular. His dark hair was cropped closer than Pete remembered, but those thick brows anchoring his forehead to his face were just the same. As were his piercing black eyes, which never wavered from Maria. The man was all about attention to detail and stone-cold deadly patience. Just like always.

Pete knew Busir wouldn't make a scene—he was too cunning for that—but it didn't lessen Pete's desire to get the hell out of the auction house and away from these two thugs as soon as possible. Whatever they were doing here couldn't be good, and his days of wheeling and dealing with the likes of them were long gone.

With growing impatience, he waited until Maria pulled a business card from her small white handbag and handed it to Busir. Before she could delve into a description of the Institute's latest technological advancements, he grasped her arm and this time didn't let go. "The car's waiting."

Outside, he took a deep breath of crisp November air

and waited while the valet signaled his driver. Trees void of leaves and wrapped in white lights for the holiday season twinkled in the night, giving the street a Norman Rockwell–ish flair he could have given a rip about. Cars whipped by on the wet pavement. A thin layer of slushy snow covered the sidewalk.

Maria frowned as she buttoned her coat. "I don't understand what the rush was about."

No, of course, she wouldn't. "I'm tired, Maria. It's been a long day, and I was ready to go. You want to go back in, be my guest."

She stopped fidgeting and stared at him. "Peter."

The sleek black Mercedes pulled to the curb. When the driver got out, Pete waved him to stay in the car. He opened the door himself and waited while Maria slid into the backseat.

After the door closed, he gave the driver directions to the apartment Maria kept on the Upper West Side, leaned back against the plush leather and closed his eyes.

Silence filled the car. He knew she was wondering why they weren't going back to his hotel, but he didn't feel like explaining. He wasn't upset with her, but for some reason the thought of being cooped up with her all night was just a little too close for his taste right now.

Cloth rustled next to him as she wiggled out of her coat. The seat dipped to his left, and his skin warmed when she curved toward his body. Some designer floral fragrance drifted his way. "You look tired, Peter. Why don't you let me relax you?"

His stomach tightened at the offer. He was damn tired and in serious need of relaxation. But he knew where this was headed, and for reasons he didn't want to investigate, he just wasn't interested.

He sat up and reached for the bar. Just his luck, the only alcohol was an open bottle of champagne, not the beer he really craved. With nothing else to drink, he poured two glasses and handed her one, hoping it'd keep her roving hands busy and off him until they got to her place.

"Have a drink, Maria." He took a long, deep swallow and blinked twice when the fizz went right to his brain.

Maybe he just needed to drink himself into a stupor. It'd been a long time since he'd been on a bender. Get toasted, pass out, wake up in the morning with this whole night just one bad memory.

"Peter, what's bothering you?"

"Nothing." He drained the rest of his champagne, leaned forward and refilled his glass.

"I can tell when you're upset. Let me help." Her hand ran up his leg, hovered on his inner thigh and drew long, lazy circles against his slacks. He managed one last swallow before she took the flute from his hand and set it in the drink holder to her left. Rolling to her side, she draped her leg over his, slid her hand inside his jacket and drew his earlobe into her mouth.

He was trapped. That was how he felt, at least. Trapped with no way out and no good reason to go.

Warm wetness met his ear. A deep, lust-filled purr radiated from her throat. Just as she was moving to slide onto his lap, the car braked hard, hurtling them both forward. They crashed into the seat in front of them, then hit the floor. Dazed, Pete glared up at the driver's rearview mirror.

"Sorry," came a quiet voice from the front seat. "Red light."

He was just about to lay into the guy for not paying attention when he caught sight of familiar brown eyes peering back at him in the mirror, highlighted by streetlights shining in from the outside. Dark brown eyes. Like molten chocolate.

He squinted to see clearer, sure his mind was playing tricks on him, but no, they were still there. Shimmering starbursts he'd looked into hundreds of thousands of times before.

A long time ago.

A lifetime ago.

Tonight.

He opened his mouth to speak, but the privacy glass went up before he could get the words out. The car lurched forward again, throwing him back once more.

No way that just happened.

"I can't breathe . . . Peter."

It took a moment for Maria's words to register, but when they did, he realized he had her pinned. He quickly eased up and pulled her to the seat. "Sorry. Are you hurt?"

"No. I think I'm okay." She glared at the dark window separating them from the driver. Color tinged her cheeks. Always the professional, though, she smoothed her hair and lifted her chin as if she hadn't just been flat on her back, spread wide with her legs straight up in the air.

Pete fixed his shirt in silence, more shaken than he liked. By the time he was done, the car was pulling to a stop in front of Maria's building.

"Well," she said, reaching for her small handbag. "That was an interesting ride."

Interesting was an understatement. He waited while the chauffeur opened the door, then slid out of the vehicle and took Maria's hand to help her out. "Wait here," he said. "I won't be long."

He caught up with Maria just as she was going inside. The bellman held the door, tipped his hat and smiled a friendly greeting as they headed for the bank of elevators. The double doors opened with a ping, but Maria didn't make a move to step inside, and neither did he.

"You're not coming up, are you?" she finally asked.

A pang of guilt shot through him at the hurt he thought he heard in her voice. "No."

She turned his direction and looked up with dark, unsurprised eyes. Eyes that were very calm and, luckily, not the slightest bit upset. "Who was she?"

It was his turn to be shocked. "Who?"

"The woman at the auction. The one you went running after. Who was she?"

Nobody he'd ever talk about. Not with her. Not with anyone. "Just someone I thought I recognized."

"Hm." She pursed her lips as if she didn't believe him. Then her expression hardened. "I realize our relationship is not exclusive, Peter. But in the future, if you call *me* for an evening, I'd appreciate it if you wouldn't go off chasing other women."

Okay, he'd been wrong. She was pissed.

"Maria—"

"And another thing," she said, stepping into the elevator and placing a hand on the door so it wouldn't close. "Do not get between me and a client. Ever. Are we clear? Date or not, that's not your call."

There was the hard-as-nails businesswoman he remembered. Take a punch, come back up swinging. She was good at that. It was one of the reasons she was so successful, a big reason he liked to hook up with her now and then. She was the exact opposite of what he used to be attracted to. It was also the reason she wouldn't ever be anything more than an occasional lay.

He stiffened, thankful he was on his way out and not up, not tempted in the slightest to argue with her on this point. "I'll remember that. Good night, Maria."

To her credit, she didn't try to stop him with any whimpering female apologies. No, not Maria. In that respect they were way too much alike.

That thought churned in his head as he headed for the front door. Brisk air whooshed around him when he stepped out onto the street. Snow had begun to fall again in big white, chunky flakes that were quickly sticking to the sidewalk and vehicles parked along the road. At this time of night, and with the crappy weather, there were few pedestrians out and about. A single car passed by, tires squishing through the slush.

He looked up to discover the limo was gone. Then had a moment of, *what the hell?*, only to realize the driver had pulled up about three car-lengths, probably to make room for another drop-off. Shivering in the cold air and growing increasingly frustrated by the minute, he crossed his arms over his chest and tucked his chin to block out the cold as he headed for the car.

And as he moved, he thought of those eyes he'd seen tonight. So dark. So mesmerizing. So much like Kat's.

Even though he fought it, her perfect face flashed in his mind, tightening his chest like a vise. Memories of the first day he'd met her and all the mistakes he'd made before and since then ran through his head. And distracted by her now like he'd been from the beginning, he didn't notice the shadowy figure step out from the alley until it was too late.

CHAPTER THREE

Six-and-a-half years earlier
Valley of the Kings

Pete hung at the back of the group and waited, trying to look entranced by a Middle Kingdom pottery shard resting on a workbench at his side. Worth maybe twenty bucks, he figured, if he could hock it. There was no market for crap like this, though, and so far he hadn't seen anything even remotely exciting in the last four tours he'd signed up for.

Christ, it was hot. He lifted the wide-brimmed hat he'd

purchased from a street vendor in Cairo, wiped his brow and replaced the damn thing. It was late March—high tourist season in Egypt, when the temperatures were supposed to be bearable—but out here in the desert it was still hotter than sin. Pretending to be the tourist he wasn't, he pulled his camera from his backpack and snapped a picture of the workbench and its smattering of useless artifacts. Then he lifted the lens and photographed the worksite. The tomb's entrance. And lastly, the crew meandering around.

This tomb would probably end up being a bust like all the others he'd visited so far this trip, but he'd learned long ago that sometimes a photo picked up things you missed on first examination.

And if there was one thing he was meticulous about, it was his research.

Unfortunately, that research had all been for crap so far. And his contacts were giving him shit as well. If he didn't score big soon, he was gonna be flying coach back to Miami.

"All right, ladies and gentlemen, if I can have your attention. The tour is about to begin."

Pete turned like the rest of the herd and looked toward the sun shelter where a woman dressed in khaki pants, a work shirt and boots was giving directions to the group in both Egyptian Arabic and English. He couldn't see her face, shielded by a worn Mariners cap pulled low over her brow, but her voice had an unusual lilt that piqued his interest.

One, it was American, and anytime there was an American woman working the site he was scanning, he had an immediate in. He hadn't met one who'd been able to see through his bull.

But two, and most importantly, she had the kind of voice that did it for him. Smooth and direct, but hinting of sinful sex all at the same time.

He lifted the camera and snapped her picture. Maybe this tour would be different from the others after all.

He shifted his pack to his back, looped his camera strap around his neck and moved the equipment so it hung down his chest. Then he slipped his hands into the pocket of his cargo pants and waited to be bored out of his mind.

Except he wasn't. As the tour progressed and their guide—a Katherine Meyer—showed the group of mostly American tourists the worksite and outlined the project's goals, he found himself intently listening. The woman knew her stuff. She managed to make the dull artifacts they were unearthing sound mysterious and exciting. And when she hinted that the tomb could possibly be the last resting place of Nefertiti, she had the entire group *ooh-ing* and *ah-ing* like she was Jacques Cousteau about to uncover buried treasure from the bottom of the ocean.

Half an hour into the tour and he still hadn't gotten a good look at her face, but he had the impression of dark eyes and hair, a slim body and graceful hands.

She gave directions for the group to enter the tomb and move down the corridor, then to the right where they would enter the first burial chamber. Pete knew the really exciting stuff would be cordoned off from tourist view, so he listened carefully to what she had to say about the religious texts and images adorning the closest chambers. It often gave clues to what or who was buried deeper within.

But as she stood at the entrance to the tomb and the group filtered past her, disappearing down into the darkness, Pete found himself strangely stunned into stupor. Up close she wasn't just attractive, she was a knockout. Mahogany hair that fell to her shoulders in a gentle wave, dark chocolate eyes, a straight nose and one damn sexy mole on the upper right side of her perfectly pink mouth.

He put the two together—that sultry voice he'd been

listening to all morning and those sinful lips he was now staring at—and even roasting in the hundred-plus-degree heat, he grew rock hard.

"Are you all right, sir? You look a little pale."

He nodded slowly but couldn't seem to get his brain to click into gear so he could stop staring.

"Here." She pulled a water bottle from the pack looped around her waist and smiled. The sweetest grin he'd ever seen. Which only jacked him up another ten degrees. "Take mine. It just gets hotter once you get inside."

Holy hell, she had no idea.

He took the bottle she held out for him, waited while she passed by and headed into the corridor. Then guzzled the whole damn thing as he watched her sexy ass sway as if for his eyes only.

Normally he'd be thinking of all the ways he was going to get her flat on her back so he could seduce her into talking about the site, the relics and what was really going down. But for some reason, watching Katherine Meyer walk away right now, he wasn't just thinking about tonight.

He was thinking of a whole lot more.

And wondering what the hell had just happened to him.

Present day
New York City

Kat bit her lip as she sat behind the wheel of the luxury car, waiting for Pete to come back from dropping off his date.

Date? Good God. That woman wasn't a date. She was a piranha. The way she'd pawed at him in the backseat? Kat was sure the woman was going to eat him for dessert right there on the expensive leather upholstery. Just what did she see in a woman like that?

Oh, yeah, right. Kat clenched her jaw. Like she couldn't tell? Big boobs, skinny butt, class and sophistication and money.

All things Kat had never had and wouldn't ever attain.

Not your problem. Don't go there. What he does and with whom isn't why you're here. You don't even care, remember?

A car honked behind her. Kat jumped and whipped around in her seat. It took moments to realize it was just another limo wanting her space. She put the car in gear and pulled forward until she was halfway up the block. Two women dressed in clingy silver outfits and sky-high heels climbed out of the limo and headed for the same building Pete had disappeared inside.

Kat blew out a breath and tried to refocus as the car behind her pulled away from the curb and turned the corner. But thinking about her current situation did little to quell the nerves in her gut bouncing around like Mexican jumping beans.

She rubbed her forehead. Seeing Pete again had thrown a major kink in her plans. She'd just committed a theft of major proportions, and now she could also add car-stealing to her list of little misdemeanors. It wouldn't take long for Pete's real driver to put out a notice on the missing vehicle. She'd lucked out that he'd left his cap and jacket on the front seat when he'd gone in to take a leak, but lifting this limo was *completely* off the plan chart.

If she wasn't careful, she'd have the cops on her in a matter of minutes. Like she needed that on top of everything else?

She pinched the bridge of her nose and closed her eyes tight. Why hadn't she just walked away?

Tired of arguing with herself, Kat dropped her hand and eyed the building again. He'd been in there too long. What if he'd gone upstairs with the piranha? What if he wasn't coming back down like he'd said? What if—*oh, shit*—what if he was having wild jungle-sex with her right this minute?

Definitely not going there.

A shadow in her rearview mirror caught her attention. Thoughts of Pete slipped to the back of Kat's mind as her instincts jumped to alert. Slinking down in her seat, she reached up slowly and tipped the mirror so she had a better view behind her.

It was a man. Broad shoulders, long legs. Tall. Wearing a full-length dark coat. He glanced around the empty street several times before crossing the road and heading for the piranha's building.

He stepped under a streetlight for a brief moment, then eased back into the shadows. But not before Kat saw his arm lift toward the sky. Metal glimmered in his hand. Seconds later, the light went out with a near silent pop.

But one second was all it took. In that moment he'd been in the light, Kat had a clear view of his face. Of his close-cropped hair. Of his beady eyes.

Busir.

The hair stood up on her arms, but she didn't avert her eyes. Not even when he slinked into the shadows along the building and then stopped. Slowly, she reached for the backpack she'd set on the passenger seat, flipped it open and pawed around until she found her 9mm. Her fingers closed over the cold metal with stunning force. Though she was expertly trained in how to use the firearm, a rush of adrenaline swept through her. Would she be able to take a life after all?

She wasn't sure. If she did, it would put her on the same level as the men who had killed Sawil and Shannon.

She knew only one thing for certain: Busir and his goons had come for Pete just like she'd predicted. Her conscience wouldn't let her sit back and do nothing.

After slipping the Beretta into the pocket of her jacket, she searched the backpack again for the small stun gun her self-defense instructor had suggested she buy. She'd much rather use that if she could. Gripping it and an extra cartridge in her hand, she climbed out of the car, careful to stay low and silent.

A quick glance back confirmed Busir wasn't alone. He'd brought a friend, though not the same one she'd seen at the auction. This one looked American. Kat inched her way around parked cars, well out of both their view, until she got to the alley. Once there, she kicked up her feet and ran down the wet pavement, made a trip around the block until she came up from the south behind their car.

She was breathing heavily as she ducked out of sight and moved close to the vehicle. Busir was still waiting in the shadows. His counterpart sat in the driver's seat, awaiting his signal.

Long seconds passed while she waited. Her breathing slowed, but the adrenaline rush sent the blood pounding in her ears in time with her heart. She let instinct and years of training finally sink in, tried to block the self-doubt on the fringes of her subconscious. Logic told her she couldn't take out both men on her own, but she had surprise on her side. And she'd make the most of it.

Pete suddenly emerged from the lobby, head down and arms crossed over his chest. A frown cut across his face when he looked up to where the limo had been. One quick glance around, and then he turned toward the car. Tucking his chin against his chest, he headed up the street, oblivious to what was about to go down around him.

Perspiration dampened Kat's skin. It nearly killed her, but she waited until she saw Busir make his move.

Then she made hers.

As Busir slinked out of the shadows and followed Pete up the sidewalk, Kat gripped the driver's door and pulled. The man in the front seat jolted around to face her. She was sure she'd never seen him before, but that didn't stop her. She gripped the stun gun and hit him hard, right in the neck to avoid his coat. He jerked and yelped, but she held her ground and counted to four.

The man seized, then fell over on the front seat. He wasn't unconscious, but he was incapacitated. At least for the time being.

And for a moment, Kat's eyes widened at what she'd just done. Images flickered through her mind like a silent movie. The tomb. The sounds. The struggle. And running.

She closed her eyes tight and took large breaths to calm her nerves. But two was all she could afford. She opened her eyes, ready to find Pete. And that was when she noticed the empty vial on the console. She reached around the man's body and lifted the small glass container.

Lorazepam.

Oh, dear God.

A loud crack, followed by a grunt, jerked her attention away from the vial and toward the street. She looked up just in time to see Pete and Busir disappear into the alley.

Her feet skidded on the icy sidewalk. She nearly lost her balance twice before she reached the entrance to the dark alley.

Where her mouth fell open.

If she'd thought Pete needed protecting, she'd been wrong. He had Busir pinned against the side of the brick building and was easily in complete control of the situation. Blood trickled down his temple. Redness and the beginnings of what looked to be a nasty bruise were forming near his eye. But what stopped her cold was the look of pure malevolence in his eyes as he stared into the face of a killer.

This was the side of him she hadn't known. The side that turned a blind eye to what was right, negotiated deals on the shady side and stayed one step ahead of the law along the way. It was also the side that contracted with rapists and murderers and men who would do whatever it took to get what they wanted.

No.

She didn't realize she'd spoken the word out loud until Pete's head whipped her way.

Surprise and confusion raced across his bruised features. "What the hell?"

Busir used that moment to take the upper hand. He lifted his arm, and with a move Kat barely tracked, plunged a hypodermic needle into Pete's neck.

Pete hollered, jerked his attention back to Busir. His eyes flared. He reached up, pulled the needle from his neck and stared at it. In the split second of Pete's confusion, Busir shifted out from the wall and plowed his fist into the side of Pete's face. Pete hit the wall, ricocheted off. He lunged at Busir, taking them both down to the ground hard.

Kat screeched and jumped back as the two grappled. Fists flew, and bodies smacked the hard concrete. She knew she needed to do something, but she was too stunned to do more than stare, especially because Pete was handling his own and beating the crap out of Busir.

Until, that is, he threw a punch that missed its mark by a foot. And another. And another.

Oh, God. That needle had to have hit an artery or a vein. He was fading fast and losing whatever advantage he'd just gained.

Blood and sweat dripped down Busir's face. When Pete blinked and gave his head a swift shake, Busir wriggled out from under him and pushed to his feet. Back to her, looking down at Pete who was fighting to stand himself, Busir let out a low chuckle. One Kat had heard years before and would never forget. It was all she needed to shock her right back to reality.

She charged before she could change her mind and hit Busir hard in the back with the stun gun. He jolted, screamed, whipped around. And she hit him again dead in the chest without even a second thought.

She gritted her teeth and held on to the stun gun even as his coal black eyes focused on her. His body jerked and seized. His eyes rolled back in his head, and then he fell to his knees, finally slumping forward on the ground where he continued to twitch as electrical impulses flickered through his body.

Slick with sweat and breathing heavy, she stared down at what she'd done for the second time tonight. Not an inkling of remorse rushed through her. At that moment, she understood how men could kill. He deserved that and so much more for what he'd done to Sawil. To Shannon. To her.

Tires spinning on slush out on the road pulled Kat back to the present. She had mere seconds before Busir's buddy in the car revived; minutes before Busir came to or his other friend from the auction showed up to help.

She hurriedly stepped over Busir and dropped to the ground next to Pete, slumped back against the wall, his head and eyes tracking her like he was operating in serious slow motion. Confusion drew his brows together as he stared up at her with wide eyes.

"We've got to get out of here," she said quickly, checking to make sure there weren't any bones sticking out of his body anywhere.

"Kat?" he croaked.

"Can you walk? I don't think I can carry you."

"Whoa." He gave his head a hard shake and leaned it back against the wall. "Real . . . real . . . trippy dream."

A nightmare was more like it.

His words were slurring together, and she knew the drug was taking effect. She had to get him up and out of this alley before it was too late. "I need you to stand."

She stepped over him, slipped both her arms under his and around his back. A grunt tore from her chest as she used every last bit of strength to help him to his feet. Good God, he was nearly dead weight already. And smelled . . . *oh, heaven* . . . so incredible. She took a deep whiff of his scent and was bombarded by a thousand memories she'd put out of her mind years ago.

"You . . ." He set both hands on her shoulders as she pushed him back against the concrete wall and used her shoulder to brace him up. "You look like som'un I know."

Definitely losing it. She needed to hurry.

"I get that a lot." She shifted around, looped his arm over her shoulder. It slid down her back as his head fell back against the concrete again.

"Motherfucker . . . I feel like shit."

That made two of them.

She grabbed his arm with her left hand and held on tight as she slipped her other arm around his waist and pulled him away from the wall. Her back and shoulders immediately screamed in protest. Panic set in when she looked up and saw how far away the car was. "Pete, you have to help me here. I can't do this on my own."

Somehow he listened. Though his head lolled around and his feet moved like there were bricks attached to the soles of his shoes. How the hell would she get him to the car before Busir and his muscle woke up? And what was she going to do once they got there? Just like he'd done once before, Peter Kauffman was suddenly turning her world upside down.

She maneuvered them around Busir, said a quick prayer the man was still paralyzed, and inched them both toward the sidewalk.

"I look as . . . bad as 'im?" Pete asked when they reached the icy walk.

"Not quite." He looked like Adonis to her, even bloodied and bruised as he was. And as dangerous as a king cobra where she was concerned. This was the dumbest thing she'd ever done. And that was saying a lot, considering her history.

"No more champan' for me, 'kay? I don' like hang . . . overs."

Sweat slid down her temple as they moved. "Don't worry. Something tells me a hangover is the last thing we'll both be worrying about in a few minutes."

CHAPTER FOUR

Six-and-a-half years earlier
Valley of the Kings

"Your secret admirer's back."

Kat hefted her backpack up on a worktable outside the tomb and flipped open the top. She had a killer headache from not enough sleep the night before and the relentless heat, which, after three months, she still wasn't used to. She popped two ibuprofen and downed them with a gulp of water. "He's not my admirer."

Shannon Driscoll rolled her eyes and gathered tools for the day's work. "Fifth time in a row he's taken the tour. I'd call that an admirer."

"Fourth. And you don't get a vote."

"You forgot Sunday. He was here, found out you weren't leading and left."

Kat frowned at her roommate and reached for her hat. "Coincidence. And besides, even if for some strange reason he is here because of me, which he's not," she said with a pointed look, "I'm not interested. There's obviously something wrong with the man. That or he's after something specific."

"I'll say," Shannon muttered. Blonde hair fell over her shoulder as she reached for a pick. "And I have a pretty good idea what that specific is. By the way, you have a smudge of dirt on your cheek."

Kat whipped around and rubbed her palm over her face. "Where? Did I get it? Is it gone?"

Shannon let out a hoot of laughter. "Yeah. And for the record? I'm totally buying that whole not-interested thing. I'll see you after your tour with lover-boy."

Kat frowned again as Shannon headed down the slope toward Dr. Latham, the site leader, who, with his trusty clipboard, was doling out assignments for the day. Just Kat's luck she'd been relegated to tourist duty—again— like the grunt she really was.

Boy, this was an exciting job, wasn't it? She loved the digging and research, but the catering to the public stuff really grated on her nerves. Now and then was fine. Days in a row? No, thank you.

She hated to admit it, but as much as she enjoyed being a part of the project, she was really looking forward to getting everything she needed and getting gone. Especially lately. Tensions were high on the dig. Several pieces they'd excavated over the last few months had mysteriously disappeared. Consensus among the crew was they'd simply been miscataloged, but Kat wasn't so sure.

She let out a deep breath, wiped the dust from her forehead, and told herself not to worry about it so much. There wasn't a lot she could do without proof, and as her colleague Sawil had told her repeatedly, it wasn't her responsibility. Especially since she really was nothing more than a grunt. What she wanted most was to finish her dissertation. And she wanted to go home for a few weeks and see her mother. It'd been too long already.

Knowing that was several months off at least, she blew out a long breath and smashed her hat down on her head, then turned toward the group of tourists fifty yards off waiting for their guide. And just like Shannon had pointed out, there was the sexy American again, hanging at the back of the group like he'd been every other time for the past four—correction, five—days.

He was the kind of guy a girl would have to be blind to miss. Tall, blond, deliriously handsome. With eyes that were a strange color of gray. Today he was dressed in a white camp shirt and khaki pants, with scuffed boots that looked like they'd been around and back a few times.

He wasn't a tourist, she'd bet her grad school tuition on that. Though he had the necessary gear—spiffy new hat, shiny camera and a map of the Valley in his back pocket— the shoes were a dead giveaway. As was the confidence and calculating calmness about him. He rarely spoke to anyone, always kept to the back of the group, watched everything with eagle eyes she doubted missed a thing. And she knew, too, because while he'd been studying everything else, she'd been watching him. Closely.

Sure, he was easy on the eyes, but this guy was after something. Something specific, like Kat had told Shannon only moments before. Only she was sure it wasn't her.

Today she intended to find out just what that was.

She came up behind him and tapped him on the shoulder. "I'd like a moment with you if you don't mind."

He turned her way, and the surprise she'd hoped to see on his face was anything but present.

Dammit, he'd been expecting her.

"Dr. Meyer. It's nice to finally meet you in person."

"I'm sure it is. Look, Mr.—"

"Kauffman. Peter Kauffman. But my friends call me Pete."

"Right. Mr. Kauffman, like I was saying. I'm sure you

could give this tour yourself." She paused to take a breath, only when he turned the full force of those eyes on her she realized they weren't just gray, they were a rolling smoky blue-gray that reminded her of the Caribbean during a hurricane. And just as crazy, they made her think of a lounge chair on a swirling, sandy beach with the guy in front of her catering to every one of her fantasies.

Those mesmerizing eyes swept the length of her body. Lingered on her sweat-dampened shirt, clinging to her already overheated skin. The blood rushing from her head at his obvious admiration was a clear reminder that even in the sweltering heat she was a woman, not just a scientist.

Which, right now, was a bad thing to have click into her brain.

His brows slowly lifted. "Are you offering me a job, Dr. Meyer?"

She swallowed at the sexy sound of his voice. Smooth and deep and way better than she'd expected. Dammit. That voice was only going to fuel her already out of control fantasies.

She gave herself a mental slap. "No, actually, I wasn't. And it's not 'doctor.' Not yet, anyway. I was simply going to point out there's nothing new at this site you can learn, so your time would be better served back in Cairo. The tours of the Pyramids are astound—"

"I've taken the tours. They're not nearly as interesting as this one. Trust me."

Oh, man. Just the way he looked at her with that twinkle in his eyes and that sultry half grin made her think of sex. Which was a very bad thing to be thinking of right now.

Remember, he's not a tourist.

"Mr.—"

"Pete." He took her right hand before she could protest,

ran his fingers over her palm and looked down at where he held her. "Your skin is soft. Way softer than I expected considering the hours you must spend out here."

"I . . ." What was he doing? Though it was nine gazillion degrees, a shiver ran down her spine. "I use a lot of moisturizer," she managed before she realized how stupid she sounded. "You know, working . . . out here."

Whatever. Now she sounded like a complete moron.

"I'd like to hear all about it."

Irritated with herself, she looked up into his eyes to let him have it, then stalled out when she felt that pull. The same one she'd felt every time he'd looked at her over the past few days. The one that made her stomach flop all over the place and her heart kick up in her chest to the beat of a marching band.

"You already did," she managed. "You've heard about it every day this week."

He smiled then, a slow and easy curve of his lips that highlighted the deep dimple in his left cheek.

Oh, boy. The man had dimples. She was in deep trouble here.

His finger traced a lazy circle against her palm. The tiny movement shot electricity up her arm, straight to her belly. "I want to hear more about you."

"I don't think that's such a good—"

"Trust me." He glanced at her name tag, then back to her face. "Katherine."

She swallowed, unable to pull her hand away or move back when he took a step closer. People were watching them, but part of her didn't care. Damn, he smelled good, too. Clean, fresh. A hint of leather and something spicy. She fought to keep from closing her eyes and drawing in a deep whiff.

"I generally go by Kat." Why was she telling him this? "To my friends. Not to, you know. Everyone."

Dear God, she was losing it.

"Kat. Yeah, that's better. Fits you." He moved closer still. "But I like Kit-Kat more."

Why did that insane nickname sound so damn sexy coming from his lips?

"Look, Pete. Um. Mr. Kauffman." Wow. She liked how his first name sounded way too much. "You seem like a nice guy." Oh, Lord. She was going to hell for lying. He seemed like a sex god, not in any way, shape or form a nice guy. "And I'm flattered. Really. But, um, I think you have the wrong idea about me."

"What idea would that be, Ms. Meyer?"

The twinkle in his eye said he was baiting her, and part of her wanted to go on playing. But common sense took control. "I'm working here."

He studied her a long moment. "I'll tell you what. It's clear I'm distracting you and that you'd prefer I quit hanging around your tomb, right?"

She nodded slowly, not entirely sure where he was headed.

"I'll make you a deal then." He smiled again, let go of her hand, and damn if that dimple didn't wink at her. "Have dinner with me tonight."

"What?"

"Dinner. With me. Tonight. I pick the place. If you do, I'll stop bugging you. If you say no, well then . . ." He shrugged and tucked his hands into his pockets. "I'll just have to keep taking this tour until you change your mind."

The man was insane. He was willing to suffer through her boring tour and this sweltering heat just to get her attention? That was what he was doing here?

Shannon had been right.

"Well?"

She reached up to touch the chain that ran around her neck and disappeared beneath her shirt as she stared into those mesmerizing eyes. She should say no, but any guy who was willing to go through all that deserved to have a bone thrown his way. And it was only dinner, after all.

It wasn't like one meal would change her life.

Present day
Cairo, Egypt

Omar Kamil wasn't happy with the interruption.

He leaned across Rehema's long, naked body and reached for his cell phone, the one he'd left sitting on the nightstand just in case something urgent came up. He didn't bother to glance at the number, instead flipped it open and growled, "*Matha?*"

"We've got movement."

The heavily accented voice speaking English on the other end of the line drew his immediate attention, and he sat up.

Busir.

"Tell me," he said in English as well.

"She came out of hiding at the auction. You were right."

It was about damn time.

Omar let out a long breath and leaned back against the ornately carved headboard in the Nile suite at the Cairo Four Seasons. Out the window across the bedroom, palm trees framed a view of soaring high-rises across the river, sparkling in the late afternoon sun. Minutes before he could have cared less about the view. Now it was the most gorgeous picture he'd ever seen.

Six fucking years he'd been waiting for this call.

Rehema slid her hand across his abdomen, smiled a lusty grin and pressed her lips to his belly button. When she eased away as if to give him space for his conversation, he threaded his fingers into her long black hair and pulled her head back to his stomach. She wasn't getting away now, not when he felt like celebrating. Especially not when she didn't understand a lick of English.

Knowing what he wanted, she slid lower and took him into her mouth. The breath that slipped from his lips was pure victory.

"Where are you keeping her?" he asked in a relaxed voice.

"We're not."

He lurched up. "What?"

Rehema gagged and fell backward against the mattress. A series of coughs racked her body, but Omar barely noticed. He leapt out of the bed and strode naked to the window. "What kind of idiot are you? She finally shows up and you lose her? Of all the goddamned—"

"We had a . . . situation. The limo she's driving has a GPS tracking device, though. The service is paranoid about security. We've already got someone on it and have narrowed down her location. It's only a matter of hours before we apprehend her."

Omar could feel the blood pounding in his brain. His hand wavered as he ran it over his brow, mopped up sweat that had popped out on his forehead. The tightness in his chest made it hard to get air, so he focused on breathing deep. Slow. *One, two, three.*

He couldn't afford another heart attack over this. Not after he'd finally changed his diet and started exercising. He'd lost twenty fucking pounds from his beefy frame as a result, but weight loss hadn't been his goal. Staying alive was. He'd worked too long and hard to throw it all away now.

When he was sure his voice was calm, he said, "Explain to me how you lost her in a limousine, in downtown New York City. She's one woman in a car the size of a goddamned boat!"

So much for calm. He took another deep breath.

"There was a . . . rush after the auction. We lost her in traffic. But we know where she is."

He was dealing with imbeciles. Didn't matter their affiliation or who they took their orders from. They were imbeciles just the same.

He rubbed a hand over his balding head in utter frustration. "You've mentioned that already. If that's the case why are you jabbering to me about it instead of going after her?"

"A nor'easter moved through the region. Roads are closed and power's out over a large chunk of the area. She's hunkered down to wait out the storm, but we've got her. We'll have her and the boyfriend within twenty-four hours."

The boyfriend.

Omar stared out at the city he'd grown up in, but hated with every fiber of his being. Keeping tabs on Peter Kauffman had finally paid off, just like he'd predicted. Did the man know she'd been in hiding all this time? Or had he been in on it with her right from start? Anything was possible, but one thing was certain. Keeping the antiquities dealer alive in the hopes that one day he'd serve as bait had been a stroke of sheer genius.

A wicked smile spread across his face.

Twenty-four hours. One day, and then he'd be free.

Once Katherine Meyer was safely back in Egypt, he could dispose of her as he'd fantasized for six long years.

The only question left was who would do it. Should he let Minyawi have his way with her first? Or would he do the deed himself?

A thousand different scenarios ran through his mind. And all sent his adrenaline surging.

Northern Pennsylvania

The bitter cold woke him.

A shiver ran through Pete, rousing him from sleep. He blinked, opened his eyes and peered into utter darkness. For a moment he didn't know which way was up. Then he registered the frigid leather beneath his cheek and the dead weight of his arm pinned beneath his body.

He pushed up slowly and immediately regretted the movement. The dull throb he'd felt behind his eyes when he'd been lying down kicked up to the roar of a Dolphins game when he moved upright, and he closed his eyes again. He rubbed frozen fingers against his temples to abate the pounding in his skull and cringed as pain sliced through his skin.

What the . . .

He pulled his hand back, tried to squint to see what the wetness was on his fingers. It felt sticky and cold. Blood?

Okay, drinking himself into oblivion had been a really dumb idea, although he couldn't remember drinking anything after dropping Maria off at her apartment. He must have fallen somehow and hit his head. Regardless, a thirty-eight-year-old man should know better.

When he felt certain he wasn't going to black out, he opened his eyes and quickly realized something else wasn't right.

He was still in the limo. He could feel the cold Italian leather cradling his body, the hard floor at his feet. Around him was a blanket of some kind. He reached a hand out to test his surroundings and met vinyl and wood surrounding the wet bar.

He paused and listened, tried to figure out what was going on. The limo wasn't moving, the engine wasn't on, and there were no voices or even sounds for that matter.

Where was he? In an underground garage? If so, then where was the driver? Why had he been left in here all alone? And who had put this blanket on him?

His adrenaline shot up, and he moved closer to the window, cupped a hand against the glass and peered outside. Nothing. A black void met his eyes.

Slowly, and with cautious movements because his stomach was rebelling with every shift, he moved to the other side of the vehicle and did the same. Through the tinted glass, he could just make out what looked like a dim light coming from a distance away. A door? It looked like it, cracked open a few inches. If so, he was definitely in some kind of garage or building.

He pushed toward the Mercedes' back door, caught the handle and gave it a shove. The exertion sent the pounding in his head up another notch, and he groaned. As he eased out of the vehicle, he wondered if staying inside hadn't been the smarter choice. It was fucking freezing out here.

He wrapped his arms around himself, pulled the tux jacket tight against his body to conserve heat, and took slow steps toward the door ahead. The light was soft, as if from a lamp, and warmth radiated from the room before he even reached the threshold.

Heat was good. No matter what was on the other side of that door, it was better than staying out here and freezing his nuts off.

He placed one hand on the solid wood, more to steady himself than anything else, and pushed.

It was an apartment of some kind. The room stopped churning long enough so he could make out a TV in the far corner. Beat-up furniture filled the space. His wobbly gaze landed on the figure curled up in a ball on the sofa.

"Hey," he said in a raspy voice he barely recognized. He cleared his throat as the figure stirred. He'd tear off someone's head if he didn't get the hell out of here and back to his suite at the Waldorf pronto. There was an Alka-Seltzer there with his name on it. "What the hell is going—"

The figure sat bolt upright, blinked several times and stared at him with big, brown, stunned eyes. And suddenly he couldn't remember just what he'd wanted to know in the first place.

"Oh, shit," he whispered.

The blood rushed from his head and went due south, leaving him lightheaded and shaky. No way this was happening. He was still drunk. That was the only explanation. He was tripped out on some seriously bad champagne and hallucinating because *this* wasn't real. He wasn't staring at Katherine Meyer alive and in the flesh because she was *dead*.

She rose slowly from the couch.

Stunned into silence, all he could do was stare as she rubbed her hands against her thighs and took a cautious step toward him.

It looked like Kat. A variation anyway. This woman's hair was nearly black and cut short as a boy's. But the face—holy hell—the face was the same. The same wide doe eyes, the same pouty lips, the same dark mole on the upper right side of her mouth.

"Pete. You startled me. I . . . are you okay?"

It sounded like her, too. His eyes widened in disbelief.

Her gaze darted over his face. "You look a little better. How do you feel?"

How did he feel? Like he'd just been hit by a bulldozer, head-on.

He barely managed to catch the door handle for support before his legs gave out. His mouth dropped open, a thousand questions fired off in his brain, and though he tried to form words, he couldn't get his lips to work.

Hallucinating. You're hallucinating, man. That's the only explanation.

"I tried to move you, but you were like dead weight, and I, well, I'm a little tired after everything else. So I got you a blanket and left the door open. I know it was cold out there . . ."

Her words trailed off. And she closed her mouth quickly at what he knew had to be his stunned expression. Then sank her top teeth into her bottom lip the way Kat always had when she'd been shy or uncertain about something.

"I guess you're ready to chat. I think it's safe to say you look a little surprised."

Surprised?

No fucking way.

The room jackknifed. He knew he was going under like a class-A pansy, but he couldn't stop it. His vision blurred and darkened until the only thing left was utter blackness and the sound of a voice he'd never been able to forget.

CHAPTER FIVE

"Pete. Oh, Pete. Please wake up."

He knew that voice.

Through a fog, Pete struggled to consciousness. He'd been here before. Knew he was dreaming. Knew it was stupid to let himself get sucked in again because he'd invariably wake up feeling ten times worse than he did now.

But her scent was strong. Clean, fresh, reminiscent of the night-blooming jasmine she'd always loved. Yet somehow . . . bolder, spicier, more *her.* Before he could stop himself, he reached out to wrap his fingers around her arms and draw her close.

Her skin was as silky soft as he remembered, her heat warming the coldest space deep in his chest. His eyes drifted open, and through a haze he saw her face. Her perfect, familiar face.

Okay, dumb, but . . . even if it was a dream, it was still her.

"Kat." He slid his hand around her nape and pulled her mouth to his.

Then groaned at the first touch.

She hesitated. He felt it, then pushed the thought right out of his head as he tightened his arms around her. Her soft purr as she melted against him spurred him on. He kissed her again, fell back onto the floor and brought her with him.

"Pete," she said against his mouth. "Oh, I shouldn't . . ."

Yeah, he shouldn't either. He was gonna have the mother of all wet dreams on his hands when he woke up, but who the hell cared anymore?

His fingers found the hem of her sweatshirt, and he pushed it up, ran his hands along the smooth skin of her back, around to her ribs. She drew a breath at the slight touch, let it out. Whatever protest had been on her sweet, tempting lips faded as she kissed him back.

His erection sprang to life. He clutched her hips and pulled her tight against him. That sexy purr coming from somewhere deep inside her turned to an achy mew he knew from experience meant she was as desperate for him as he was for her.

He deepened the kiss, knew he'd never last if she kept rubbing up against him like she was doing, if she didn't lose those clothes and set his pounding arousal free, climb on top of him and take him right here, right now.

Hell, he didn't even care that in this twisted fantasy he was lying on a cold cement floor, that his head was still throbbing from a monster hangover or that his toes were nearly numb. All he cared about was getting her naked and burying himself inside her until that hot sweet scent of hers surrounded him and she screamed his name and came with a ferocity that . . .

Wait. He could *smell* her.

Time seemed to stand still as the impact of that realization plowed into him.

His heart ratcheted up a notch. She continued to kiss him while he went cold all over.

In all his delirious fantasies about being with Kat again—the ones he'd never cop to, no matter what—he'd always been able to see her, to feel her, even to taste her to some degree. But never, not once in all the times he'd had this recurring dream, had he ever been able to *smell* her.

Now he could.

She was also on fire. Like liquid heat against his skin where she burrowed closer to him.

You couldn't smell dreams, and they sure as hell weren't warm.

Confused, caught between a dream state and reality, he gripped her arms, pushed her back and squinted to look up into a face he'd never expected to see again in this lifetime.

"Kat?" He croaked out the word, didn't dare move as those wide, molten chocolate eyes ran over his features.

"Yeah," she whispered. "It's me."

No way.

He bolted, not sure what was happening. All he knew for certain was his kinky sex fantasies had never taken this detour into insanity before. He scrambled from the floor and was nearly knocked over by a wave of nausea that made him grip the door handle again to keep from falling to his knees.

She was up and next to him before he could catch his bearings. "I know how this looks, but if you just give me a minute, I can explain." She sounded frantic. A little scared. And completely wigged out.

Holy fuck. That made two of them. "What the . . ." The pounding hit his skull again with the force of a jackhammer, and he pressed his fingers against his temples. "This isn't real," he muttered to himself as he gave his head a strong shake. "Can't be real. I'm hung over. Really hung over. That or I've got a brain tumor." He squeezed his eyes shut. "MRI. That's it. I need a goddamn MRI."

She reached out for him. "Let me—"

He flinched and jerked away from her hand. If she touched him again he was afraid he wouldn't be able to think straight. And right now he really needed to clear his damn head so he could figure out just what the hell was going on.

She dropped her arm like he'd burned her, reached up with one hand to wrap her fingers around a pendant of some kind hanging from her neck. "The least you can do is listen to what I have to say, Pete. Believe me, I wouldn't have dragged you into this if there was any other way."

He barely heard her words but registered the bite. Though at that moment the only thing he could focus on was the charm hidden in her fist.

He pushed her hand away and fingered the silver medal between her breasts.

St. Jude. Patron saint of lost causes. Kat had always worn it. Never took it off. And the sudden memory of that medal falling against his chest as they made love was as vivid and real as the warm and solid weight now in the palm of his hand.

His eyes shot to her face.

She was real. This was happening, and, holy hell, she was *alive*.

The world fell away. He let his instincts rule his body. In a move so fast she gasped, he grabbed her hard, pulled her tight against his chest and kissed her with everything he had in him.

"Kit-Kat," he mumbled against her lips.

But as quickly as the joy and elation erupted inside him, it fizzled and died.

She was alive. Had been all this time and hadn't tried to contact him. Not once in six years. Not when he'd blamed himself for what had happened or bawled like a baby over her death or wished like hell he could trade places with her. No, instead of finding him like he would have done if the situation had been reversed, she'd been living somewhere else, healthy and happy and obviously . . . whole.

He broke the kiss, pushed her to arm's length and stared down at her. "You're alive? After all this time? You're . . . alive?"

Her muscles went rigid beneath his hands. "I know this is hard for you to grasp, but I have reasons for everything I've done. I didn't plan any of this tonight. I didn't plan for you . . ."

She looked down at his shirt and closed her mouth.

Plan this. Tonight.

Her words ricocheted around in his head as his memory came back in a rush. And with it, reality formed a knot in the pit of his stomach.

"You were at the auction house. You're the woman I saw in the crowd." The one he'd chased after like a love-sick fool.

"I—I'd hoped you hadn't seen me."

Hadn't seen her? He dropped his arms. That knot twisted. His brain skipped ahead, flashed on Maria's mouth against his in the limo, how they'd tumbled to the floor and he'd looked up into the rearview mirror to see eyes that were the same exact color and shape as the ones he was staring into now.

"And in the limo. Was that you, too?"

She nodded slowly. "After I saw them, I just needed five minutes to talk to you. I swear that's all I wanted, but then everything went to hell and back and," she threw up her hands, "then I didn't have a choice."

A choice?

He suddenly didn't like where this was heading. This wasn't the reunion he'd always fantasized about.

Kat tensed, obviously reading his expression. "Before you go getting those half-cocked ideas of yours—"

"Half-cocked ideas?" he snapped. "You're alive and yet you couldn't once pick up a goddamn phone and call to let me know you *hadn't* died in a car bomb in Cairo after all? What, did it slip your mind?"

His headache took that opportunity to stab him right in the middle of his forehead. He slammed his eyes shut, pressed his fingers to his temples and bent over at the waist to ease the throb. "Son of a bitch."

"Oh, Pete." She rushed toward him. "Don't pass out on me. I can't handle that again. I don't even know how much they gave you."

"Gave me? What the hell are you talking about?"

She stopped inches from touching him with a nervous look in her eyes. "I . . . um. . . ." When he raised his head to stare at her, she lifted her arms and finally dropped them on a sigh. "A sedative. I don't know how much you got, but you've been out cold for the last five hours."

He eased up slowly. "Whoa. Wait. Are you saying you *drugged* me?"

She opened her mouth to speak but closed it quickly without answering.

That was when it all hit him. The auction, the limo, the dark, the cold, and her here alive, alone in this room. She hadn't sought him out. She'd been at the auction for another reason entirely, and something had happened there to force her into ambushing him. In fact, the more he thought about it, the more he realized she'd obviously been playing him from the moment he thought she'd died. Maybe even before that.

And wasn't that just fucking ironic?

At that moment, with his head pounding and his stomach weak, he didn't give a flying fuck what she wanted from him or why she'd brought him here. All he could think was that she'd been alive all this time while he'd been . . . half dead inside.

"I'm outta here."

He moved back out the door he'd stumbled into, ignoring the shock that flashed across her face. Light from the room behind him poured into the garage, highlighting the limo and the wall of tools on the far side.

"Pete, wait."

Yeah, right. Not in this lifetime. Not ever again.

He headed for the massive door on the far wall. Footsteps echoed behind him as he fumbled with the lock, but he didn't turn, didn't look at her. Tried like hell not to think of her.

A wave of snow blasted across his face when he managed to get the door open. He held up his hands to block the biting wind, took a few tentative steps out into the snow.

Where was he? No city lights twinkled in the distance. His dress shoes sank into eight inches of powder. He stumbled.

The darkness and never-ending flakes slapping his face made it impossible to see, but the rational side of his brain said if there was a garage—wherever he was—then there had to be a house. And houses had phones.

"Pete! Please come back inside. You'll freeze out there!"

As juiced as he felt, he didn't think it was possible to freeze. And no way in hell was he going back in there with her.

Okay, this was stupid.

Kat shivered in the cold air, wrapped her arms around her waist and tried to breathe.

How long had Pete been gone? Two minutes? Three? She couldn't see him anymore, had no idea at this point which direction he'd gone. He was dressed in a tuxedo, for crying out loud. Considering the frigid temperatures, he wouldn't last out there long, and he didn't know where he was or where he was going. Besides all that, there was no way he could see in that blinding blizzard.

He'd figure that all out, right? There were no houses within miles of this property. Woods bordered the north side, pastures and farmland the other three. Common sense would tell him to come back to the warmth of the garage, wouldn't it? Even with her there?

She gnawed on the end of her thumbnail, completely unsure what he would say or do next. In her head she rationalized this was a good thing. She finally had the golden pharaoh. He knew she was alive. If something happened to him now, well, at least he'd be partially prepared. He wasn't her problem anymore. Never really had been, come to think of it.

Her traitorous heart, on the other hand, screamed this was bad news. He could die out there in the cold, or worse, escape and then be found by Busir. Either way, by bringing him with her tonight, she'd just signed his death certificate.

And wasn't that a peachy thought? Everything she'd done the past six years meant nothing because he was too proud to give her five minutes of his frickin' time.

She shook off the thought and told herself he'd be back. Once he discovered they were isolated and realized there was no one around to help but her, he'd have no other choice.

At least she hoped so.

She toyed with the medal at her chest. And stupidly thought of that kiss.

Hot came to mind. Reminiscent of the kisses he'd drugged her with in Cairo, but more urgent. Immediate. Her cheeks heated at just the memory. And like the fool she'd been back then, she'd fallen for it again tonight. Opened for him like a flower, sank into his body. Hadn't even thought to fight it.

Twice!

Idiot.

Hadn't she learned her lesson where he was concerned?

Kat stared out into the snow once more and finally gave in to common sense. She couldn't leave the door open any longer. Every minute she did, the temperature in the building dropped in increments.

She flipped on the outside light so Pete could find the building in the snowstorm and closed the door. Then she backtracked into the apartment and cranked the furnace up higher, grabbed blankets from the closet and laid them by the register to warm. She went into the closet-sized kitchen, found a teakettle and filled it with water.

Having something to do made her feel marginally better. When the water was on the stove heating, she went back to the door to the apartment she'd left open and leaned against the jamb while she waited.

Fifteen minutes passed. Twenty. No sound but the wind howling outside.

Where was he?

As a clock somewhere in the apartment ticked off the long seconds, she bit her lip. Toyed with her medal some more. And though she tried to fight it, couldn't help but think of the way he'd looked at her tonight when he'd discovered she was really alive. Of the way he'd looked at her from the very beginning.

CHAPTER SIX

Six-and-a-half years earlier
Valley of the Kings

She'd been right. Peter Kauffman was trouble. The kind that came in flashing capital letters and needed a warning label slapped all over it.

Kat stared across the table of the dimly lit Italian restaurant as Pete talked about his business and felt the same electricity flow through her veins she'd been trying to tamp down the last few hours.

Hell, the last few days for that matter.

It wasn't so much what he said—though she did enjoy hearing about his gallery in Miami and the buying trips that sent him all over the globe—it was the way he looked at her. With those smoldering eyes, like she was grade-A prime-cut beef and he was dying to sink his teeth in her.

Heat rushed to her cheeks. She eased her hands under the damask tablecloth and wiped her sweaty palms on her black slacks like she'd done several times during the meal.

He really was gorgeous—all blond and tan and sexy in that white dress shirt and those charcoal slacks. His shoulders were broad, his waist narrow, and those hips? Perfection. He was also so totally focused on her she wasn't entirely sure he was real. She'd been wary at first, careful not to divulge too much about her work site just in case he was one of those treasure hunters the crew had warned her about, but he'd barely seemed interested in her dig. And a big part of her was relieved. She really didn't want to get into the scandal surrounding her site and the artifacts that had been slowly disappearing the last few months. Instead he'd steered the conversation to her months in Cairo, her interests, what she did in her free time and what she wanted to do with her life.

And that was what really did her in. No one had ever seemed so genuinely interested in her before. Especially not an Adonis like him.

At some point she realized she needed to open her mouth and say something intellectual so she'd stop focusing on that sexy dimple in his cheek and the subtle curve of his lips. He'd been doing most of the talking, and it wasn't going to take him long to figure out she was practically drooling. So she picked the one topic she knew would get her mind off hot, sticky, sweaty sex and what he looked like underneath those fancy clothes.

And regretted it minutes later when he only stared at her without responding.

"I'm boring you, aren't I?" Kat reached for her wineglass. "Not everyone's as excited about Egyptian history as I am. Sorry."

Pete chuckled, the sound so deep and rich, she was sure she felt the vibrations all the way across the table and into her toes. "You're not boring me at all. I could listen to you talk all night long."

She frowned, knowing he was simply playing her, and told herself not to read too much into his words. But when his grin widened and those damn eyes of his sparked, held on hers and dropped to her mouth, she wasn't so sure anymore. There was definitely something happening between them. Something sultry and electric she'd never felt before. And damn if it didn't excite and scare her to death all at the same time.

The waiter brought his receipt then. Pete signed the slip of paper and pushed his chair back. "Are you ready?"

"Yes." Happy for the distraction, she grabbed her purse, slipped the strap over her bare shoulder and headed toward the front of the restaurant.

Outside the air was balmy, with a slight breeze blowing off the water. Beside her, Pete tucked his hands in the pockets of his slacks and gestured with his shoulder. "You want to walk for a bit?"

She was more relieved than she wanted to admit. Walking meant she'd get to spend more time with him before they said good night. "Yes. I'd love to."

They strolled the streets of downtown Cairo and talked about sports and politics and what it was like to be an American living and working abroad. Eventually they ended up along the banks of the Nile where lights from high-rise office buildings shimmered over the water, contrasting with mud-brick houses and donkey-drawn carts.

Cairo wasn't a gentle city. It overwhelmed the senses with its noise and chaos, pollution and sixteen million people. But Kat loved it. Sure, there was too much of everything here—too much progress, too much history, too many dangers lurking if you weren't careful—but it was a magical place. Never more so than it was this night.

It was close to an hour later when they finally made their way to her flat. The building was in an older neighborhood, but well-kept and safely lit.

"This is me," she said as they slowed near the front entrance and the five steps that led to the building's main door.

"Nice area." She noticed he took it all in—the other buildings, the modern cars on the street, the security system blinking just inside the glass door of her building—and approved. The man missed nothing.

"Yeah. One of the guys on our team has been in Cairo a long time and has a flat here. He told us about it when a unit opened up. Personally, I think it's because he has a crush on Shannon and he wanted to keep an eye on her, but I'm not complaining. Beats living in a mud hut or a tent."

He smiled and looked down at her. And that spark passed between them again. A jolt she hoped he felt as strongly as she did.

She swallowed and watched as his eyes followed the line of her throat, lower to the skin revealed by her open collar, lower still to the St. Jude medal that fell just above her breasts.

Her pulse pounded under that sultry gaze. And she made a choice she never would have even considered before, right on the spot. "Do you want to come up? I think Shannon was hanging out with some friends tonight. She won't be back until morning."

Those smoldering eyes ran up to hover on her lips, higher still until his gaze locked on hers and it felt like he was looking all the way into her soul.

"I'd like to," he said softly. "But I can't. I'm flying to Rome tonight."

Her stomach fell like a stone weight. "Rome?"

He nodded slowly.

"When will you be back?"

"I'm not sure."

"Oh."

She looked down at her hands, noticed they were shaking and clasped them together. Maybe she'd read him wrong. Was she really that stupid?

His hand closed over both of hers before she saw him move. "Thank you for the nicest dinner I've had in longer than I can remember. I'm glad I met you, Katherine Meyer."

A slight tremble ran through his touch, one she tried not to misread but couldn't ignore. She chanced a look up. And knew she hadn't been completely wrong. Regret and disappointment reflected deeply in his eyes.

And odd as it was considering she wanted him more than she could remember wanting anything else in her life, a strange sense of relief pulsed along her nerve endings.

Something she couldn't define was pushing her toward him. Something deeper than a sexual connection and a thousand times hotter. He was the most dangerous kind of man because he was the first who made her feel with her heart rather than think with her mind.

Lucky for her, something was holding him back. Something she didn't understand but knew instinctively had just saved her from major heartbreak.

"I'm glad I met you too, Pete." Her throat grew thick. "I wish we'd had longer."

She forced herself to let go and step back before he said

something that would make her stop. Without a doubt, the secrets in his smoky eyes would stay with her long after he was gone. "Good luck in Rome."

She turned, hustled up the stairs and with a click of her key left him standing alone on the street.

Present day
Northeastern Pennsylvania

"Forecast shows snow slowing in the next hour or so."

Aten Minyawi looked up from the handheld GPS he was studying and gave a brief nod toward his counterpart, Hanif Busir, who was seated at the small table in the motel they'd scrounged up, studying the weather on his computer. Minyawi refocused on the picture in front of him. The GPS dot hadn't budged in the last three to four hours. Katherine Meyer was hunkered down, feeling safe and smug.

She wouldn't be smug for long. It was only a matter of time before he caught up with her. And finished what she'd started six years ago.

"That's good," Busir mumbled with a scowl that said he was talking to himself.

Minyawi ignored him. Thoughts of Kat's large brown eyes slid into his mind. Of the way she'd looked at him back then. Of the way she'd been so trusting. So naïve. He'd pegged her wrong from the start, though. He wouldn't do so again.

He ran a finger down the scar on his left cheek. No, she wasn't naïve. She'd taken away the only thing he'd ever truly cared about. Made him the killer he was today.

He shut out the memories and emotions he no longer felt. His training had hardened him into nothing more than a machine. And it had saved him.

He stood. "We go now."

Busir glanced up. "But the weather—"

"We go now," he said again. They'd been sitting on their asses too long as it was, holed up in a motel in the middle of bum-fuck America, and he was sick of it. Sick of waiting, of watching. Of planning. "Take care of the clerk while I contact Usted and Wyatt. They'll go in from the north side. We'll take the south."

Their partners on this excursion were hired American thugs, but Minyawi didn't care. He'd been at the auction house looking for Kat when she'd gotten the jump on Busir and Wyatt. Morons that they were, they'd let her slip through their fingers. But Minyawi still needed them. At least a little longer.

"Aten—"

He turned hardened eyes on Busir. The man quickly closed his mouth.

Indecision brewed in Busir's eyes. He was debating whether to ask a question or bite his tongue.

Minyawi relaxed his jaw. Though he ran the show, he liked that this unlikely brother-in-arms had a brain and knew how to use it. It could be an asset in the future.

Busir closed the laptop and slowly rose from the metal chair. "We're two hours from her location. With the snow yet, it'll take us twice that. Usted and Wyatt are an hour behind us. She's not going anywhere. If we wait—"

Of course, there was using a brain, and then there was overkill.

"If we wait," Minyawi said through clenched teeth, his accent punctuating each word, "she could decide to leave. We'll secure the perimeter and hold for the others. Now do as I say."

Busir's lips thinned, but he didn't press the issue. With a frown he pulled the semiautomatic from the holster at the small of his back and screwed on the silencer. His footsteps echoed across the tile floor, followed by the muffled sob of the night clerk bound hand-to-foot in the back room.

Minyawi glanced at the GPS one last time before pocketing the instrument. He wouldn't let her get away. Not this time.

A muffled pop echoed from the back room. Then . . . silence.

Loose ends.

In the military when he'd been nothing more than a boy, he'd learned to consider all his options. Prepare for the unexpected, never underestimate your enemy. He'd overlooked Katherine Meyer the first time he'd met her.

He wouldn't again.

He now knew her weakness. A weakness he no longer had. She had no family left, no friends. Nothing. But she was loyal.

And that loyalty, luckily, was going to lead him right to her.

CHAPTER SEVEN

Present day
Northern Pennsylvania

Kat straightened from the doorjamb where she'd been leaning. Okay, Pete had been gone for thirty minutes. Enough was enough. She was going out to look for him.

In a closet off the kitchen she found several parkas, gloves and a flashlight. The exterior garage door opened just as she reached it.

Pete shivered as he stumbled through the opening. Snow covered his body. Ice crystals stuck to the shadowy beard on his jaw. As she took in his nearly white skin, she couldn't help but think he looked like a well-dressed pop-sicle.

Relief and irritation warred inside her as she grabbed him and helped him inside. "Smart move, Indiana."

"F . . . f . . . freezing out there," he chattered as he stomped snow off his feet.

"No kidding. It's called a blizzard. What were you thinking? You could have been killed."

"Looking for . . . h . . . house."

She used one arm to close and lock the outer door, made sure to flip off the exterior light and then led him into the apartment. After easing him into a chair in front of the register, she took his frozen jacket, wrapped one of the heated blankets around his shivering shoulders and rubbed his arms to stimulate circulation.

And felt a twinge of sympathy for him.

Okay, being a bitch just because that kiss had thrown her for a loop wasn't going to accomplish much. They were stuck in here together until the storm passed. Might as well make the best of it.

"There isn't one," she said as she shrugged out of her coat. "It burned to the ground about three years ago. The nearest house is at least a mile away."

His teeth continued to knock together as she rubbed his arms, then his legs and finally his feet after she removed his shoes and socks. He was soaked to the skin. She'd seen extra clothing in the closet and knew she'd have to get him out of his wet tuxedo before long.

She glanced at his sodden slacks, the ruined dress shoes on the floor. Armani. She didn't live in a hole in the ground; she knew when she saw money. And he had it. More than he'd had when they'd been together. Judging from how well all those stolen artifacts had done at his auction tonight, a whole lot more.

Don't go there.

"Wh . . . where are we?"

Before she could answer, the kettle whistled. Relieved at the distraction, she rose, went to the kitchen where she poured a mug of tea and brought it back to him.

"Northern Pennsylvania," she said as she handed him the steaming mug. He took it with two hands, pressed it against his right cheek and closed his eyes.

His color was slowly returning, but he still looked like death warmed over—which was ironically how she felt. Dry clothes could wait a few minutes. He looked like he needed a moment to catch his bearings.

So did she for that matter.

He kept the cup against his cheek, took slow and rhythmic breaths. He hadn't looked at her once since he'd come back into the room. Though he'd accepted her help, hadn't pushed her away when she'd guided him into the apartment, she sensed he was struggling to keep his emotions in check.

She had a brief flash of his enraged face in that alley tonight, and a shiver ran down her back. No, she really didn't know this man, not the parts that mattered. Considering what she knew he was now capable of, she thanked her lucky stars he was in such control.

On a deep breath, she sat on the couch across from him and bit the inside of her lip. This was going to be a long night.

"Warming up?" she asked to cut the silence.

There was no response save a slight shift in his breathing. His eyes were still closed, the cup still pressed against his cheek. For a minute she wondered if he'd fallen asleep, but then decided he couldn't have, not sitting upright like that.

"You weren't on the guest list," he said in a raspy, deep voice void of any kind of emotion.

"No," she said quietly. "I wasn't."

Silence.

"What were you doing at my auction?"

How much could she tell him without putting both of their lives in more jeopardy? How much of the truth could she really trust him with?

Not much, her conscience screamed.

"I guess you could say I was curious. I . . . bypassed security."

A humorless sound came out of him. A cross between a huff and a laugh. "Fitting, I guess," he mumbled. "Karma's got a badass sense of humor."

Kat frowned. Oh yeah, good ol' karma. When you considered the fact *he* was the criminal and *she'd* been the one doing the breaking and entering, it was more than just a little ironic.

"Answer me one question," he said. "Why a bomb? I mean, if you'd wanted to hide from me, you could have easily done it without the theatrics."

Hide from him? Was that what he thought? She'd been in hiding *because* of him.

"I didn't really have a choice."

The look he shot her screamed *yeah right.* "You mentioned that before. Everyone has choices, Kat."

Not her. Hers had dried up the day she'd met Peter Kauffman.

She looked away. "It doesn't matter anymore."

"I've got nothing but time, thanks to you." He sipped his tea as if all was well, but the bite in his voice told her to watch her back. "And I think I have a right to know. You owe me that much at least."

Her resistance wavered. She didn't owe him a thing, not as far as she could see, but some small part of her knew he wouldn't let up until he had at least a smattering of the truth. She decided giving him the basics wouldn't hurt.

"I'm sure you remember Dr. Sawil Ramirez."

He thought for a moment, took a sip from the mug. "Dark-haired guy. Brazilian, wasn't he?"

"Yes." He'd lived in the apartment above her and Shannon, and Pete had met him several times. "I talked to him about the relics I suspected were taken from the tomb. He was surprised I'd kept such a close eye on it all. But in the end he was thankful."

Tension seeped back into the room with just those few sentences. His hand tightened around the mug.

Kat crossed her arms over her chest. She would *not* feel guilty about this again. If he didn't want to hear the truth then he shouldn't have asked.

"One night while you were away on one of your 'business trips,' Sawil showed up at my apartment. He said he had the proof I needed and that I wouldn't believe who was involved."

Pete's jaw clenched and unclenched. Kat knew what he was thinking, but he wasn't denying it, so she went on.

"He'd taken what I'd told him to the Supreme Council of Antiquities himself. Filed his own report. The man he'd filed the report with, Amon Bakhum, was conveniently killed in a car accident the following day."

The Supreme Council of Antiquities was the government body that oversaw all archaeological excavation in Egypt. They were supposed to keep Egypt's treasures safe. In this case, they'd let the ball drop. Big-time.

She paused, thought back to Sawil's wary eyes the night he'd come pounding on her door. He'd been a quiet man, and his crush on Shannon had endeared him to Kat. Repeatedly he'd tried to talk her into leaving things alone, told her it was none of her business. But when she hadn't, when she'd persisted in looking for answers, he'd tried to warn her. He'd seen her coming and going with Pete, and he'd been worried their association would eventually cost her her life.

It had, but not in the way Sawil had predicted.

She bit her lip, debated how much else to say, then figured, *what the hell?* Pete already knew most of this. He'd been privy to it from the other side.

"One of the men I saw at the auction tonight ran stolen artifacts on the black market in Egypt."

"Let me guess," Pete said calmly. Too calmly. "Ramirez told you I knew the guy."

A knot formed in her stomach as she remembered back. At the time, she hadn't wanted to believe what Sawil had told her. The man she'd fallen in love with couldn't possibly be involved in an artifact-smuggling operation. She'd told Sawil that much.

But that was before she'd seen the proof herself.

The betrayal that cut through her now was as sharp as the day she'd realized she'd been duped. Played, from the very start.

"He didn't need to tell me," she snapped.

Pete's gaze shifted her way, not a flicker of emotion anywhere on his face. No, that wasn't true. There was boredom in his flat eyes. Boredom and indifference.

And it cut her. Just as much as his reaction had that day.

"Move on," he said. "What happened next?"

She drew a deep breath. "Sawil had an idea. A way we could get the last bit of evidence we needed, and I, well . . . I was curious. He asked me to go back to the tomb with him that night." Her stomach pitched as memories of that night flooded her mind.

"Kat?"

She flinched at Pete's voice. His brows lowered as he watched her. Was that concern in his eyes? Concern or just mere curiosity at her silence?

She didn't know. But ultimately, she'd been in that tomb that night because she'd wanted some kind of proof Sawil was wrong and Pete was innocent. She hadn't found it.

"We didn't know they were still there. We surprised them."

"Who?"

"Two men. One was at the auction tonight. The other—I never saw his face. Sawil, he . . ." She swallowed around the lump that formed in her throat. "He didn't make it out."

Pete's jaw flexed, but he didn't say anything, and it was impossible to read his expression.

"Somehow I made it back into Cairo," she went on, refusing to think about the details or what she'd heard from the shadows of the tomb. "I was afraid to go home. I didn't know what to do. I tried to call Shannon, to warn her not to go back to our apartment. I got worried so I . . ." She took a breath. "I called Marty."

Pete's cup paused halfway to his mouth. It was no secret he hadn't liked her ex, Martin Slade, who worked for the CIA. Of course, she hadn't put two and two together as to *why* until after everything had gone down and she'd realized what Pete had really been into.

It was obvious Pete liked Marty less now than he had back then. That should make all this easier considering the circumstances, right? Only for some insane reason, it didn't.

"Marty . . . he told me they would have her picked up. That they'd protect her. But they couldn't."

Kat glanced toward the radiator and focused on the tarnished metal. To this day, she still couldn't let herself think of the horrible things those two men had done to her roommate.

"Whoever they worked for was so important," she said, "they were willing to kill anyone who got in their way. That SCA agent. Sawil. Shannon. Me. They used Shannon to get to me."

"So why the bomb?"

"Because I was in over my head. I was the last one to

see Sawil alive. I didn't have an alibi for being gone that night, and people at the tomb had heard me arguing with him earlier in the day." They'd been arguing about Pete and his possible involvement, though she didn't say that now. "Several of the missing artifacts were found in my apartment, along with Shannon's body. Shannon and Sawil were practically a couple by that point. And they both died on the same night. According to Marty, I was already under watch because of my job and my association with you."

He glanced away, but she stiffened her spine and went on. "And then I heard from them. They knew everything about me—about my mother, where I lived, where I worked, what route I drove to the university when I was home. They threatened . . . my family, and after everything . . . I knew they'd make good on it."

When he looked at her with blank eyes, she knew he didn't believe her, and that treacherous heart of hers dropped. Did she expect his sympathy? She really was more pathetic than she realized.

"So, let me guess," he said. "Good old Marty faked the car bomb."

She nodded.

"And Shannon's body was in the rubble, not yours."

Sickness welled in her stomach again just like it had that day. "Not Shannon's. But someone else's. I don't know the details, but Marty handled it. He figured an Egyptian investigation would just raise too many questions. Whoever it was . . . He made sure the dental records matched."

"Jesus Christ." Pete looked away in disgust.

Kat squared her shoulders, lifted her chin. There wasn't anything she could do about the past. All that mattered— all that ever mattered—was what she did now.

"Look, I don't expect you to understand. You asked. I answered. I did what I had to do to stay alive."

He stood, wobbled and reached out to grip the chair. She quickly rose to help him, but the fire in his eyes had her thinking twice about touching him. She pulled her hand back.

"No, I don't understand, and I don't want to. Sounds to me like everything that happened was a result of you being too stubborn and impulsive to listen to reason."

"Wait a minute—"

"No, I'm done waiting," he snapped. "Why the hell am I here now? Not because you need anything from me. I'm here because you fucked up—again—and this time dragged me into it."

She couldn't believe he was just going to stand there and act like he hadn't played a part in what had happened. She opened her mouth to say just that but stopped.

He was right about one thing. She had dragged him back into this mess. If she'd stuck to her plan and not gone into the Worthington's lobby last night, neither of them would be here right now.

"I didn't mean to—"

"What you meant to do and what you did are two very different things, then and now. Aren't they, Kat?"

Her mouth snapped closed.

"And now I suppose you're going to tell me these guys, the ones who were at the auction tonight, saw you and now know you're not really dead. Which means they're looking for you because they want to have a nice little conversation about what you remember. And because you showed your face at *my* auction, that means I'm now fucked because they'll try to find me to get to you. Is that about right? Please, by all means, fill me in if I missed anything."

It was more than right, and his sarcasm proved just how ticked he really was. She sensed now wasn't the time to tell him the pendant she'd mailed him just before disappearing six years ago held the only evidence that would prove her innocence and possibly put a murderer in jail.

And that when she was forced to turn it and herself into the authorities tomorrow, she'd have to explain everything she knew about his involvement as well.

He waited long seconds for a response she just couldn't give. Finally, he rubbed both hands over his face. "This is all I need right now."

All *he* needed? *Get in line, buddy.*

He turned and looked around the room. "I'm soaked."

"There are extra clothes in here." Happy for the excuse to get away from him, she moved to the small closet and pulled out a fresh towel. "Not fancy, but dry."

"Whose property is this?"

She froze. It was the one question she'd hoped he wouldn't ask. She could tone down the violence of what had happened in that tomb. She could keep her emotions out of it when she told him the story. She could even fudge on the whys of what she'd done. What she couldn't do was lie to him. Not about this. Because it had been an issue between them even before those last few days.

"Whose property, Kat?"

"Marty's."

"Oh, man. This is just fucking fantastic."

He stalked toward her, jerked the towel from her hands and shoved the bathroom door open. "Why am I surprised?" he muttered. "Considering everything else, I shouldn't be."

"Oh, for God's sake, Pete, it's not what you—"

"You know what?" He stepped into the small bathroom. "I don't even want to know. Who the hell you screw isn't my problem anymore. When the storm breaks, I'm gone."

Her back went up. She wanted him gone, right? Then why was her chest suddenly stiff?

"That pickup in the back of the garage work?" he asked.

Startled, her mind flashed to the beat-up blue Ford F-250 she'd parked the limo next to. "Yes, I think so."

"Good. Then I'll take that and be out of your hair."

"They'll come looking for you."

"Oh yeah?" When he glanced down at her, his eyes were hard and cold and the same steely gray she'd seen tonight in the alley when he'd had Busir pinned to the side of that building. This was the man she didn't know, a side he'd kept carefully hidden from her. She'd never been afraid of him, but right now, she was. He looked like he could commit murder and enjoy it. "I can't wait."

"Pete—"

She never got to finish her statement. The door closed in her face. He didn't slam it, didn't even snap it shut like she'd expected. He simply clicked it closed and forced her out.

Then turned the lock so she couldn't get near him again.

CHAPTER EIGHT

Present day
Barcelona, Spain

His phone had a habit of ringing just as he was about to crash for the day.

Martin Slade groaned at the shrill notes and flopped onto his back. If it was important, whoever had the bad sense to bother him would leave a message. A man deserved two hours of shut-eye without interruption.

His phone ran through the high-pitched notes twice more before it stopped. On a deep sigh, he rolled to his side, bunched the pillow over his head and closed his eyes. Two seconds later, the sharp sound woke him again.

"Goddammit." He threw the pillow aside and reaching for his cell on the nightstand. "Somebody better be dead."

"Somebody already is."

The agitation rushed out of him in a wave and was replaced by that familiar thump, thump, thump in his chest.

"Kat."

"Hey, Marty," she said softly. "Sorry to bother you."

Katherine Meyer.

He pushed up in the pillows, rubbed a hand down his face. The beard he hadn't shaved in three days itched, so he scratched his jaw in a crazy attempt to think of anything besides Kat's angelic face and the fact she was the last person he expected to hear from and the only one he ever wanted to talk to. "No, you're not bothering me. I was just trying to catch some Z's, although it's so damn light here, I wasn't getting many even before you called."

"Oh? Where are you?"

Shit. Open mouth, insert foot. He faltered. "Um . . ."

"It's okay," she said. "I understand."

He knew she did, and it relaxed him. He leaned back against the scuffed headboard in his hotel, tucked his right hand against his opposite side and thanked God for the sweet distraction she created. Didn't matter the reason she was calling, just that she had.

He tried to think of a way to keep her talking. Her voice had the softest lilt when she said his name. "Sunny here today," he mumbled. "Way too bright in this dingy room."

"I'm sure it's better than snow. I'd trade sunny for just about anything right now." He heard the brief smile in her voice and smiled himself.

"Snowed in, huh? How many inches?" Right now he'd love to be snowed in anywhere with her.

"Close to a foot already. And not letting up much."

"Where are you?" he asked. "There's an echo."

"Oh, ah, I'm in a garage. Sorta."

It wasn't her answer that put him on alert, but the worry he suddenly heard in her voice.

And it dawned on him. It had been six months since he'd heard from her. Six very long months. Just before she'd called the last time, he'd been considering a trip to upstate New York himself to make sure she was all right. Which he knew was the last thing on earth he could do.

"Kat, is everything okay?"

"I . . ."

Her slight hesitation was all he needed to know she was in trouble. "Something did happen. What's going on?"

"I . . . I ran into a small problem tonight. In New York City."

His nerves coiled tight as she ran through the events at the auction house, as she relayed the drive through the Pennsylvania countryside in the midst of a major blizzard. He heard, clearly, just why she'd finally come out of hiding and risked her life. And knew, even before she said it, who she'd dragged along with her.

A string of curses whipped through his head, but he bit them back.

None of this should surprise him, but for some asinine reason it did. It wasn't like she was going to beg him for a second chance after he'd been the one to break things off with her so long ago in Egypt. Not when she'd fallen for Kauffman shortly thereafter. And especially not when she was legally dead and her old friend Marty Slade was the rogue CIA operative who'd put her there.

Damn. He was screwed no matter how he looked at it.

If he went with his instincts right now, she was better than dead. No way he could protect her, and some small part of him felt he owed her for how he'd used her when they'd been together.

But knowing she was with Kauffman right now? Yeah, it set off a strange protective surge in his chest. And reaffirmed the fact his day was heading straight for the shitter.

"I can't get to you, Kat. I'm too far away."

"I know. I . . . I messed up. I just didn't know what to do next."

Okay, think. She'd just changed everything by coming out in the open. Her cover was blown, and there wasn't anything he could do about that now, but he'd help her where he could. He owed her that much at least. Reports he'd seen over the past few days confirmed Minyawi was on the move, which—now he realized—meant news of her appearance had already spread back to Egypt.

Could he protect her and finally wrap up that goddamn op? If he did, he was going to take a serious hit. The agency would come down hard on him for what he'd done six years ago. And there was a chance she was going to be in some serious trouble herself. But keeping her alive at this point was more important than what came after.

With his mind running a mile a minute, he kicked off the covers, rose and reached for his secure PDA from the dresser across the room. She'd just blown the whole thing wide open. "Okay, here's what I want you to do." He paged through screens until he found what he needed. "I've got a colleague where it's always sunny. Can you get to Philadelphia?"

"Yeah, I think so."

"The truck's in the garage. Tank should be full. If not, there are a couple red gas cans on one of the shelves, at least enough to get you to a service station. I want you to call this number." He read off a name and contact. "When you get close to the city. Not before. Do you understand?"

"Yes."

"I'll get in touch with David and let him know what's happened. Don't say his name over the line, just tell him you're a friend of mine." He paused, looked out the window toward a bicyclist speeding down the middle of the street and knew his career was headed for the toilet with what he was about to do next. "Kat, you realize you have to come in, right? We'll put you in protective custody. There might be consequences."

"I know."

"It's different now," he said, hearing the quiver in her voice. "You're in the States, we can finally finish this. We can protect you."

"Like you did Shannon?"

His stomach seized. "You know that was—"

"I know," she said quickly. "And I'm sorry. I shouldn't have said that. I don't blame you, Marty. I know there's no guarantee and that you did everything you could for her. I just—" She paused, drew in a shaky breath. "It's not just me."

Marty clenched his jaw, and not for the first time, considered telling her everything he knew about Kauffman. All the really ugly stuff, too, not just the rumors. But he couldn't. Because it wouldn't hurt Kauffman. It'd only cut her.

He hoped like hell the POS knew how lucky he was to have her back in his life.

"We'll do what we can, Kat. Just get to Philadelphia. As soon as the weather breaks. Don't wait."

"I will. Thanks, Marty. I owe you so much. I don't know what I'd do without you. I . . ."

Not exactly the response he wanted, but the best he was going to get. "Yeah, well, when this is all done, you can buy me a beer. Or a case. We'll call it even then."

"Thank you," she whispered.

"No sweat. You take care, Kat. And . . ."

"Yes?"

"Be safe."

"I will."

The line went dead. He stood in the middle of his grungy hotel room dressed in nothing but boxers long moments after he closed the connection, cell pressed against his forehead, knot twisting in his stomach.

Be safe, Kat.

He hoped like hell she would be. But he had a feeling things were about to get a helluva lot worse before they got better.

He pulled the phone away from his face and dialed again.

CHAPTER NINE

Six-and-a-half years earlier
Cairo

"If you let me have the first shower I'll do your laundry for a week."

Kat chuckled at Shannon's comment as they hauled their gear out of the tomb on Friday evening. They were both covered in an inch of dust, hot and sweaty from working belowground, but giddy with excitement. Dr. Latham had finally given Kat the break she'd wanted. He'd assigned her and Shannon to the most recently discovered burial chamber. After three and a half months on site, she was finally getting a taste of what working the dig was really like. She'd never been more excited. Or as tired.

"As tempting as that is," she said with a grin as they headed up the last set of steps toward the fading light, "I'm going to have to pass. You still owe me for convincing me to go out with Pete, remember?"

Shannon huffed behind her. "I still think you must have done something to make him run. He was way into you. Did you pick your teeth or talk about your ex too much or drone on and on about Nefertiti? Because you have a habit of doing that, you know."

Kat sent her roommate a look in the dim light. "I have a habit of picking my teeth?"

Shannon rolled her eyes and pushed past her. "Droning on and on about Egyptian history. It gets old."

"I do not."

"Yes. You do. If I'd known you were going to embarrass yourself I would have given you pointers."

"I can't wait to hear these," Kat muttered, following behind. Shannon was a man magnet, and she knew it. Shoulder-length, curly blonde hair, green eyes that drove guys nuts and a confident ability to flirt with just about any guy without feeling self-conscious. She knew how to work men, and she did it well, but she was also one of the sweetest people Kat had ever met.

"I'm an Egyptologist," Kat said in defense of herself. "Of course I'd want to talk about Egyptian history. And he's an art dealer. Trust me, he was interested."

"In you or what you were boring him with?"

Kat opened her mouth, then closed it when she realized she didn't know the answer. Had she bored him? She knew she hadn't picked her teeth, and she definitely hadn't talked about Marty, so maybe Shannon was right. Maybe Pete had realized by the time dinner was finished that he just wasn't interested anymore.

The thought depressed her way more than she liked. She'd spent more time than was healthy over the last two weeks thinking about the way he'd pursued her, what she'd thought was an amazing dinner and the fact he'd cut and run as fast as possible after.

"Okay," Shannon said as they neared the last step. "I'll admit my lack of coaching might have played a role in your dismal date. Since he's gone and there's no chance for a second go—there is no chance, right?"

"None at all." *Dammit.*

"Okay, for that I'll make a concession and let you hang out with me tonight. How about that?"

Kat couldn't help it. She laughed at Shannon's pathetic offer. "Ruin your date with Sawil in addition to first dibs on the shower? I accept."

"It's not a date. It's just a movie. You know he's not my type. And the bath thing wasn't part of the deal, you sadist."

"You're still not getting the shower first, Shannon. You had it first last time."

Shannon stopped just outside the tomb, and her voice took on a very confident quality. "You sure about that? How about a little wager?"

"I'm very sure," Kat said, stepping out behind her roommate, catching the faraway look in Shannon's eye. "What the heck are you looking at?"

"Oh, nothing," Shannon said with a wry smile. "Just another tourist."

Kat followed Shannon's gaze across the desert and squinted as her eyes adjusted to the increase in light, then froze when she saw the shiny silver Land Rover parked fifty yards ahead with a man leaning back against the hood, looking their way.

It took several seconds before she realized who it was, and then her heart jumped in her chest.

"A bit of advice," Shannon said close to her ear. "This time don't bore him to death." With a nudge, she pushed Kat forward, then headed toward the modular that served as the site's command station, where Latham and Sawil were talking in the late afternoon sun.

Kat's nerves rolled around like dice in her stomach, but she forced her feet forward. She was blindingly aware that Pete was freshly showered, dressed in clean slacks and a white button-down rolled up to his elbows and she looked like death warmed over, covered in layers of grime from the bowels of the earth.

Not exactly the impression she'd wanted to hit him with if she ever saw him again.

What the heck was he doing here?

She stopped a few feet from him, ran a hand over her dusty hair and swallowed her courage. Since she couldn't see his eyes through those spendy Rēvos, she couldn't tell what he was thinking, and that only unnerved her more. "If you're here for another tour, I'm afraid you're too late."

He slid off the glasses and tucked them into his breast pocket. "Is this a new fashion statement for the tour guide?"

She looked down at her filthy jeans and T-shirt. And wished she'd been doing anything else today, even though she'd loved the work. Embarrassed, she glanced up and got the full effect of those stormy eyes. They were sparkling with amusement as they gazed down at her.

Warmth spread all the way to her belly. "Um. No. I'm not doing the tours anymore."

The corner of his mouth twitched, but he didn't smile, and she longed to see that dimple flash at her like it had so many times during their one shared dinner. "Lucky for me I took the tour when I did."

Shannon walked up to them then and, like the pushy friend she was, stuck her hand out. "I'm Shannon Driscoll. Kat's roommate. We haven't met."

Pete straightened from the car long enough to return her handshake. "Peter Kauffman."

"Guy with a tour fetish. I heard all about you."

"You did, huh?" Pete's eyes resettled on Kat. No matter what she tried, she couldn't look away. "Are you done for the afternoon?"

Kat managed a nod.

"She's off tomorrow, too," Shannon interjected. "Just in case you're wondering."

"Shannon," Kat warned.

"What?" her roommate said quickly. "It's true." She looked at Pete. "She hasn't taken many days off in the last month so she's due. In fact, I could cover for her Sunday if she needed an extra day. Did she tell you she'd been dating this other guy for a while and that they broke up not too long ago?"

"Jesus, Shannon," Kat muttered. There was mortification, then there was Shannon.

"No," Pete said with an obvious smile in his voice. "She didn't tell me."

Kat's cheeks heated as she felt Pete's eyes on her and Shannon kept rambling. "It wasn't like, serious or anything. And they're still friends. He comes around now and then. Personally, I think he still has the hots for her. Come to think of it, didn't Marty mention something about stopping by tonight, Kat?"

Kat groaned and closed her eyes. She knew exactly what Shannon was doing, but it wasn't going to work. If Pete was really interested, she'd have heard from him before now.

"Too bad she has other plans tonight."

Kat's eyes snapped open. Next to her, Shannon grinned.

"Good boy," Shannon mumbled.

"I'm afraid your ex is going to be disappointed you're not around."

"He is?" Kat asked in a whisper as her heart began to pound.

Electricity crackled between them, and Kat waited for Pete to reach out and touch her, but he didn't. He just stood there studying her with those sexy eyes.

"So," Shannon said in the silence, "I'm thinking first dibs on the shower are mine after all, huh?"

"Um—"

Pete finally tore his gaze away from Kat and looked toward Shannon. "I've got the shower thing covered." He slipped on his glasses. "She'll be home tomorrow. If she decides she wants to take Sunday off, she'll let you know."

"Wait a minute," Kat said, enjoying the way he'd swept in here and surprised her, but not entirely sure she liked his making decisions for her. Before she could further protest, he was pushing her around the shiny vehicle and opening the car door for her. "I'm a mess, Pete. I need to go—"

"Don't worry about it." He nudged her inside. "You look great. And where we're headed, what you're wearing won't matter."

Her stomach tightened. Just what did that mean?

He shut her door, moved around the Land Rover and glanced toward Shannon. "She'll call you tomorrow."

"She'd better."

Kat's heart was hammering as Pete slid into the vehicle beside her, smelling sexier than she remembered. She looked out the windshield at her roommate, who held up her hand to her ear like a phone and mouthed, *you can thank me later.*

Kat only frowned at her friend.

Pete put the car in gear. "Ready?"

She slowly turned his way and took in his broad shoulders and strong arms, the line of his jaw and all that blond tousled hair. He was a man who did what he wanted and took charge of everything around him as if he owned it all. Apprehension sent her nerves jangling. "What if I said no?"

His smile was pure victory as they tore out of the site, leaving a cloud of dust in their wake. "Then I'd say, good girl."

"Not on your life."

Kat stared straight ahead as Pete killed the ignition and popped open the driver side door. A wave of heat blasted into the interior while a man dressed in the traditional white Muslim *salwar kameez* walked in front of their car and disappeared inside the entrance to the Mena House, located in the Giza district of Cairo.

"Come on." Pete climbed out and handed his keys to a

valet who rushed over, then walked around the car and opened Kat's door.

Kat immediately grabbed the handle and jerked the door closed, then clicked the locks so neither Pete nor the confused valet could get in.

Pete regarded her with raised brows. "Open the door, Kat." When she didn't, he knocked on the glass until she lowered the window an inch. "What's wrong?"

"This is a five-star hotel."

"I know."

"I can't go in there.

"Why not?

"Because I'm a mess!"

He chuckled and leaned closer to the window. "It's the desert. People expect you to be dusty."

"Not at the Mena House!"

His eyes and voice softened. "Come out of the car, Kat. I guarantee no one's going to care what you look like."

She cared. More now than she had when she'd foolishly climbed into this vehicle.

"There's a better shower in my suite than I bet your roommate's getting back at your flat."

Oh, right. Like that was going to work on her.

Kat chewed on her lip in indecision. It wasn't simply that she was covered in dirt and grime from the tomb. It was also the fact he'd brought her to a hotel. A very expensive, ritzy and romantic hotel located at the base of the Pyramids. The move was clearly calculated and blatantly sexual, and she knew exactly where this would lead if she got out of the car. Straight to his suite, into his bed, without a second look back.

Though she burned inside and wanted to go with him, that part of herself that had been molded at St. Thomas's Orphanage was wary. For two weeks she'd been telling herself the fact he'd disappeared was really a good thing in retrospect. The attraction she felt for him was like nothing she'd experienced before. It was the kind that burned hot and consumed everything in its path. She'd heard people talk of falling in love at first sight, but she'd never expected it to happen to her. One dinner, though. That was all it took. He'd breezed into her life and set her world spinning, and cowardly as it was, she was almost afraid to see where it would go.

She looked through the window and felt her stomach tighten as a slow smile spread across his lips. And in that moment she knew she was lost.

She released the locks and slowly climbed out of the vehicle. When she was standing in front of him, looking up at all that bronzed beauty, she swallowed. "I don't have anything else to wear."

His smile widened until that dimple winked at her and turned her insides to lava. "Don't worry about it. I've got you covered."

They headed into the hotel. He didn't hold her hand like she expected, but she felt his commanding presence next to her as they crossed the ornate lobby toward the bank of elevators on the far side. "People are looking at me," she mumbled as they moved.

"That's because you're fidgeting."

She slanted a sideways look. "And that's a line from *Pretty Woman*."

"Never saw it. Though I can't imagine any woman being prettier than you."

Her cheeks heated as they approached the elevators. He still hadn't touched her, and she was all atingle with nerves. As the door opened and they stepped inside the small car, once again she was reminded how dirty she was and how fresh and clean he smelled.

They rode in silence, her nerves bouncing all over. Then the doors opened, and Pete held out his hand to let her exit first. "All the way at the end."

The hallway was lush and dramatic, with plush carpeting and gilded sconces on the walls, but it paled in comparison to what came next.

Kat found herself instantly swept up in a world of luxury as soon as she stepped into the suite. Gold and burgundy carpets, hand-carved wooden furnishings, heavy fabrics and enormous windows that looked out over a view of the Pyramids, so close it felt like you could reach out and touch them.

"Oh, my."

"Like it?" he asked from behind her.

She eased farther into the room and felt herself immersed in opulence, like Cleopatra for the day. "It's amazing."

His footsteps sounded behind, and then he was in front of her, heading toward heavily carved double doors at the far end of the large living room. "Bathroom's through here."

The bedroom suite was more magnificent than the living area, with an enormous canopy bed and a pile of golden pillows. Kat's stomach tightened with anticipation as she looked at the bed and imagined lying on it with Pete, but he barely spared it a glance.

He pushed the door across the room open. Behind him she had the impression of miles of marble and gold. "Any kind of toiletry you need should be in there." He pointed to a set of closet doors on the opposite side of the room. "And there are a few things over there you can wear." His eyes ran over her. "I had to guess on size. We'll see if I was right."

He moved past her, back toward the main door of the bedroom suite, leaving her standing in the middle of all that lavishness. "I have some paperwork I need to do. Take your time."

Then he was gone.

Alone, Kat's brow drew together. What exactly was going on here?

She'd thought he'd brought her here for sex, but he hadn't once touched her. Aside from saying she was pretty in the lobby, he hadn't actually done anything to indicate he was really interested in anything other than friendship. Come to think of it, the night of their dinner, he hadn't touched her other than to shake her hand and wish her good night. Sure, he'd sent her heady looks, but what if she'd been misreading him?

Growing more confused by the minute, Kat scratched her head, only to come away with a handful of grit. She turned for the bathroom, flipped on the light and discovered she'd been right. The entire room was done in white marble and was the size of the living room in the flat she shared with Shannon. Though there were female toiletries galore on the counter, there was nothing that indicated a man had stepped foot in here. No used towel, shaving kit or even a comb on the counter. In the car, Pete had told her he'd arrived in Cairo earlier in the day, checked into his hotel, showered and changed. But that didn't look like the case to her eyes.

Just what kind of game was he playing?

Apprehension growing, Kat peeled off her clothes, started the water and stepped into the glass-enclosed shower. The heat and steam immediately relaxed her, and with each passing minute she convinced herself she was overreacting. Maybe he just didn't want to touch her until she'd cleaned up. That made more sense than her thinking he had ulterior motives. And it was highly likely the maid had straightened up after he'd had his shower.

Twenty minutes later, when her fingers were wrinkled and her skin was warm and dewy, she climbed out and wrapped herself in a plush terry robe. The cotton was soft against her skin, and she felt worlds better than she had only moments before. Feet bare, she padded out into the bedroom and moved to the closet to find something clean to wear.

She gasped at what she saw inside. Two pair of slacks—one black, one brown—silky blouses in a variety of colors and low matching sandals. All pieces made from sumptuous fabrics, bearing expensive designer names any moron would recognize.

She swallowed hard, knowing the few outfits alone hanging in this closet probably cost more than her entire wardrobe, both here in Cairo and at home.

But something wasn't right.

Kat backed up until her legs hit the bed and crumpled beneath her. And staring at the extravagant clothing and the opulence of the room, she had a flashback to the offhand *Pretty Woman* comment Pete had made in the lobby.

Things started to click into place. Each of the pieces hanging in the closet was beautiful, but they weren't overly sexual in any way. Not the kind of thing a potential lover might buy for a woman. With sinking suspicion, she realized he hadn't brought her here for sex like she'd thought. Instead, he'd brought her here because he wanted something from her. Wanted something so much he was willing to try to buy her off with trendy clothing and posh luxury in lieu of his body.

In a rush she remembered the way he'd been eyeing the artifacts in the tomb during his first few tours, and the way he'd watched everything around him with a keen eagle's eye.

Her stomach tightened as reality smacked her in the face. Tomb robbers did indeed exist in this day and age. And there was an enormous belowground market that traded in ancient antiquities. She'd even heard stories of shady dealers scouting out tombs, passing themselves off as tourists and doing whatever they could to get information from workers. And with the pieces she suspected had gone missing from her site . . .

Oh, God. She'd been stupidly naïve. She'd been so

sucked in by his good looks and charm she hadn't even questioned what he was really about.

Heart pumping, Kat rose on unsteady legs and opened the bedroom door. The living room appeared empty at first, and though she wanted to rush out of the disgustingly beautiful suite she'd at first envisioned as a lover's palace, now all she wanted were answers.

Her jaw clenched when she spotted Pete sitting at a desk facing windows that looked out toward the Pyramids, his back to her, his hand busily moving over a piece of paper. Dusk was just settling over the desert, and the lights were only now coming up, spotlighting the massive stone triangles against the dimming sky.

"Just what the hell's going on here?"

He turned sharply and looked at her, obviously not having heard her march across the floor. For a moment she was sucker punched again, only this time with that familiar lust she'd been experiencing since he'd shown up. He was still wearing the same clothes as before, but he'd added a pair of wire-rimmed glasses that for some reason made him look damn sexier and even more rugged than he already was.

His eyes swept over her as he swiveled his chair and leaned back, taking her in from wet hair to bare feet. "Nothing fit?"

She fisted her hands on her hips and ignored the playful tone of his voice. "I didn't try any of it on."

"You didn't like the clothes?"

"I'm not some hooker you can buy off."

With slow movements, he set the pen he'd been holding on the stack of papers at his side and regarded her like a lion tamer considering the foolishness of trying to coax a fresh steak from his growling pet. "You're going to have to explain that one for me. I'm a little behind."

"I'm getting at *that*." She pointed to the bedroom, then lifted her arms to indicate the entire room. "And *this*.

Why did you bring me here? It's pretty clear it's not because you're dying to jump into bed with me."

"Whoa. Wait a minute." He rubbed a hand over his jaw and had the audacity to look amused. "I think you've got the wrong idea."

"Oh, no, I have the very right idea. A woman knows when a man's not attracted to her, so don't talk to me like I'm stupid. Just come out and say what it is you want from me and stop playing these games."

He rose from his seat, the leather creaking beneath him, and hesitantly stepped toward her. "What makes you think I'm not attracted to you?"

"A woman knows."

"How?" His eyes were soft and hypnotic through those lenses, and she fought to keep her common sense in check. "Tell me how you know, specifically, that I'm not interested, Kat."

She crossed her arms over her chest. "For one, you haven't touched me once today."

"I didn't want to startle you. You've looked a little nervous."

"You barely touched me the night we had dinner either."

"True. But not for the reasons you're thinking."

Her eyes narrowed. "There's not a sexy thing in that closet of designer labels you bought."

"In the first place, I didn't buy them. I happen to have a . . . friend who's got an in with some of those designers. And in the second, I disagree. Those clothes might not look sexy on the rack, but I'm willing to bet on you they're amazing."

He was throwing her off with those lusty looks, but she knew she was right. There was something about Peter Kauffman that just didn't add up. "A guy who's interested in a woman *acts* like he's interested."

He smiled then, a slow and confident grin that turned her insides to Jell-O, but he didn't so much as respond.

Her stomach tightened. "And it's obvious you aren't staying in that room you pushed me into because there's nothing of yours in there."

"Do you want something of mine in there?"

Kat faltered, and he saw it. She hated the fact he was getting to her like this when she knew better. She lifted her chin. "That's not the point."

"I think it's exactly the point." He moved closer until she felt the heat radiating from his body, but she refused to let him intimidate her, so she didn't step back. "In fact, I think the point here is that I'm different from the other men you've been with, and it's confusing you."

He was absolutely right about that. He was completely different, but she wasn't about to tell him that.

"I know that shouldn't thrill me," he went on, "but I can't help it. Because you're completely different from the women I've been interested in, too, and in my defense, I haven't known exactly how to deal with that."

She watched in slow motion as he ran his finger down the length of her sleeve. Even through the thick terry her skin tingled.

"As for not touching you." He shook his head. "I've been dying to touch you since the first second I laid eyes on you."

He lifted the finger that had just stroked her arm and pointed over his shoulder toward a door she hadn't noticed behind him. "This suite has two bedrooms. My suitcase is in there. I didn't want to put any pressure on you."

He took off his glasses, and when he looked down at her she was hit with the full impact of those stormy, suddenly serious eyes. "I don't live here, Kat. I'm based out of Miami where my gallery's growing like a toddler. I get to Cairo maybe three, four times a year on buying trips or when a colleague calls with something of interest. I wasn't planning on coming back until the fall."

She took a breath, because the air was suddenly hot and sultry, and she had a strange feeling maybe she'd jumped to the wrong conclusion way too fast.

"That dinner we had? The one where you were convinced afterward I didn't want to see you again? Furthest thing from the truth. I suggested we go for a walk because I didn't want to take you home, and once we got to your flat all I could think about was dragging you against me and kissing you senseless. I would have given up my left arm to go upstairs with you, but I forced myself to leave instead, because I didn't want you to be a one-night stand."

One-night stand? *Oh no.* "Then . . . why am I here now?"

His gaze ran over her face, down to her lips and back up to her eyes. "Because I haven't been able to stop thinking about you since that night. About how soft your skin is, about how sweet you smell, about the sound of your sexy voice. Just the memory is enough to drive me mad."

Her toes curled against the carpet.

"I have to be in Barcelona in three days," he said. "I have a mountain of paperwork from my last trip that I never finished, and I left a buyer high and dry to fly out here last night. I don't have time to do the normal dating ritual of dinner and a movie and an 'I'll call you' goodnight kiss. I brought you here today because I wanted time alone with you so we could get to know each other better before I have to leave again. To find out if this spark between us is real or imagined. And my bags are in that room because I didn't want you to feel pressured to do something you weren't ready for." His voice deepened. "But don't for one minute assume I'm not dying to get inside you in any way you'll let me right this second. Because I guarantee you'd be wrong."

Liquid slid through Kat's veins, then pooled in her stomach until she felt like she would burst. "And, um, what did you discover?"

His brows drew together to form a slight crease between his gorgeous eyes. "About what?"

"About us. This spark. Is it . . . is it still there after I made a fool of myself a few minutes ago?"

One side of his mouth curled in that sexy half grin, the one she'd been itching to lick off his face through their whole dinner. "Oh yeah. Definitely there for me. What do you think?"

She finally drew a breath. "I think if you don't kiss me soon, I'm going to die."

His arms were around her so fast, she gasped. And when the long, lean line of his body came into contact with hers, she knew she'd been wrong. He was hard as stone and very obviously aroused.

Warmth spread between her thighs, and even as she berated herself for being a fool, her heart jumped in time with his pulse.

He leaned down, but he didn't kiss her. His mouth hovered over hers until she thought she'd scream. She curled her fingers in his dress shirt, trying to draw him closer.

"This is going to be complicated," he whispered.

"The good things always are."

He brushed his thumb over her bottom lip, sending sparks of desire straight to her center. "I'm not looking for a one-nighter with you. Fair warning, Kit-Kat, I want a whole lot more."

Oh, so did she. She barely knew him, but one thing was clear: he was going to change her life.

His lips settled over hers, gentle at first, but with growing urgency. As his tongue slid into her mouth and desire exploded in her core, she responded with everything she had in her.

When they were both breathless and his mouth finally parted from hers, she slipped her hands up into his hair and stared into his smoldering eyes, knowing there was no going back for her. "So, um, you showed me my room but not yours. I'm curious what the rest of this suite looks like."

His answer was a lusty groan followed by strong arms sweeping her off the floor to carry her across the room.

CHAPTER TEN

Present day
Northern Pennsylvania

It had to be the longest night of his life. Or the longest few hours to daylight.

Take your pick, Pete thought. *Shit in one hand, piss in the other.* Either way he looked at it, the end result was still the same. Every muscle in his body twitched in time to the second hand on his watch as dawn inched closer.

In the shower, he hadn't been able to stop thinking about the night he'd ignored the God-given gift of common sense that had kept him alive for thirty-two years and gone after Kat at her tomb. Dammit, he should have stayed away. If he'd thought with his big head that day instead of his little one, none of this would ever have happened.

Scowling at the memory, he finished showering and reluctantly emerged from the bathroom only to find the tiny apartment empty. He suspected Kat was in the adjacent garage, but he wasn't interested enough to go searching for her. And to be honest, he was relieved at the silence. His brain was still working around everything she'd told him.

Yeah, well, he wasn't about to go overanalyzing any of that now, was he?

But he still had questions. Like how the hell she'd gotten the jump on him and why his face looked like it had been used as a battering ram recently.

With a towel wrapped around his waist, he pawed through the small closet next to the kitchen. He didn't feel as sick to his stomach anymore, but his brain was still pounding away at his skull, and he knew this time it wasn't due to sedatives or any alcohol he'd consumed earlier but from reality crashing down around him. Pulling out a pair of worn jeans and an NYU sweatshirt, he frowned.

"Goddamn hand-me-downs," he mumbled. As if the situation weren't bad enough, he had to actually wear Slade's clothing.

Muttering curses at no one in particular, but with no other options, he pulled on the jeans and refused to think about the fact he was going commando in another guy's pants. He tugged the sweatshirt over his head, found a pair of wool socks in a basket on the shelf and pushed his feet into a pair of hiking boots in the bottom of the closet.

"Oh, this just figures." He bent down and shoved his foot around as he tied the laces as loose as possible, the whole time glowering at the size tens that were—just his luck—one size too small. When he stood up too quickly, his head spun, and a wave of nausea hit him hard.

Food was a good idea at this point. Soak up the drug, sober up his head. He turned for the small kitchen only to find most of the contents were frozen foods and packaged meals.

He didn't have the patience or inclination to actually cook right now, so he pawed through the cupboard until he found a jar of peanut butter and decided that was better than nothing. As he pulled a frozen loaf of bread from the freezer, he couldn't help wondering when the hell Slade had been here last. The guy was probably off on ops half the time, but you'd never know it by looking at the supplies he kept on hand. Or maybe he'd left the agency and been in hiding with Kat all these years.

That thought was enough to send the blood roaring to Pete's head. *Not going there. None of my business anyway.*

With more force than necessary, he grabbed two slices of frozen bread, slapped peanut butter on one and smashed them together. One bite told him his stomach wasn't going to like the combination, but he figured, *screw it.* Anything was better than this drugged-out feeling.

After he choked down the sandwich and polished off a cola, he went back to the closet, found a gray parka that looked like it would fit his shoulders and tugged a black wool cap over his head. He shoved a pair of fingerless gloves into the coat pocket, then searched the closet some more. A little metal box up on the top shelf drew his attention.

He pushed propane canisters to the side, reached for the box and pulled it down. The locking mechanism on the front was child's play, really. Just enough to deter a kid or a halfwit. Frowning, he carried the box into the closet-sized kitchen, set it on the counter and dug through the drawers until he found a metal skewer.

Not a pick, but it'd work in a pinch.

It took him longer than he'd have liked to pop the lock, and he knew his buddy Rafe would have laughed his ass off if he'd been watching, but the end result was still the same. The lock gave with a soft click. Pete tossed the skewer on the counter, lifted the lid and let out a low whistle when he looked inside.

At least one damn thing was going his way. The 10mm was high end and probably the most expensive thing in the whole apartment. He lifted the black metal, turned it from side to side and checked the chamber. Like an old habit, he pocketed one magazine, snapped the second into place, then tucked the firearm into the back waistband of his jeans.

And as he did he had a sudden flash of doing the same damn thing time and again, in a lot shittier places than this.

He'd been in tight scrapes before. A man in his line of work ran into shady characters in some of the worst corners of the world. It went without saying that the poorest and least policed countries had the biggest treasures and the greediest suppliers, and he'd capitalized on that fact over the years. Sure, his business was pretty much on the up and up now, but six years ago, when he'd met Kat? That was another matter entirely.

Since he didn't want to think about anything remotely related to Kat, he ran a hand over his face, scratched his jaw and wished like hell for a razor.

Metal banging around in the adjacent garage echoed through the room. He eyed the clock on the wall in the small living area. 5:15 a.m. The sun would be up in a few hours. He couldn't hear the wind whipping against the building anymore, and he hoped that meant the mother-f-ing storm had finally passed.

Pete looked at the ratty sofa. If he were smart he'd lie his ass down and get an hour of shut-eye before he had to go outside and dig himself out of this mess. He'd need all his energy so he could make tracks back to civilization as soon as it was light.

More banging drifted to his ears. Followed by a curse.

He bit back the eloquent French retort that jumped to his lips and glared toward the garage door. And knew he wasn't getting any sleep now or anytime soon. He was about to make matters worse.

He stepped into the garage only to be greeted by a familiar view that socked him hard in the gut. The hood of the rusted Ford he'd planned to use as his escape vehicle was up, and Kat was leaning over the thing doing God-knows-what to the engine. What stopped him wasn't the fact she was tinkering with his only means out of this hellhole, but that she'd changed into jeans, her heart-shaped ass filling out the worn denim as if it were a second skin.

And staring at her there, light from an unshaded bulb highlighting each and every curve, he had a sudden memory flash: pressing his lips to the twin dimples on her lower back, running his hands over the smooth skin of her gorgeous backside, clutching her hips tight with his fingers as he sank inside her from behind and bent to kiss her neck.

Warmth he grudgingly recognized as arousal speared him in the stomach, drifted lower until he had to shift his feet around to relieve the pressure in his groin. And that was when he realized his body obviously wasn't up to speed with his brain quite yet. The little man in his pants didn't know sex with her was no longer an option.

He clenched his jaw and fought back the arousal that only pissed him off more, then unleashed all that pent-up anger on her. "Just what in the hell do you think you're doing now?"

Kat's head hit the top of the hood with a crack that echoed through the garage and sent stars firing off in her line of vision.

She bit her tongue to keep from swearing and jerked away from the engine block. Rubbing the back of her throbbing skull, she glanced behind her and saw Pete, freshly showered and smelling just as good as she remembered, looking more pissed off than a chained pit bull.

"I asked what you think you're doing," he barked.

Okay, his shower hadn't done much to improve his mood. His tight shoulders were bunched for battle in that worn gray sweatshirt. Deep frustration lines marred his forehead beneath that black wool cap covering his hair. He had one heck of a shiner around his eye which, for reasons Kat couldn't explain, made him look that much more dangerous and sexy as hell.

He clenched his jaw as he waited for her to answer, and her gaze dropped to his mouth.

Yeah, that sweet and tempting mouth that had kissed her silly before was now set in a grim line. He was downright ticked she was anywhere near the vehicle he planned to use as his escape.

Escape. Right. That was exactly what he planned to do. And from the looks of it, sooner rather than later.

"I was just checking to make sure it runs," she said as she massaged her scalp.

He eyed her like he didn't believe her, then moved to examine the engine himself. Careful to step around her so their bodies didn't come close to making contact.

Definitely still pissed. Although at the moment she wasn't sure why he thought he had the market cornered on that emotion.

She waited while he pulled the dipstick out and checked the oil level. She held the rag out for him as a peace offering, but he ignored it, instead wiping his grimy hands on the thighs of his jeans.

Oh right, not his jeans. *Marty's jeans.* No wonder he was in an extra-foul mood.

He walked around the side of the truck without speaking, climbed behind the wheel and started the ignition with the keys she'd left in the cab. His eyes narrowed on the dash. Then he killed the engine and climbed back out. "There's less than a quarter tank of gas. How far to the nearest town?"

"Keeneyville's about ten minutes down the road. In good conditions. But there's only one gas station, and it might be closed due to the storm."

"Great." He perched his hands on his narrow hips and glanced around the garage as if considering his options.

She touched the medal at her chest and thought about her own. She'd found the gas cans Marty had mentioned on the phone, but there still wasn't enough fuel for two vehicles to get out of here, and considering the weather, the limo was pretty much useless at this point. It had barely made it the last ten miles to the farm when the snow had been seriously piling up. So that left the truck. She needed to get to Philly, and he wanted out of this garage.

Indecision warred within her as she bit her lip. She really wanted to tear into him for being such a dick but knew that wouldn't get her anywhere. So she tried for sweetness instead. "I know where we can get some fuel, but I'm going to need a favor from you first."

He slowly turned her direction with eyes that could have burned a hole right through her and felt like they had. Refusing to shrink from that look, she shifted her feet and lifted her chin in defiance. So he was ticked at her. So she'd lied to him. So what? He'd done some pretty awful things, too.

"Oh, this should be good," he muttered, crossing his arms over his chest and spreading his feet wide in an aggressive stance. "Lay it on me. I'm all ears. What could I possibly do to help you out, Kat? Please. Tell me. I'm *dying* to help."

No, not just a dick. Now he was being a complete asshole. She refused to drop to his level. "I need to go to Philadelphia."

"And that impacts me how?"

She glanced at the pickup.

Understanding dawned in his eyes. "In this truck."

She nodded.

"My truck," he said again.

"The limo won't make it in this snow. And besides, there's not enough gas for both vehicles to leave here. So . . . I was thinking we'd go together. I can't leave you out here stranded without transportation."

"Generous of you." His brows dropped low. "Why do you need to go to Philly?"

She hesitated, sure this would only make things worse, but really, what were her other options? "I made a call. A friend of a friend has agreed to help me. Us, if you want. But we have to get to Philadelphia first."

"A friend," he said with guarded suspicion. "Someone with the government?"

"Something like that."

He studied her a beat. "Your friend of a friend wouldn't happen to be an acquaintance of Slade's, would he?"

She bit her lip. "Maybe."

"Maybe," he repeated. Then he shook his head, disgust running across his face. "No, I think definitely. You just wanna keep rubbing my nose in it, huh?" He turned away to study a shelving unit across the room.

"It's not like that," she said quickly.

"I don't care what it's like," he said sharply. "All I want right now is to get the hell out of here."

His tone was straight and to the point, but his body language belied something else: frustration, anger . . . jealousy?

Definitely not the latter. Not after the way he'd walked away from her so easily all those years before. "Pete—"

A loud popping pierced the quiet. Metal blasted off metal in a long series of bursts that sounded like a garage full of cars backfiring all at once. Wood panels on the exterior wall across the room cracked and split with an echoing *thwack*.

One minute Kat was standing on her feet ready to dig her heels in over their transportation situation, the next Pete dove for her, taking her down hard on the cement floor. Her back and shoulders took the brunt of the fall. Her skull cracked against the unforgiving concrete. A wooden shelf behind them splintered as bullets ripped it to pieces. A can of nails flew up in the air, raining bits of metal down around them.

Kat shrieked. Pete moved more of his body over her, shielding her head with his arms and tucking her face against his neck. The seconds that passed as the garage was ripped to shreds by flying shrapnel felt like hours.

In the brief lull that followed, Pete muttered, "Holy fuck."

His weight was a solid force pushing down on her, his breath hot against her skin, but all she could focus on was where she'd gone wrong and how in the name of God they'd been found so fast.

"Are you hit?"

She registered his hands gripping her arms hard, his eyes intense, only inches from her own, boring right into her skull. She glanced down at where he held her, then back up again. Somehow, she was able to shake her head. "No. No, I'm not hit. I . . . oh, God—"

"Katherine Meyer!"

Kat froze at the deeply accented Middle Eastern voice.

"We know you're in there," it yelled again. "Come out now so we can settle this in a civilized manner."

Busir.

"Civilized manner, my ass," Pete whispered. "Don't you move a goddamn muscle."

Perspiration popped out on Kat's skin. Without warning she was back in the tomb, a knife at her throat, a hard and evil man at her back, holding her tight by her hair.

"No, no, no," she muttered, struggling underneath Pete. Panic washed away her common sense. She had to get away. She couldn't stay here. She had to . . . what? What could she possibly do? A groan tore from her chest.

"Pull it together, Kat," Pete said softly. He locked his

legs around her thighs to stop her struggling, holding her tight against his body. Bracing one forearm across her chest to keep her pressed to the cold concrete, he clamped his free hand over her mouth. "Shh!"

The flight response was so strong, his words and strength barely registered. But when they did, and she realized he was carefully listening to Busir's movements outside, she went utterly still.

"That's it," he said in her ear. His hot breath tickled the soft skin behind her ear, ran like rivulets down her neck. Or maybe that was the perspiration from her adrenaline rush. She couldn't tell anymore.

"Two out front. They're checking the main door. It's locked, right?"

She couldn't find the words to speak, so she nodded instead.

"I'm going to let go of your mouth. But you better stay quiet. Nod for me if you understand." When she did, he slowly eased his hand off her face.

She forced herself to swallow back the mind-numbing fear. So much for all her training and years of preparation for this moment. Her gun was yards from her, and when it came right down to a life-or-death moment, she'd frozen, just like she had in that tomb.

What would she have done if Pete hadn't been here?

Pete pushed up just enough to peer around the large, metal freestanding tool chest that had saved their lives. Footsteps echoed from the side of the building. From somewhere behind his back he pulled out a very big, very black gun she'd had no idea he carried.

She let out a small gasp of surprise. He held his fingers to his lips and pointed toward the apartment door. "Exterior access?"

Common sense was finally filtering back into her mind. She shook her head and swallowed. "Not there. Back of the garage. There's another door for rear parking."

He gave one nod, then lowered himself so he was close to her ear again. Electricity zipped along her nerve endings at both the rush of adrenaline and his skin brushing hers. "I think there are two more. They're circling the building and reloading. Can you get inside the cab without making any sound?"

Her heart skipped a beat when she realized he wasn't going to save his own ass and leave her here for Busir. Regardless of everything they'd done to each other and how he felt about her right now, he wasn't leaving her behind.

Stupid-ass tears that had no purpose stung the backs of her eyes. She nodded quickly, blinking in rapid succession to avoid turning into a hysterical woman in the midst of a crisis. She was so not that woman anymore.

"Good," he said. "I'm going to create a diversion. When you hear it, gun that engine and make sure the passenger door is open for me."

Just what did he have planned?

"Wait. Are we going out the front or back?" she asked.

He thought for a second. "You know this area better. With the amount of snow that's come down, your best guess is a helluva lot better than mine."

Her best guess. Crap, her best guess had nearly killed them both. Refusing to think about that, she swallowed again. Hills ran close to the building along the back side. If they went that way, their odds of getting stuck in the fresh powder were much, much greater. "Front," she finally said, knowing it was their only hope.

"Front," he agreed with a nod, staring into her eyes.

For a second, she felt the connection they'd shared earlier when he'd kissed her spark up again, the same one they'd had in Cairo.

"Then we pray like hell you can drive this damn rig so we don't end up spinning our wheels," he added.

He eased off her slowly, in increments so their movements wouldn't be heard. Pushing up to a crouch behind the tool cabinet, gun lifted near his head, he waved for her to get up.

Kat was rattled as hell, and she knew she was going to be sore from hitting the cement floor, but she forced herself up and somehow managed to get to the side of the truck with barely a whisper. When she glanced back at Pete, though, she gasped. Blood stained the back of his torn sweatshirt in several places.

She bit down hard on her lip to keep from calling out to him, then prayed the fresh spots of blood were only shrapnel wounds and not bullet holes.

He'd used his body as a shield for her.

The heroics were so at odds with what she knew of him. But she couldn't think about that now. She had to get into the truck and get ready for whatever it was he had planned.

Using both hands, she reached up and lifted the door handle, pausing when the soft click seemed to echo through the vast garage like a cannon exploding on the horizon.

"Katherine Meyer!" Busir yelled again. "This is your last warning. Come out now peacefully or we come in after you."

Kat didn't waste any more time. Busir was a man of his word. She'd learned that a long time ago.

She pulled the door open and quietly rejoiced when the hinges didn't creak. In jerky moves, she crawled across the seat and slid behind the wheel. Her pack with the pendant of the crouching pharaoh nestled inside was already secured under the seat—a precaution she'd made earlier, just in case. She glanced up to let Pete know she was in position, but by the time she looked he was already gone.

Fear iced her veins. She had no idea where he was or what his diversion was going to be.

An explosion from within the small studio apartment rocked the truck and entire garage. Flames shot out of the doorway. Kat ducked her head and stifled a cry just as gunshots whipped through the air again in rapid succession.

The world felt like it had caught fire. But from somewhere far off, she heard a familiar voice yell, "Go, go, go!"

She twisted the keys in the ignition and revved the engine. Just as she was about to step on the gas, Pete threw himself into the cab of the truck and yelled, "Now!"

She gunned it. Their bodies jerked back at the sudden momentum. The Ford's tires squealed on the cement. Seconds later they crashed through the wooden door at the end of the garage and tore off through the snow.

Two bodies Kat barely saw leaped out of the way of the truck. The tires slipped, and the back end whipped around on a thick layer of fresh powder. Miraculously, they somehow gained traction.

Gunfire ignited behind them. Pete rolled over the seat, gripped her head and pushed. "Stay down!"

Kat tightened her hands on the wheel, leaned down as low as she could and tried to focus on getting to the road without killing them both. When a blast of cold air rushed through the cab, she realized Pete had opened his window and was firing back. She couldn't spare a glance to see if he'd hit anyone. They were about to reach the road.

"Hold on!"

She pulled hard on the steering wheel to make the turn. Pete fell into the seat, rammed into her shoulder. The back end slid again, this time as if the tires were on an ice rink. And in the split second that followed, Kat realized in a moment of utter clarity that unless a miracle struck, they weren't going to make it.

They were going to spin. Right there in the middle of

Hwy 249. Before they could correct, Busir would be on them.

Oh, God. This was it.

After six long, lonely years, she was really going to die in a car accident after all. This time in the middle of a blizzard. And she was taking the man she'd once loved with her.

CHAPTER ELEVEN

The tail end of the truck whipped across the ice-covered road and sent Pete and Kat spiraling to the left. Pete gripped the dash hard as the tires slipped, then caught in the powder and the old vehicle corrected itself, shooting out of the drive.

When they finally turned a corner and were out of direct sight of the farm, Kat let out an audible breath. Her hands tightened on the steering wheel until her knuckles turned white. She darted a glance into the rearview mirror at the old barn, now half-engulfed in flames and partially hidden by trees.

"What was that?"

"Propane," Pete said. "Small tank in the kitchen." He ditched the spent magazine from the Glock he'd found, snapped the new one into place and darted a look behind them. It was hard to see much through the surrounding forest and early morning darkness as they shot down the barren road, but the red glow of flames was still visible through the canopy, as was the smell of burning rubber through the open window at his side.

Wouldn't be long before those fireworks were spotted

by some locals. For their sakes, he hoped Kat's thugs were gone by then.

Shit. How had Busir found them so fast? The other guy, the long-haired one from the auction, had been there, too. The one Pete knew he'd met before but just couldn't place.

They rounded several bends in the road before Kat glanced in the rearview. Breathing easier, but obviously with enough adrenaline still rushing through her body to run a marathon, she said, "I don't see anyone behind us."

"Not yet." He repositioned himself on the torn fabric bench seat and wished like hell they had a Hummer like the bad-asses behind them. Just his luck to get stuck in a rusted-out, beat-to-hell-and-back pickup. "I think I shot out at least one, maybe two tires on that big rig. We've got a bit of a head start. But they'll be coming."

Dawn was just rising over the hills. He figured they had fifteen minutes, maybe less if she didn't pick up her pace on these snowy back roads. "Speaking of which. How do you think they found us?"

She shook her head but stayed focused on the road. "I don't know. We had a run-in with them outside the pir—" She stopped abruptly and pursed her lips. "Your girlfriend's apartment."

His brow lowered. And though he couldn't quite make sense of the scenes popping through his mind, he had a vague recollection of being in an alley, wrestling with someone who looked suspiciously like Busir. Then being shocked into stupor by Kat's presence.

He reached a hand up to run fingers over his bruised eye. "A run-in, huh? Was this before or after you drugged me?"

"Before. And I didn't drug you. They did. I just made sure they didn't take you with them. Their interrogation techniques aren't pretty."

She wouldn't look at him, and the sickness sliding across her features struck him as completely at odds with the tough-as-nails liar he'd pegged her as earlier. When he'd come to in Slade's garage apartment, he'd been so focused on what the hell she'd done to him that he hadn't stopped to wonder how she'd actually gotten him all the way to Pennsylvania in the first place. Was it possible she'd somehow saved him from a much worse fate?

What exactly had she witnessed in that tomb? What had Busir and his crony really done to her roommate?

He wasn't sure he wanted to know. Because if it was as bad as he was starting to envision, it gave her a damn good reason for disappearing into thin air for six years.

"How far to the nearest town?" he asked instead.

"Eight miles, maybe more. But there's nothing there. A gas station. A store. Both of which will be closed this early in the morning, especially after a storm like last night's."

Just what he was hoping for. He glanced back over his shoulder. Still no sign of Busir. He figured that had to be a plus, all things considered.

"Where'd you learn to drive like that?"

She seemed surprised by the question, which made him realize it was the first time he'd asked anything personal about her in the hours they'd been locked up together.

"Upstate New York. You either stay locked in your house six months out of the year or learn to drive in snow. Since I tend to go stir-crazy indoors, I learned how to drive in the snow."

So that was where she'd been hiding. And why she'd so easily shown up at the auction in New York City.

"Where'd you learn to shoot like that?" she asked a few minutes later.

He glanced sideways across the seat. The early-morning glow illuminated her profile. He still did a double-take when he saw her with that short black hair, but her face was just as he remembered. As if she hadn't aged a day beyond the twenty-five she'd been when he'd known her.

A heavy tingling started low in his stomach and inched its way south. He stiffened and shifted the Glock to his other thigh, palming the cool metal in the process to give his body a different sensation to focus on. "Good skill to have in my line of work."

He glanced out the window at the sun rising slowly over the white-covered hills and told himself he didn't care about her reaction.

She kept her eyes on the road as she made the sharp S-turn, but he heard her mumble, "Job security."

He looked her way again. And thought about the kind of men he'd dealt with before he'd met her.

She had no idea about job security and what he'd done.

Silence filled the cab. He propped an elbow on the windowsill and ran his hand over his mouth, contemplating what she'd say if he told her.

Then frowned. She wouldn't say anything. Even after their steamy months together, after everything he thought he'd meant to her, he knew she wouldn't care. And why should she? If her story was at all close to the truth, she had every reason to hate his guts.

The truck rounded a bend, and the small town of Keeneyville came into view. As Kat drove down the main street, he sat up straighter and refocused on the here and now.

Like she'd mentioned earlier, the downtown consisted of nothing more than a smattering of homes, a two-tank gas station with a flapping green-and-white sign advertising overinflated prices and a hole-in-the-wall market where the locals probably bought beer and cigarettes and gossiped about the local high school football team like they were the Super Bowl champs. There were no people milling around at this early hour, no other cars on the road for that matter either. The one stoplight in town was blowing gently in the wind and flashing yellow as if the power had gone out during the storm.

"Turn in there."

Kat's eyes widened, but she didn't question him, simply pulled into the lot behind the market and parked next to a blue, early-90s Pathfinder covered in snow. Pete popped the truck's door before she came to a complete stop.

"Hold on, Pete. You're blee—"

He hopped out before she finished her statement, the too-small boots crunching in the snow as he moved. A quick glance in the passenger window confirmed there were no keys, but no alarm either.

He looked down for a rock to smash in the window as he walked around the vehicle but couldn't see anything useful through the snow that filled the lot. When he reached the driver's side, he lifted the door handle on the off chance whoever had left this POS here had forgotten to lock it. And wouldn't you know it, the damn door pulled open.

Maybe things were looking up for him after all.

He'd just slid into the Pathfinder and leaned down to look under the steering column when he heard footsteps scuffing across the snow, followed by Kat's surprised voice.

"What are you doing?"

He popped the panel, found the two wires he figured were the right ones and pulled. "Saving my ass," he said as he sat up. "Your friends back there are going to be looking for a rusted-out Ford. Not a beat-up Nissan."

He used his fingernail to strip the wires, made the connection and smiled as the engine burst to life, the sound like music to his ears.

"So you're just going to *steal* it?"

"Yep. Now back away, or you're going to get run over."

From the corner of his eye he caught her startled expression, but he ignored it. They were away from the farm.

She had her own means of transportation. They didn't need each other anymore.

He sent her a two-finger salute as he pulled out of the lot and turned onto the street.

And then made the mistake of glancing in the rearview mirror.

Kat stood in the middle of the snowy lot, staring after him with eyes that were flat and resigned. She'd expected him to leave her like that. And he'd just reaffirmed every one of her beliefs about him.

He hit the brakes at the end of the block, gripped the cold steering wheel with both hands and dropped his head.

Fuuuuuuck.

If he'd seen hurt or even disbelief on her face he could have sped off without a second thought. But not with that look of . . . cold indifference etched into her features.

Muttering curses at her, at himself, at the whole situation in general, he circled the block and slammed on the brakes in front of the market's empty lot. Kat was still standing in the same place, watching him with impassiveness.

He leaned over the seat and popped the passenger door. "Get in."

She stared at him for a long moment, then turned and rummaged in the truck. When she reemerged seconds later, she was carrying a backpack he hadn't noticed before and a small white box.

She climbed in next to him and shut the door without a word.

"What's that for?" He nodded toward the first-aid kit.

"You're bleeding," she said without looking his way.

He eased around to get a good look, pulled the worn sweatshirt out at his back but couldn't see anything more than a few red smears on the gray cotton.

She still wasn't looking at him. And if he expected to

see gratefulness that he'd come back for her or concern for his well-being on her all-too-familiar face, he was barking up the wrong tree. She looked like she could give a rat's ass about him or the car or anything besides herself right now.

"We should go before we're spotted."

Her voice was dull, her eyes anywhere but on him. As he stared at her determined, perfect profile, he couldn't help wondering what had happened to the sweet and sensuous woman he'd changed his whole life for.

"She died."

He hadn't realized he'd spoken out loud until he heard her voice. He looked back up to her eyes, but her expression hadn't changed. If anything, it was even more resolute.

Yeah, the woman he'd known had died. This one was a stranger.

Pete put the car in gear and eased his foot off the brake, slowing as they reached the end of town. "Which way?"

Kat hesitated just long enough to make the hair on the back of his neck tingle. "Straight. Toward Wellsboro."

Which would then take them toward Philadelphia. Not back to New York.

Dammit, he wasn't the ass she thought he was. He didn't know why he felt the urge to prove to her he had a decent bone left in his body, but he did.

Before he could change his mind, he punched the gas. "I'll take you to Philly, but from there on out you're on your own."

"Fair enough," she said quietly as they sped down the road. "Thank you."

Pete frowned. Screw fair. And he didn't need her thanks.

It hit him then, the irony of the situation, as a memory

of the first time he'd left her flashed in his head. At one point he'd have done just about anything to be locked anywhere with her, but now? Now all he could think about was getting as far away from her as possible.

"Don't thank me yet," he muttered. "We still have to get there first."

Six-and-a-half years earlier
Cairo

"I think I left a mark."

"Hm?" Pete sat on the side of Kat's bed, tying the laces of his boots. "Where?"

Still tucked into the covers and looking deliciously rumpled, Kat eased up and ran her finger just underneath the collar of his blue button-down. A tingle raced over his skin where she touched him, and a shot of renewed lust kicked him in the stomach as he watched the strap from her camisole slide over her bare shoulder. "Right here. I don't think I've ever actually given anyone a hickey before."

His stomach tightened at the memory of her mouth on his skin, licking, kissing, sliding lower. He smiled and rose, then proceeded to load the last of his things in his travel case. "I'm glad I could be your first at something."

She settled back into the pillows on a sigh, her dark hair fanning out around her. With her heavy-lidded eyes focused solely on him, it was all he could do to keep packing instead of diving back under the covers for a repeat of the way he'd awoken her from the inside out only an hour ago.

Man, he couldn't get enough of her. Loved being beside her, inside her, loved touching her and listening to the sounds she made when she came apart around him. And that was new for him. He liked women, but he'd never had the desire to be so close to one before. And definitely not for so long.

He'd already stayed in Cairo longer than he'd planned, and if he didn't leave soon he was going to stay a helluva lot longer. They'd spent two nights locked in his suite at the Mena House, then the last two at her flat. She'd had to go to work yesterday, which gave him a chance to reschedule his appointments and get some much-needed paperwork done on his own, but he couldn't put off his meetings any longer.

But the not-knowing-when-he'd-be-able-to-get-back-to-her thing? Yeah, already eating at him.

Had it only been four nights ago he'd rolled into Cairo and swept her off her feet? It seemed like months. There were a thousand things he still wanted to know about her even though he felt like he'd already known her forever.

She was still watching him with those come-get-me eyes, and he knew if he didn't say something to distract them both he was definitely going to miss his flight.

"Admiring your handiwork?" he asked as he threaded his belt through the loops of his khaki pants, then tossed his shaving kit in his bag.

"Yes. Does it make you nervous?"

"Makes me hot. Don't look at me like that." He buckled his belt. "I'm already late as it is."

Her kiss-me lips spread into a warm smile. "You're the one who insisted on having a shower. We could have gone for round four if you'd skipped it. Or was it five?"

He zipped his bag. "Tease me now and you'll pay later."

"Promise?"

His eyes shot to her darker ones, and he saw the same things reflected there he felt. She was putting on a good face, but she was hating this as much as he was.

Damn, but he should have listened to that little voice

going off in his head the night they'd had dinner and stayed away from her.

He lifted the bag from the foot of the bed and dropped it near the door, then came back to sit next to her on the mattress. "Should I be worried about this ex of yours Shannon keeps talking about?"

"I don't know," she said with a sultry grin. "Are you worried?"

"A little," he admitted. "He's here, and I won't be."

She ran her hand up his forearm. "Marty's just a friend, Pete. We dated for a while, but it wasn't serious. He's married to his job."

"What does he do?"

She looked like she wasn't going to answer, then shrugged. "He works for the U.S. government."

"Here in Cairo? Doing what?"

"Antiterrorism stuff."

Pete's brow lifted. "Like with the CIA?"

"I don't know for sure. He didn't talk about it much, but yeah, that was my guess."

Shit. Pete looked at the pink wall across from him. Her ex was CIA. Fabulous.

Walk away.

That teasing returned to her voice. "So long as you haven't committed any crimes, you don't have to worry about Marty at all."

New plan: Don't just walk away. Run.

Pete fought to keep from frowning as he stared at the wall and tried to picture all the spooks he knew in the area. "Good to know," he mumbled.

Her finger traced a lazy circle on his forearm. "Um, I have a confession to make."

He looked over and watched her bite her plump lip in a way he'd learned the last few days meant she was nervous or worried about something. "What?"

"It's nothing. Silly, really. You'll get a kick out of it. But," she bit into her lip again, "when you took me to the Mena House that first day and I, uh, got the wrong idea about you—"

"About me not wanting you? I think we cleared that up."

She blushed. "Yeah. Well. I was worried you were only interested in me so you could get information about my work site. Artifacts have disappeared from some of the neighboring tombs, and there's talk of a smuggling operation in the area. Some of the crew's on edge about it."

Pete stiffened, though he hoped like hell she didn't notice.

"Crazy, huh?" she said with a chuckle. "I mean, that you would do something like that? I don't know what I'd been thinking. I guess I was just nervous."

Pete turned fully toward her. "I'd never use you like that, Kit-Kat. Never. You know that, don't you?"

Her smile faded. She sensed he was making her a promise, and though she couldn't understand the enormity of what he'd just given her, she did realize it was an important moment between them. "Yes, of course I do."

Her hand tightened around his forearm. "When do you think you'll be back?"

For your sake? Hopefully never.

He brushed a lock of hair back from her cheek, marveled at how soft her skin was and called himself ten kinds of stupid.

Why her? Why was she the one woman to get under his skin when he'd avoided letting any woman inside all these years?

All he knew for certain was that there was something special about her. Something pure and fresh and wholesome he hadn't ever experienced before. Something that made *him* feel whole and fresh and pure. And corny as that sounded, he only wanted more of her. "I don't know."

She put her hand over his on her cheek, tipped her head into his touch in a move that was so tender his heart pinched. "This is really stupid, isn't it? We don't have a shot in hell at making this work."

"Yes, we do," he heard himself say, even though he knew it was a mistake. "Because what we've got going here is a lot more than most couples who live in the same city have."

"And what's that?"

"Everything."

Her dark eyes held his as if she were searching his soul for some truth he couldn't prove. Then she leaned up and wrapped her arms around his neck. Her face slid into the hollow between his throat and shoulder in a way that felt like she'd been made just for him. "I'm very glad you took my tour four times in a row, Peter Kauffman."

He closed his eyes and held her tight. And hoped she'd still be saying that a month from now.

Before he thought of a reason to change his mind, he eased back and reached for his bag on the floor. "There's something I want to give you."

He watched her closely as he handed her the small wooden box he'd been debating over giving her, then held his breath while she opened it.

Her doe eyes widened, then darted up to his face. "How did you—"

"It came from a private collection," he said quickly, hoping to God that was the truth. "I found it in Europe last week, and, well, it made me think of you." Carefully, she lifted the chain. The gold crouching pharaoh pendant peeked over the edge of the box. "I've got the provenance on it, and all the paperwork, just so you know."

She didn't seem to hear him. "This has to be worth a fortune."

It was. But seeing her reaction to it now, the awe in her

eyes as she stared at the piece, there was no way he could ever sell it.

"I want you to have it, Kat. It means more to you than it would some stuffy old collector."

"Look at the detail." She ran her fingers over the gleaming gold. "It's so beautiful. Made for a queen. This should be in a museum."

Gently, he took the chain from her hands and draped it over her head so the golden pharaoh fell over her St. Jude medallion and hung between her succulent breasts. "It looks to me like it was made for you. And it doesn't even come close to being as beautiful as you are."

Her eyes lifted to his, and his heart turned over at the tenderness he saw there. At the trust. And when she whispered, "Pete," and tugged him close with a hand that felt like heaven and he knew from experience could take him there, he gave in and brushed his lips softly over hers.

He meant the kiss to be gentle, he really did, but the moment her hands came up to cradle his face and she opened to his mouth, his restraint broke. He pulled her tighter against his body, opened and stroked his tongue against hers until they were both breathless and frustrated beyond words. Then he pressed his forehead to hers and waited until the last possible second before he finally let go and stood.

He lifted his bag from the floor. "It's clichéd to say I'll call."

She hooked her arms around her knees. "But you'd better if you know what's good for you."

He smiled at her lusty grin and the mischievous twinkle in her eyes and squashed forever that little voice telling him to walk away. He couldn't now, even if he wanted to. "I will, Kit-Kat. I promise. Think about me lying next to you when you go to sleep tonight."

She let out a contented sigh. "God, I love that."

Outside her building, he opened the door of the cab he'd called earlier and paused to glance up. She stood in the second-floor window, watching him with a look of longing in her eyes, the golden pharaoh hanging around her neck. And he knew right then, aside from his gallery, he'd never had anything all his own he'd ever truly wanted to hang on to. Now he did.

He waved, then climbed into the car.

"Airport?" the driver asked.

Pete rubbed his chin as they pulled away from the curb. Any doubt he'd had about what he was about to do next disappeared forever. "No." He gave the driver the address of a bar in a dilapidated area of Old Cairo. "I have one last thing I have to finish."

CHAPTER TWELVE

Present day
Philadelphia

In a run-down apartment in the heart of Philadelphia, Dean Bertrand lifted the gun in his hand and stared down at the lifeless body of David Halloway. Blood from the shot to the man's head was already seeping into the carpet.

He unscrewed the silencer from the end of the 9mm with care and placed it in his jacket pocket. Then he tucked the gun in the holster hidden in the back waist-band of his pants and eyed the dead man like a cat eyes a writhing mouse. Funny that most would have considered

Halloway his friend only moments before. If, that is, Halloway'd had any friends.

No one would come looking for ex-FBI Agent David Halloway for days. He'd been the solitary sort, no girl-friend, no wife, no kids watching out for him. He'd dedicated his life to the Bureau, and what had he gotten for it? A piss-poor pension and a date with the devil.

Dean shook his head as he watched the color of the carpet change before his eyes. He figured eventually the stench would seep out into the hall and someone would investigate. Probably that elderly neighbor next door who kept her TV up too loud and let her damn cats wander the hallways. Maintenance would find him when she insisted he was cooking drugs or something else altogether repugnant in his apartment. The police would come, and a case would be opened. Only the authorities would never locate Halloway's killer.

Because like a silent shadow, Dean Bertrand had never been here.

Turning away, Dean lifted the untraceable cell phone from the coffee table and dialed a number he knew by heart but hadn't used in years.

He waited while it rang. The link he'd forged so long ago had finally panned out. When Halloway had IMed him moments before and told him of Slade's phone call, he'd known the two years of watching and waiting had finally paid off. He'd been here within minutes.

A clipped female voice answered. "It's been a long time, Dean." Her Middle Eastern accent was strong, her tone all business. Just as it always was.

"Yeah. A long time." He stared out the dingy window at a pigeon balanced precariously on the railing of the fire escape as he thought about the best tactic to use with her. Some women were easily swayed. This one wasn't. A shark with claws, that was the way he'd always thought of her and still did. "I have something that may interest you."

"Oh, really?" Traffic rumbled in the background. A horn blared. "Must be pretty important for you to come out of the dark. Jameson's death last fall didn't even rouse you. We thought you'd fallen off the face of the earth."

Not quite. But he'd wanted to. More than once. He'd seen and done things in his fifteen years with INTER-POL he wasn't proud of.

Of course, none of that was relevant now.

He ignored her taunt. "I know where Aten Minyawi will be in roughly three hours."

Static crinkled across the line, followed by clicking footsteps, then silence, like she'd entered a building or found a quiet corner to continue their conversation. Oh, yes. Now he had her attention.

"That does interest me," she said. "How, exactly, did you come by this information?"

He glanced at Halloway's lifeless body on the floor. "A mutual acquaintance informed me of his movement. Katherine Meyer will be calling shortly."

Silence.

Yep. That was what happened when you dropped a bomb like this one. He definitely had her attention now.

"So Meyer is really alive," she said in a quiet voice.

"Alive and on her way to meet me."

"You?"

"Our mutual contact is unavailable, you could say."

Silence again as she processed the information. Then, "Minyawi is a top priority for us."

"I know. Of course, he's really just a small fish in a very big pond, isn't he?"

"He is. But not for you."

No, not for him. Dean had been hunting Minyawi for years. It was why he'd left INTERPOL and gone out on his own. The man who'd murdered his wife was his *only* priority. And this was as close as he was ever going to get to the sonofabitch.

"You want to make a deal," she said.

"Don't I always?" He imagined her tapping her toe and twirling the ring on her finger as she thought through her options. He'd watched her do it numerous times in the past.

"If you're calling, it means you must need my help. You wouldn't be telling me any of this simply out of professional courtesy."

She'd always been a smart broad. Smart and savvy and deadlier than a snake. On that he could match her inch for inch. And Kelly had paid dearly for it.

His jaw tightened. "Leak the information Meyer is alive and on her way to Philadelphia to meet with an FBI contact. It'll get out eventually if it hasn't already, but if you jump-start it, Minyawi will come running, guaranteed. And then he's yours."

Silence.

He held his breath as he waited for her response. Did she suspect his real intentions?

"And what of Meyer?"

No, she didn't suspect anything. Not yet at least.

He breathed slowly as he thought about the dark-haired Egyptologist he'd seen pictures of in Halloway's file. He'd memorized every angle of her face, every word in her dossier.

Halloway had seen her once six years before in Cairo, when she'd gone to the SCA to report her suspicions of an artifact-smuggling ring linked to the tomb she'd been working in. He had been at the SCA office in Cairo that day because of an ongoing, unrelated investigation in which the FBI had cooperated with INTERPOL. Though her story had momentarily intrigued Halloway, he hadn't done anything about it. Hadn't reported it to his FBI superiors, to his comrades at INTERPOL, even though the woman had looked flustered and had easily been on edge. Instead, he'd left it in the hands of the SCA.

And that was his first mistake. Because if Halloway had reported it, Minyawi may have been apprehended sooner. And Kelly might still be alive today.

Yeah, Halloway was more than an acceptable sacrifice.

"She's yours to do with what you want," he said.

Her end of the line was silent again, and then finally she said, "Give me a specific location."

His relief was bittersweet as he recited the rendezvous point he intended to use.

In the quiet that followed after he ended the call, he stared out the window at the Philly skyline and thought about Kelly's sunny smile, her bronze skin, her long, silky dark hair. Traffic whizzed by on the road below, while the low echo of cars braking and horns blaring bounced around the walls of the drab apartment five stories up. The pigeon stared back at him, as if it knew every one of his secrets. Then with a great flutter of wings, disappeared into the sky.

Up to Kelly.

He closed his eyes. Took a deep breath. Freedom and peace were but hours away. He'd failed Kelly in life. He wouldn't fail her in death.

He sat down to wait for Katherine Meyer's call.

CHAPTER THIRTEEN

Present day
Central Pennsylvania

The two plus hours it took to get to Williamsport felt like the longest of Kat's life. The snow had lightened up the farther south they drove, but it was still slow going. The iced-over roads were slicker than snot.

Kat tried to sleep, but it didn't work. Her mind was a tumble of activity. Shifting on the seat, she glanced at Pete through hooded lashes, and try as she might, she couldn't help focusing on his bloodstained shirt. More than once she'd told him to pull over or lean forward so she could have a look, and more than once he'd told her he was fine.

Fine.

There was a word to focus on. Irritated, on edge, frustrated as hell . . . all described him way better than *fine*. But his emotional state wasn't her problem anymore, was it?

Something loosened inside her chest as she watched his profile while he drove. Shafts of sunlight illuminated the shadowy beard on his jaw, the lines and angles of his face. He was older now, fine lines fanning out from his eyes, creasing the skin around his mouth, but he was still classically handsome in every sense of the word, even with that shiner.

She thought about the way he'd left her in that lot, then come back for her for no apparent reason. She knew it wasn't guilt driving him to take her to Philly, but if not that, then what? He could have just as easily driven away and never looked back. Then she remembered the ease with which he'd used that gun back at Marty's farm. And knew the Peter Kauffman she'd loved years before was a far cry from the gun-toting car thief she sat beside now.

If she expected to understand him in any way, she was fooling herself.

His gaze drifted her way. "What?"

She straightened, bringing her seatback upright. "Nothing."

He didn't press her for a better answer, and she was glad she didn't have to explain. She glanced out the front windshield again and told herself to stop wondering about whether he was innocent or guilty of being associated with those crimes in Egypt and focus on what really mattered. Namely, staying alive.

And she really needed to get in touch with Marty's contact before they reached Philadelphia.

"I need to find a pay phone and a set of yellow pages," he said, breaking the silence. "Hopefully there's a car rental agency in this town."

"A pay phone's fine. I need to make a call, anyway." She darted a look into the side mirror. "Do you think we lost them?"

Pete easily changed lanes and glanced in the rearview again like he'd done routinely the past few hours. "Yeah. For now. But just to be safe, let's not dawdle."

He eased the car into a gas station and killed the engine. While he went to look up the rental location, Kat slipped out of the vehicle and walked into the convenience store. A bell above her head jingled as she entered.

She didn't waste any time. She grabbed a couple of sodas and an assortment of snack foods she hoped would last them the rest of the trip, then carried her selection to the counter. As she reached for the cash in her pocket, she eyed a rack of T-shirts just to her right.

Outside, Pete was using the pay phone. A quick burst of panic washed over Kat when she stepped out into the cold and saw him standing with his back to her, the receiver pressed to his ear. Who could he be calling and why? A friend? A business contact? Was he telling someone where she was?

Then she had a sickening thought, one that oddly struck her as worse than knowing he might be turning on her. What if he was calling the woman from last night? The one in the limo.

Stomach flipping over, she deposited her purchases in the backseat, then climbed into the front and waited. Pete was deep in conversation with whoever was on the other end of the line. He waved his arm as he spoke, ran his hand through his hair and angled away from her so she couldn't see his face.

The car door opened as she was studying a young mother holding a gallon of milk while dragging a toddler along with her through the parking lot. Pete slid behind the wheel, his sudden closeness breaking her train of thought. Her blood warmed, and she drew in a breath as she remembered the sensation of his skin against hers, his hands on her body, his lips capturing hers.

"There's a Hertz dealer about ten blocks from here," he said as he pulled the door closed.

"Girlfriend know you're okay?"

"It wasn't my girlfriend. It was my business partner. I was due back in Miami today."

"Oh," she said, hating she'd jumped to conclusions but still needing an answer as to who he'd been talking to. "What did you tell him?"

"Just that something came up. I figured the less he knew, the safer he'd be, in case your friends went looking for me in Miami."

That made sense. And it meant he wasn't turning her in. At least not yet.

"Turn around," she said quickly to give her something else to focus on. "I need to check your back."

"I don't think now—"

"There's never going to be a good time. It'll just take a minute." She reached into the backseat and grabbed the first-aid kit and shirt she'd bought. "Besides, you can't go walking around with those bloodstains all over your sweatshirt. People will notice and ask questions."

With a frown of reluctance he took the shirt she offered, turned away and lifted the cotton over his head. The unease in Kat's stomach was quickly replaced with a rolling heat that trickled through her limbs with every inch of skin revealed.

Narrow waist, roped muscles, broad bare shoulders and golden brown skin from hours in the sun. She drew in a sharp breath and reached out to see if he was as soft as she remembered.

"That bad?" Pete asked, angling his head over his shoulder to get a look himself.

Kat flinched at his words and stopped millimeters from touching him. Embarrassed that she'd almost forgotten what she'd set out to do, she dropped her hand and quickly rifled through the first-aid kit for the supplies she needed. "No, it's fine. Just a few cuts. They look like they're already starting to scab over."

In silence she used an antiseptic wipe to clean the few cuts, then gently applied a topical antibiotic just to be safe. Since the wounds didn't need bandages, she blew on them gently to air-dry the antibiotic.

Pete's back arched. Goose bumps broke out on his flesh. And something between a gasp and a moan slipped from his lips, a sound that kicked Kat's pulse up at least two notches. Though he hadn't flinched or reacted at all when she'd touched the cuts with her fingertips, the sensation of her breath against his skin had obviously affected him.

And her, too.

Oh, boy. She was playing with fire here.

"There. Um, you're done." She held up the tube of antibiotic cream with fingers she tried to keep from shaking as he turned to face forward. "You might need more of this later, though."

"Thanks." Pete pulled the plain black tee over his head, and Kat caught a quick glimpse of rock-hard abs, chiseled pecs and a body she'd once kissed and licked just about every inch of.

Lord, she didn't need that image in her head. She ran a hand over her brow.

Oblivious to what he was doing to her, Pete repositioned himself in his seat, but his voice was hard when he spoke. "If you need to use the phone, make it quick. I want to get back on the road."

Kat quickly opened the car door, thankful for the chance to get away from him. "I got a few things, in case you're hungry." She headed for the pay phone as he turned to look in the backseat.

She dialed the number Marty had given her, careful not to look back. The line rang twice before a male voice answered and asked for her by name.

Confusion rushed through her, but then she remembered Marty had probably called ahead.

"Are you being followed?" he asked.

The man was direct and to the point, which for some reason calmed her. She turned to look around the sparse parking lot. "No, not that I'm aware, Agent . . ."

"Just David. Technically I'm retired, and if anyone but Marty had called, I'd have said no to this little meeting."

"I see." Though she really didn't. She wasn't even sure which agency this *David* worked for. She knew Marty was CIA. In the short time she'd dated him and through the course of their lasting friendship, though, he'd never talked about his colleagues or connections, and certainly hadn't ever mentioned this man to her in their brief conversations.

"You're sure it was Busir last night?" he asked.

Like she could ever forget that face. "Yes. Absolutely."

"Describe the other one."

She went through Busir's accomplice's description. Keys clicked in the background.

"Minyawi," he finally said. "Has to be. His involvement with Busir is new, and interesting. Busir disappeared from radar about two weeks ago. Intel's been monitoring his location for some time. The fact he's with Minyawi can't be good."

She wanted to ask *Intel from where?* but bit her tongue. That kind of question could get her into trouble. And she already had enough trouble to last a lifetime.

"There were more." She told him about what had happened at Marty's farm.

"Well, now," he muttered in a surprised tone. "You're one popular woman, Ms. Meyer. This is about more than tracking down one measly female witness to a decade-old crime, isn't it?"

Kat didn't answer as she glanced backward at Pete, who was watching her carefully through the windshield. Marty may trust Halloway, but her instincts screamed not to reveal too much to this man too soon. Especially not over the phone. And she wasn't entirely sure where this would all lead. It wasn't just her safety on the line here.

"You could say that."

Computer keys clicked again. "We'll meet at Fairmount Park, Lincoln Parking Area. There's a footpath that leads out from the parking lot. Follow that. I'll be waiting at the bridge. How soon can you get here?"

She turned back toward the storefront. "If the weather holds, about three hours, I think."

"Three hours." He recited another phone number. "You can't make it, you call this number and I'll give you a new rendezvous point. And, Ms. Meyer?"

"Yes?"

"Don't jerk me around. I'm going out on a limb here simply by stepping out in the open on this one. If you even suspect you're being followed, you don't show. Do you understand?"

Something in his tone sent a chill down Kat's spine. Just how high did this run if an ex-CIA operative—assuming that was what he was—was wary of being seen in public with her?

The line went dead before she could ask.

A shiver of foreboding rushed over Kat's skin as she hung up the phone and walked back to the car. "Three hours," she said after she climbed in. "Fairmount Park."

Pete eyed her a long minute like he wanted to ask what else they'd discussed, then finally started the ignition and backed out onto the street without another word.

What would happen in Philadelphia? Would this David be able to help them? And would Pete go in with her or leave?

"Stay here," Pete said as he parked in the shadow of a large tree in the corner of the car rental lot and killed the engine. "I'll be right back."

Kat did as she was told only because it was easier and was relieved when he came out of the office ten minutes later with a key dangling from his fingers.

He pulled open the back door. "Grab everything you brought with you. The car's in the lot around back. I'm going to ditch this thing on a side street and meet you back there in a minute." He reached into the backseat for the small bag of groceries.

"And here I thought you'd grown attached to this thing," she said as she climbed out. "Just where did you learn to hot-wire a car anyway?"

He held the car door open for her with one hand. Hesitated long enough to make her think he wasn't going to answer, then surprised her when he said, "I had a friend in high school who taught me a thing or two."

"Your parents didn't care?"

"My parents were dead."

His declaration was so matter-of-fact, it made her pause. It also made her realize they'd never talked much about family. At least not about his.

He grasped her arm to help her out of the vehicle. "It's no big deal. My grandmother was too busy with her volunteer work and social clubs to pay much attention. And child rearing was the last thing my grandfather had in mind during his retirement. He spent most of his time on the golf course."

"What happened to your parents?" she asked in what she knew was a shocked voice.

"Car accident. They were killed coming home from a political fund-raiser when I was fourteen. Lauren was nine."

"Lauren?"

"My sister."

He had a sister? How could she have never known that?

And then it hit her. She hadn't known because in all the months they'd been together, they'd either been in bed or talking about being in bed.

A lump formed in her throat. "Your parents were in politics?"

"No. One of Dad's friends. My father ran a fledgling art gallery in St. Petersburg. Oils, mostly. A few watercolors. Nothing spectacular. When he died, we went to live with his folks."

That explained his love of art. "What happened to his gallery?"

"It closed up. My grandparents never really supported it. No one even noticed it was gone."

There was more to it than that. But in the silence she thought she understood. His father's dismal success and ultimate lack of legacy had obviously stuck with Pete.

"That's . . ." Kat searched for a word that fit how she felt hearing about his past. She couldn't help imagining him as a renegade teen, missing his parents, running with the wrong crowd, hot-wiring cars to gain attention from his uninvolved grandparents. When she couldn't think of a single word that worked, she finally settled on one she'd heard time and again about her own childhood. "Sad."

He shrugged. "Depends who you ask. Things hadn't gone down they way they had for me and Lauren, we wouldn't be who we are today."

Wasn't that the truth?

His sister's name finally clicked, and her eyes snapped to his. "Lauren Kauffman? As in, Lauren Kauffman the underwear model?"

He frowned in a clear hint of disapproval. "It's called lingerie, or so she tells me."

She stared at him as images of Lauren's face from numerous magazine covers Kat had seen over the past few years flashed in front of her eyes.

He pursed his lips as if he knew what she was thinking. "Yeah, you're right. She looks a lot better in her underwear than I do."

Kat tried to speak, but nothing came out. And dammit, her cheeks heated in what she knew was an obvious blush.

If he noticed her reaction, he didn't show it. Instead he handed her the bag of groceries and the key dangling from his fingers. "It's a green Taurus around back. Guy at the front said you can't miss it."

Happy he'd let the subject of his near nakedness drop, Kat took the key and groceries, watched as the muscles in his arms and shoulders flexed with his movements. Hearing him talk about his family confirmed there was a whole side of him she hadn't known existed. And though it was counterproductive to her ultimate goal, she wanted to hear more. For some reason, needed to.

"Taurus, huh?" she said, hoping to keep him talking and enjoying the fact he'd finally dropped that ticked-off tone with her. "And here I pegged you as a sports car kinda guy."

"I left my Porsche in Miami. The Taurus will have to do."

One side of her mouth curled. Yeah, not nearly as ticked off anymore. "I guess it'll have to, if that's the best you can do."

His eyes ran over her. And something hot flashed in their depths. "I can do a helluva lot better, Kat. I always could."

A tingle ran down her spine. She suddenly wasn't so sure they were talking about cars anymore. "I suppose a Taurus is probably less conspicuous than a Porsche."

"Yes, it is. And we both know green is safer than sin-city red any day."

Her skin warmed. She imagined him behind the wheel of that wicked car, tanned and sleek and sexy, the wind ruffling his hair as he rocketed down the highway. The image, combined with the intense way he was watching her, made her mouth go dry. "Being safe is important."

"It is. But it's not near the adrenaline rush." His voice dropped to a whisper. "And it'll never be as satisfying."

That tingling slid lower, into her belly. Lower still. She swallowed and forced herself to speak. "It's just a car."

His gaze dropped from her eyes to her lips in a move that sent those tingling sensations shooting straight between Kat's thighs and reminded her of the thousands of times he'd looked at her like that in the past. "Men do love their cars."

"Of course," he added in that same husky timbre that made her remember steamy sex and sweaty bodies and long iniquitous nights, "sometimes all it takes is one test drive to know what you like."

And what you don't. The unspoken words were reflected clearly in his fathomless eyes.

"Maybe once isn't enough," she heard herself say before she could stop the words spilling from her mouth. "Maybe sometimes it takes more than once to know what you need."

"Maybe."

The air crackled between them. His gaze held hers, a thousand questions brewing in those stormy pools. And her heart thumped wildly in her chest. Though she knew it was foolish, she expected him to move forward, to touch her, to drag her close and kiss her like he had in Marty's garage.

She waited for all that to happen, and some insane part of her wanted it, no matter what she knew to be true about him.

Then a muscle in his jaw tightened, and he looked away. And the spell he'd just woven around her broke like ice shattering against hard, cold cement.

"Maybe," he said again. "But I doubt it."

A breath Kat hadn't realized she'd been holding rushed out of her like a balloon being deflated.

He shifted the backpack on his shoulder before she realized he was taking it with him and walked around the car. "I'll meet you in the back lot in five minutes."

Then he climbed in the old Pathfinder and pulled away from the building.

Standing there in the frigid breeze, Kat remembered when he'd looked at her like that in Cairo. Like he still wanted her but didn't know what to do about it. Like nothing between them would ever be the same.

Because it hadn't been. That day, in her apartment, everything had changed between them. She knew now that had been the beginning of the end.

She let out a long breath and turned for the back lot. He was stirring up feelings and memories she'd buried long ago. And she wasn't sure she was strong enough to deal with them all. Not now. Not with him so close.

She prayed in a matter of hours, she wouldn't have to deal with them ever again.

CHAPTER FOURTEEN

Six years earlier
Cairo

"Thanks for meeting me on such short notice. I know you're busy."

"Never too busy for you, Kat. You know that." Martin Slade pulled the chair out for Kat and waited while she sat at the small bistro corner table. Outside on the street, cars honked and jockeyed for space amongst industrial trucks spewing exhaust and donkey-drawn carts darting through traffic. Inside, the predominantly European clientele clinked cups and saucers amidst a steady hum of chatter and afternoon caffeine.

"I just wish I had more to tell you," Marty said as he moved around the table and sat down.

Kat set her purse on the floor and waited as a waitress came and took their order. As Marty was speaking with the young girl, Kat's eyes moved over this man she'd once been intimate with. Funny, but she didn't feel anything for him now except friendship.

It'd been several months since she'd seen him, but he looked good, albeit tired. Then again, Marty always looked tired. It was as much a part of him as were those broad shoulders and that solid frame and the secrecy that hung around him like cologne. Today he wore a white button-down and a pair of black slacks that accentuated his toned body. His dark hair was longer than she remembered, but still stylish and well-kept as it set off his dark eyes and what looked to be a day's worth of stubble he hadn't bothered to shave.

He was an attractive man. One she'd been interested in, but never head-over-heels about. Not like she was with Pete.

Her heart turned over at just the thought of Pete. It'd been six months since their first night at the Mena House. Since then he'd come and gone from her life, never with any warning or regularity. Weeks would go by where she didn't see him, days between phone calls when she had no idea where he was or what he was doing. She'd imagine the worst, tell herself this crazy relationship wouldn't last because there were so many things left unsaid and unexplained between them, but then he'd magically appear on her doorstep, and all her rational thoughts would slip away.

When they were together, all she could see and feel was him. And she knew he felt the same. It was in his eyes every time he touched her, every time he kissed her. Every time he sank his body deep into hers and held her close. He'd never told her he loved her, but she didn't need the words to know what was in his heart. She felt it.

And that knowledge made everything else so much harder to bear.

She knew very little about his business, about what he did when he was gone. She'd asked, of course, time and again, but each time he'd sidestepped her questions by telling her he was working on something important for the future and that he didn't want to waste their moments talking about work when there were other things more important to do.

His aversion to letting her into such a large part of his life hurt, but she never pushed him. He was right, their time together was already so limited, she didn't want to do anything to tarnish it. Now, though, sitting across from Marty, she knew she was fooling herself. Sawil had already warned her.

As the waitress moved away, Marty's eyes resettled on hers. The closest table was too far away for anyone to overhear their conversation, but he spoke in a low voice anyway. "A couple of the pieces you described to me showed up in a gallery in Turkey."

Kat closed her eyes. Pete had called from Istanbul last week.

"Turkish officials are working with the Supreme Council of Antiquities to return them to Egypt. No one's talking about how they got there."

Kat looked up at the mention of the SCA. "You have a hunch, though, right?"

"Technically, Kat, I'm not even supposed to be talking about this since it's not my area. I passed on what you told me, but I'm only here out of courtesy given our friendship."

"I know, and I appreciate it. I just didn't know what else to do. I told Sawil about my suspicions, and he talked to Dr. Latham about it, but so far the SCA hasn't done diddly."

What she didn't say was that Sawil had warned her about Pete the night she'd gone to talk to him. When she wouldn't let the subject drop after Sawil's repeated attempts to tell her to just let it go, he'd finally admitted he suspected the trouble at their tomb and Pete's appearance in Kat's life were too close to be a coincidence. He'd argued Pete was an antiquities dealer. Even if he didn't work on the shady side, he knew people who did. He had to.

She'd told Sawil he was crazy, that Pete would never be

involved in something like that, but some small part of her had been knocked off kilter by the accusation.

Because there were too many things she just didn't know about Pete. And even now, sitting across from Marty, she remembered the way Pete had checked out her tomb during those first few tours, not like a tourist, or a man who was simply pursuing a romantic interest, but like he was after something special.

She supposed that was why she'd called Marty. So he could reassure her Pete was clean and someone else was responsible for the thefts.

This news didn't help.

"Did Latham increase security around the tomb?"

"Yes," she said. "But if what you just told me is true, it doesn't matter. Someone's getting in anyway."

His lips thinned. "This isn't a U.S. matter, Kat. The SCA's closed-lipped. They like to handle things from within."

Her shoulders slumped.

"If you have evidence, that's another matter. But my suggestion now would be to file a report with the SCA yourself. Even though Latham's handling it, if more people come forward you might see an increased response from the SCA."

She nodded, knowing he was right.

Their coffees were served, and they managed to talk about the more positive aspects of her excavation instead of the missing relics.

As dusk settled in, Marty walked her back to her flat, four blocks away. She felt no better than when she'd left to meet him. She still had a thousand questions, and she desperately wanted to see Pete to have these insane doubts put to rest. She hadn't talked to him in a week, and every day that passed without word made Sawil's warning that much more ominous.

They turned the corner onto her block, and Kat's heart

rate increased as she looked toward her building. Pete rose from the steps where he'd been sitting, waiting for her. A duffel bag sat at his feet, and his hair was mussed. His rumpled blue shirt and worn jeans looked like he'd slept in them.

But it was his face she focused on as she approached. Exhaustion lines marred his skin, making her wonder when he'd slept last. She picked up her pace to close the distance between them, only to falter when she saw the dark and chilling look in his eyes as he glanced between her and Marty.

He didn't move toward her, just watched her with narrowed eyes.

"Pete," she said when she was only a few feet away. She eased in to hug him, and he returned the brief contact, but it was stilted and reserved, not the hot-blooded greeting he usually gave her with his mouth and tongue and teeth. Her stomach tightened, and in the obvious tension between them, a little of her doubt solidified into place. "What are you doing here?"

"I had a layover. Thought I'd surprise you." His voice was hard and unfriendly, and his eyes skipped right over her to land on Marty. "You obviously had other plans."

Her pulse pounded as she turned toward Marty. "Um. This is Martin Slade. Marty, this is Peter Kauffman. My, uh, friend."

"Last time I checked," Pete corrected in that same hard tone, "we were a lot more than friends."

Kat's face heated.

Marty glanced from Pete to Kat and back again, then held out his hand. "Nice to meet you. Kat and I were just chatting about her work site."

Pete didn't answer, and he didn't return Marty's handshake. In his hard eyes there was no mistaking the warning: *hands off.*

Guilt for something she hadn't done quickly morphed

to frustration. He was the one who left her for weeks at a time without word and was then upset when she had friends? Six months of not knowing where he was or what he was doing or when he'd be back compounded and transformed into anger.

Marty dropped his hand and looked between the two of them, obviously sensing the strain. "I'm going to take off, Kat. If anything else comes up, let me know, and I'll see what I can do."

She smiled for his benefit, though she felt her cheeks crack with the effort. "Thanks, Marty. I will."

Kat waited until Marty headed up the street and disappeared around the corner. When she turned toward Pete she could practically feel the animosity radiating from him. "That was a little childish, don't you think?"

She pushed past him and moved up the steps of her building.

"I don't know. You tell me." He jerked his bag from the ground and followed close at her heels.

"If you expect me to apologize for having coffee with him, you're high." The main door snapped shut behind them as she headed up the narrow flight of stairs to the second floor.

"Why would I expect you to apologize?" he asked coldly at her back.

She ignored his question as she shoved her key in the door lock, twisted and moved inside, seething the whole time. Thankfully, Shannon was out for the afternoon.

Dammit, he had no right to be upset with her. None at all. She tossed her purse onto the couch as he came in behind her and pushed the door shut. His bag dropped to the ground in the entry, but he made no move to come farther into the apartment. "When did you get here?" she demanded.

"Two hours ago."

Oh, geez. He'd been sitting on her stoop in that wretched

heat for two hours? No wonder he was pissed. "If you'd told me you were coming I would have—"

"Is this a normal thing for you? Running off to meet your ex when I'm not around?"

Shock rippled through her. "Of course not. I haven't seen him in months."

His hard eyes screamed he didn't believe her. "Why'd you rush off to meet him today? I did interpret that right, didn't I? *You* were the one who called *him?*"

Kat's heart stilled. There it was. The accusation she'd expected. He didn't trust her. And the irony in that one thought hit her right beneath the breastbone until even drawing a breath hurt.

"Yes. But only because I wanted to talk to him. Nothing else happened. I'm not interested in him anymore. And he's not interested in me."

"Right," Pete scoffed and rested his hands on his hips. "Talk to him about what?"

"About . . ." She faltered. "About the missing pieces at my tomb. I thought maybe he could use his contacts and find out what's going on."

"Let me guess. He doesn't have a fucking clue."

Why did he sound so sure of himself? She'd tried to talk to him about what was happening at her tomb a few times, but he'd always brushed it aside, just like he did whenever their conversation turned toward work for either of them. What if he knew what was happening there? Was he hiding something?

Sawil's warnings came back to her in the silence between them, coupled with the unknowns about Pete and his aversion to letting her into his life.

"How did you know?" she asked quietly.

His shoulders tensed. Something very much like disbelief raced across his face, then settled into his eyes as disgust. "Why don't you just ask me what you really want to know?"

She swallowed hard as dread unfurled in her stomach. A tiny voice screamed, *don't do it*! But she had to. She couldn't stand the secrecy between them anymore. And more than anything, she needed to hear his innocence from his own lips. "Did you have anything to do with those missing artifacts in my tomb?"

She regretted the words the moment they were out. His stormy eyes hardened, and the light she always saw there when he looked at her darkened.

His mouth barely moved when he spoke. "You think I had something to do with that?"

"No." *Yes!* "I don't know." She lifted her arms, dropped them. "There's just so much going on and so much I don't even know about you. Every time I try to talk to you about it you clam up. I just want you to open up to me and tell me the truth."

"You're not going to believe me no matter the answer, so why bother?"

"Yes, I will," she said quickly. She wanted to touch him, but more urgent was the need to hear his answer.

His eyes blazed into hers. An eternity seemed to pass. The air in the apartment grew hot and stifling. For a moment she wished he'd lash out at her, just give her some indication this mattered to him, but he didn't. He didn't even move.

"No," he finally said. "I didn't have anything to do with those missing relics."

Her relief was swift and consuming, and she moved toward him, desperate to have his arms around her, only to stop when she saw the warning flash in his eyes. He reached down and snatched his bag from the floor. "Where are you going?"

"I'm outta here."

Panic set in. "Wait. Pete, let's talk about this."

"There's nothing to talk about. You just told me everything I need to know." He jerked the door open and left.

Kat stood in the middle of her living room as his receding footsteps pounded on the steps in the hall. A sick feeling settled in her stomach as her heart hammered against her ribs.

What had she just done? She'd let her aggravation over the scene with Marty, her fear over where her relationship with Pete was headed and her worries over everything happening at the tomb sway what she knew about Pete deep in her heart.

The hundreds of ways he'd loved her over the past six months flashed before her eyes, the whispered promises late at night and the tenderness in his eyes when he looked at her. Her heart cracked wide open.

She loved him. If she hadn't known it before, she knew it now. She loved him, and she was losing him.

She tore out of the apartment and down the stairs. Her hands shook as she pushed the heavy front door to the building open and paused on the top step, breathing heavily, searching up and down the sweltering street for him. *Please don't let him be gone yet.*

She couldn't see him. A Muslim family crossed in front of her building. A garbage truck burped out exhaust as it ambled down the street. A man sped by on a bike.

Where was he? *Please God . . .*

Then she spotted him, a block up with his bag over his shoulder and his head down, striding away from her.

"Pete!"

He turned sharply at the sound of her voice, and she didn't even hesitate. She threw herself into his arms, wrapped herself around him and held on tight.

"Don't go. Not like this. Please." A sob caught in her throat. "I'm sorry. I'm so sorry. Please don't leave."

He hesitated, and for a frightening moment she thought he was going to push her away. Then his bag hit the concrete, and his arms wrapped tight around her until his embrace squeezed the air out of her lungs.

"Dammit, Kit-Kat."

A tear slipped down her cheek as his mouth crushed over hers, hard and possessive and bruising in its demand. She returned the kiss with everything she had in her.

Somehow they made it back to her flat where they made love with an urgency that bordered on the violent. When it was over, they lay sweaty and breathless in the bed they'd shared so many times she'd lost track. But this time was different. Though they were skin to skin and his arms were around her, Kat felt the distance between them as wide as the ocean that normally separated their continents.

She closed her eyes and snuggled closer, trying to bridge the gap. "What are you thinking?"

Silence. Then, "I have to go soon."

Her heart pinched at the emptiness of his words. She wanted to tell him she loved him, but she knew now wasn't the time. He wouldn't believe her. Not after what had happened earlier. She'd have to wait. But in the meantime, she'd show him.

She eased up on her elbows and looked down. He was staring at the ceiling, lost in his own thoughts. Slowly his gray eyes shifted her way, clouded with the same turmoil she felt.

"Not yet," she whispered as she leaned down and kissed him. Once. Twice. Drawing him into her mouth and deeper into her soul. Hoping he could feel what he meant to her with every beat of her heart.

His hands came up to frame her face, and his fingers slipped into her hair. "Not yet," he repeated against her mouth.

CHAPTER FIFTEEN

Present day
Philadelphia

Pete's instincts went on high alert the closer they got to Philadelphia. He couldn't shake the feeling something about this meeting Slade had set up was wrong.

During the last few hours, Kat had sat stoically in the passenger seat of the midsized sedan he'd rented, staring out at the scenery as if she were a thousand miles away. Considering their last conversation at the rental lot, he figured maybe that wasn't such a bad thing. It gave him time to think about what was really important, like what the heck was about to go down next.

All he knew for certain was she was meeting with one of Slade's contacts. He assumed that meant CIA, though she hadn't said for certain. Most definitely it wasn't Slade, and he wasn't entirely sure if he should be ticked or relieved by that fact.

Questions about Slade lit off in his brain as he pulled to a stop in the Lincoln parking area of Fairmount Park and killed the engine. The sprawling 1400-acre park was full of leafless trees and dense underbrush. Ahead, abandoned play equipment sat like dinosaur bones in the brisk November breeze. Though no snow covered the ground here, the temperatures were near freezing, keeping even the most active kids indoors.

He glanced over his shoulder at the trees on the opposite end of the parking lot. They framed a pathway running up a gentle slope. He thought he could hear the rush of water over rock somewhere close. There were no other cars in the lot. No signs of life anywhere in the park.

That didn't exactly put him at ease.

Kat sat still, staring out at the play equipment. He took in her tense features and hard eyes and knew without even asking something was definitely off here. "What now?"

She checked her watch, and then her eyes swept the landscape. "He should be here anytime. He said to meet him near the bridge."

He caught her hand before she could open the door. "We'll go together."

For a second he thought he saw something like relief flash in her dark irises. "Okay."

He steeled himself against the stab of tenderness he felt for her, reminded himself what she'd done to him and refocused on the here and now. "Just stay close."

She nodded, and when he let go, she slid out of the car and reached for the parka she'd stuffed into the backseat.

They headed toward the path in silence. Pete scanned the trees for anything out of the ordinary. Nothing but branches swaying in the wind and the slight echo of traffic rushing by on the street two blocks over.

As they came over the rise, Kat's feet stilled. He looked toward the bridge that held her attention and noticed a figure standing deep enough in the shadows to prevent anyone from seeing his face.

Not Slade. Even Pete could tell that from this distance, and he hadn't seen the guy in six years. This man was built like a linebacker.

Kat took a step forward, but he caught her arm again, stopping her momentum. "How do you know you can trust this guy?"

The muscles in her upper arm tensed beneath his hand. "I . . . Marty knows him. He trusts him. That tells me he's secure."

That didn't reassure Pete any. "And what if *Marty's* wrong? Take a good look. Do you recognize this guy at all?"

Her eyes narrowed on the man pacing slowly across the footbridge. His hair was slightly gray, but his face was hidden in the shadows. He stopped and looked in their direction.

So much for blending. They'd been spotted.

"No," she said warily. "But I don't think I would. He's retired."

"Retired what?"

"CIA."

"You're sure?"

She hesitated just long enough to tell him she wasn't entirely sure of anything. And that little piece of news kicked his nerves up a level. He reached back with his free hand to adjust the gun at the small of his back. "Stay close to me."

"I thought this was what you wanted. In a few minutes you'll be rid of me for good." Her eyes flickered with uncertainty, and a muscle in her cheek twitched like her nerves were in high gear.

Well, that made two of them. His had been on overload since he'd awoken in Slade's garage and found her alive. And the last few hours with her in the car had been enough. He'd remembered too much, been aware of too much, and the way his body still heated up in reaction to hers pissed him off to no end. The smartest thing he could do was get the hell away from her before he did something really stupid. Like shook her until she screamed.

Or kissed her until he did.

He beat back a temper that seemed to be building from nowhere. "That *is* what I want. I'm just hoping like hell we don't get caught in a crossfire because your boyfriend set us up."

He let go of her arm and took a step around her.

"He's not my boyfriend," she said behind him.

"Yeah, you said that once before," he mumbled. When he'd been stupid enough to believe everything she told him.

Her shoes shuffled along the path at his back. "And I was telling you the truth. Then and now."

"You'll understand if I don't jump for joy at that news." Jesus, how the hell had he let the conversation take this side trip into insanity? They should both be focused on the meet-and-greet that was about to take place.

"Marty's not my boyfriend," she said again as if saying it enough would prove a point he knew was a lie. "He hasn't been since before you and I were together."

"You said a lot of things, Kat. And look how many of those turned out to be true."

"If I lied to you, it was for a very good reason. Someday, maybe, you'll understand."

That did it. He stopped, wheeled around and faced her. She nearly ran into him before slamming on her own brakes and stopping mere inches from his chest.

"Lay it on me. Gimme your good reasons for fucking my life up, not only once but twice. I'm all ears."

"I did it for . . ." Her eyes drifted from his face to his chest, her expression one of utter regret and extreme hurt.

And oh, yeah. His chest tightened as he stood there watching her. He could kiss her senseless. Dive right in, not bother to come up for air. Overwhelm the both of them so neither remembered what the hell they were arguing about in the first place.

But then he'd be in an even worse place than he was now. He was smart enough to know getting away from her here was the only way he was going to save himself.

"You know what?" he said, trying to get a handle on

the conflicting emotions racing through him. "Everyone's got reasons for what they do. You got yours and they make sense? Good for you. Everything you did got you here, didn't it? So you tell me, Kat. Isn't this where you want to be?"

She stared at him. Long and hard, battling some internal war she'd never share with him. He waited for her answer, felt she was on the verge of telling him something he might need to hear, but then her eyes dropped from his, and she nodded slowly. "Yeah. Everyone's got reasons. And you're right, Pete. This is the only place I can be."

He felt like she'd just sucker punched him in the stomach. But he wasn't surprised. It wasn't like he expected her to confide in him after everything that had gone down between them.

And it wasn't like he'd even know what to do if she did.

She started walking, and with no other choice, he followed.

As they approached the bridge, the man stepped out of the shadows. "Katherine Meyer?"

They stopped at the end of the bridge. Pete shoved his emotions into a lockbox and turned the key so he could focus. He kept his arms at his sides in case he needed to grab his gun. Kat glanced his way briefly, then looked back toward the man. "Yes."

The man stepped into the light. He was easily fifty years old, but in superb physical shape for his age. "David Halloway. You probably don't remember me, but we met briefly once. In Cairo."

Her brow dropped as she thought back, but Pete could tell no recognition flared in her eyes. "No, I don't remember you."

He shrugged a little. "Not a surprise. I have one of those faces that tends to get lost in a crowd."

"Good feature for a spook to have," Pete interjected.

Halloway looked his way. "And you are?"

"Peter Kauffman."

Halloway studied him, and like wheels clicking into motion, recognition dawned in his eyes. "I thought you looked familiar. Your dossier came across my desk more than once."

He had a dossier? *Fabulous.* His day was just getting better by the minute.

"And for the record," he continued, "I'm not a spook."

Pete glanced at Kat and back again. "You're not CIA?"

Halloway shook his head. "Retired FBI. I worked with the Art Theft Crime Team near the end of my career."

"So how do you know Marty?" Kat asked.

"We worked together on a few cases. Interagency co-operation. Art theft and antiquities smuggling tend to be international affairs. I spent my fair share of time overseas."

"What do you know about Busir?" she asked. "And this man Minyawi you said was with him."

He focused in on her, and his expression went from conversational to serious in the space of a nanosecond. "More than you want to know. Busir's small time, really. A middleman, nothing more. Does what he's told for a price. The fact he's working with Minyawi is more interesting.

"Now Minyawi," he went on, "he's a catch, that one. Is on the wanted list in several countries because of what could be described as less than humanitarian methods of obtaining information. Man's been on a killing spree for nearly five years. Rose in the ranks of his group like wildfire spreads across a dry valley. He's careful, goal-oriented and smart. And I've never heard of a single person who's given him the slip. Which makes me wonder what's so important about you that he would take the time to track you down. Either you're the smartest hit he's ever had, or you've got the luck of the Irish on your side, girlie."

Kat tensed.

"You know something about someone Minyawi's indebted to," Halloway added. "Or afraid of. That makes you priority number one for him. Enough to get him to risk coming into the U.S., which is something he's steered clear of until now."

Kat didn't answer, but her expression confirmed Halloway's words. Pete's eyes narrowed as he watched her. Just what did she know? And how high did this run to have both CIA and FBI involved with her case? He wasn't naïve enough to think she was anything more to the government than a pawn in a very large chess match.

"Of course," Halloway said when it was clear she wasn't going to answer, "doesn't really matter to me. All I care about is bringing him in."

"Why you?" Pete asked Halloway. "If you're retired, why did Slade call you?"

Halloway looked thoughtful for a moment, then said, "Minyawi was involved in one of my last cases. Martin knew I'd want a crack at him."

Pete knew better than to believe that. There was something else going on here.

"Okay," Kat finally said as if she had all the explanation she needed. "What now?"

Halloway looked her way again. "Now we take you in, put you in protective custody. Your location will most likely be leaked so they can draw him out. You'll be completely safe, of course."

Of course, Pete knew that was a big fat lie. But what could he do? This didn't concern him, and ultimately, it was her choice. But man, big red warning flags were popping up all over in his mind.

Kat glanced Pete's way, uncertainty and the slightest bit of fear in her eyes. She looked at the wood beneath her feet, then glanced up at Halloway again. "Okay. But you have to take both of us."

"What?" Pete and Halloway both asked at the same time.

She ignored Pete and instead said to Halloway, "You and I both know he'll go after Pete to get to me."

"Look," Pete cut in, all her quiet time in the car suddenly making sense, "I don't need—"

Halloway ran a hand across his chin. "She's probably right."

Pete shot a glare at Kat, then nodded toward Halloway. No way he was being dragged anywhere else he didn't want to go. He'd had enough of that to last him a lifetime. "You'll understand if I don't kick up my heels in delight at the thought of going anywhere willfully with the Feds. The State Department did dick for me when I was stuck in Afghanistan."

Halloway scratched the top of his head. "I read about your situation there, Kauffman. Ticked off the wrong people on that little trip."

Kat's brow wrinkled as she looked Pete's way, but he ignored it. "Yeah, and when the U.S. cracked down on militant uprisings in the country I got stuck. Six weeks. No one did shit for me then."

"INTERPOL had you listed on a blue notice," Halloway said. "Your extenuating circumstances were a plus at the time. The Afghan government cooperated out of necessity."

"You mean INTERPOL wanted to keep an eye on me, and the Afghanis didn't have a choice."

"Pretty much." Halloway said. "There was a lot going on then."

Pete's jaw clenched. For him, too. A three-day meeting had stretched into six weeks until the U.S. Embassy had finally gotten him out. He had less-than-happy memories of the way he'd been treated on that trip. Especially because it was right after Kat had died, and he'd had his nose to the grindstone. Shit, he'd been careful *not* to piss off the wrong people on that trip, though he had on numerous ones before.

"Pete," Kat said. "It won't be forever."

"Is that what Slade told you?"

Her expression dropped. Okay, low blow. But dammit, he wasn't about to give up his life over this. Not again. Not even for her.

"Pete—"

He shook his head and worked to keep his jaw from tightening. "I'm not going in with you."

She glanced at Halloway. "Can you give us a minute?"

Halloway checked his watch. "A couple. Then we need to go."

As he walked toward the opposite end of the bridge, Kat turned Pete's way again, and he had a sudden realization that by not agreeing to go with her, this was good-bye for them.

Closure. Hell, how many times had Lauren told him that was what he was missing, why he couldn't ever seem to get over losing Kat in the first place? Now, faced with it, he felt like his skin was being peeled off his muscles one slow inch at a time.

Ironic, considering that was how he'd felt when he'd thought she'd died. If closure was supposed to make a person feel better, then it was a crock of shit as far as he could see.

"Are you sure about this?" she asked. "They'll come looking for you. The fact they were at the auction confirms they've been watching you a lot longer than I thought."

Pete realized that as well, but it didn't change his decision. "I'm not going into protective custody." In fact, he actually hoped this Minyawi character came after him. Minyawi and Busir both.

Her eyes settled on the gray parka he was wearing, and she bit her lip as if there was more she wanted to say, but couldn't.

And damn, he knew just how she felt. There were a thousand things he wanted to say to her, questions he needed answered before she walked out of his life for good, but he couldn't find the words. Never in his wildest dreams had he thought being with her again could leave him feeling more empty than he'd felt when he thought she was dead.

"Are you sure about this?" he asked, turning her question back around because it was the only thing he could say without unleashing a firestorm neither had the time or desire to deal with.

"It's about time, don't you think? Now that it's all out in the open, there's really no reason to hide anymore."

No, there wasn't. No reason to hide. No reason to stay, either.

"I'm sorry you got dragged into this," she said, looking up with more resolve than he'd seen in her eyes in nearly twenty-four hours. "Yeah, you know. I'm . . . I'm sorry for a lot of things, but mostly that. If I could go back and change what happened, I would."

His chest tightened as if in a vise. And words shot around in his brain like a Ping-Pong ball.

Don't let her go.

She took a step away before he could think of a good reason to make her stop. Then another. And another. And as he watched, paralyzed by pride and anger and the slightest hint of something that felt oddly like fear, his insides twisted into a knot. "Take care of yourself, Pete."

She made it halfway across the bridge before she paused and looked back. Though it made him a complete and utter schmuck, his pulse jumped in response.

She was careful not to look him in the eye, instead focusing on a spot somewhere near his feet. "You were right, you know. That last day in Cairo? In my apartment when we argued? You were right when you said I didn't know how to trust people. I don't know that I ever learned. I wish I had. I wish . . . yeah. I wish a lot of things."

Her gaze slowly drifted up. And when her chocolate irises locked on his, it was like looking into his past. At a lifetime of things he shouldn't have done and wished he could change. And being hit with the knowledge there wasn't a damn thing he could do about any of it now. Especially anything that had to do with her.

She was gone before he could respond.

Pete stood in the same place, on the end of the bridge in the cool December breeze, watching as she and Halloway climbed the path on the opposite side of the small creek and disappeared over the knoll. She didn't bother to look back again, and part of him didn't really blame her. Over the past twenty-four hours, he hadn't done one thing to see her side of the issue. Sure, he'd listened to her story, but then he'd mocked her motives and made it clear he didn't want to have anything to do with her. Yeah, he'd driven her to Philadelphia, even engaged in a little chitchat, but when she'd clammed up, he hadn't pressed her to open up so he could understand what she was going through. And he hadn't offered her a single thread of help.

When he couldn't hear their voices or footsteps anymore, he took a deep breath. And knew what it felt like to be filleted from the inside out.

He headed back the way he'd come. Head down to block the bite of wind, hands stuffed deep into the pockets of jeans that weren't his. When he reached the rental, he slid behind the wheel, closed the door and just sat in the silence.

Kat's scent lingered in the interior of the car, and for some insane reason he had a memory flash. Her naked, fresh from the shower, sitting at the little vanity in her apartment, slathering that purple, jasmine-scented lotion she'd always loved all over her skin. Smiling at him over her shoulder when he offered to help. Turning and handing him the bottle with a sultry grin that did wicked hot things to his blood.

Did she still use it? Did she think of him when she rubbed it all over her body?

He glanced at the empty seat where she'd sat and noticed her backpack. In her rush to meet up with Halloway, she'd left it behind.

Giving it back to her *wasn't* an excuse to see her one more time. There wasn't anything he could say to her to change anything anyway. But at least it was one way he could make up for being a total ass this whole last day.

He leaned over and lifted it. Then paused as a thought occurred to him.

How many women would think to grab their purse when they were being chased by psycho killers? When had she slipped it into the truck? And why had she clutched the damn thing to her chest like it was her last vestige of hope?

He pulled the top flap open and peered inside. Then lowered his brow in confusion. Two wigs. One blonde, another a dark auburn. A small container of colored contacts. Passports, three different ones, all with her picture and different aliases. A series of driver's licenses from various states that looked like her but had different names. And a gun.

A Beretta.

He lifted the firearm, turned it to check the magazine. When he replaced it, he felt something hard brush his fingertips.

The crouching pharaoh he withdrew from the pack was one he'd seen a hundred times before. Because it was his.

Gold. Egyptian. Small enough to fit in a coat pocket, but intricate and ornate. It had been part of the auction.

She'd stolen it. That was what she'd been doing in New York. But why?

His confusion was interrupted as three motorbikes jerked into the empty parking lot. Out of their line of sight, he eyed the trio as they parked near the playground. When the first driver removed his helmet, light glinted off his shaved head.

Busir. Here. Already. He watched as another man dismounted and tugged off his helmet. A fall of dark hair reached his shoulders and hid his face from view.

This one had to be Minyawi.

Pete's adrenaline jumped. His brain clicked into gear as another man dismounted and a fourth bike pulled in behind them. Somehow he and Kat had been followed. Or some*one* Kat was with right now had ratted them out.

The four men ditched the bikes and took off at a slow jog across the park. When they reached the trees on the far side, Minyawi pulled a gun from his back pocket and checked the magazine. Busir and the other two did the same.

Suddenly the whys didn't matter. Pete closed Kat's pack. In a matter of minutes neither of them would need protective custody anyway.

CHAPTER SIXTEEN

"Hold on. I left my backpack in the rental car."

Kat paused on the path to look back over the two small hills that hid the parking lot from view. Would Pete have left already? She needed that pack. She had to go back.

"We don't have time, Ms. Meyer." Halloway gripped her arm at the elbow.

"It'll just take a few minutes, I promise." Kat lifted her

arm to free his hold but discovered his grip was solid. What was this?

"I don't think you understand the severity of the situation." His fingers dug into her arm. "We don't have a few minutes. Now let's go."

Kat looked up into his very hard, very black eyes as his words on the bridge filtered through her mind.

It wasn't so much what he'd said as how he'd said it. His tone had been laced with anger and very, very personal.

And he'd called Marty *Martin*. No one called Marty Slade by his given name.

Now we take you in, put you in protective custody. Your location will most likely be leaked so they can draw him out.

Not they. *Him.*

Oh, God. She wasn't walking out of this park.

The tree trunk to her right splintered into a dozen pieces as a bullet whizzed by and struck with a resounding *thwack.* Kat yelped and jerked to cover her head when she realized what was happening. Before she could dart out of the way, Halloway had an arm around her waist and was yanking her down behind a collection of boulders just off the path.

"Stay down!" he yelled, bracing his arm on the top of the boulder to return fire.

A series of bullets ricocheted off wood and rock around her. Trembling, Kat scooted as close to the shelter of the rocks as she could to protect herself.

But as quickly as the gunshots started, they stopped.

"We want no trouble with you," a heavily accented voice finally yelled. "Just give us the girl, and you can walk away!"

"No deal!" Halloway yelled back in a very definite British accent he hadn't had before. "You want her? You're going to have to come and get her yourself!"

A low chuckle came from what seemed like only yards

away. "Well now, Bertrand, I never expected to run into you here. With her."

Bertrand? Sweat broke out on Kat's forehead. Just what in the name of God was going on?

Brush rustled to her right. In the waning light she couldn't see anything more than trees and shrubs. Could she make a run for it while these two duked it out with words and bullets? She looked back at Halloway . . . or Bertrand . . . or whoever the hell this man was and knew with a sinking reality she wouldn't make it very far. For whatever reason, he was here because of her, and he wasn't about to let her out of his sight.

"You underestimated me, Minyawi!"

Another chuckle. Followed by footsteps. Close. Closer. The brush rustled mere feet from her. Kat sank back against the rocks.

Out of nowhere Bertrand whipped around and fired into the brush at her side. Kat jerked and shrieked. Her ears rang from the popping sounds. A man she hadn't seen approach fell to the ground at her feet, his wide, lifeless eyes staring out at nothing.

Oh, God. *Oh, God.*

Bertrand whipped back and fired again over the rock. "One down! How many more you got, Minyawi? We can do this all night. But I guarantee I'll kill the girl myself before I'll give her to you!"

In the distance there was a low rumble, like thunder, though the sky was clear.

More laughter, this time from a different location in the trees. "She begged me to kill her. Did you know that? She's one I will never forget."

Bertrand went rigid all over. His face morphed in rage, his hands tightening on the gun as he searched the park with lifeless eyes. And for a second, Kat was sure she'd heard that voice before. But where?

"Go ahead, kill the girl," Minyawi yelled. "You save me the trouble of having to do her myself. It makes no difference to me."

Kat tensed.

"You son of a bitch!" Bertrand started firing rapidly into the brush, and Kat took that as her cue to cut and run.

She jumped to her feet and ran at breakneck speed through the woods. The rumbling grew louder, but she didn't pause to look back, couldn't because she knew she'd fall and didn't want to see if they were closing in on her. Her heart pounded in her throat, echoed in her ears. At any moment she expected to be gunned down, but she wasn't going out without a fight. Not after all this time.

She ran hard, darting around trees and rocks and skidding in the dirt. Shouts and voices and an eruption of gunfire echoed behind her, but she kept running. The thunder was now a resounding echo in her ears that she couldn't get away from, until suddenly she thought she heard her name being called on the wind.

"Kat!"

Stumbling over rocks that seemed to come out of nowhere, she fell, took in a mouthful of dirt, rolled quickly and jumped to her feet again, ready to tear off into the trees. Until she realized the rumbling wasn't thunder or a helicopter, but a motorcycle rushing toward her. And driving? A big blond hulk of a man she never thought she'd see again.

She was too scared to spend much time thinking about the reasons Pete had come back. She simply leapt off the path as he approached to make room. He didn't stop the bike, and she didn't wait. With one swift move as if they'd practiced it a hundred times before, he grasped her arm in one hand and pulled her onto the back of the bike as she jumped with all her might.

"Hold on!" he yelled.

She did. Finding the footrests on the axle, she wrapped both arms tight around his waist and buried her face against his strong, muscular back. They sped off into the depths of the park with the wind whipping her hair, away from Minyawi and their second brush with death in only a matter of hours.

And it wasn't until they reached the parking lot on the opposite end of the park that she realized her hands weren't clenched tight around Pete's belt buckle, but around the base of a backpack he was wearing backward against his chest.

Her backpack from the car.

Pete revved the Honda's engine and sailed through the streets of Philadelphia. At his waist, Kat's fingers dug into his skin through his jacket. He knew they were being followed. The last two times he'd checked there'd been a motorbike hanging with them some distance back.

Weaving in and out of traffic, the bike hiccupped, and he glanced down, realizing in a rush they were almost out of gas. Didn't it just figure the bike he'd picked to lift was now operating on fumes?

When the bike coughed again, he turned onto a side street and quickly darted into an alley. He parked behind a Dumpster as far out of sight as he could, killed the engine and hit the kickstand.

Kat let go of his waist and sat up. "What happened?"

"Out of gas." He climbed off the bike, switched the pack to his back and grabbed her hand. "Let's go."

She didn't argue, instead gripped his hand in hers and ran with him. The alley spilled out onto a dimly lit street. Darkness was just settling in as they wove through pedestrians on the sidewalk. They kept close to the buildings in the less-than-desirable neighborhood and tried to blend in.

Didn't work. Minyawi's muscle was still behind them

and closing fast, so lollygagging down the sidewalk wasn't gonna cut it. When Pete heard the rev of a motorbike behind them, he didn't bother to look back. He clenched Kat's hand hard and pulled her into the first open door he could find.

Smoke and darkness surrounded them. Kat coughed in the thick haze as Pete's eyes and ears adjusted to the pulsing lights and rhythmic bass echoing out of speakers hidden in the walls. His first thought was nightclub. Then he took in the surroundings, the hour, and knew he wasn't so lucky. And that speculation was confirmed as he pulled Kat behind him down a long dark corridor and they were met by a scantily clad woman in a rhinestone-studded halter top, black skirt that barely covered her ass and eight-inch spike heels.

"Ten-dollar cover," she announced. Her dark hair was piled high on her head, and her silver top formed a revealing vee all the way to her naval.

Definitely not your local nightclub.

Kat's eyes widened as she too realized where they were. But when the door around the corner was jerked open and a blast of frigid air swept into the lobby, she pushed Pete forward. "Pay the lady already."

The three-hundred-pound bouncer built like an Eagles linebacker eyed them as if he had a sixth sense about their situation. No doubt he'd seen everything working in a place like this. "We don't want no trouble in here."

Pete nodded, pulled a twenty from his back pocket, thanked his lucky stars the guy wasn't going to frisk him and slapped the money on the high counter. "We're just here for the entertainment." He didn't wait for the woman to stamp their hands, instead grabbed Kat and pulled her around the corner into the heart of the strip club.

They paused long enough to get their bearings. The smoke was thicker in here, the music a body-thumping beat that made it impossible to hear conversation going on around them. Neon lights pulsed across the club's floor, spotlighting the three elevated stages where girls in various states of undress were grinding and gyrating for both men and women seated around them.

Kat's fingernails dug into his palm, and Pete darted a look her direction. Her eyes were wide as she took it all in, and he knew if he didn't do something quick, she was going to attract unwanted attention real fast.

He gripped her hand and pulled, knowing there was one place they could blend in that might just save their asses. Skin joints all around the world were the same. He'd been in enough of them, cutting deals with seedy dealers he'd never look twice at back in Miami.

The VIP area was one floor up, set back from a balcony that overlooked the action below. He led Kat up the winding stairs and tried like hell to stay close to the wall and in the shadows. When they got to the second floor, he pointed at the first dancer walking out the door and said, "You'll do. In there."

She eyed him up and down as she pulled her glove-fitting, siren red dress back into place. Then she shot a quick glance in Kat's direction, and a knowing smile slid across her heavily made-up face. "Sure thing, big guy. You watching or is she?"

Kat tensed at his side, and she opened her mouth to protest, but her words were cut off by a ruckus going on below them.

Pete eased close to the railing to look down. His adrenaline spiked. "Fuck," he muttered.

Alarm spread across Kat's face, and she stepped closer to look over the railing herself. Her pulse jumped in the skin of her hand still pressed tightly against his when she spotted the burly-looking, dark-haired man below arguing with one of the bouncers they'd passed on the way in. Not Minyawi or Busir, but definitely one of their cronies from Slade's property.

Before he could react, Kat pulled him back from the ledge and made a beeline for the private room. "Him. I'll watch."

Pete nearly tripped over his feet, both at her command and the way she was tugging him like a woman on a mission, but he managed to shake his head at the dancer as Kat pulled him into the room. "No, you dance for her."

He figured all around that was safer. He wouldn't be distracted that way, and he could keep an eye on the door just in case. Plus, he didn't want the stripper inadvertently finding the 10 mm lodged in the waistband of his jeans.

Another NFL-worthy bouncer closed the door behind them and slid into the shadows. The blonde in the skin-tight number pointed toward a plush couch in the far corner. Two other dancers were earning big bucks as they shook their hips and naked breasts at the men seated in front of them. No one seemed to notice they'd come into the room.

To her credit, Kat managed not to look shell-shocked, but she did shoot Pete a big what-the-fuck over her shoulder before she parked it on the unoccupied couch and stared up at the dancer following closely at his back.

And Pete's brain took that opportunity to throw a big ol' what-the-fuck at him then as well. Twenty-four hours ago he'd had a pretty ordinary life. Work and the occasional date. A party here and there. Nothing overly exciting except for a few work-related overseas trips he took each year. But even those had tamed down, spread out as he'd cleaned up his act.

Now he was on the run from a homicidal maniac, about to watch the girl of his dreams, who he'd thought was dead, get a lap dance from some anonymous blonde he could care less about. Holy shit, this was so not what he'd envisioned when he'd climbed into that limo last night, closed his eyes and wished for something different.

Nerves thumping as the music changed tempo, Pete sat on the couch, close enough to keep up their ruse as a couple simply out on the town for a good time, but with enough distance so he could see around the dancer toward the door. He dropped the backpack at his feet and heard Kat draw in a sharp breath as the blonde leaned forward and whispered something in her ear he couldn't hear.

He looked her direction, caught Kat's eyes widen as she gave her head a small shake in response and darted a quick look his way. But the dancer only smiled a knowing grin and eased back. Then the woman licked her lips and winked at Pete as the show started and her hips began to move to the beat of the drum.

His blood warmed. He knew a possible killer was just downstairs, but seeing Kat's reaction to what the dancer had whispered made his groin tighten. Obviously, it had something to do with him from the way she'd looked at him, but hell if he could imagine what the woman could have said to put that color on Kat's cheeks.

Or maybe he could. His blood went white-hot at the erotic images suddenly kicking off in his brain.

Oh, shit. This was a really bad idea.

The music swelled, distracting him from his thoughts. The blonde undulated her hips to the rhythm, sliding her hands up her rib cage to cup and mold her barely covered breasts. Eyes closed, she rolled her head to the side and pulled the clip from the back of her hair so her long blonde locks spilled down over her shoulders in a seductive move a man would have to be impotent not to react to. Her hands ran lower, over her abdomen, slowly, inch by inch until she widened her stance, leaned forward to give them a teasing shot of surgery-enhanced cleavage and rubbed her inner thighs like they burned. In a very calculated and well-practiced move, she lifted one stiletto-clad foot and placed it on the armrest at Kat's right.

Pete's jeans grew incredibly tight. But not because of the blonde or what she was doing. No, he barely saw her. His attention was glued instead to Kat and her reaction to what she was seeing. Eyes wide as saucers, her mouth open in a little "o," she watched the dancer in front of her, riveted by the scene. Once or twice she shifted against the cushions of the couch, as if uncomfortable with the situation, but she barely blinked. And the series of glances she kept shooting his direction, as if to gauge his reaction as the stripper gyrated and ground her hips around, only made him hotter with every passing second.

Had she ever been in a strip club before? He didn't know. But the way she licked her lip, the way her top teeth sank against her bottom lip, nearly sent him over the edge.

Damn, he really didn't need this. He needed to be watching the door, not her. He tried to look away, but then the stripper turned, bent over at the waist and lifted her dress high up her thighs, giving them both a clear view of her itty-bitty thong. Kat's eyes grew even wider. The blonde ran her hand down the back of her leg and glanced around at Kat with a coy smile. Then she dragged her hands up her ass and pumped her hips in time to the beat.

Kat looked directly at him, and he didn't miss the unmistakable flash of arousal in her eyes, would have had to be dead not to feel the electricity buzzing in the air between them. His erection jerked to attention in response, and he wondered if she was thinking of him as she swallowed and slowly went back to watching the dancer.

He didn't know. But when she unzipped her jacket, lifted her hand to the silver medal hanging from her neck and rubbed her fingers against the warm metal and the edge of her white T-shirt, Pete knew he was lost. He couldn't look away if his life depended on it.

She drew slow, easy circles over her peachy skin, each

time going a fraction of an inch lower toward her plump breast until Pete thought he'd explode. The whole time she was touching herself as if she had no idea what her own fingers were doing. At some point, Pete realized the stripper had ditched her dress, but he barely noticed. Heat colored Kat's cheeks now, and the arousal he saw on her face forced him to adjust his own position on the couch to keep the pain of his growing erection at bay.

It could have been the music. It could have been the fact they were running for their lives and no doubt both had enough adrenaline in their systems to power a small city. Most likely it was the sex-charged atmosphere and the surging woman in front of them that was changing things. But whatever the cause, as Pete watched the stripper move closer to Kat and give her what he knew was her first lap dance, he still wanted her.

He might have every reason in the world to be ticked at her, but that didn't change the fact he wanted *her* dancing for *him* like that right now. He wanted *her* wriggling her naked breasts in his face, *her* hands stroking over his shoulders, *her* ass grinding into his erection. And he wanted *her* mouth pressed hard against his as he thrust deep inside her.

A thousand visions of the two of them together spilled into his mind, igniting a rush of memories of the way they'd made love those months they'd been together. Slow and sensual by candlelight one night; swift and rough when he couldn't think of anything but getting inside her as fast as possible the next. He swallowed hard as he continued to watch her breasts rise and fall under her T-shirt and her breathing grow more and more shallow.

The blonde straddled Kat then and leaned close. Her naked breasts brushed Kat's cotton-covered ones, and she whispered something again in Kat's ear. Mesmerized, Pete shifted for a better view.

Kat's face turned the color of ruby red wine at whatever

the woman said, and she moved her head sharply to look his way. Emotions rushed across her features, and a desire he hadn't seen in years flared in the depths of her eyes. And oh, yeah, he knew she was thinking of him.

Then the dancer cupped Kat's cheek, turned her face back to hers and brushed her lips softly against Kat's. Kat flinched, and her eyes went bug-wide, but she didn't fight the gentle kiss.

Pete, however, almost came in his pants.

And just like that, the dance was over.

The music faded, and the blonde leaned back with a victorious smile as she reached for her gown from the floor. "So, big boy. Did you enjoy your show?"

Holy shit, had he.

Pete sat up straight and ran a hand over his face. Jesus, he was sweating. And so juiced he could barely sit still. For the first time, he realized the stripper was wearing nothing but stilettos and a G-string, but he really didn't care as she pulled her clothing back into place. The woman he was solely interested in was suddenly studying the carpet like it might just jump up and bite her.

And he wasn't entirely sure it wouldn't. Considering what had just happened here, he was starting to believe anything was possible.

He stood, careful to tilt his hips and the raging hardon in his pants away from Kat's line of sight as he pulled a wad of cash from his pocket. He had no idea how much he gave the blonde, but he wasn't coherent enough to count right this minute. All his brain activity was focused elsewhere on deflation techniques.

"Is there a back door out of this room?" he asked. His voice sounded like gravel, a clear indication he was turned on to the max. He coughed once to cover it but knew it didn't do jack to make him sound normal. The stripper smiled proudly, like it was all her doing, but it wasn't.

Not even close.

As he waited, the blonde looked down to count the bills in her hand, and her eyes flew open wide, like she'd just hit the mother lode. "Sure, that door there." She nodded toward what he'd thought was simply a wall.

No, not just a wall. A well-disguised door they probably used to kick the touchy-feely guys out of the VIP area. Maybe their luck was improving after all.

Kat stood, careful not to look at either of them, as the blonde pulled a business card she'd hidden like Houdini somewhere in her dress and slipped it into Pete's jacket pocket. "I do private dances, too." She glanced Kat's way and winked. "I like her. Anytime she's up for getting a little wilder, call me. I love threesomes."

Kat's wide-eyed gaze shot up, held on the stripper's face, then jumped to Pete's. He didn't have a clue what she was thinking as color stained her cheeks, but when she quickly jerked toward the hidden door, he knew better than to dawdle and followed right at her heels.

The door slammed shut with an echoing snap. A long white hallway stretched ahead, contrasting sharply with the dim room they'd just been in. Pete blinked several times as his eyes adjusted. Muffled music seeped into the space from the club's blaring sound system on the other side of the walls. They made it halfway down the corridor before Kat stopped abruptly and whipped back to face him.

Oh, crap. Here it came.

He braced himself for her outrage at what he'd just put her through, but instead of lambasting him with an onslaught of words, she shocked the hell out of him by grasping the lapels of his jacket, thrusting him back against the wall and closing her mouth over his in a kiss that nearly sent him to his knees.

The blood rushed out of his head and went due south to pool hard in his groin again. And all rational thought about lies and betrayal and would-be killers slid right out of his head. All he could think about was her and what she was about to do to him.

He just hoped she'd do it fast before he could think of a reason to say no.

CHAPTER SEVENTEEN

Kat was on fire, her blood a screaming roar in her ears. Every inch of her skin burned. But it was nothing compared to the searing need going on deep inside.

She shoved Pete back against the wall and kissed him hard, knowing it was a bad idea but unable to stop. The sexual tension had been building between them for hours, and she was in serious need of release. And at the moment she didn't care how she got it.

His back hit the wall with a thud, and his body tensed as she crushed her chest against his, as their legs and hips came into intimate contact. His arms closed around her waist as she continued to kiss him, more to keep them both from hitting the ground, she knew, than for any other reason. But it still didn't deter her. She was swept up in some insane arousal that consumed every part of her.

Frustrated when it wasn't enough, she pushed her hands beneath his jacket to slide over his hard chest, changed the angle of the kiss and used her tongue to lick the seam of his lips.

He opened as if on reflex, and she used the opportunity to thrust her tongue into his mouth and kiss him deep. Liquid heat rushed through her veins, and she moaned at the first taste. Wanting more, she rotated her hips and rubbed her aching body against the zipper of his jeans.

Something shifted inside him. She felt it in the way his

muscles relaxed. Out of nowhere he let out a growl from deep in his throat, and suddenly he was kissing her back. Stroking his tongue hard against hers and tightening his arms around her waist.

Yes, yes, yes. This was what she wanted. She pressed her hips against his again and felt his erection swell inside his jeans. He tilted his head to kiss her deeper, then slid his hands down to cup her ass and pull her tight against him.

She moaned again and shifted for a better angle so he hit her sweet spot with every rock of his hips. Tingling sensations shot through her core. He continued to kiss her as they rubbed up against each other in the empty hall. She knew if they kept this up she was going to come right there.

Visions of the erotic scene she'd witnessed earlier crashed into her brain, and the stripper's whispered words filtered back through her mind. *Look at the way he's watching us. He's not looking at me, he's looking at you. He wants you. Right now. Right here. Would you let him take you here if you could?*

Oh, she was about to. She wanted Pete to fill her. Wanted to feel him erupt inside her when he came. She'd seen how turned on he was during that dance. She could feel it now as he hitched her up higher and pushed a hand inside her jacket to grasp her breast through her cotton shirt.

Electricity shot through her skin at the touch, sending a thousand pulsing waves straight to her center. Did it matter that he was only aroused because of what he'd watched? It shouldn't. She'd been aroused by that scene as well. It wasn't what the stripper had done or what the woman had looked like that had made Kat hot, it was the knowledge Pete was watching and enjoying the show. She knew it was wrong to take advantage of his aroused state to get what she wanted from him, but she was beyond caring.

She continued to rub against him, to delve deeper into his mouth with her tongue, to get as close as possible. From somewhere in the back of her mind—though, she fought it like hell—common sense pushed through the sexual haze and came to a grinding halt in the front of her brain.

They were standing in the back hall of a seedy strip club, about to have wild, rough, against-the-wall sex. Anyone could walk in on them at any moment. Busir and Minyawi were likely still close by, and if they found them, she and Pete were no better than dead. On top of that, though Pete was obviously sporting a massive erection and was kissing her back, she knew deep in her heart he would only regret it later.

It nearly killed her to break the kiss and pull back, but she did. Breathing heavily, she dropped her head to his chest and held on to his coat to steady herself. Just for a minute. Just until she was sure she wasn't going to hit the floor.

His heart thumped hard against her ear, and he drew in ragged breaths like a man starved of oxygen. One of his hands was still wrapped tightly around her waist. The other had slid into her hair, where it was rubbing tiny circles against her scalp as he held her against him and tried to regulate his breathing.

Oh, she wished that was what he was doing. Just holding her tight because she mattered.

Her eyes slammed shut. "I'm sorry. God, that was . . . ," *stupid, idiotic, the best sex I've had in longer than I can remember,* ". . . not what I meant to do."

His hand suddenly stilled in her hair. Then he quickly released his hold on both her head and her waist. "Yeah. I'm sure you didn't."

His voice was thick and gravely, but there was a clip to it she hadn't heard before that made her grimace. She was almost afraid of what she'd see on his face when she glanced up.

But she didn't see anything. When she stepped back and looked, he was scrubbing both hands over his eyes. And when he dropped them, it was like a wall had come down.

Though his body still sported signs of arousal, his eyes were flat. She didn't think it was possible to make him think any worse of her than he already did, but after that little nympho attack, she was obviously wrong.

"Pete—"

"Don't sweat it," he said again in a nonchalant voice. "We should go."

That was it?

She stood stock still as he picked up her backpack from the floor and headed for the back stairwell at the end of the hall. He was going to act like nothing had happened? Part of her was shocked. Another part was weary. Weary from fighting the emotions brewing inside her. One minute he was the man she remembered, holding her close, kissing her with a burning passion she'd never felt from anyone else, saving her life when he could have easily looked the other way. And the next he was like a stranger, cold and calculating and brushing her off like she meant nothing to him.

She struggled to put the two together, had no idea if she ever would. And couldn't help questioning why he'd come back for her in the first place.

As she watched him walk away, she knew she was back at square one with no one to turn to, wondering who she could trust.

So what do you do now, Kat? What have you always done?

She reached up to grip the St. Jude medal at her chest and thought back over her life. Her goals had always saved her. As long as she'd had something to work toward, she'd been able to get through anything.

When she'd been an orphan, flitting from foster home to foster home, she'd paid attention and learned as much as she could so that one day she could make her own choices. When she'd been working on her doctorate and professors had told her she didn't have what it took to be an Egyptologist, she'd muscled in and studied harder. And when she'd gone into hiding, decided to give up her entire life in one heart-wrenching moment, she'd taken it one day at a time, knowing that by staying in the shadows, she would keep the people she loved safe.

Goals. That was what she turned to when she needed strength. That was what she'd turn to now.

Her mother was gone. Marty wasn't an option any longer because he was compromised. And her head screamed she couldn't trust Pete either, no matter how much her heart wanted to.

"Pick up your pace, Kat," he said from the end of the hall. "We need to make tracks. That goon's probably still hanging around."

Make tracks.

Suddenly, she knew just what she had to do next. Yeah, it would tick Pete off, but they'd both be better off in the long run.

The only question was finding the right time to do it.

Pete sensed something was up with Kat the moment they stepped out onto the street.

An ordinary person probably wouldn't see it, but he'd known this woman better than anyone in his life.

At first he thought her shift in mood was related to what had happened in the strip club. Then he'd revamped his thinking and decided it was what had happened *in the hallway* of the strip club that had obviously thrown her so off kilter. Hell, it had certainly thrown him for a loop.

Especially her little revelation that she hadn't *planned* to jump his bones, it'd just . . . *happened.*

Talk about an ego crusher. Ever since he'd first seen her, his body had been lit up like a roman candle anytime he looked her way, and here she was telling him she didn't really *want* him, she'd just simply been responding to her environment? Christ, this whole situation just got crappier by the minute.

He darted a look her way as they put distance between them and the strip club and noticed the change in her demeanor. It was subtle. A squaring of her shoulders, a lifting of her chin, a hardening of her eyes. She didn't look worried or concerned about his or anyone else's safety. She seemed determined, like she was in the midst of a major attitude adjustment.

Or she was planning something.

That didn't sit well with him. Her planning something on her own had bad news written all over it as far as he could see. The last time she'd planned something, his life had hit the skids and stayed there for a long-ass time.

They walked four blocks in silence, sticking to the shadows as much as possible in the rundown neighborhood before they finally hailed a cab that took them over the Delaware River and into Camden, New Jersey. Thinking they were far enough away from Minyawi's muscle and confident they weren't sporting a tail, Pete signaled the driver and had them dropped off at some podunk diner off I-676 that served breakfast twenty-four hours a day. He couldn't remember when he'd eaten last, and his stomach was growling.

There were only a handful of patrons in the diner when they stepped inside. A bell on the door chimed, and a dark-haired waitress looked up from the lunch counter where she'd been talking to a man in a 76ers cap. She nodded their direction. "Seat yourself," she said. "I'll be there in a minute."

Pete scanned the room, with its Formica tabletops and cracked plastic red booths. Darkness pressed in through the wide, streaked windows, but a neon green motel sign across the street with its flashing vacancy notice made it through the grime. A couple who looked to be in their eighties sat near the window, forks in hand, watching them as if they'd never seen strangers before. A middle-aged man was reading the sports page at a table in the middle of the floor and eating french fries doused in ketchup. He, at least, didn't bother to look up.

Figuring the place looked relatively harmless, Pete gestured to a booth in the far corner where he could keep a close eye on the front door, just in case, and where they had instant access to the emergency exit in the event they might need it.

Kat slid onto the bench seat, the plastic creaking as she moved. She shrugged out of her parka and reached for a menu propped between the sugar dispenser and the salt and pepper shakers at the end of the table. "I'm starving," she said with way too much enthusiasm.

Pete frowned as he sat, dropped the backpack at his feet and reached for his own menu. Just what the heck was up with her? She'd gone from being scared shitless in the park to insanely aroused at the club to perky Paula here, all within a matter of hours? He wasn't buying it.

"What'll it be?" the waitress asked, stopping at their table with a pen and pad in hand. She eyed them with a bored look.

Pete glanced at his watch. 9:52 p.m. The sign on the door stated the diner was open until ten thirty, which meant the waitress's shift was coming to a close.

"Coffee," Pete said and smiled, though it did little good. The waitress lifted her brows and regarded him over the top of her glasses. "Two." He held up two fingers.

"I'll have to brew it." She glanced at Kat and sighed. "Anything else?"

Kat scanned the menu with ravenous eyes. "Let's see. You're still serving breakfast, right?" Without waiting for an answer, Kat said, "I'll have two eggs, sunny side up. With wheat toast, hash browns and sausage links." While she continued looking at the menu, the waitress rolled her eyes and glanced Pete's way, ready for his order, but Kat stopped him before he could open his mouth. "Do you have those silver-dollar-size pancakes?"

The waitress nodded, glanced at her watch and heaved out a sigh that blew her too-long bangs out of her face. Suddenly amused, Pete slung one arm over the back of the booth and watched with familiar interest.

Kat still had a hefty appetite. That obviously hadn't changed in six years.

"Great," Kat went on. "I'll have those with blackberry syrup. Oh, and a bowl of fresh fruit if you have it. A tall glass of milk, too." She looked toward Pete.

The waitress's pen paused on the paper as she looked up. "Instead of the eggs?"

"No, with the eggs."

The waitress glanced between them. "Is that for both of you?"

Pete fought back a smile and closed his menu. "Cheeseburger and fries for me."

The waitress looked back at Kat with wide eyes, almost as if she assumed there'd be more, and when Kat only smiled and closed her own menu, the woman shook her head in dismay and finally headed for the kitchen.

It was a scene he'd witnessed before. He didn't know where Kat put all that food on her slim five-foot-seven frame, but he figured she had to have some superhuman metabolism to burn off all those calories because it definitely didn't show on that compact body of hers.

And yeah, now he knew exactly what her body felt like thanks to that little foray in the strip club's back hall. How firm her breasts were, how tight her ass was, how hot she was between her thighs.

He shifted on the bench seat to release the sudden pressure in his jeans at just the memory. He'd had his hands on her back at Slade's garage, but then he'd been too drugged up to notice the difference he'd clearly felt only a few minutes ago.

What else was different about her now?

He watched her carefully across the table. She sat still, her hands folded on the Formica, staring out the window across the room. She wasn't looking at him, but she hadn't been avoiding eye contact either, which was another major tip-off something was up. In the park she'd barely been able to look him in the eye.

He waited until the waitress brought their waters and two steaming cups of black coffee and then walked back into the kitchen before he leaned forward and placed his forearms on the table.

"That guy in the park wasn't FBI."

She looked his way with clear eyes. Clear and very focused dark brown eyes. "I know."

"You see him before?"

She shook her head, lifted her water and took a sip. "No, but he knew plenty about you and me. CIA maybe?"

Pete reached for the cream. "I don't know, but one thing's for sure. Whoever he was, he definitely knew this guy Minyawi."

Kat pursed her lips. "Yeah, but how did Busir and Minyawi know we were in Philadelphia? That was fast, even for Busir."

Pete shrugged, stirred his coffee. "Maybe the guy in the park called him after you talked to Slade."

Kat's brow lowered. "Marty would not have turned me in. I refuse to believe that. Somehow the guy in the park knew Marty, which leads me to think he's somehow connected through the government. But I'm sure Marty didn't know what he was up to."

Pete sat back with a frown, hating the way a quick stab of jealousy shot through his chest anytime she mentioned Martin Slade. Jesus, why did it bother him so much?

"I don't think you can assume anything at this point," he said. "Busir has obviously stayed under the radar all these years because he has high-powered contacts. You said yourself the SCA didn't or wouldn't get involved back when your supervisor went to talk to them. We slowed their guy down with the explosion at the garage, but they never lost our trail."

He hesitated, then added, "The other guy, Minyawi. You recognize him?"

Kat shook her head. "I never got a good look at him. But there was something about his voice. I don't know. It was familiar."

"Yeah, that's what I thought, too. I'm pretty sure I've seen him before, I just can't place where."

Kat's cup hesitated halfway to her mouth as she glanced at him. The waitress came back with ketchup and Tabasco. She set the bottles on the table and moved away again.

"Why did you come back to the park?" Kat asked in a quiet voice as she set her cup on the table.

Pete bit the inside of his lip as he mulled over her question. He'd been asking himself that same thing since he'd jumped on that bike and raced through the trees looking for her. And he still didn't have an answer he liked. Because the only one that came to mind went against his better judgment.

"It was the right thing to do," was all he said.

Their eyes held in the silence that followed, and then she said in an achingly soft voice, "For whatever reason, thank you. You saved my life."

His heart thudded in his chest, a reaction that both

confused and ticked him off. "Thank you for saving mine back in New York. I'm still not entirely sure what went on there, but I have a feeling if you hadn't stepped in, I wouldn't be sitting here right now."

Emotions he couldn't read rushed across Kat's face, and she opened her mouth to speak, but the waitress returned with an armful of plates, interrupting her. It took the woman two more trips before Pete had his burger and the rest of Kat's order was overflowing the table.

Kat picked up her fork and looked down at her food. "It was no big deal. Really. I just . . . surprised them."

She didn't look like she wanted to give details, so he didn't press. She dove into the food like a woman starved, and Pete almost chuckled as he reached for the bottle of ketchup. Same old Kat. The first few times he'd taken her to dinner in Cairo he'd been shocked by how much she could put away. Then he'd been pleasantly thrilled when she'd spent the remainder of the night working the calories off with him between the sheets of his bed.

Damn. He shifted again on the bench seat in discomfort. Clenched his jaw at what the memory did to his pants and the little bit of gray matter left between his ears.

"So Minyawi," he said as he picked up a fry and tried to forget about his raging libido. "If we go by what this Halloway said in the park, he's the mastermind, not Busir. And he knows we're together. It's possible he's tracking us with my credit card."

Kat swallowed around a mouthful of food. "I hadn't thought of that, but I guess it's possible."

"Not likely, though," Pete went on as he picked up his burger. "The more likely scenario is he's got someone on the inside who's connected to Slade, but we'll use cash from here on out just to be safe."

Kat set her fork down, lifted her coffee and took a long sip. Something in her eyes said she wanted to ask him a question but didn't know how to broach the topic.

"What?" he finally asked when his curiosity got the best of him.

She reached up to run her fingers over the medal at her chest. "What happened in Afghanistan?"

Ah, so that was what the mood was about.

Pete leaned back and carefully wiped his mouth with his napkin. As he did, he glanced around the restaurant. The cook had come out from the kitchen and was now deep in conversation with the waitress and the man still seated at the lunch counter. The elderly couple who'd watched them with curious eyes earlier was standing to leave. No one was listening to their conversation or paying one iota of attention to them anymore.

Which was a good thing. Except it left way too many opportunities for intimate questions such as this.

How much should he tell her? How much did she already know? She'd once accused him of buying and selling on the black market, which he knew wasn't too far off the mark. So what did it matter if he told her the truth now?

It mattered, he realized, for the same reason it had mattered back then. Because somewhere inside he didn't want her to know the whole truth about him.

"I got delayed," he said, figuring that was the safest answer he could come up with.

"What were you doing in Afghanistan in the first place?" She lifted her fork again and resumed eating, but he could tell by the set of her chin she was curious and she wasn't about to let this conversation drop.

He went back to his burger and shrugged. "You know I trade in antiquities. Cairo wasn't the only place I went looking for a deal."

"In Afghanistan? I thought the Taliban cracked down on foreign trade after the war on terror heated up."

"They did. Doesn't mean you couldn't get in."

He knew he was giving her the bare bones and that she

was growing increasingly frustrated, and out of some strange sense of guilt he heard himself adding, "Look, there was nothing shady about it. I had a contact there who told me of a collector who wanted to sell a few of his pieces. I went to meet with him. It was all on the up and up."

Which it had been. That time, at least.

"So why wouldn't they let you leave?"

He lifted his water and took a long swallow. Oh, maybe it was because he *had* dealt with some pretty slimy characters in the past who *had* traded on the black market. Or maybe it was because he *had* turned a blind eye a few times when he'd known the provenance on a piece had been faked. Obviously INTERPOL knew that as well, or else he wouldn't have been stuck in that Afghani armpit to begin with. Or it could have been because this time—though he'd done it all the right way—he hadn't been quite as careful about who he told he was headed to Afghanistan in the first place.

A thought suddenly occurred to him. "Halloway knew about the blue notice."

She looked up, brow creasing because he'd changed the subject so abruptly. "What's a blue notice?"

"It's a color-coded lookout INTERPOL sends to its member countries to assist law enforcement in their investigations. A green notice means they're looking for some kind of dangerous career criminal, a yellow notice is sent out when they want to locate missing persons, red's issued when they're seeking the arrest of fugitives, and blue goes out on the wire when they want to locate people in certain criminal investigations."

"You seem to know a lot about how INTERPOL works."

"When you run with some of the people I have, you keep your ear to the ground and pay attention."

Her brow lowered, and she studied him as if looking at a stranger. Then her eyes grew wide, and she held up her hand as she made obvious connections. "Wait. You were involved in a criminal investigation with the International Crime Police?"

He grimaced at the suspicion he heard in her voice and told himself it didn't matter, though it stung to know she now thought her original assumptions of him in Cairo hadn't been too far off the mark. Stung a lot. But what mattered most here was the fact Halloway knew about the notice.

"No," he said emphatically. "The blue notice was a watch. It meant the Afghan government could keep me in one place while they checked me out. It meant I couldn't leave and the U.S. couldn't do anything to get me out until the notice went down." He eyed her. "And it did go down, Kat, obviously, because I'm here now. I'll admit in the past I've worked with some people I probably shouldn't have, but on that trip I didn't do anything wrong. They knew it, which is why they finally had to let me go."

She touched the medal again, and he saw the flash of doubt in her eyes as she thought about what he'd said, coupled with questions she wasn't sure she should ask. "So why are you surprised Halloway knew that? If he worked for the FBI, wouldn't he be privy to blue and green notices or whatever you called them? The U.S. has to be a part of INTERPOL, right?"

"Yeah, they are. There are something like one hundred eighty-six member countries, and the U.S. is definitely a part of that. And if this guy really worked for the FBI, then yes, he'd know. But he said he worked for the Art Theft Crime Team and that they were watching me then."

"So? Isn't that part of the FBI?"

"Yeah, but the Art Crime Team wasn't established until *after* I was in Kabul."

Kat glanced around the empty restaurant while she ingested that information. "So he definitely wasn't FBI."

"I'm thinking not. He could have been at one point, but my gut says no. He'd have known when that division was established."

"So who was he then? CIA? Why would he play like he wasn't?"

"It's possible he could have worked for Uncle Sam. It'd gel with how he knew Slade, but I doubt it. My guess is he's connected to INTERPOL." A breath of excitement rushed through him. "And if so then we just got our first break, because I have a way of finding out."

He quickly checked his watch. Too late tonight. But tomorrow was another story. When he popped a fry in his mouth and looked up, Kat was biting her lip and playing with her medal again.

And Pete stopped eating because that look was back in her eyes. The determined one that said she'd made her mind up about something.

"What?" he asked again.

She hesitated, then finally said, "If someone from IN-TERPOL's involved in this, they would have been privy to Sawil's original complaints filed with the SCA."

"Yeah, I thought of that. Your list of missing relics might not have gotten out on the wire. And if that person was in on it with someone from the SCA, your complaint never would have gone anywhere."

She stared down at her half-eaten plate. "I went back to the SCA that morning before Sawil and I went into the tomb. They brushed me off." A visible shudder rushed through her, and she opened her mouth to say more, but then closed it suddenly.

She'd been in the tomb the night Ramirez had been killed. Pete wanted to ask exactly what she'd seen, but he sensed this wasn't the time or place to do that. He did, however, know she was holding something back.

"Ramirez must have talked to someone else," he finally said. "Maybe he was the link to the guy at INTERPOL."

"I doubt that."

He dipped a fry in ketchup and went back to eating. "Too bad we don't know who the other person was you said you heard in that tomb."

Pete looked up at Kat's silence. "What?"

"I . . ." She quickly reached for her backpack at his feet and scooted out of the booth. "I have to use the restroom."

Frowning at her strange and sudden exit, Pete watched her walk to the bathroom and had a momentary thought that maybe he should check to make sure that was exactly where she was going. The woman looked like she might just bolt.

He froze, fry halfway to his open mouth. And nearly lost his dinner.

She wouldn't do that to him again, would she?

He lowered the french fry to the plate and wiped his suddenly sweaty hands on a napkin. He kept his eyes glued to the women's restroom door, mentally ticking off the minutes she'd been gone. When he got to five, he had a sinking suspicion she'd just screwed him again, and not in the way his body wanted.

Holy hell. How stupid did he have to be not to see the signs? She's been planning to bolt since they'd walked out of that strip club.

Disbelief and a resurging sense of rage he thought he'd clamped down bubbled up in his chest as he gripped the edge of the table and started to slide out of the booth. Just as he was putting his weight on his feet, the women's restroom door opened and Kat walked out.

Relief plowed into him hard at the sight of her, and he dropped back onto the bench seat on an adrenaline rush.

Idiot. Fucking idiot. He raked a hand through his hair and took a deep breath to settle his blood pressure. No way she'd ditch him again like she'd done in Cairo. Whether she admitted it or not, she wanted his help. Otherwise she'd already be gone.

Gone.

That thought kicked him in the gut as he watched her walk across the restaurant and slide into her seat again, all long legs and lanky build, dark, tousled short hair and even darker, mesmerizing eyes he'd thought he'd never see again. Somehow he had to figure out a way to put the past behind him so they could work together and live through this . . . whatever it was.

From there . . . he eyed the silver medal hanging at her chest, followed it to the vee of her T-shirt and the bit of exposed cleavage there without even meaning to, and remembered their last sultry week together. When he'd gone to Cairo with the sole purpose of fixing their tattered relationship. When she'd blown his mind with her hands and mouth and every inch of her body.

When everything between them had imploded in on itself.

She stared down at her food as if she hadn't seen it before. "I'm really not that hungry anymore."

Neither was he. Not for cheeseburgers and fries anyway.

He lifted a finger and signaled the waitress. "Check, please."

Kat looked up as he climbed out of the booth. "Where are we going?"

He nodded toward the flashing neon sign across the street and pulled cash out of his wallet. "To bed. I think it's been long enough, don't you?"

CHAPTER EIGHTEEN

Six years earlier
Cairo

Kat was waiting for him when he walked out of security at the Cairo International Airport. Standing amidst a sea of people, looking so goddamn gorgeous in her jeans and sleeveless blouse, she made his heart turned over in his chest. It was the first time she'd ever met his plane.

Then again, it was the first time he'd ever told her he was coming in.

He saw only her as he approached, and the moment her eyes found his through the crowd that spark they'd had from day one flared hot and bright.

"Hi." She rose slowly on her toes when he reached her, wrapped her arms around his neck as he pulled her close.

"Hi, yourself," he managed. She felt so good. Smelled like heaven. It'd been two weeks since that horrible scene in her apartment. He'd flown from Cairo to Bangkok that day with the weight of the world on his shoulders, and before he'd even landed in Thailand, he'd known what he was going to do. Maybe he'd known it from their first night at the Mena House.

His mother's antique ring was a solid presence in his pocket, and he itched to give it to her, but this wasn't the time. They still had a thousand things they had to deal with first. And most importantly, it was time he laid it all out on the line to her.

She eased back, and in her mocha eyes he saw relief and a whole lot of uncertainty that tightened his chest like a fist. "How was your flight?"

"Long."

"You look tired. Were you in Europe?"

"No. Miami."

She threaded her fingers in his as they headed through the terminal. "How long are you staying?"

"Two weeks."

His arm jerked, and he turned when he realized she'd stopped. Confusion drew her brows together. "How long did you say?"

"Two weeks," he said again.

"What about—"

He knew what she was thinking. He rarely stayed a week at a time when he visited, and he was always rushing off unexpectedly when he got word from a seller or a buyer that there was a deal to be had. That was going to change, but she didn't know it yet. He'd worked his ass off the last six months to get his gallery to the place it was now, and he wasn't about to blow all that he'd built if it meant she wasn't going to be around to enjoy it with him. Being here now might set him back a few weeks, but he'd stay a month if it meant fixing what was broken between them.

"I cleared my schedule, Kat. No business meetings. I didn't even bring my BlackBerry." She looked so damn cute with her brows drawn together and that little crease in her forehead, he moved closer. "I know you have to work, but I've got two full weeks off, and I want to spend them with you. However I can. If, that is, you'll have me that long."

She stared at him like he'd grown a second head, and just when he was sure she was going to ask what he'd been drinking on the plane, she threw her arms around his neck and kissed him. "Yes. Oh, yes. I even have some time off coming to me. Not a full two weeks, but—"

Thank you, God.

His arms tightened around her. "Doesn't matter. I'll take whatever you can give me."

She laughed against his throat, a warm, relieved, loving sound that tingled all the way to his toes and told him they were good. This was right. They'd make it work. "Oh, Pete. Two full weeks. I can't believe it. I've missed you so much."

He held her close, buried his face in her hair and breathed in her sweet jasmine scent as people continued to rush around them.

And knew she couldn't possibly miss him as much as he'd missed her.

Camden, New Jersey
Present day

Kat stared at the bed in the middle of the room—the only bed in the run-down, forty-nine-dollar-a-night motel room—as her pulse jumped. From the bathroom, she could hear the shower going and knew if she was going to make her move, now was the time.

So how come her feet were cemented to the floor? How come she couldn't take her eyes off that damn mattress?

Moron.

The erratic *thump, thump, thump* of her heartbeat echoed in her ears like the roar of a 747 on takeoff. Without a word to her, Pete had paid for the room with a wad of cash, ushered her inside, then announced he needed a quick shower. And since he'd disappeared behind the bathroom door, she'd been staring at the sheets in front of her, thinking of the hundreds of times they'd lain together, right up until the end. Then, it had been right.

Now? Now she didn't know what the heck was happening.

When had he changed his mind about what he wanted from her? Yeah, he'd been primed in the strip club, but that wasn't her doing. That was because of little-miss-blonde-big-boobs. The man had made it more than obvious every chance he got that he clearly couldn't stand her anymore. So what was this? A pity fuck? A way to work off some tension? Or was it simply a way to prove to her he was calling the shots now, and she'd better shape up and listen?

Her pulse skyrocketed again at just the thought of being dominated by him. On her back, tied down. On her hands and knees, pinned from behind. Didn't really matter how or where, the end result was always the same.

Sweat broke out on her forehead, and she lifted a shaky hand, wiped her fingers across her brow. Okay, now she was officially sick. Because even though she knew this—whatever he planned to do to her on that one, lone bed—wasn't about rekindling an old romance or even attempting some sort of reconciliation, she knew she wasn't going to say no to him.

She closed her eyes, breathed deep, and told herself she should walk out now. Forget about waiting for him to fall asleep. There was something about Peter Kauffman that made her knees weak, made her rethink simple logic, made her bend every one of her rules. He'd done that to her in Cairo years ago. He was doing it to her again now.

The water shut off, and a crackling sound followed, like the shower curtain being pulled back.

Kat stiffened and realized she'd been standing in the same place for the last ten minutes. She needed to get a hold of herself. Lifting her hands to her cheeks, she felt the heat there and knew Pete was going to see it as soon as he stepped out of the bathroom.

Please don't let him walk out of that bathroom naked.

The door pulled open before she could move, and a wave of heat and steam preceded him as he eased into the bedroom. She drew in a deep breath, inhaling the scent of Ivory soap and sweet, wet male skin, and dared one quick look his way. Then wished she hadn't.

His chest was bare. Light from the bedside lamp glinted off his hard, firm abs. Her eyes dropped lower, to his belly button and the thin line of hair that narrowed and darkened, pointing like a flashing arrow downward until it disappeared beneath the waistband of the same low-slung, worn denim jeans he'd been wearing earlier. As heat rushed back into her cheeks, she dropped her eyes to the floor and noticed his bare feet peeking out from beneath the frayed cuffs.

Oh, Lord, even his toes were gorgeous.

Not good. Not. Good. At. All.

He rubbed a towel over his hair, mopping up water, then down over the nape of his neck. "Shower's all yours. I washed out my shirt, laid it over the towel bar to dry. Until we can hit a mall or something tomorrow, we'll have to make do."

Kat's eyes flashed back to his bare chest. Make do? Oh, man. She was almost afraid to ask what he meant by that.

He tipped his head, eyed her with a quizzical expression. "You got something on your mind?"

Kat gave her head a small shake. Tried like hell not to blush again. No luck. She could literally feel the blood rushing to her cheeks. "What? No. I'm fine. I'll be out in a few."

Happy for the brief escape, she made sure to take a wide berth around him and slipped into the bathroom. Since there was no lock on the door, she silently cursed that he could walk in on her at any moment but figured he probably wouldn't. No, he wanted her to sweat, which was exactly what she was doing, wasn't she? Whatever he had

planned was going to happen out there. In that other
room. In that very, very small bed.

She groaned, braced her hands on the sink and dropped
her head. A series of deep breaths helped settle the nerves
in her stomach, and when she looked up, all she saw was
a foggy mirror and a blurred image.

Better that she not see her wanton reflection. It would
only reaffirm what she knew was true. She was danger-
ously close to jumping his bones.

Well, that wasn't going to happen. With a shake of her
head, she squared her shoulders and hefted the backpack
up onto the edge of the sink. She opened the latch, reached
inside and pulled out her Beretta. The metal felt cool in
her hands, solid and familiar. Out of habit she checked the
magazine, snapped it back into place and made sure
the safety was set. She was prepared to use it if she had to,
though deep inside, she really, really hoped it wouldn't
come to that.

Funny, she thought as she tipped her head and studied
the gun in her hand. The whole time she and Pete
had been running over the last few hours, she hadn't had
a chance to pull her weapon. Or maybe she just hadn't
thought to do so. A gun she hadn't once forgotten to slip
in the nightstand beside her bed in more years than she
could count. A gun she never went anywhere without.

She knew why instantly and hated the reason. Because
no matter how many times she questioned his ethics, she
still felt safer with Pete than without him.

Heaving a sigh at the emotions that thought stirred in
her, she slipped the gun back into her pack. Her fingers
brushed a fabric pouch, and she drew out the necklace
she'd stolen from his auction.

For a moment she thought about opening it but then
changed her mind. This wasn't the time. Just like the
bathroom at that rundown diner hadn't been either. When
she was alone and could think without this sex-charged

brain fuzz, then she'd take the time she needed and look at what she'd hidden inside.

Her shower did little to settle her nerves, and when she stepped out and dried off, the idea of putting her dirty clothes back on made her cringe. But she wasn't going out there naked, and she hadn't thought ahead far enough to stick a change of clothing in her pack back in New York.

The bra was a necessity, but the two-day-old panties were not. She tossed them in the trash and pulled on her jeans.

One deep breath and she knew she'd spent as much time in the bathroom as she could. Kat picked up her pack and opened the bathroom door. The bedside lamp was off, a low hum echoing through the room from the heater under the window. From the light in the bathroom behind her, she could see Pete laid out on the mattress, the blankets and sheets pulled down to the foot of the bed, one arm tucked behind his head as he eyed the door.

One bed. One bed. He'd gotten a room with *one* bed.

"Are you coming or what?" he asked in a thick, sexy voice that sent heat rushing through her body.

Oh, geez. What a question. To be taken in several different ways.

Use your brain, Kat. You know, that thing taking up space between your ears?

But still she didn't move. Only breathed deep and was sure he could hear every pull and draw of air in her lungs.

He sat up slowly and dropped his legs over the side of the bed. "I know it's not the Ritz, but my cash reserves are running low, and until I can replenish, I didn't want to risk using my credit card. You can make do for one night."

Kat opened her mouth to speak, but nothing came out.

Before she could get her mouth working, Pete's expression eased. "They didn't have a room with two beds, and

I wasn't about to let you stay by yourself. At least not until we know Minyawi's out of the country."

She should have felt relief. Instead she was still so keyed up she didn't know what to think. He didn't want to sleep with her after all? The knowledge was almost harder to deal with than thinking he had something sinister planned.

"Lie down, Kat," he said, his voice hard. "You're not going to be any use to me tomorrow if you're dead on your feet. We're both tired. We need to sleep while we can."

Her eyes cut from the mattress to him. And she knew she was stuck. When he lay back on the pillow again and crossed his bare feet at the ankles, she flicked the bathroom light off and walked around the bed to the far side.

Okay. She could do this. Lie here beside him. Not think about touching him or kissing him or having wild jungle sex with him. She was tough, after all. She'd proved it over the past six years, hadn't she?

Her pack hit the floor with a soft thud as she sat on the edge of the bed with her back to him. The mattress was firm, and she gave it a bounce to see if it softened. No luck.

Carefully, she eased back on the pillow, well on her side of the bed and away from Pete's near nakedness. She lay still, listening to his breathing, waiting for it to deepen and indicate he was asleep.

It took forever. While she waited, she quietly crossed her arms over her chest, dropped them to her side, folded them over her middle. She was hot. It was too damn warm in the room, and her skin felt prickly. She eyed the heater and thought about getting up and turning it off.

No, she'd just live with it. If he was starting to drift off, she didn't want to do anything to rouse him.

She blew out a long breath and crossed her feet. Uncrossed them. Her skin itched, and she reached up to scratch her arms. Then her side. Her thighs. She thought about the mattress they were sleeping on. The run-down motel. How many other people had slept in this same room. What lived on the mattress.

Damn. This wasn't working.

Before she could stop herself she jumped up, reached for the edge of the fitted sheet and pulled it back from the corner of the mattress.

Pete eased up on his elbows, looking irritated beyond belief. "What are you doing?"

"Nothing. Just . . ."

The mattress was clean. She checked the edges. The creases. Pulled the sheet far enough back to look under where her pillow lay.

"Kat?"

Nothing.

She retucked the sheet. "I watched a special on 60 Minutes about bedbugs in motels." She reached for the flimsy faux wood headboard. "They're often massed behind the—"

She pulled the headboard away from the wall, half expecting to see it alive with creepy-crawlies, but there was nothing.

"Kat, lie down."

She stared at the headboard some more. Bit her lip. Felt like crawling out of her own skin.

God, this was awful.

"Kat." He sat up straighter. And softened his voice enough to make her look his way. "Come back to bed. Nothing's going to bite you. Not even me. I promise."

Dammit. He knew what was bothering her. And she was a complete idiot for letting it get to her like this.

Thankful he couldn't see her bright red cheeks, she settled back onto the mattress, knowing there was no way in hell she'd be able to sleep.

She closed her eyes tight. Opened them. Bit her lip hard so she couldn't sigh and stared at the ceiling.

"Ditching the shoes might help," he said into the dark.

Right. Yeah. Like shoes on wasn't a dead giveaway she was ready to bolt.

Kat toed them off and sat up to move them by her pack on the floor. She lay down again. Waited. Rolled to her side. Eased onto her belly. Rolled back again as quietly as she could.

Oh, man. This just wasn't working.

The sheets rustled as Pete moved on his side of the bed. Then she felt him scoot close to her. Her adrenaline jumped, and she stilled quickly.

"Lift your head."

Not knowing what he wanted, she obeyed, all sorts of thoughts going through her head. Was he giving her his pillow? Taking hers away? Kicking her out of the bed after all because she kept tossing around like a mix-master?

Then she felt his arm slide under her nape, and he pulled her close so she was suddenly snuggled up to his side.

He was warm and hard against her skin, yet safe and unbelievably comfortable. And when he tugged her closer so her head rested against his chest, she didn't fight it. Instead she let out a little sigh of contentment and finally felt her body begin to relax.

It was wrong on so many levels, but oh, it felt right.

His hand ran over her hair in a soft, barely there caress. "Close your eyes. You need sleep."

She was suddenly more tired than she'd been in years, the weight of every one of her decisions weighing heavily on her shoulders. She chanced a glance up to his face and through the dim light coming from a crack in the curtains saw his eyes were closed, yet he continued to stroke her hair and her neck, to run his hand down her arm in a soft, gentle motion that was so at odds with the way he'd treated her over the past few hours, it confused her. Way more than thinking he wanted to use sex to punish her.

She finally couldn't stand it anymore. "Why are you being nice to me?"

"Momentary lapse in judgment," he mumbled.

There was humor in his voice, and dammit, it made her smile.

"Besides," he went on, "I figure if you don't get to sleep, then I don't get to sleep, and it'll be bad news all around if we're both bleary-eyed in the morning."

What he didn't say, and what tugged on her heart, was that this was how she'd often fallen asleep with him in Cairo. Snuggled up tight and warm. Usually after making love, but not always. When she'd been stressed or antsy about her job, when things hadn't been going well between them, being in his arms had always calmed her. And he remembered.

Kat looked down at his bare skin. Watched the rise and fall of his chest as he breathed. Thought about the events of the day. There was no reason for him to come back for her in the park, but he had. He could have walked away after they lost their tail in the city, but he hadn't. He didn't have to be holding her now, but he was.

And then out of nowhere, she remembered the flowers. Big bouquets of lilies and roses and spears of white freesia. And him.

"Thank you," she whispered.

"'s okay," he mumbled in that sleepy, sexy voice. "Long as you stop tossing. I'm good."

She smiled in the dark. "No. Not for that. Though thank you for that, too." She sobered. "I meant thank you for the flowers."

His hand stilled in her hair, and his chest rose and fell a few more times. She knew he was dozing off, but that was okay.

"Flowers?" he asked in a slur out of nowhere, as if his brain had finally caught up with the conversation and didn't want to give up to sleep yet. "What flowers?"

"The ones you sent to my mother's funeral."

Silence. Then, "You were there?"

A pang of regret snaked through her, and she closed her eyes. Her adoptive mother had been a nurse for over thirty years and healthy as an ox. Kat had never thought someone as strong as Jane Meyer could fall to something as ordinary as a heart attack. Or as fast.

She should have been with her mother the day she'd collapsed, not hiding in upstate New York like a scared rat. Maybe she would have gotten Jane to the hospital in time. Maybe the doctors would have been able to revive her. Maybe she'd still be here now.

Tears stung Kat's eyes, but she forced them back. Regrets. Yeah. She had them. She had enough to last a lifetime and then some.

"No. Not for the service," she managed. "But I was there before. At the funeral home when no one was around. I saw them then. They were beautiful."

Silence hung between them like a steel barrier, and then he said softly, "I didn't see you."

Her heart bumped. He'd been there?

"It was a nice service. You . . . you would have liked it."

Kat's chest squeezed tight, and her throat grew thick. In the quiet she didn't know what to say. And she was thankful when he went on and she didn't have to say anything.

"There were a lot of people. Standing room only. Your mother had a lot of friends. I think the whole staff of the hospital was there. Big gray-haired guy—Dr. Carter?—spoke about the first time she brought you in with her on one of her shifts. Scrawny ten-year-old with a heap of attitude, that was what he remembered about you. He thought for sure she was making a mistake by adopting a kid who'd been through so many foster homes and in and out of that orphanage. And when she made you sit at the nurses' station all night with a history book to read while she worked, he told her that was cruel and unusual punishment, even for her, and that you'd turn out to be the worst kid ever."

Kat smiled as she listened. Remembered back. At the time she'd thought that was cruel and unusual punishment herself. It'd taken her a long time to trust Jane, and she knew now the trust issues she had as an adult stemmed from her early childhood, but when she'd finally opened herself up to her new mother, she'd found the family she'd always dreamed of.

"Addie Walker talked about how Jane didn't have money for a sitter and how she hoped taking you to the hospital with her night after night would get you interested in medicine. She wanted you to become a doctor. But you were too focused on history by that point and were more interested in the dead than the living. Then when you got accepted into your doctorate program, she ran up to Dr. Carter and waved your acceptance letter in his face. Told him the scrawny, obnoxious Meyer kid was going to be a doctor after all."

A wave of adoration rushed through Kat as she listened. She hadn't known her mother had done that to the cranky old doctor, and her heart squeezed tight. Her mother had been her biggest advocate. Whenever Kat had thought she couldn't do something, Jane Meyer had set her straight. *You're smart. And you're resourceful. Where you came from doesn't matter. You'll find a way.*

And she had. Most of the time.

"They told a lot of stories about her," Pete said into the darkness. "About you. It was strange being there. Sort of like the memorial service she had for you after . . ."

Kat's heart pinched again, this time with her own discomfort. Because hearing him say it suddenly made it all real. She'd never thought about the fact Janie Meyer would have had a memorial service for her only daughter, but of course she would have. Even in her grief, she would have had a big party with all her friends to celebrate her daughter's life.

But what also hit her, as she laid there next to him, listening to his words, was that he'd been at that one, too. He'd gone to Points Bluff, Washington, population 1,257, two hours from Spokane, not only for her mother's funeral, but for *her* memorial service. Even after that horrible last argument in Cairo. After he'd walked out the door without looking back.

He'd gone to comfort her mother. A woman he'd never met and had no obligation toward.

Words lodged in her through. "Pete—"

"I'm really tired, Kat." His voice changed. Hardened. Grew distant. "We have a big day tomorrow, and I need to sleep. You do, too."

He was right, but the fact he'd cut her off stung.

He didn't make a move to push her to her side of the bed, and she didn't volunteer to go. So she closed her eyes and breathed deep, inhaling the scents of soap and fresh cotton and his unique musky scent. Reveled in it for a few more hours at least.

She must have slept, though she had no idea how much time passed. When Pete moved his leg on the mattress, she startled awake.

Bleary-eyed, she looked over him toward the digital clock on the bedside table and felt her heart drop. 2:34 a.m. If she was going to escape, she had to do it now.

She slowly pushed up on her elbow, pausing when the mattress creaked. One look confirmed Pete was still sleeping. His head was tipped her way, his mouth slightly open. The little bit of light coming through the slit in the curtains highlighted blond hair falling across his forehead, the shadow of beard on his jaw. Even his long eyelashes, blond at the root, darkening to a warm brown at the tips. She listened to the steady draw of his breath, watched as his bare, muscular chest rose and fell, and felt a little of her heart break all over again.

She was doing the right thing. Leaving now before it was too late. Before he was more embroiled in this whole mess. She now knew Busir was just a hired thug, that this went higher than she'd thought, into the SCA, possibly into INTERPOL. If this was ever going to be over, she had to figure out who was behind it all. What she'd seen and how it all meshed together. She knew where she had to start, and she knew she didn't want Pete tagging along. Not when she was starting to question his involvement from the very beginning. What if she'd been wrong about him?

He'd gone to see her mother.

She was trapped miserably between her heart and mind as she closed her eyes, fought back the tears, opened them again and stared down at his features. But even with that debate still raging, she knew, deep in her heart, that he was the one. The love of her life. The happily-ever-after she'd never have. It didn't matter what he'd done or who he'd been before they'd been together. When he'd been hers, he'd been everything she'd ever wanted.

She held her breath as she leaned close to brush her lips softly over his. Just a whisper of a touch. Just one last kiss.

Through wet eyes she moved to climb off the bed.

And gasped.

CHAPTER NINETEEN

"I don't think so."

Kat's pulse jumped against her skin where Pete gripped her wrist. In the dark, he could see the whites of her eyes glow like halos all around her dark irises.

"Where do you think you're going?"

She opened her mouth to answer. Stared at him. Closed it quickly.

She hadn't thought he was awake, he realized. And granted, he hadn't been. Not until she'd laid her lips on his.

Then he'd come immediately awake. Had grown instantly aware.

She trembled beneath his touch. He sat up slowly, let his eyes adjust to the dark, raked in the sight of her there in front of him. Hair tousled from sleep, dirt-streaked, white T-shirt she hadn't rinsed out in the bathroom creased from where she'd slept on it. Eyes sultry and filled with a yearning he'd recognize anywhere.

His blood rushed hot in response even though he knew it was a bad idea.

She drew in shallow breaths, but she didn't once look away from him, didn't ease back, didn't try to get out of his hold. And he saw then the same thing he'd seen in the diner earlier. A decision that flashed in her eyes and sucked him in.

He knew that look.

Bad idea. Really fucking bad idea.

He let go of her wrist. Made a move to slide away from her. But didn't make it more than a fraction of an inch.

Her body sank into him. Her lips brushed his. Once. Twice. As soft as before but with an urgency he'd missed in his groggy state.

He tensed. Thought about pushing her away. Knew he couldn't.

Oh, sweet Jesus.

That heart he was sure had cracked and shattered years ago swelled inside his chest with the first taste. And shoving away the thousand reasons this was wrong, he let her draw him into her warm, wet mouth. Deep, deeper. Until he felt her body quiver, felt her firm breasts press against his bare chest, felt her muscles tighten and loosen and her heart jump beneath her ribs.

He didn't think. Just savored her in his mouth. Ran his hands over her back and around to her waist. Pulled her closer. The position was awkward, so he gripped her hips, lifted her easily, guided her to straddle his lap so he could kiss her deeper yet. Then nearly came when she settled herself on her knees over him and lowered until she was sitting on his throbbing erection.

And ah, hell, being with her like this was like coming home. Like leaving the dark and coming into the light. Like finding where you were meant to be.

Neither of them spoke. The heater hummed in the background. Every now and then a car passed on the freeway outside. But all he could focus on was the roar in his head that screamed, *now, now, now,* followed by a tightness in his chest that warned, *take it easy.*

He listened, though it nearly killed him. Moved slowly. His hands slid to the edge of her tee, up under to the bare skin of her abdomen, higher until his knuckles brushed her bra. All the while he kissed her, licked into her mouth and bathed himself in the sweet taste of her on his tongue again.

She was hot, and he was burning. She was soft where he was hard as stone. He broke the kiss long enough to pull the T-shirt over her head and drop it on the floor, nearly groaned at the sight of her practical cotton bra. No bells and whistles, no lace or see-through cups. Sturdy. Practical. Like her.

Her heavy-lidded eyes stayed on his as he worked the bra free. The back hook gave with a soft pop. She drew in a breath, then helped him by wriggling out of the straps. It fell into his hands, landed next to her T-shirt on the floor. He licked his lips in anticipation as he cupped her perfect breasts, flicked his thumb across her nipple and watched as her eyes slid closed and her head fell back in pleasure.

That roar returned, louder than ever. He kissed her jaw, scraped his teeth along her throat, worked his way south. With one hand supporting her, he lowered her onto her back so her head was near the foot of the mattress, then resumed his foray across her body.

His lips closed over one breast, and he drew lazy circles around her nipple, sucked her deep into his mouth until she writhed beneath him.

"Pete," she whispered.

He loved that needy, sex-charged voice. Loved the way she melted beneath him. Didn't realize how much he'd missed it until right now. He moved to the other nipple and tasted the sweetness of her skin. She reacted by lifting her foot, kicking her heel into the mattress and digging her fingers into his biceps with a death grip until pain shot through his arm. But the moan that came out of her made up for any discomfort he felt, so he kept driving her harder, closer to the edge, greedy for the sound of her pleasure.

"Pete. Oh . . ."

"More?" He didn't wait for an answer, drew her nipple into his mouth, scraped his teeth over the tip until she groaned long and deep. "Or stop?"

"No. No. Don't stop. Whatever you do . . . don't stop."

Good thing, because he wasn't sure he could. Even if she begged.

Sliding lower, he kissed his way down her belly. He flipped open the top button of her jeans with the other hand and brushed his lips over the sensitive skin beneath her waistband.

She moaned again, arched her back in approval. He quickly released the other three buttons, then with both hands, pulled the jeans from her hips and slipped them off her legs.

And groaned himself when he saw she was naked beneath her denim.

Her tummy was flat, her hips a gentle flare that fit her shape. Her legs long and lean and athletic. She was everything he remembered and more. Toned and fit and muscular where before she'd been merely slim skin and bones. She worked out now. Hard by the looks of it. A woman's body on the girl he'd loved and lost a lifetime ago.

"Pete?"

Her soft voice pulled at him, and he looked up to find her watching him with confusion and the slightest bit of worry in her dark eyes.

He climbed over her, fueled by some need he didn't want to name, braced his hands on the mattress and lowered to take her mouth again. She cradled his face in her palms and kissed him back. Long and slow and deep.

His hand found her breast again, then lowered to her hip, her thigh, and finally to that sweet, sweet spot between her legs. She opened for him on a sigh, groaned into his mouth as he slid his fingers into her folds and found her burning, slick center.

Oh, she was wet.

Her breath hitched when he rubbed over her tight knot. He circled and swirled, took her higher. When she kicked her head back and moaned, he closed his mouth over her neck and licked the sweet, dewy column of her throat the way he knew she liked until her body tensed and her muscles quivered with her release.

She was quiet. So quiet. But he knew the signs. Knew her body so well. Even after all this time. As she slid down the other side of her climax, he shucked his jeans, reached for his wallet on the nightstand and pulled out a condom, then used his knees to push her thighs wider to make room for him.

Her hand snaked out. "Let me."

It nearly killed him, but he waited. Gritted his teeth as she rolled the latex on, groaned out loud when she wrapped him fully in her hand and stroked up and down his arousal. She found his mouth with hers again as she tugged him closer and lined him up with all her slick, female heat.

Oh, yeah, she was wet. Drenched from her release. And hotter than anything he'd felt before.

"Slow," she whispered against his lips. "Just . . . slow."

He clenched his jaw tight on the verge of thrusting hard and deep inside her. Electricity raced down his spine. Sweat broke out on his forehead. He pushed slowly until just the head of him was buried inside her and then stopped.

She was tight. So damn tight he was afraid he'd hurt her if he moved too fast. Nothing he remembered had ever been like this.

He looked down to find her lids were closed tightly, her lips compressed. He wondered just how long it had been for her.

Quite a while. Years maybe.

If she'd left him for Slade, she hadn't been seeing the guy recently. Hadn't been seeing anyone recently.

And he was a son of a bitch for being thrilled by that knowledge.

"Kat," he whispered. "I don't want to—"

She gripped his ass with her hands when he would have eased back and kissed him again. "No. Don't stop. Please. Don't stop. I need . . . I need . . ." She shifted her hips so he slid in another inch, groaned at the friction. "You," she finished on a deep breath.

He dropped his forehead to hers and drew air into his suddenly shaky lungs. When he felt steady, he licked his finger, got it good and wet and slid it between them to find her sweet spot again.

The flick of his finger, the push and pull of his hips soon had her moaning and writhing beneath him. And with one final thrust he was all the way in.

Okay, he'd been wrong. *This* was coming home.

"Kit-Kat," he whispered against her mouth. He wanted to remember the feel of her clenched around his length. Wanted to memorize each sigh and sound and movement she made so when he was ninety he could look back and remember how he'd felt at this moment.

Whole. Not broken. Not empty. Nothing but complete.

Then she was moving beneath him, and all thought rushed right out of his brain. He matched her thrusts until the little tugs were long strokes and they were both sweaty and breathless from exertion.

He had to grit his teeth to hold off his climax, but the instant he felt her muscles clench around him and her back bow in pleasure, he let go. Erupted deep inside her on a long groan. And in the process let go of six years of emptiness and anger and bitter betrayal.

He just didn't know if it would be enough to get past what had happened between them.

Six years earlier
Cairo

By the end of the first week, Pete knew he was in trouble.

Shannon had made herself scarce as soon as Pete had

arrived in Cairo, staying with Kat's friend Sawil Ramirez two floors up, but it hadn't cut the tension. When Pete wasn't making love to Kat, they were walking on eggshells around each other.

He hated the strain. Hated the way she was censoring what she said and did around him. He knew she was afraid to talk about anything serious for fear of another eruption like the last time they'd been together.

It nearly killed him, because there were things they needed to get out in the open, but he decided not to push her. Instead, he smiled when she told her silly jokes, held her hand as they played tourist and scoured the Abdeen Palace and the Sharia al-Muski street market, even managed to laugh when they took a belly dancing class that made him feel like a complete idiot. But always in the back of his head was the weight of what he needed to tell her and the fear she may not be as thrilled with his plans for the future as he was.

Her dig would be over in three months—at least for her. They'd talked briefly about what she planned to do when her time was up. She'd given up her apartment in Maryland when she'd come to Cairo, so she didn't have one to go back to. After a year away, she wanted to go home to Washington and see her mother for a while, and then she needed to get busy on her dissertation. She could do that anywhere, he knew. She didn't need to be back in Maryland to write. In his head, he'd already worked out the details.

Convincing her to come to Miami, though, was small potatoes compared to what he had to convince her about himself. And after a week, he felt like he was running out of time.

She rolled over in bed and snuggled into him on a sigh, and as he wrapped his arms around her and drew her closer, he told himself he'd do it today. She'd taken a week off to be with him, and she had to go out to the site this morning to work, but tonight, when she came home, he planned to lay it all out for her. Strip himself bare and hope what she felt for him was strong enough to overlook everything he'd done.

"You smell good," she said in that sleepy, sexy voice of hers he loved hearing.

"You feel good."

She smiled against his neck, slinked on top of him in all her naked glory and pressed her lips against his throat. His blood pulsed. He grew rock hard as the St. Jude medal she always wore fell against his chest. "How good?"

He groaned at the feel of her silky wetness already sliding against his length, placed his hands on her thighs and spread her legs so she could settle herself on his erection. "Like paradise. Let me take you there."

Their lovemaking was slow and sensuous. But reserved. He felt it in the same way he'd felt it for the last seven days. She was holding back, and the urgency to break through her barrier only reinforced what he needed to do tonight.

"I could get used to you being around like this," she mumbled later when she collapsed onto his chest, slick with sweat and breathless.

"Could you?"

She nodded slowly.

"Good. Because I plan on being around. A lot."

She went still. Then pressed her lips against his chest before climbing off and heading for the shower. "What's your plan for the day while I'm gone?"

Pete pushed himself up in the pillows and watched as she brushed her teeth, telling himself her avoidance technique wasn't a bad sign. Not completely. "I thought I'd veg on your couch, rot my mind with Egyptian television and drink what's left of that crappy beer in your refrigerator."

She turned, toothbrush in mouth, and smiled. "Sounds like a full day."

His eyes ran over her naked flesh. "After the way you've worn me out the last few nights, I need the rest."

Her reaction was masked as she turned back to the sink, rinsed and grabbed a towel from the rack. "Then you'd better rest up for tonight. We're having dinner with Shannon and Sawil. And after, I plan on wearing you out all over again."

He said good-bye to her at the door with a long, lingering kiss he hoped she'd think about as much as he knew he would, then watched her leave from the window. When he was alone, he looked around the sparse living room she'd called home the past year and wondered if she'd like his house in Miami. He did, but what if she wanted something smaller? Or less modern? Shit, she was an Egyptologist. She liked old things.

His cell phone chimed in the bedroom, and he moved across the floor with a smile, knowing it was her on the other end of the line. If she was planning on getting him all hot and bothered, two could play at that game.

"My girlfriend would be upset if she knew you were calling me," he said into the phone.

"Then you'd better not tell her," a deeply accented male voice responded.

Pete went on instant alert. *Busir.* "I thought I told you I was out."

A deep chuckle echoed over the line. "You said that. But I have something that just might interest you."

He should have said no, hung up and turned off his phone. If he had, he could have avoided everything that happened next. But he didn't. Because there was a small part of him—a part he was working hard to bury—that flared with excitement at Busir's words.

He shifted the phone to his other ear and sealed his own fate. "Tell me what you've got."

CHAPTER TWENTY

Dreams woke him. Or memories. He wasn't sure which.

Pete was at Lauren's fancy house on Key Biscayne. Sitting on her back stone patio, beer in hand, staring out at the beach and the open ocean beyond.

His sister was there behind him, on one of her many mini-vacations, as she called them, between photo shoots. She stood just inside the wide patio doors, in the kitchen she never used, on the phone ordering a pizza as he listened to the lap of water, the cry of a gull, the whisper of palms blowing in the warm gentle breeze.

It should have been peaceful, but it wasn't. It should have relaxed him, but it didn't. He'd told Lauren the whole story. Beginning to end. From the moment he'd met Kat at the tomb to that night she'd come home early from work and found him in her apartment packing, with a full box of artifacts at his feet.

The ones he'd purchased from Busir that afternoon. The ones he hadn't known had been from her tomb.

She'd instantly accused him of being involved in the smuggling ring. Hadn't listened to his side of things. Just kicked him out. Ended it all. Right there.

And when he'd realized how badly he'd fucked up, he hadn't bothered to fight back.

What else could he have done? Stayed there and listened to her trash him? Watch what she'd felt for him grind to dust in her eyes?

Nope. He couldn't do it. Didn't want to watch that happen.

So he'd left. Flown back to Miami. Come here. Licked his wounds, had a few beers and gotten good and pissed. Time did that. Reduced the pain to duplicity. Alcohol helped.

Six months of trying to go straight, down the toilet because of one mistake. One major-ass, fuck-up-your-life mistake he didn't have a clue how to fix.

Go back and tell her the truth.

He grimaced at Lauren's words. Lifted the third beer—or was it the fourth? Drank long and deep.

Didn't really matter what the count was up to. He was on the road to getting good and wasted tonight anyway. Go back? After everything Kat had said to him, and the way she'd looked at him like he was nothing more than gum stuck to the bottom of her shoe that she couldn't wait to scrape off? Going back would be the equivalent to slicing open a vein and bleeding out all over the floor. Of course, the fact Lauren was right, and that it was the only thing he *could* do, only made him want to speed up that whole get-shitfaced-drunk-and-forget-the-whole-nightmare process.

Then his cell rang.

He glanced at the display—unknown number—and considered letting it go to voice mail. He wasn't really sure why he answered. Only knew he regretted it the moment he flipped the phone open.

The rest was a blur. Him rising, his beer bottle hitting the ground, shattering at his feet to spill cold, golden liquid over his shoes. Lauren rushing out of the house to ask what had happened. Slade's voice—of all people—echoing in his head. And a blinding pain right beneath his sternum.

It was the pain that brought his eyes open now. He felt it as sharp and real as he had then. Staring up at the water-stained ceiling, he gasped in a breath and rubbed the heel of his hand over his chest to ease the sting.

And then had a major-ass moment of confusion.

Not Lauren's house. Not the blue sky he'd looked up at when he'd finally opened his eyes on that cold, stone patio after going under like a pansy.

No, now he was in a room. It was dark. A sliver of light formed a crescent shape on the wall straight ahead. A poorly painted beach scene hung at an angle directly in his line of sight.

He lifted his head, eyed the headboard that should have been behind him but was now near his feet. Then remembered the dive motel he'd paid cash for. The shower. The sheets. The bedbugs. The sex.

Kat.

Warmth spread through his whole body, slid down his chest. Pooled in his groin until he was hard all over again. He tipped his head, noticed he was alone and shot a look toward the bathroom. The door was closed, but he could just hear the hum of the fan running and saw light burning where wood met worn carpet.

Bathroom break. Smart. He needed one, too. When he could move.

He eyed the clock and noted it was almost six a.m.

Last night had been a really bad idea. Monumentally bad. The last thing he needed was to get twisted up with her again. Six years ago it had nearly killed him. Except, lying here now, with her scent all over his body and the taste of her still lingering on his tongue, it didn't feel half bad. It felt . . . oddly right.

He kicked his foot out from beneath the sheet, absently wondering when he'd had the sense to pull the damn thing up. Wondered if she'd done it for him, or if he'd just used her body as his blanket until she'd finally climbed out of bed this morning.

Shiiit. *Really* bad idea.

He rubbed both hands over his face. Then looked back at the closed bathroom door. She'd been in there a long time.

Reaching out a hand, he touched her side of the bed only to find the sheets were already cold.

Something in his stomach tightened as he sat up slowly and swung his legs over the side of the bed. He really didn't want to surprise her if she was on the toilet, but he also didn't like the direction of his thoughts.

He rapped his knuckles on the door, leaned close to listen. Didn't hear anything other than the hum of the fan.

"Kat?" When there was still no answer, he took a chance, turned the handle and pushed.

Light burned his eyes. He closed them quickly. Blinked until the spots faded from his vision. Then stared into an empty room.

The shower curtain was pulled back, an empty tub reflected in the mirror across the space. The counter was clean. Only his T-shirt hung over the towel bar.

"No fucking way."

Surprise hit first. Then shock. Then abject disbelief. He turned quickly, flicked on the bedside lamp and discovered her backpack, clothes and shoes were gone as well.

Stunned, he stood there, staring into the quiet room, putting pieces together in his head. Her change in attitude last night at the diner. Her nervousness when they'd been going to bed. The way she'd kissed him when she thought he'd been asleep. The hesitation when she'd discovered he was awake. The decision she'd seemed to make before they'd made love.

No, he realized. That wasn't making love. That was a goddamn diversion.

His vision dimmed, and that all-too-familiar sense of betrayal clawed its way up his chest.

She'd just fucked him again. And this time she'd done one helluva good job.

Omar Kamil hated exercise. Unfortunately, it was keeping him alive. Just about the only thing at this point.

Sweat poured down his forehead as he pumped his legs on the elliptical machine. Across the room, CNN ran nonstop on the flat screen mounted to the wall. He kept an eye on the ticker at the bottom, searching for any news on Katherine Meyer.

Nothing. No body. No death. No unexplained shootings.

That was both good and bad news as far as he was concerned. He drew in two deep breaths and felt his muscles burn with the effort of his workout

His cell chimed, and he flipped it open without slowing his feet. "Yes?"

"Not good," Busir said. "We had a little trouble in Philadelphia. Bertrand showed up."

Omar punched stop on the machine. "In fucking Philadelphia? What the hell is INTERPOL doing in on this? He's *retired*."

"Not so much, apparently. No matter, though. Fucker's dead now."

"Dammit." That would draw major international attention.

"She got away in the scuffle. With Kauffman."

That brought Kamil's focus back around. His vision blurred, and he had to step off the elliptical to keep his balance. He was dealing with incompetents. How hard was it to find one measly woman?

"And your solution?" he asked calmly.

"He's not using his credit card. We think he'll try to take her to Miami. Where he can watch out for her on familiar turf."

Omar snapped a towel from the table and rubbed it

over his face. "Or maybe not. Don't you think he'd know that's the first place you'd look for him?"

Silence.

Omar bit back the curse on his tongue. This was one fucking nightmare that wasn't getting better. If he'd done the job himself six years ago, they wouldn't be in this clusterfuck to begin with. And Minyawi—the dick—could bet his ass his payout was taking a cut for each one of his major screw-ups where Katherine Meyer was concerned. The man's personal obsession with her was fucking up everything.

"They won't go to Miami. He won't risk it." He thought about his options, then had an epiphany. "She'll go to Latham."

"Why?"

"Because she wants answers. He was the project leader, and he's the only one still alive who worked that tomb."

"And if she doesn't go there?"

"Then she'll head back to New York."

"Why?" Busir asked again.

He really was dealing with imbeciles. But that was okay as long as they took the fall and he didn't.

"Worthington security said they had an unidentified woman sneaking around the storage room. I'd bet my ass she stole something from the auction. A statue, a container, an urn big enough to hide the film from the camera she had that night in the tomb."

"Her camera was in her bag the night of the bombing. She ran with it."

Omar's entire faced tightened. "That's what she wanted us to believe. But she wasn't in that bombing after all, was she? Which means her camera wasn't there either. She must have hidden it, possibly sent it to Kauffman for safe-keeping just before she disappeared. Look at it from her perspective. She finds out he's going to sell it after all this time, she realizes her one chance at freedom's about to go in the toilet. She shows up at the auction house to get it back."

He snapped his fingers as links clicked into place. "I'm betting she hasn't even looked inside yet. Or if she has, what's in there is inconclusive or damaged. If it wasn't, she'd already have gone to the CIA, and I wouldn't be standing here now."

"So if it wasn't in the piece she took, where is it?"

Omar paced the small exercise room. "It wasn't in any of the ones you purchased at the auction. I already had someone check them carefully. He paused as a thought occurred. "Athens. The Institute woman. She purchased several of the pieces herself, didn't she?"

"Yes, but that doesn't make sense because Kauffman would have had it the whole time."

"Maybe he didn't know he'd had it."

Busir was silent. Then he said, "You want us to check out the pieces the Greek woman purchased?"

"No. I'll send another team to do that. I have something else in mind for you and your partner."

"What?"

"I'm coming to America. We have a collection about to be shipped on loan to the Metropolitan Museum. I was going to send an assistant, but I believe I will accompany them this time instead, maybe drop in on Dr. Gotsi and see how she's doing."

"And what is it you want us to do in the meantime?"

"Get Minyawi and pay a visit to Kauffman's sister. If he won't cooperate, we'll find a way to draw him out of hiding one way or the other."

"What if Meyer goes to Latham?"

"Send Wyatt and Usted."

"Usted's dead."

Omar gritted his teeth. "Then send Wyatt."

Silence. Then, "Minyawi won't like giving up the hunt for Meyer. He's got a score to settle with the woman. It's personal."

Omar didn't give a flying fuck about Minyawi's personal goals. He wasn't paying the man to go after his own vendetta. And as far as Omar was concerned, that went for Minyawi's associates as well. He'd made them a lot of fucking money over the years for their cause. They could suck it up and step back on this one.

"He'll get his chance. Just bring the Kauffman woman to New York."

"I understand."

"And Busir?"

"Yes."

"Bring her to New York unharmed. Do not let Minyawi touch her."

"That's easier said than done. Minyawi is unpredictable."

All the more reason to get this over with as soon as possible.

"Then you watch him. And if he gets out of control, you know what to do. I want Katherine Meyer, and I want that evidence she has. Nothing gets in the way of that goal. Are we clear?"

"Crystal."

CHAPTER TWENTY-ONE

If she could shoot her new secretary and get away with it, she just might turn to a life of crime after all.

Hailey Roarke frowned as the door to her office was pulled closed and thought wistfully of her service revolver.

Too bad she'd had to turn the damn thing in when she'd taken her leave of absence from the Key West police force to come to this hell known as Roarke Resorts.

Her intercom beeped, and Gail-the-grim-faced-gate-keeper-Florentes's nasally voice echoed through the room like a thousand fingernails scraping down a chalk-board. "Ms. Roarke. You have a call on line three. A Mr. Kauffman. I don't recognize the name. Your nine o'clock appointment has been waiting to see you for over ten minutes."

Hailey didn't miss the implied lecture. *Peter Kauffman isn't Roarke-related business, or I'd know. That means the call is personal, and that's unacceptable. Make it quick. Your father's lawyer is waiting.*

On this one thing, Hailey knew she'd win. For the first time that day, a smile spread across her face. No way she'd ditch Pete for her father's stuffy lawyer. She pushed the intercom button. "Thank you, Mrs. Florentes. Get Mr. Arnold coffee or anything else he'd like and make sure he's comfortable. I need to take this call, and I may be a while."

A disapproving harrumph came over the line. Hailey only smiled wider.

She picked up the phone, kicked back in her father's plush leather chair and swiveled to look out the seven-teenth-story window at the skyline of downtown Miami. "Now this is a surprise. Word is you're hunkered down nice and cozy in New York with the Euro-babe."

"I should be so lucky."

Hailey smiled wider. As her ex-husband's business part-ner at Odyssey Gallery, Pete was one man she knew well and trusted implicitly. She considered him a personal friend and always would. "Of course, it begs the question. What are you doing calling *me* when you've got the Euro-babe all to yourself? Come on, Pete. Make my day and tell me she's not enough woman for you or any other man."

"Sorry to disappoint, but I'm not with Maria."

Something in his voice made her sit up and shuck the sarcasm. Pete was rarely serious. A joker. A playboy. Everyone's friend. He had those good-boy looks and that old-school attitude that put people at ease right from the start. Underneath that laid-back personality, though, Hailey had always sensed a hint of something dark, a past he never talked about. Which was why his suddenly serious tone set off big red flags in her mind.

"Well, now," she said. "That's a surprise. Lisa told me Rafe's been trying to get in touch with you."

"I lost my cell. How's Rafe's mom?"

Lost his cell? Pete? Uh-huh. Riiiiight.

Hailey watched a news helicopter circle the downtown area. "Stable. For now. She's hanging in there. But they're not sure how much longer."

"Dammit. I should be there for him."

Hailey's chest grew tight as she thought about Teresa Sullivan. A woman who'd been more of a mother to her in a few short years than her own mother had been to her in all her thirty-four. Though Hailey and Rafe had divorced shortly after their impromptu never-should-have-happened Vegas wedding, they were still friends. And Teresa would always be family.

"Where are you?" she asked, pushing aside the pain just the thought of Teresa's illness brought.

In the background she heard springs squeak, like from a mattress. "I don't know. Somewhere in south Jersey, I think."

"You don't know?" Just what was going on? Last she'd heard from Rafe, Pete had left the wildly successful auction with the Art Institute of Athens's slinky Maria Gotsi in a fancy limo and disappeared into the snow. Rafe had told Hailey he suspected the two were on the verge of something serious, though they all hoped that wasn't the case. Maria was a tiger shark.

"It's a long story."

Hailey thought about what waited for her on the other side of the door. "Start talking. I've got lots of time, trust me."

It didn't take as long as she'd expected, but she had to finally shut her mouth so she'd stop saying, *really?* and *are you serious?* Because she was slowing down the flow. And because even she recognized she was beginning to sound like a broken record.

She knew about Pete's shady past dealings. Hell, she'd been married to a thief who'd worked for him, so none of that was a surprise. She also knew he'd cleaned up his act over the past few years. So it wasn't what he was saying that had questions firing off in her brain, rather what he was omitting.

Which, of course, piqued Hailey's interest. On both a personal and professional level.

"You get a good look at the guy in the park?" A burst of excitement rushed through her. She'd been off the police force now for three weeks while she stepped in to help her father's company during his illness. He'd asked for her help specifically, and she'd agreed only out of some morbid sense of guilt. This was not the job she wanted to be doing. And her father knew that. As soon as he was better, she was on her way back south.

"Yeah. Stocky. Medium height. About fifty, I'd say. Good shape for his age. Gray hair. Said his name was David Halloway."

She made a note on the pad on her desk. "You don't think he was FBI after all?"

"No. Definitely not. Hinted he was, though. Somehow he knew Slade, so he could have been CIA, but I doubt it. Gut feeling says INTERPOL."

"Hm. Interesting. I've got a friend with INTERPOL. Jill Monroe. She used to be with the Miami PD."

"That's why I called."

She didn't miss the frown in his voice and smiled. It was sappy and pathetic considering she was now running a multimillion-dollar company, but it felt good to be needed. Not just used.

Hailey made another note. "I'll call her. See if she can look him up."

"I'd appreciate it. I also need some background information. I'd do it myself, but I've got a few other things I need to wrangle, and considering what's happening with Teresa, I don't want to bother Rafe."

"I'm happy to help out. What do you need?"

"Cash first of all. I don't want to use my credit card in case they're tracking me, and I'm about zapped out of funds. Can you get to Odyssey and have Liddy wire me some money?"

She made a note to call his assistant. "No problem. What else?"

"I need a list of addresses for the people Kat worked with in Cairo."

Hailey scribbled on the pad at her elbow as he read off names. "I can do that, too. But why don't you take the easy route and just ask her where these people are?"

He didn't answer, and his silence made her pen stop its furious chicken-scratching. "Oh," she said as understanding dawned. "She's not there, is she?"

"Bingo."

"What did you do to her?"

"Why do you assume it's something I did?"

She smiled again. "Wild guess."

"Well, on this one you're wrong." There was definitely a defensive tone to his answer. And it made Hailey sure there was more he wasn't saying. A lot more.

Not that that was any of her business, though it was an interesting twist of events. Pete the ultimate bachelor had the hots for some wily Egyptologist, and she'd just ditched his ass for greener pastures. No wonder he was pissed.

"I'll look them up for you," she said to cut the guy a break. "Anything else?"

"Yeah." He hesitated. "I could use a plane."

Her brow shot up. "You want to take the Roarke Resorts' Bombardier for a test flight while the bad guys are out there tailing your girl?"

"It's not for a test flight," he said. "I need to find her. Fast."

Whoever this Katherine Meyer was, she'd done one helluva number on Peter Kauffman. "I don't know," Hailey teased, leaning back in her chair. "I could get into serious trouble appropriating company resources for private use like that. It goes against Roarke Resorts' company policy."

"Screw company policy. Like you've never broken the rules before?"

"Me?" She feigned shock. "I'm a police officer, Kauffman."

"*Was* a police officer, Roarke. And not a very good one to begin with. Look, can I have the goddamn plane or not? I don't have time to charter my own, and I don't have a fucking clue where I'm headed yet."

Desperate. Oh, yeah. He was seriously fucked.

"Relax. Don't get your panties in a bunch. Of course you can use it. I'll call right now and have Steve fly up to Philly. He'll take you wherever you need to go." She dropped the teasing since it wasn't doing much to lighten his mood and steered back to what was important. "Where will you be in an hour? I can probably get everything you need by then."

"I'm not sure." He hesitated. "Tell you what, I'll call you. It'll give me time to get a disposable phone and do a little research on my end."

"Okay. Will do. And Pete?"

"Yeah?"

"She was wrong. Not to trust you. You're one of the most dependable men I know."

He was quiet so long, she wasn't sure he was still there. Then she heard static, and his voice, filled with something that sounded oddly like regret. "Yeah, well, I never gave her many reasons to trust me."

Before she could ask what that meant, his voice hardened. "I'll call you in an hour, Hailey. And thanks."

Then he was gone.

Hailey set the receiver down and stared at the notes she'd just made. She had roughly sixty minutes to do all the things Pete needed done in addition to running background checks on Katherine Meyer, David Halloway and Aten Minyawi. She'd definitely heard that last name before, she just couldn't remember where.

As she reached for the phone again, she briefly remembered her father's lawyer was sitting outside waiting to see her. *Screw it.* He could just go on waiting. She had more important things to worry about than Daddy's will. There would always be tomorrow.

Kat stared out the bus window as she passed through the quiet streets of suburban Raleigh, North Carolina. Dusk was just settling in, and her butt hurt from the hours she'd spent on the Greyhound that had brought her here.

She'd switched to a Capital Area Transit bus once she'd reached Raleigh and was now tooling through North Raleigh on her way to the Brentwood neighborhood she'd marked on her handy little map. She seriously hoped the address she had for Charles Latham was still correct. It had been six years. It was possible he'd moved. Or died.

She prayed it wasn't the latter. Of the four other archaeologists who had worked the tomb with her in Cairo, he was the only one left alive. A chill spread down her spine at the thought, but she pushed it aside. Car accident, heart attack, stroke—all normal ways to die. All ways that didn't attract attention or cause questions. Even for men in their forties and fifties.

Convenient.

Too convenient as far as Kat was concerned. She'd kept tabs on everyone for safety reasons over the years. And when her colleagues had mysteriously started dropping off the radar, she'd known things still weren't safe. It was part of the reason she'd stayed in hiding so long. Last she'd heard, Charles was still alive—though barely. He had cancer—inoperable—and was slowly dying. Had Busir let him live because the SOB had known Charles's days were numbered anyway?

Possibly. Or the more likely answer was he'd been in on the smuggling ring with Busir from the very beginning.

Kat shifted in her seat, unsettled by the thought. Someone had to have been feeding Busir's group information. Since her life—and Pete's—was on the line, she intended to find out who that was. Even if it meant facing Charles Latham and wringing his dying neck to get the info out of him.

Kat glanced at her watch. It was nearly four o'clock. She wondered how long Pete had slept before he'd realized she was gone. He'd been exhausted, had nearly passed out after they'd made love.

Warmth rushed over her skin at the memory, and she closed her eyes and breathed deep. It had definitely been the wrong thing to do, but when he'd looked at her . . . oh, man, every one of her arguments had crumbled in her mind. She suddenly hadn't been able to remember why she couldn't have him. He'd tasted so good, felt so divine, and the things he'd done with his fingers and tongue had driven her completely wild until every no was a yes and she'd been begging for more.

The driver called out the stop as the CAT bus slowed, and Kat's thoughts wound back around to what she had to do next. She grabbed her backpack from the floor and stood. The doors slammed shut behind her as she stepped off the rig, and the bus let out a whir as it pulled away from the curb. She glanced around the aging neighborhood and checked the map she'd picked up at the transit station. Three blocks over, one block up.

"About time you got here."

Kat's pulse nearly stopped at the familiar voice, and she looked toward the bus stop where a man she couldn't see was sitting on a bench reading a paper. As the paper slowly lowered, she drew in a sharp breath. "What are you—"

"Doing here?" Pete finished. "What the hell do you think I'm doing here?"

He rose, crumpled the paper and tossed it in a garbage can next to him.

He'd changed. He wasn't wearing borrowed jeans and an old parka anymore. He was decked out in tan slacks, a white button-down and a slick leather jacket. He looked of power and money and ultimate sex appeal.

And there wasn't one thing friendly in those eyes of his when they stared her down.

"How did you find me?"

"You mean after you fucked me senseless and left?" His eyes flashed. "That, by the way, was a great diversion. Can't just wait for me to fall asleep on my own, so you screw me until I pass out and speed the whole process along. I'll have to remember that one for future reference."

Oh, yeah. This guy was way past irate and moving into livid territory. "That's not what I—"

"You *really* don't want to push me right now, woman. Because if you do, I guarantee one of us is going to get hurt and the other's gonna get tossed in jail."

She drew a sharp breath at the bite in his words and cut off her apology. Okay, she'd been wrong. His anger at Marty's garage was nothing compared to what he was showing her now.

She swallowed around the lump in her throat. "How did you find me?"

"I know how to do research, too."

Right. Of course he did. And he'd known who she'd worked with in Cairo because she'd told him and because he'd met many of her colleagues when he'd dropped by her work site. "Why are you here?"

"Two reasons." He eyed her with flat, emotionless eyes. "One, because any way we slice this, I'm screwed. I go back to Miami now, pick up my life, and I'm gonna have some Middle Eastern badasses hunting me down trying to get to you. That's not my idea of fun. So I don't particularly see much choice in where I go or what I do. Until we figure this out, you're stuck with me."

Which obviously pissed him off, judging from the way that vein pulsed in his temple.

"And the second?" she asked warily.

He clenched his jaw as his eyes took a slow stroll across her features. "The second is because I want my pendant back."

That wasn't the answer she'd expected.

"You know," he said in a slightly amused voice, "I couldn't quite figure out why you were at the auction. When I first saw you in Pennsylvania, I stupidly thought it was because of me. But we both know that wasn't the reason, was it?"

Kat opened her mouth to answer, but he cut her off.

"Then," he went on, "after you left me in the park, I realized you'd forgotten your bag. I opened it. Hell if I know why. I just did. And that's when I saw it." His eyes sharpened. "You weren't at that auction to see me. You went there to steal from me."

"That's not what I—"

"Don't *lie* to me, Kat. Not now. Not after everything I've been through because of you."

He was right, but it wasn't the *whole* truth, and if she

told him the real reason, she knew he wouldn't believe her. In his current mood, she figured it was better not to add more fuel to his fire.

She closed her mouth quickly.

"It took me a while to figure it out," he said, "but I've had a whole day to do nothing but think things through. Why is the pendant so important, Kat?"

There was no reason not to tell him, so she didn't even try to hedge. "It was hollow. I tucked a memory stick inside. From my digital camcorder."

"Why?" It wasn't a question but a demand, and he wasn't asking because he was curious, but because his life hinged on the answer.

She glanced up the quiet neighborhood. Porch lights were flickering on here and there, but there wasn't another soul out this evening. And while the temperature in Raleigh was a good fifteen degrees warmer than it had been in Philadelphia, Kat was frozen inside.

Frozen because of the icy look of revulsion on Pete's face. She'd much rather remember him in the throes of passion than like this.

"After that SCA agent was killed," she started, "and nothing came of the report Sawil filed about the missing artifacts or Dr. Latham's complaints, I decided to set up a camcorder in a corner of the collection room just to see what was happening after hours. It had a motion sensor, so I knew it wouldn't trip unless someone was in there."

"Did Ramirez know about the camera?"

She shook her head. "I didn't tell him about it. Then that night, after you . . . left." She swallowed hard, pushed that particularly horrid memory away. "He came and told me he'd found something I needed to see. I didn't think of the camera until we got to the tomb. I only went with him because . . ."

She hesitated, unwilling to dive back into the root of her problems with Pete.

"You went to see if I was in the tomb," he finished for her.

Her chest squeezed tight because that was exactly why she'd gone there that night. "Yes."

"Then what happened?" he asked with no reaction whatsoever to her revelation.

"Then," she said, forcing herself to go on because it was clear he didn't want to rehash anything regarding their relationship, "we heard Busir and his partner. They weren't in the collection room. They were deeper in the tomb."

"And?"

She looked down at the ground.

"Don't think about lying again, Kat. I want the whole truth this time. Not the watered-down version you fed me before."

She took a steadying breath so she could get through it. "I didn't want to go farther inside, but Sawil said we needed the proof. I . . . I followed. It was dark. I couldn't see more than an inch in front of my face. Sawil disappeared. I didn't know where he'd gone. I called out to him, but there was nothing. Then . . . the next thing I knew, someone had me by the hair. I heard two voices. Shouting. And someone growling in my ear that I was ruining everything. I was scared, and I fought back. I remember struggling, hitting the wall, going down. Then heavy breathing, like he was coming for me. I reached out, and luckily, somehow managed to grab a pick one of the workers had left behind. I struck. I'm . . . pretty sure I got him in the face.

"I ran. I could hear the other man behind me. Yelling. But I couldn't hear Sawil. I didn't know what had happened to him, and I knew I couldn't wait for him. When I reached the collection room, I remembered the camera. I . . . I grabbed it, just in case, and slipped it into my pocket.

"I couldn't go home. I was afraid they'd find me. So

I left a message for Shannon. Told her to get out of the apartment and wait to hear from me. By the time I got hold of Marty hours later to ask him what I should do, someone had already found Sawil's body. They killed him in that tomb. Because I'd dragged him into the whole mess."

Pete's jaw tightened, but otherwise he showed no emotion.

Refusing to be hurt by that, she went back to her story. And this time had to close her eyes because the pain she felt at just saying the words was as awful as it had been the day she'd heard the news. "Shannon never got my message. She'd been out with friends that night. When she got home, they were waiting for her."

Silence settled between them. A silence Kat couldn't read and didn't want to. Marty had told her he'd make sure Shannon was safe. Ultimately, he'd been too late. They both had.

She pushed the emotions aside as best she could and finally said, "I mailed you the pendant with the camera card hidden inside because I knew it would be safe with you. I never looked at it, so I don't even know if there's anything useable on it, but I figured if I ever needed to get it, I could."

"Why didn't you just turn it in then? Why the theatrics?"

What could she tell him that wouldn't sound insane? "After they killed Shannon, I knew I was screwed. Two dead bodies, linked to each other and me. My involvement with you. People knew there was tension between me and Sawil. All the evidence was pointing my way, and I had no solid alibi. Then I heard from them. They'd gotten a hold of my cell phone. They threatened my . . . family, and I didn't know who or how many were involved. I was scared. I thought disappearing was the safest thing I could do. Marty agreed. After the car bomb, though, and after everything died down," she shrugged, "there really wasn't any reason to go after it again."

"Until I put it up for auction."

"Yes." She finally looked up. "I couldn't let it fall into the wrong hands, and I couldn't afford to lose track of it."

He studied her with stormy eyes she just couldn't read. And she waited for the inevitable questions: *Why did you send it to me instead of Marty? And why didn't you come for it sooner?* But he never asked.

Instead, he said, "Well, go ahead. Open it. Show me this precious card you risked my life for."

Here? She stared at him in utter shock, then finally realized he was serious. He wasn't moving until she did just that. She glanced nervously up and down the road again. While there was no one around that she could see, it wouldn't be long before some nosy neighbor took notice of two strangers arguing on the corner of a quiet residential area.

She perched the backpack on her knee, leaned over and pawed through the bag until she found the pendant. Light from the streetlamp above highlighted the crouching pharaoh. She turned the statue over and looked at the flat bottom.

It was just as she remembered. With just enough pressure the false bottom would slide forward to reveal the hidden compartment inside. Only when she pushed, nothing happened.

A chill slid down her spine as she lifted the pendant for a closer look. No, not a false bottom. This thing was solid.

Dread started at the top of her head and rushed down her body like a tidal wave.

"Nice going, Kit-Kat," Pete purred in a mocking tone. "You stole the wrong necklace."

CHAPTER TWENTY-TWO

He was being a complete jackass, and he knew it. But as soon as he'd seen her step off that city bus, all those rational thoughts about playing it cool went sailing out the window.

"I . . ." Kat's wide eyes darted up to his. "Where is it?"

"I gave it away."

"What?" Disbelief pushed her voice higher.

"To a friend," he said casually. "A thanks, if you will, for convincing me to finally auction off all that Egyptian crap I'd been collecting over the years that was eating up room in my storage facility."

"You . . . you gave it to someone? Just like that?"

Was she upset because he'd given away her precious evidence or because she thought the necklace held some kind of sentimental value for him since it had come from her?

He couldn't quite tell. And he wasn't about to admit the reason he'd given that particular piece away was because it *did* hold a trace of sentimentality. It was the last thing she'd given him. The last thing she'd touched before—he thought, mistakenly—she'd died.

"Where?" she asked. "Where is it?"

"Someplace safer than your backpack."

He could see her wheels turning as she glanced around the empty street. Dusk was quickly fading to dark, but her worried features were clearly highlighted by the streetlamps above. "We have to get it back. You don't understand. If the wrong person finds it—"

"They won't. I'm more than confident it's locked up safe and sound. So tell me about Charles Latham."

Obviously resigned to the fact she wasn't getting rid of him, she dropped to the bench. "He was the director of our site in The Valley of the Kings."

"I already know that much."

"He . . ." She rubbed a hand over her brow. "I think he might have been in on the whole smuggling operation somehow. Sawil said he'd talked to Latham about what he suspected, but nothing ever happened. Latham never took Sawil's concerns to the SCA like he said he would. I know, because I checked with the SCA after Sawil's death."

"Maybe he was scared people were on to him."

"Maybe. Looking back now, Latham was acting strange those last few days. Watching Sawil, sneaking around almost. I didn't think much of it at the time, you know? I mean, I was distracted by what was happening with . . . us. But yeah, after, I knew something just wasn't right with Latham."

"So you came here to talk to him? If he's in on this, he could call Busir and this Minyawi freak and let him know where you are."

"Yeah," she nodded. "That's a possibility, but I wasn't intending to give him a chance to do that."

He thought of the gun he'd seen in her backpack. Just what the hell was this woman willing to do to save her own skin?

"Besides," she said before he could ask, "I don't really care what happens to me anymore. I just want it over."

Something unsettling rippled through him. If she didn't care about what happened to her, why was she going through all this in the first place?

"Then come on," he said, trying to push that thought aside. "Let's go find out."

The Latham house was a sprawling two story on the corner of a quiet street. A porch light shone through the darkness. Pumpkins left over from the fall holiday were still sitting on the front steps.

Pete grasped Kat's elbow before she could ring the bell. "Just so we're clear. Anything funny happens, you stick with me. None of this running-off-on-your-own crap again."

She nodded, and he knew she'd obey because he had the one thing she wanted: the necklace.

They waited thirty seconds, and when there was no answer, Kat rang the bell again. Just when Pete thought it was a dead end, he heard footsteps from inside the house.

The door pulled open a crack, and a middle-aged woman peered through the space. "Can I help you?"

Kat moved to the side so the woman could see her better. "My name's Katherine Meyer. I'm sorry to bother you so late, but I used to work with Charles Latham. This is my colleague, Peter Kauffman. We were wondering if we could speak with Charles for a moment about a project he was involved with several years ago."

"You used to work with Charles?"

Kat nodded. "Yes. A long time ago."

The woman's eyes darkened, and she pulled the door open farther. She was dressed in jeans and a black sweater, and though she looked tired, Pete had the impression of a striking woman in her midfifties. "In that case you must not have heard. Charles passed about a week ago."

Kat darted a look Pete's direction, and he didn't miss the how-convenient flash in her eyes. "I'm so sorry," she said to the woman. "I didn't know."

"Katherine Meyer," the woman said as if trying the name on for size. "Charles spoke about you." Her brow wrinkled, drawing a lock of salt-and-pepper hair forward to brush her cheek. "That would have been years ago, when he worked in Egypt."

"Yes," Kat said. "In the Valley of the Kings."

Pain, or maybe worry, crossed her face as the woman pulled the door open wider. "Why don't you come in? It's freezing outside."

Pete and Kat exchanged glances before stepping into the house. The entry opened into a sunken living room decorated in dark woods and burgundy furnishings.

"My name's Ann, by the way. Charles and I were married for twenty-two years." She gestured toward the sofa for them to sit. "I don't think we ever met, but I do remember Charles speaking about you after he came home."

"I heard he was sick. I'm sorry."

"Yes." Ann folded her hands in her lap. "It was a long illness. Cancer. In the end . . ." Pain etched her face as she looked toward a photo on the shelf across the room. "In the end he went peacefully, and I guess that's all I could ask for."

For a moment, Pete was transported back. To sitting on Lauren's patio. To flying up to Washington to see Kat's mother. To suffering through a memorial service he hadn't wanted to attend. He knew exactly what this widow was going through, because he'd lived it.

"Has anyone else Charles worked with in Egypt come by to see him in the past few weeks?" he asked.

"No, I don't believe that they have. Our daughter's here, visiting from Atlanta. She might know, but I'm sure she would have told me."

"You said he mentioned me," Kat said. "Can you tell me what that was about?"

"Not specifically, no. It was a long time ago. I do remember your name, though. A problem with the excavation, though he never elaborated." She ran a hand over her shoulder-length hair. "Those were some tough times. After he came home from the project in Egypt, he was withdrawn. We went through a rough patch, marriage-wise. I always knew something had happened there, but he didn't speak of it, and after a while I stopped trying to figure it out. He went back to work for the university after that, started teaching once more. He never went into the field again."

Kat looked Pete's way, and he knew she was thinking the same thing he was.

He glanced back at Ann Latham. "He didn't happen to save any of his research from the tomb he was working in, did he?"

Ann pursed her lips. "He might have. I'm pretty sure there's a box out in the garage with some of his work from that time. Would you like to look at it?"

Pete fought from jumping up and saying, *hell yeah!*

Kat, thankfully, was more tactful. Her smile was warm and sympathetic. "If you wouldn't mind."

"Actually," Ann said, rising, "you'd be doing me a favor. I wasn't sure what to do with it all, and I just can't look at it anymore. It brings back way too many memories."

She gestured for them to follow her. They passed through a sparkling kitchen with cherry cabinets and granite countertops, then through a door that led to the garage. Ann reached around the corner and flipped on the light. The two-bay garage was filled with boxes, some open, many closed and labeled in red marker. A chair was stacked on a desk. An old, ratty couch was pushed off to the side.

"My daughter and her husband spent all day emptying Charles's office at the university." Unshed tears filled her eyes. "I just don't know what I'm going to do with all of it. I swear I can still smell him in here."

Before either of them could answer, she turned to her left. "It's right over here. Some of these have been sitting out here for years. This particular box," she pushed a car-ton around, wove between a stack of cardboard until she found what she wanted, "was one he never took to the school. Ah, there it is."

"Here, let me." Pete stepped up to help her. The box she pointed to was labeled *Luxor*.

Pete pulled the box down so Kat could flip through it. Most of the contents were of little interest, but a small notebook caught Kat's eye. She lifted it, and when she glanced at Pete he saw the spark of excitement.

"You're more than welcome to take that with you," Ann said. "I don't know if it will help you with your continued research, but Charles was a stickler for details. If you're looking for some specific documentation, I'm sure it's in that journal."

"Thank you," Kat said. "That's what we're hoping for."

Ann Latham walked them to the front door. Pete handed the woman a business card as Kat stuck the journal in her backpack. "My private number's on the back. If you think of anything else, we'd appreciate if you'd call us. Anytime."

Ann Latham looked down at the card. "I will."

Before they left, Kat gave the woman a quick hug. "I'm very sorry for your loss."

"Thank you. Charles was a good man deep down. Oh, he wasn't perfect, and he had his demons, just like we all do, but he tried to live a decent life. And whatever wrongs he did, I forgave him for them a long time ago. It doesn't do any good to hold grudges. Life is too precious."

Kat smiled sadly. "I wish everyone were as wise as you, Mrs. Latham."

"It's not being wise. It's facing the loss of something you didn't realize you couldn't live without that makes you reevaluate your priorities."

Ann's words stuck in Pete's head as the door closed at their backs and they headed down the dark sidewalk. Kat was quiet as they moved, and Pete wasn't sure what was going through her head.

He pointed toward his rental two blocks down. When they reached the sedan, he unlocked the passenger door and waited while Kat climbed inside. He slid in next to her and sat staring out at the darkness, while Kat flipped on the overhead light and opened the notebook.

Thing was, he wasn't sure what was going through his own head at that moment either. Somewhere between ringing Ann Latham's doorbell and right now, all that anger he'd been stoking since she'd run out on him this morning had slowly seeped away until he just felt . . . empty.

"Oh, my God," Kat said at his side. "Look at this."

Pulled from his thoughts, Pete glanced over to where she was pointing to a list of dates and numbers. No, not numbers, he realized. Amounts. In Egyptian *gineih*, or pounds. Hundreds of thousands of pounds. And corresponding dates that referenced what looked like payments.

"He kept a log of his take?"

"No." Kat shook her head, and her voice dropped to a whisper. "You were right."

"About what?"

His eyes followed her finger as it ran up to the top of the page and the letters *P-A-N-E-K*.

"What's 'Panek'?" Pete asked.

Kat closed her eyes and tipped her head back against the headrest. "It's Egyptian. It means serpent in the old language. It was a joke, or so he said." Her face paled "Because he was tall and slim and could slink into caverns Latham and the others couldn't."

"Who?"

She opened her eyes and looked at him. "Sawil. Everyone called him Panek on the dig." She pressed her hand against her temple. "He really was in on it with Latham, like you suspected."

Pete looked over the multitude of numbers in her lap. No, not just in on it. From the dates, it looked like Ramirez had been filtering relics from the site long before Kat had even arrived in the Valley of the Kings. "That's why your accusations went unsubstantiated."

Kat nodded.

Pete thought back to Busir and that very well-timed call that had sealed Pete's fate and ruined his relationship with Kat. "Ramirez knew we were a couple. If he was working with Latham, then he knew Busir." And Ramirez had probably been adding fuel to Kat's paranoia over Pete and his possible involvement. "They set us up." When her eyes darted his way, he added, "You blew the whistle, and you weren't going away. They had to get rid of you."

And Pete could see two ways to do that. One, set her up to take the fall if the SCA did get involved and started sniffing around, or two, kill her. Busir had known Pete would take the bait that day, and that explained how they'd gotten the relics into her apartment. Then Ramirez had lured her to the tomb that night when Pete had walked out, to finish the job. He suspected they'd planned to kill Shannon all along, because of her involvement with Kat, but kept that little gem to himself.

"I don't . . ." Kat shook her head. "I can't believe that. If Sawil was involved, if what you're insinuating is even remotely true, then he had to have changed his mind. They *killed* him."

"How do you know?"

"What do you mean how do I know? I was there!"

"Did you see his body?" When she opened her mouth to protest he added, "Because trust me, dead doesn't always mean dead."

She stared at him. Closed her mouth. Then slowly shut the notebook in her lap and looked down at her hands. "He was declared dead. It was all over the news the next day. And he . . . he was my friend," she whispered.

"He wasn't your friend, Kat. He was using you."

Pete's words hung in the air between them, and he

realized in the silence, she was thinking the same thing about him. That he'd used her, lied to her. That when it came right down to it, he was no better than Sawil Ramirez.

And why that suddenly left a hole the size of a baseball in his chest, he didn't know. He reached for the key in the ignition to give him something else to focus on.

The front windshield shattered with a deafening crack that sent glass raining over both of them before he had a chance to start the engine.

CHAPTER TWENTY-THREE

"Pete!"

Kat was lying across the console underneath him, the backpack clutched to her chest, pure terror in her voice.

"I'm okay." He lifted his head just enough to look through the now missing windshield and spotted a man stepping out from behind a nearby tree with something metallic glinting in his hand beneath the streetlight.

"Go, get out of the car right now!"

He half pushed, half pulled her out of the car. They both hit the pavement on his side of the car just as another shot fired off, flew through the rental and took out the back windshield.

Bits of glass littered the street and felt like they were stuck in his clothing. He looked up at Kat's wide, frightened eyes, and realized, yeah, they were both dead if they didn't get out of here ASAP.

"Are you hit?" she asked in a frantic voice.

"No. I'm . . ." *Fuuuuck*. ". . . okay. Are you?"

She shook her head fiercely as she scrambled to her feet, careful to keep low behind the car. She stuffed the journal they'd taken from Latham's house into her backpack. One quick glance around and he knew they'd have to make a stand or hoof it. He grasped the gun at his back, racked the slide to chamber a round and inched around the vehicle to get a good shot. "When I say go, go."

"Pete—"

"Don't argue with me." He saw the man, ten yards closer than he'd been before. And oh yeah, this one had been at the farm in Pennsylvania. No doubt about it. When the guy lifted the gun and pointed their way, Pete let off a round and yelled, "Go!"

She must have listened, because before he knew it, she was gone. He got off a couple more shots, heard a yelp, followed by a string of curses, and said a prayer he'd hit the SOB someplace where it did serious damage.

Then he took off after Kat, heading for an open gate he spotted between two houses. Something whooshed by his ear a fraction of a second before wood splintered in the fence directly in front of them.

Shit.

He ducked to the side. Realized he'd never be able to stop and set up again before the guy got off more shots. If their pursuer was injured, though, they could outrun him. Ahead he could just barely see Kat racing in the shadows. Good idea.

He kept running. They streaked through backyards, avoided barking dogs, up over fences and down the other sides. His shoulder hurt like a bitch where he'd hit the pavement, but he had to hand it to Kat, she didn't look back once, not even to see if he'd gotten away or if he was with her now.

When they were a good mile away, she finally slowed and leaned against a tree to take a few breaths.

"I think . . . we lost him," he said, sucking back air. Damn, but the woman was in good shape. Better than him.

"Did you get a look at him?" Her chest rose and fell as she glanced around the quiet street they'd just crossed, but she wasn't huffing nearly as badly as he was. "Was it Busir or Minyawi?"

He shook his head and leaned forward on his knees. Okay, he was starting up his running program again. As soon as this whole nightmare was over. "It was . . . one of the guys from the park. I think I may have hit him. I'm not sure."

"They couldn't have followed us. They must have figured I'd try to see Latham."

He nodded and continued to breath deep. "Yeah . . . that'd be my guess."

"Are you sure you're okay? You don't look so good."

"I'm . . . fine," he said again, just as the disposable cell he'd bought rang. He pulled it from his pocket, knowing only one person had this number, and took another long breath. "Talk to me."

"Hello to you, too," Hailey said smugly. "Bad day?"

"You don't want to know."

"For some reason I believe you. Word to the wise, though. I think your day's about to get even worse."

"Wonderful. Lay it on me."

"I finally heard back from Jill Monroe at INTERPOL."

As Hailey talked, Pete glanced at Kat, who was studying him with intense eyes. "And?"

"Egyptian Liberation Army. Mean anything to you?"

"I've heard the name in the news," he said warily. "What's that got to do with this?"

Hailey blew out a long breath. "Aten Minyawi is a known hit man for the ELA. They're thought to be an offshoot of the Egyptian Islamic Jihad. Al-Jihad, the EIJ, the Jihad-group, the Jihad-organization. Call it what you will, anyway you say it, it adds up to really bad news."

"Christ," Pete muttered, rubbing a hand over his hair.

"Yeah, well, you might want to think about saying your prayers, Pete. Because it looks like your girl there is the only witness to what could possibly be a major international fiasco."

Kat reached up to play with the medallion at her chest as she watched Pete on the phone. He was looking at her, but the way he'd gone on alert as soon as he'd answered told her whatever he'd just learned couldn't be good.

He motioned for her to keep walking as he continued his conversation. "Yeah, I got it. What else?"

They walked another block, then approached a major thoroughfare. As if luck were on their side, a cab approached. Kat waved it down, and they slid inside.

Pete eased the phone away from his mouth and gave the driver directions, then went back to whoever was on the other end of the line.

Kat tuned out his conversation and stared out the dark window and the blur of lights rushing by. Her heart was still pumping a mile a minute.

The cab pulled into what looked like a small municipal airport. Without a word to her, he paid the driver, popped the door and gestured for her to join him, all the while talking into his phone. "Yeah, I'm sure, Hailey. See what you can find out about his contacts. And see if you can get a photo. This cheap phone I got can accept photos, just can't send them."

Kat had to pick up her pace to keep up with him. They moved across the parking lot, into the small terminal and out through another set of double doors onto the tarmac. A thousand questions fired off in her brain, but she didn't have the strength to ask them. Was simply thankful they'd lost whoever was taking potshots at them through the trees.

Pete pointed toward a streamlined jet, lights flashing, engines running, and tipped the mouthpiece of his phone away from his lips. "Climb aboard," he said to her. "I'll be right there."

Kat stared from him to the shiny Bombardier Challenger 850 and back again. He pushed her forward when she would have kept standing there gaping and went back to his conversation.

Alone, Kat climbed the steps of the plane. Cream-colored leather chairs, a long couch, teak woods and wide windows greeted her eyes.

She dropped her pack on a seat and bent over to look out the window. Pete was still talking on his cell. His hair was a mess, and his shirt was covered in grime. He'd lost the jacket somewhere along the way, and scrapes ran across his face from where he'd hit the pavement, but he wasn't seriously hurt. And he was alive.

This time. No thanks to her.

That thought churned in her stomach as she walked down the small aisle, past a set of four chairs with low tables between them. At the end of the corridor was a door. She eased it open. To the left sat the galley, complete with any kind of liquor a person could want and an assortment of snack foods. To the right, the lavatory. Ahead there was another door.

Her jaw nearly hit the floor when she looked inside. What could have been extra seating was in fact an elaborate bedroom suite, complete with overstuffed mattress and pillows, two dark teak side tables and a large beveled mirror hanging on the back wall.

The entire plane was bigger than the house she'd grown up in with her mother in Washington. This one room probably cost more than her apartment back in upstate

New York. Definitely more opulent, way more comfortable. And very, very enticing. Her mouth went dry as she thought about the next few hours trapped on this plane, alone, with Pete.

"We're about to take off," he said at her back.

Startled, Kat whipped around. "I didn't hear you come in."

He looked from her to the bed, then headed back to the main cabin. "You need to take your seat so we can get out of here."

For a moment she stood there. Wondered what he'd thought when he'd looked at that bed. Wondered if he'd remembered what they'd done in that motel last night.

Yeah, right. He'd nearly been killed because of her. Only an idiot would be thinking about sex at a time like this.

Kat followed him out into the main cabin and sank into a chair at his right. "Where are we going?"

He pushed a button on the console to his left. "We're all set, Steve. Whenever you're ready."

"Roger that, Mr. Kauffman," a voice replied over a speaker in the ceiling. "We've already been cleared for takeoff. We should be in the air momentarily."

Pete finally looked her way. "That was a business colleague on the phone. I asked her to do a little research for me before I tracked you down today. This is her company plane."

Kat had a handful of questions about what, exactly, "business colleague" meant and what kind of person owned their own luxury jet, but she shelved them in favor of what she was most curious about. "What kind of research?"

He used a towel he must have picked up in the galley to wipe his dirty face. "Background."

She watched for any sign he was more hurt than he looked. She didn't see it. "On who?"

He reached over and cinched her seat belt tighter, then

handed her the towel. "Your friend Minyawi. Turns out he's with the ELA."

His unconscious action would have touched her, but Kat's skin went cold at his blunt revelation. The other questions floating around in her head vanished into thin air as she gripped the towel in her hand. She barely felt the plane rocketing down the runway or the landing gear lifting off the ground as she thought back to what she'd heard about the terrorist organization when she'd been working in Cairo. "The Egyptian Liberation Army."

"Yep. They're thought to be closely affiliated with the Egyptian Islamic Jihad, whose—"

"Part of the Muslim Brotherhood," she finished for him. "The largest political opposition party in Egypt."

Pete nodded. "And a close ally of Al-Qaeda. I don't know if you've watched the news lately, but several members of the Brotherhood—some upstanding businessmen even—are on trial in Egypt right now for money laundering and what the press is calling 'financing of an illegal group.'"

"The ELA," she said quietly as links fell into place.

"That'd be my guess. The Brotherhood holds over a fifth of the seats in parliament. They'll do just about anything to undermine the Egyptian government."

Kat's eyes lifted to his. "Even to go so far as to raid their country's archaeological treasures to make their point."

"Bingo," Pete said. Frowning, he took the towel from her hand and leaned over to wipe her cheek. "And if that's the case, it means someone high up in the government is aware this is going on and either doesn't care or is making a butt-load of money through the exchange. It's the only way it could happen."

"Possibly someone with the Supreme Council of Antiquities," she said, "which is why nothing ever came of my reports."

"Yeah, that would make sense, too." He tossed the dirty towel on the couch across the cabin.

She was silent as she thought through everything he'd told her. Then looked up. "If that's true, then who was the man in the park?"

Before Pete could answer, the pilot's voice came over the intercom again. "We've reached cruising altitude. Weather should be pretty calm all the way up the coast, so feel free to move about the cabin. I'll let you know if we hit any turbulence."

Pete unsnapped his seat belt and rose. "Another bit of interesting information my contact was able to dredge up." He pushed the galley door open. Kat twisted in her seat and watched as he added ice to two glasses, poured amber liquid into each and came back. He handed her one as he sat. "The man in the park was identified as Dean Bertrand."

She took the drink he offered. "I don't recognize the name. Should I?"

"I doubt it. He's ex-INTERPOL. Used to work out of their London Branch. Three years ago he was aiding the British government after a terrorist subway bombing in London. Remember seeing that on the news?"

"Yes, I think so."

"Guess who INTERPOL thinks was involved in that hit?"

Kat's glass hesitated halfway to her mouth. "Minyawi?"

"Yep. And according to INTERPOL's records, Bertrand was the only agent who's ever gotten close to the SOB. Nearly brought him down, but the op went south, and Minyawi got away. And this part you'll love. In return for getting close to him, Minyawi tracked down Bertrand's wife when the man was out of town. Raped and murdered her, then sent the photos of what he'd done to Bertrand via FedEx."

"Oh, my God." Kat closed her eyes.

"Not a nice guy, this Minyawi," Pete said quietly.

No, not nice at all. She remembered seeing pictures of what they'd done to Shannon. Pete's description of Bertrand's wife was too close. Kat's stomach rolled.

She tried to focus on the facts and not a past she couldn't change. "How did this Bertrand know where to find us, though? Is he a friend of Marty's?"

Pete tossed back his whiskey, shook his head. "No. That's where it gets even more interesting. Late last night, a woman in Philly reported something strange from the apartment across the hall. Cops went in, found a body. Identified the victim as retired FBI agent David Halloway. He'd been shot in the head. Authorities don't have a suspect yet, but my contact's link at INTERPOL said Bertrand had routinely worked with the FBI's Art Theft Crime Team, which Halloway was a part of before his retirement."

It all started to make sense to her. "Marty was working antiterrorism in North Africa. If he suspected this link between the smuggling and the ELA, that explains how he knew Halloway. They'd worked together."

It also explained why Marty had started dating her. Though she didn't want to think about that in too much detail. The knowledge she'd been used by three men she'd cared about was a little more than she wanted to deal with right now.

"Possibly."

"And Halloway and Bertrand?" she said. "They were what, working together now? That doesn't gel."

"Or passing information back and forth on unsolved cases. For whatever reason, neither of these guys were out of the picture even though they weren't on the payrolls anymore."

"So it's possible Halloway tipped Bertrand off about my phone call."

"Looks that way."

"And Bertrand killed him? To get to me?"

"Not to get to you, Kat. To get to Minyawi."

Kat thought back to the scene in the park with Bertrand. *How many more you got, Minyawi? We can do this all night. But I guarantee I'll kill the girl myself before I'll give her to you!*

No, Pete was right. Bertrand hadn't wanted her. He'd wanted revenge on the man who'd murdered his wife.

She stared at the cream-colored leather seat in front of her as a heavy weight pressed down on her chest. This whole nightmare was bigger than even she'd imagined. How on earth could she ever expect to clear her name and keep Pete out of it in the process with what they were facing?

"So what now?" she asked into the silence that settled between them.

"Now we go get your necklace back."

Kat looked his way. "Where?"

"New York City."

Her brows drew together. "We were just there."

"Yeah."

And that was when she realized just who his friend was who had her pendant. "Oh."

The sickness she'd been fighting came roaring back as the plane dipped to the left and cut through the inky darkness. She gripped the armrest of her chair, closed her eyes and fought to clear her mind of terrorists and corrupt politicians and a faction that didn't care about anything but seeing her dead.

And she did. Because, as trivial as it was considering everything they'd just been through, the only thing she could think about right now was the fact she was heading right into the piranha's waters.

Hailey Roarke peered into the dark windows of Lauren Kauffman's fancy house on Key Biscayne. No lights shone in the entry or front rooms, but that didn't mean Lauren wasn't home. It also didn't mean she was.

Hailey knocked again and waited, and when there was no answer, pulled the key Pete had told her to pick up from his office at Odyssey from her pocket and slipped it in the lock.

The door gave with a pop, and Hailey stepped in, went to the alarm and punched in the code. When the light flashed green she kicked the door closed and stood in the dimly lit entryway, listening for any sound inside the house. "Lauren?"

The last thing Pete had asked Hailey to do was to swing by Lauren's place and make sure his sister wasn't home. And if she was, to talk her into disappearing for a while. At least until things cooled off for him. He didn't put it past the ELA to go after his sister to get to him and Kat, and neither did Hailey.

When there was no response, Hailey wove through the downstairs and checked rooms for any sign Lauren had been home from her most recent photo shoot. She had a habit of popping in and out of Miami unannounced, which was what concerned Pete most.

The kitchen was sparkling clean, as were the rest of the rooms downstairs. No tossed jackets, no shoes lying askew. None of the ten thousand bags Lauren generally traveled with littering the floor.

Feeling more at ease by the second, Hailey jogged up-stairs to check Lauren's office to see if she'd left her calen-dar laying about, possibly indicating when she might be back or where she was scheduled to be now. Pete hadn't had a clue where his sister was but wanted her found, and considering tracking down the supermodel was a lot more fun than dealing with her father's stuffy secretary, Hailey'd jumped at the chance to help.

Besides, Hailey liked Lauren. Sure, Lauren could be a prima donna, but she had spunk. And any woman who could put Peter Kauffman in his place was a friend in Hailey's book.

She pushed open the office door, flipped on the light and skimmed the calendar on Lauren's fancy glass desk. The phone rang as she was sitting in the plush leather chair, flipping pages in Lauren's datebook. Her hand stilled as the call went to the answering machine.

"Lauren, it's Blake. I know you're home. Pick up the phone."

Home? Hailey glanced up.

"Look, baby," Blake said. "We need to talk. Lauren? Can you hear me? Dammit. I know you're there." He let out a long sigh. "Just call me back, okay?"

The call ended with a beep before Hailey could pick up the receiver. She recognized the name. Lauren's life was often splashed all over the tabloids, and Blake Warner was her newest boy-toy. Something had obviously happened between the two of them. Good ol' Blake had sounded pissed. And a little desperate.

"Man trouble," Hailey mumbled, glancing back at the datebook in front of her. "Nice to know I'm not the only one." A frown cut across Hailey's face as she scanned the page, and her mind wandered to her own version of man trouble.

Which really wasn't much trouble at all because you had to *have* a man to have man trouble, which Hailey definitely didn't. The last guy she'd even been remotely interested in—a homicide detective from Chicago who she *thought* she'd forged a connection with at Rafe and Lisa's wedding just a few weeks ago—had stood her up the following morning where they'd made plans to meet for breakfast. And wasn't that just her damn luck? Her track record with men sucked. So much for that outlook improving.

The phone in her pocket beeped, and she pulled it out, looked at the text from her friend Jill at INTERPOL and smiled. She immediately forwarded the message to Pete and hoped he had his phone turned on.

Refusing to think any more about Shane Maxwell and those sexy and mysterious eyes of his, Hailey flipped the datebook closed, slipped her phone back in her pocket and stood. Considering Blake's message, it was possible Lauren was on her way home right this minute.

A car door slammed outside, the sound easily discernible through the quiet evening air. Hailey lifted her head and listened. Footsteps echoed from somewhere near the front of the house.

Bingo.

She hit the light switch and jogged back down the steps, wanting to intercept Lauren before the poor girl got the scare of her life and realized the front door was unlocked.

Hailey reached the entryway and jerked the heavy mahogany door open. Then stopped short.

The man staring back at her wasn't the blond supermodel she'd expected. This guy was easily six-foot-three, with a mane of dark hair, a full beard and black, soulless eyes. A thin scar ran down the left side of his face and gave the impression of badass to the core.

And when he smiled, his slow and evil grin sent a shiver of foreboding down Hailey's spine. She knew the face, because she'd just looked at it on her phone moments before.

"Hello, Miss Kauffman," he said in a heavily accented voice. "Your presence is honorably requested by an associate of mine."

Oh, Fuck. Minyawi.

Hailey slammed the door closed with all her strength, but Minyawi snaked a hand and foot inside and grabbed her by the hair before she got two steps away. More good luck for her. She'd left her Browning in the glove box of her car.

In a flash she was on her stomach, face pressed into those gleaming tiles she'd walked across earlier, a knee shoved hard into her back. Her phone went skidding across the floor to land behind a large potted plant. The air whooshed out of her lungs as something sharp was jabbed into her arm.

The last thought she had was Pete's teasing that she'd never been a very good cop.

No shit, Sherlock.

CHAPTER TWENTY-FOUR

"That was a wonderful dinner."

Maria Gotsi lifted her wineglass and took a sip as she regarded the man seated across from her at Per Se over-looking Central Park West. Candlelight illuminated his round features, pudgy face and dark eyes. Though she wouldn't consider him a personal friend, the fact a man of his standing had called and invited her dinner had intrigued her. So she'd accepted.

"I do have to say, though," she said as she set her glass on the white linen tablecloth, "it was a bit of a surprise."

"As much as a surprise for me," Omar Kamil said in a thick Middle Eastern accent as he leaned forward in his seat. "Not only was I stunned to find out you were in New York, but also that you were free this evening."

Maria smiled one of her coy half grins and fiddled with the stem of her wineglass. She'd learned the game early on. Give the men in this industry what they expected. That meant flirt, tease, pay attention to what they did and said around you and never ever let them figure out how smart you really were.

Then strike when they least expected it.

It was how she'd built the Art Institute of Athens from a fledgling scientific laboratory into one of the premier archaeometry centers in the world. It was also how she'd become a major player in a male-dominated field.

"Well," she said, leaning forward just enough so her black fitted jacket pushed her cleavage together in a move that clearly caught his attention, "as it turns out, I recently had a change in plans. I was due back in Athens this evening, but a situation at my warehouse here in New York forced me to rethink my plans."

"Situation?" Omar's gaze flicked from Maria's exposed breasts up to her face. His beady eyes took on an amused gleam. "What type of situation?"

Oh, yes. She'd been right. There was something going on here. A man like Kalim didn't simply phone for dinner and show up out of the blue unless he wanted something.

The question was, what could he possibly want from her?

"Nothing more than a personnel issue." She smiled again, ran her finger around the stem of her wineglass. "And how are your preparations at the Met?"

He waved a hand and eased back in his seat. "Fine, fine. Between you and me, my assistant could have handled the transfer and overseen the setup, but it was a good excuse for me to get out of the heat. And besides, it gave me the opportunity to dine with you."

"Hm," Maria said, not buying a line of his bull. "It definitely did."

He opened his mouth to reply, but her cell phone chiming cut him off.

"I'm sorry," she said, retrieving the RAZR from her sleek handbag. "With all the commotion at the warehouse, I should take this." She lifted the phone to her ear. "Dr. Gotsi."

"It's Pete."

Surprise hit her. She hadn't heard from Peter since the auction and didn't plan to talk to him anytime soon. She looked across the table at Omar, who was studying her with unreadable eyes. "You are the last person I expected to hear from tonight."

"I know. Listen, Maria, about what happened at the auction—"

"Forgotten," she said quickly. She didn't want to get into a discussion regarding Peter's auction with Omar watching her so closely, and frankly, she wasn't entirely sure how she felt about what had happened between them. Though she enjoyed Peter's company, and he had—contrary to her better judgment—become a friend over the years, she wasn't interested in a relationship in any way, shape or form. Of course, when she was out with a man for the evening, she wasn't interested in being second fiddle either. If she wasn't enough to hold his attention, then there was no sense in seeing him again, friend or not.

"I'm glad to hear it," Peter said in a clearly relieved voice. "Because I need a favor."

Something in his tone hit her as slightly anxious, and it piqued her interest because Peter Kauffman was never anything but cool and completely composed.

"Just what did you have in mind?" she asked hesitantly.

"I'll discuss it with you tonight, if you're available. I should be in New York within the hour. I'd like to come by your building, if that's all right."

He was coming to New York? Something was definitely going on. She glanced at her watch. "Yes, that should be fine."

"Great. I really appreciate this, Maria."

"Hm," was all she said. She still had no idea just what she'd agreed to.

She flipped her phone closed and smiled at Omar. "Sorry for the interruption."

He lifted his glass and took a long swallow of wine. "Boyfriend?"

With a humorless laugh she tucked a strand of hair behind her ear. "No. Nothing like that." Whatever Peter needed from her most definitely wasn't of the romantic nature. It never had been. "Just a friend."

The waiter stepped up to the table. "Can I interest either of you in dessert?"

Maria shook her head. "No, I think just the check."

"Oh, come now, Maria," Omar said as he lifted the dessert menu and shot her a wicked grin he'd developed over the last few minutes. "You have time for a little sinful pleasure, don't you?"

Something in his eyes warned her not to brush him off so quickly. And though Maria had no idea why, she complied. Peter could wait for her. After the way he'd treated her at the auction, he could just go on waiting.

Pete leaned forward in the seat as the cab pulled to a stop in front of Maria's building. Outside, rain pummeled the street in sheets, and water ran off the eaves to pour onto the sidewalk below. He handed the cabbie a wad of cash and opened the door.

With Kat's backpack in one hand, he hunched his shoulders and reached down to help her out of the taxi. The snow that had covered the sidewalk days before had long since washed away, and the gutters were steadily filling with water and overflowing onto the street. At this hour, in this weather, there wasn't another soul around.

He grasped her hand tight as they jogged toward the covered entrance. When they got there, they both shook the water from their hair.

Kat shot a worried glance toward the alley. Water dripped from her short hair down across her temple.

"What is it?" Pete asked, reaching up to wipe the droplet from her cheek before he thought better of it.

"I . . ." Her head lifted, and in her eyes he saw what looked like worry and regret and . . . something else he couldn't quite read. "Never mind." She stepped past him and into the building where the doorman held the door.

She'd been unusually quiet ever since he'd announced they were headed back to New York, and on the drive from the airport she'd avoided all small talk like the plague. It didn't take a rocket scientist to figure out she was ticked about being here.

He chanced a glance at her as they stood at the elevator waiting for the car, watched her jaw clench and unclench as she stared at the shiny doors. Her hair was damp from the rain and tousled from her fingers. Her cheeks were the slightest bit rosy—a combination of the November chill outside and a good dose of temper. His gaze ran lower, to her open jacket, to the vee of her T-shirt. To the St. Jude medal resting against her chest.

And standing there, studying her, a vision hit him. Of her above him, straddling him, smiling down into his eyes. Of that medal falling against his chest, grazing his skin as she moved. Of her leaning down and kissing him, long and slow and sumptuous until he couldn't get enough of her.

His chest tightened as Ann Latham's words ran though his head. *It's not being wise. It's facing the loss of something you didn't realize you couldn't live without that makes you reevaluate your priorities.*

He swallowed hard as the elevator door opened with a ping. A slightly balding, dark-skinned man wearing a long wool trench coat stepped out and pushed between them as he headed for the door. His shoulder smacked into Pete's already sore one, nearly knocking Pete off balance. Pain shot up his arm.

"'scuse," the man mumbled in a heavy accent as he rushed by.

Pete stepped into the elevator after Kat and turned to look back. "Excuse you," he muttered.

The man hesitated, and just as the elevator doors were closing, pivoted to look their way.

Pete turned the knob on the wall panel and punched the intercom for the penthouse suite with more force than necessary. "All kinds in this city," he mumbled. When Kat didn't respond, he glanced her way and was pretty sure he could see steam coming out of her ears.

Definitely not happy. Well, that made two of them. Bringing her here wasn't his first choice either, but they were out of options as far as he could see.

Maria's housekeeper answered the page, and Pete announced himself. Two seconds later the elevator began moving. "We'll only be a few minutes. Long enough to get the pendant and go."

"You could have left me in the car," Kat said through clenched teeth. "I didn't need to come up here."

"And leave you out there alone? Between you ditching me and guns going off, I don't think so."

The look she shot him said she'd rather take her chance with a loaded gun over him any day.

Okay, definitely ticked. And why the hell did that bug him so bad?

The elevator opened, and they both stepped out into the vestibule. Since Maria's penthouse occupied the entire floor, there was only one double door directly ahead. Kat tensed. Pete moved forward and knocked.

A young woman Pete didn't recognize but who had to be Maria's new housekeeper opened the door.

He waited for Kat to step in first, then followed. Maria appeared on the curved staircase that led to the second floor. Dark hair flowed down around her shoulders. She wore loose-fitting black silk pants and a long-sleeved charcoal tunic, looking just as perfect as she always did, even in lounging attire.

"You're later than I expected, Peter," she said as she descended the last few steps. Her black mules clicked on the marble floor when she reached the first level, and her eyes ran over him from head to toe. "And you look like hell."

From the corner of his eye, Pete watched Kat's shoulders stiffen, but to her credit, she didn't cross her arms or scowl or show any other outward sign she was upset. Pete had to hand it to her. If the roles were reversed and she'd brought him to see Slade, he'd have already decked the guy.

"Weather's pretty nasty outside. Took us longer than we expected."

"Hm." Maria shifted her gaze to Kat and extended her hand. "I'm Maria Gotsi."

Kat hesitated, then took Maria's offered hand. "Katherine Meyer."

"She's an old friend," Pete interjected.

"Hm," Maria said again as her eyes narrowed on Kat.

Tension swirled in the room between the two women. The scene in the limo the night of the auction flashed in Pete's brain. At that moment, a fifty-foot drop into a boiling ocean looked more appealing than being trapped between these two.

He opened his mouth to ease the tension, but Maria cut him off.

"I recognize you from the auction," she said, dropping Kat's hand. "Black washes out your coloring." She transferred her attention back to Pete. "Now, what exactly did you want from me, Peter, that couldn't wait until tomorrow?"

Same old Maria. Blunt and to the point, especially when a situation wasn't in her control. The barb didn't go unnoticed by Kat. From the corner of his eye, Pete watched a muscle in Kat's jaw twitch, but she still didn't utter a sound, and she didn't once take her eyes off Maria.

"We came to get the necklace I gave you a few weeks ago," Pete said. "The gold crouching pharaoh."

Maria looked between them. "Why, exactly, do you need it back?"

Pete glanced toward Kat and lifted his brow. This was her deal, really. He figured whatever she wanted to share with Maria was up to her.

Kat lifted her chin. "Because he didn't have the right to give it to you. It's mine."

Silence.

"I see," Maria finally said, brushing a finger down her neck. "However, we're in America. And possession is nine-tenths of the law in this country. So why don't you both stop dancing around the facts and tell me just what's so important about *this* necklace that has you both running here when it's very obvious my home is the last place either of you wants to be?"

Kat looked his way, and he saw the indecision in her chocolate eyes. He nodded, silently telling her unless they cooperated, they probably weren't getting diddly squat from Maria.

Kat shifted back toward Maria, and in her eyes Pete saw strength and certainty and a woman who would do just about anything to get what she wanted. Something familiar turned over in his chest. She wasn't the timid girl he'd fallen in love with all those years before. She was a thousand times sexier and a million times more intriguing. And so damn focused he wanted to kiss her senseless and drag her off to bed like a caveman and let her tame him in any way she wanted. Which was nuts considering everything she'd put him through in the last two days.

"I sent it to him," Kat said. "There's something inside that could be crucial to an international investigation." She shrugged in indifference. "Of course, it's your choice whether to keep it or give it to us. But if you keep it, the Feds could charge you with impeding an investigation. Or even collusion."

Doubt colored Maria's features. She swung her gaze

back his way. "An international investigation," she said blankly. "Involving one or both of you. Recently?"

Pete shook his head. "Long time ago."

Maria's eyes narrowed. "Why do I get the feeling there's more to this than that?"

Because there was. And because she was a smart woman. Pete didn't answer.

Neither did Kat.

Maria's mules clicked as she crossed to the sideboard and poured herself a glass of wine. She took a long swallow and looked toward Pete again. "I'm afraid it's not here."

"Where is it?" Kat asked quickly.

Maria shrugged as if she could care less about Kat's question, in the same way Kat had shrugged moments before. "In storage."

"Here in New York City?"

"Possibly. I've had several shipments sent back to Athens in the last few days. It's *possible* it was in one of those."

Kat sent Pete a worried look.

"Or," Maria went on, "It's *possible* it's still in the vault."

"Then let's go check," Pete said. "We can't wait until your shipments arrive in Greece and your employees unpack the crates."

Maria laughed. "Peter, it's nearly eleven o'clock. The building is closed, the vault is locked and even I can't get access to the security codes until the morning. I'm afraid you're stuck until tomorrow."

Kat turned away in a clear sign of frustration and glanced around the apartment. And Pete felt the first stirrings of unease.

He'd hoped to get the necklace and get Kat the hell out of New York before dawn. He didn't like being here, where they could be seen driving around the city or walking into a hotel. Odds were they hadn't been followed, but he couldn't be sure, and he sure as hell wasn't risking his life—or Kat's—on a handful of maybes. He'd seen first-hand what these guys were capable of.

The more he thought about the fact they'd been set up, that Busir had used him to get to Kat in the first place, the more determined he was to make sure she got out of this alive.

Options ran through his head. And though he knew the one that popped up strongest was the worst of the bunch, it was also the safest.

"Fine," Pete said. "We'll go with you to get it in the morning. But in the meantime, I need one more favor."

Maria lifted her brows in question but didn't respond.

"We need a place to stay tonight."

Kat whipped back toward him in a blur.

"What?" both women asked at the same time.

"Just for tonight," he said, ignoring Kat's reaction. "As soon as we have the necklace, we'll be out of your hair."

"No way," Kat exclaimed. "I'm not spending one single—"

A sly smile spread across Maria's face as she, too, ignored Kat's reaction. "That could be interesting."

She lifted a bell on the sideboard and shook it. The housekeeper scurried in from the kitchen. "Mabel," Maria said. "Show Ms. Meyer to the guest room. She"—her gaze ran up and down Kat's damp, dirty clothing—"looks like she could use a towel."

The air chilled at Pete's side, and he could feel Kat's eyes boring into him like icy daggers, but he didn't turn to look. This was the safest place for her right now, whether she liked it or not.

Maria glanced back to Pete with a victorious smile that made his blood run cold. He knew Kat saw it, just as he knew he wouldn't do a damn thing about it.

"I, on the other hand," Maria said, "would like some time alone with you, Peter. We have some unfinished business, don't you agree?"

CHAPTER TWENTY-FIVE

Maria watched Katherine Meyer stalk up the stairs. The dark-haired woman didn't bother to look back, which was just fine with Maria. She was happy to finally have her out of the room.

Maria turned toward the sideboard again when they were alone. "Drink, Peter?"

He cut his gaze from the stairs with a scowl. "You can be a real bitch when you want, you know that?"

Maria laughed, poured a finger of bourbon and handed it to him. "And you are never a man a woman can predict." She watched as he set his untouched glass on the coffee table and sank into a side chair. Alone, he looked tired. Run-down. Beat. Maria couldn't help wondering just what had happened over the last two days to steal the spunk and style from Peter Kauffman.

She perched on the arm of the sofa across from him and pursed her lips. When it was obvious he wasn't going to volunteer any information, she said, "She was the one at the auction you went after, wasn't she?"

He hesitated, then nodded.

"Former lover?"

He hesitated again, then nodded.

"Why do I get the impression there's more to it than that?"

"Why do you keep asking that same question?" he said with a scowl.

She couldn't help it. She smiled. "Why are you not being

honest with me? Have I not stuck my neck out for you several times in the past? Are we not friends? Suddenly this woman breezes back into your life, and you trust no one but her?"

Peter let out a weary sigh and dropped his head back against the cushions. "She's not just any woman," he finally said. "She's the one who changed my life."

"I see," Maria said quietly, though she didn't, not really. Peter's past was as blank to her as hers was to him, and for a moment, she considered letting the whole thing drop. True, he was her friend, but there was a reason she'd kept their relationship strictly sexual. She didn't want to deal with anyone else's baggage.

She thought of the way he'd looked at Katherine Meyer, with tenderness in his eyes and a longing she'd not seen on another man's face in . . . years. And she suddenly wondered if she'd been fooling herself. Maybe he'd been the one keeping their relationship strictly sexual. Maybe she wasn't as in control of things as she thought she was.

"I'm a good listener, Peter," she said in a softer voice.

He lifted his head and studied her with speculative eyes. Then rose and walked to the window where he looked out at the rain dousing the city in waves. "There's not much to tell," he said as he pulled the curtain to the side.

"Oh, I think there is. It's obvious she wriggled herself under your skin. In fact, I think, somehow, she broke your heart."

When he scoffed, Maria knew she was right.

And it wasn't jealousy that coursed through her as she looked at his somber face reflected back into the room by the window pane, but curiosity. No matter what he said, this woman meant more to him than just about anything else. It was written all over his face, in the deep lines around his mouth and in his haunted eyes. Though she'd vowed never to let herself get close to another like that again, she wasn't so completely coldhearted that she couldn't empathize with someone going through the same thing.

"Why don't you tell me about this pendant and what she was doing at the auction?"

He dropped the curtain and turned to look her way. "It holds evidence pertaining to a crime she witnessed in Cairo when she was working there. We met there. She's been in hiding ever since for fear of retaliation by the real criminals."

"You knew about this?"

He shook his head. "I thought she was dead."

"Oh."

And that was how the woman had broken his heart, Maria realized. Her gaze dropped to his untouched glass on the table in front of her as links to the story fell into place. "She faked her death."

"Yeah. She was afraid they'd come after her family if she just disappeared. She had to make it look like she'd died."

"Where is her family now?"

"She doesn't have any left. Her mother passed about two years ago. Heart attack."

"Why did you not know about any of this?"

"She didn't trust me with it. There were other things between us then."

"I see," Maria said again. But her brow wrinkled as she thought through what he'd said. "Why did she come back for it now?"

"Because I was selling it, and she was afraid it might fall into the wrong hands."

"But you didn't sell it."

"Nope," he said, moving to study a painting on the far wall. "I didn't. She picked up the wrong necklace at the auction."

"It seems to me a woman who can break into a Worthington auction and steal a prominent piece of art from underneath security's nose isn't helpless. You've had that pendant for years, and your security isn't nearly as rigid as Worthington's. She could have broken into your gallery at any time to get it. Why now?"

He shrugged as he straightened the painting on the wall. "I don't know. Maybe she was tired of hiding. Maybe she wanted her life back."

Maria frowned. "I don't buy that. If this evidence could have cleared her of any wrongdoing on her part, she could have come out of hiding at any time. There's something else going on here, Peter. She's protecting someone."

His hand paused on the frame of the painting, and slowly he turned to face her. Questions, and something that looked oddly like realization, raced across his classic features.

"What?" Maria asked, puzzled by his reaction.

"Nothing. I just . . ." His brow lowered. He seemed to be thinking something through. He glanced to the stairs, then back to the painting. But when he looked her way, the confusion was gone, and there was a clarity to his eyes she hadn't seen before.

"The details aren't really important right now, Maria. The bottom line is, without that evidence, she's the prime suspect in that crime she witnessed. That's why we need to get it back."

Maria let out a sigh and rose to take her glass back to the sideboard. "I'm afraid that might be a bit of a problem then."

"Why?"

"Because," she said as she set her glass down, "I wasn't entirely honest with you earlier about the status of my warehouse."

His eyes narrowed, completely clear and very focused. "I'm listening."

"Someone broke into the warehouse early this morning. The vault was breached. Several of the pieces I purchased from your auction are missing."

"And the pendant?"

"I don't know. It's completely possible it was already sent to Athens. It's also possible it's still in the vault. We haven't finished sifting through the mess that was left behind yet."

"And it's possible it was stolen," he finished for her.

She pursed her lips. "Yes. This was a professional hit. The FBI was collecting evidence all day. INTERPOL has already uploaded a list of known missing pieces from the theft to their Web site."

"You have no idea who was responsible?"

"No." She tipped her head. "But something tells me you do."

He ran a hand over his mouth and was silent for so long, she wasn't sure he would answer. Then he dropped his hand, and the urgency she saw in his eyes verified her assumption.

"I want to go down there tomorrow and take a look around."

"I can probably arrange that, though it'll likely ruffle some feathers."

"Not like I've never done that before."

She smiled a little, happy some of the lighthearted humor she liked most about him had entered his voice again. "You look exhausted, Peter. There's nothing we can do tonight regarding any of this. You'd be better off taking a shower and getting a good night's sleep. You left some clothes here. The rest of this can be dealt with tomorrow."

He glanced toward the stairs with the same longing in his eyes she'd seen when he'd walked in the door, and the bitterness she'd felt toward him for ditching her after the auction slipped away.

No matter that she didn't have much of a heart left herself. Someone else did. She wasn't about to stand in his way. "Why don't you just go ask her?" she said softly.

Surprised, smoky eyes turned to look her way. "Ask her what?"

"Whatever it is that's got you so confused about her motives." When he frowned, her smile widened. "While you're at it, you might try telling her how you feel. A woman always likes to hear she's exactly what a man wants."

His frown deepened. "I don't have a clue what you're talking about."

Maria laughed. "Yes. You do." She turned for the hallway that led to the master bedroom on the first floor. "You might also mention I'm not quite as bitchy as I come across."

"But you are," he said to her back.

Maria couldn't stop the chuckle that slipped from her mouth as she walked away. "I'll have Mabel bring you something clean to wear. Good night, Peter."

"G'night, Maria."

In her own room, Maria closed the door and listened. The floor outside creaked ever so slightly. She looked across the plush room, decorated in shades of red and gold, and figured that counted as her one good deed for the year. Sure, she'd lost a lover, but she hoped she'd kept a friend.

Lovers were a dime a dozen. Someone you could count on when you were down on your luck? That was hard to find.

And she of all people should know.

Pete showered and changed in the guest bathroom downstairs. Hot water had never felt so good, and for once he was happy he'd had the foresight to leave a few things here, even if at the time it'd seemed wrong.

Maria's words skipped around in his brain as he dressed, and questions he hadn't thought to ask Kat over the past two days fired off like bottle rockets, one after another. More than anything he wanted to barge upstairs to Kat's room and find out if what he suddenly suspected was true, but he couldn't. Not yet. There were two things he had to do first.

The apartment was eerily quiet as he made his way into the office Maria kept on the main level. Floor-to-ceiling windows looked out over trees and grass and a black void that was the park. Dark cherry bookcases spanned an entire wall, decorated with leather tomes and bronze sculptures and expensive art she'd no doubt collected over the years.

He'd always liked this room. While the rest of her penthouse was frilly and delicate, this room had the dark colors and bold woods he found peaceful. He shut the door behind him, moved around the antique French desk and sank into the plush leather chair. The immaculately clean surface held only a small lamp, a phone and a lone pen.

He sat in the dark, just staring at the smooth desktop softly illuminated by the city lights outside, thinking through everything Maria had told him. Thinking back over everything that had happened in the last two days. Man, had it only been two days since his life had been turned upside down because of Kat? It felt like longer.

Some small part of him wanted it to be longer.

Odds were pretty good Maria's break-in was related to the auction and Kat. Someone wanted to know if Maria had the pendant, and they were willing to do just about anything to get it. Odds were even better it was already long gone.

Which meant Kat was in deep shit.

No matter how Pete worked it in his head, Kat was going to take the heat for what had happened all those years ago in Cairo. If she turned herself in to the Feds without proof there'd been anyone else in the tomb with her the night Ramirez had been killed, there was a good chance she could do time. Maybe even be extradited back to Egypt.

A searing pain slit his chest at just the thought. Would Slade stand up for her? And if he did, would his pull have any weight?

Pete doubted it. One, no matter what, there was no proof. And two, Pete seriously doubted Slade would put himself on the line for her like that, regardless of how much he may still care for her.

Which left only one option. She'd have to stay in hiding. But, shit, from the way things had gone down the past few days, that wasn't much of an option, was it? How long until Minyawi or whoever the hell he worked for tracked her down? They knew she was alive now. They knew she could bury them. They couldn't let her live.

Pete ran his hand over the glossy surface of the desk and thought about his life in comparison to hers. About how smooth it had been. He'd been like his buddy Rafe's big fancy boat really, sailing along, a few waves here and there, but no major storms that had jarred him or flipped him around. Losing his parents had been hard, but he'd just been a kid then, and he'd quickly adapted. Burying his grandparents had stung, but he'd been in college by then and had his own life that didn't include them. And though it was selfish, he knew the deaths of the role models in his life had helped him build Odyssey. He'd taken his inheritance and put it all into the gallery, plodded along with ease and never looked back. Things had always come effortlessly for him. Until the moment he'd met Kat. And lost her.

Then his life had changed forever.

For nearly three days he'd been blaming her for that. Reasoning he could be so much further ahead if he hadn't gone on the straight and narrow after he thought she'd died. No question his life had been harder since that point. Emotionally as he tried to get himself on track, mentally as he came up with ways to make Odyssey profitable on the right side of the law, physically as he worked himself to the bone so he didn't have the energy to think of her or dream of her or wish things could have been different.

He remembered how he'd felt when he'd found out she was alive. Beat to hell and so utterly betrayed. Because everything he'd done because of her had been for shit.

Then he thought of what Maria had said: *If this evidence could have cleared her of any wrongdoing on her part, she could have come out of hiding at any time. There's something else going on here, Peter. She's protecting someone.*

Followed by Kat's voice at that park in Philadelphia just before she'd left him: *If I lied to you, it was for a very good reason. Maybe someday you'll understand that.*

He closed his eyes and took a deep breath and knew, if given the chance, he'd do it all over again the exact same way. No matter how any of it had played out, she'd been the one person to change his life for the better.

His heart was pounding a mile a minute as he leaned forward and flipped on the small tabletop lamp, then reached for the phone. A quick glance at the clock on the wall told him it was almost midnight, but he didn't care. He paid his lawyer in Miami an insanely embarrassing retainer for moments just like this. The guy could get his ass out of bed for all Pete cared.

Twenty minutes later, with the weight of his decision on his shoulders and no thought of turning back, he clicked off the cordless phone, turned it on again and dialed the number his lawyer had grudgingly dug up for him.

He was routed all over hell and back, then told to hang tight. He clicked off the phone one more time, sat back and waited.

Minutes passed before the damn thing rang. He picked it up on the second shrill note. "That was fast, even for you."

"Where's Kat?" Martin Slade's voice had that same superior clip Pete remembered from the one time he'd met the guy in Cairo. And it sure the hell didn't endear the SOB to Pete any now.

"She's fine," Pete said, working to keep his tone even and calm. "Sleeping. I don't have to tell you she's been through the wringer the past few days. No thanks to you."

"I had no idea Halloway was in contact with Bertrand or that he'd pass on the info I gave him about Kat's location. Surely Kat doesn't believe—"

"She's not sure what to believe right now," Pete snapped. "Any way you look at it, the government's fucked her twice now. Why the hell should she trust you?"

"Because she doesn't have many other options, does she? It's only a matter of time before Minyawi finds you both. Neither of you have any idea what you're dealing with here. This goes deeper than she could imagine."

"She already knows."

"How—"

"I've got contacts, too, Slade. And the how isn't really important. What is important is keeping Kat safe. I'm willing to do whatever it takes to make sure she stays out of harm's way and that this finally ends for her because I know I played a part in it from the beginning. But what about you? She gave up six years of her life because you convinced her it was the only way. And now she's right back where she was before. Only this time there's no easy way out. What are you willing to do to make things right for her?"

Silence.

Pete ground his teeth and though he knew it was useless, just couldn't quite keep the contempt from his voice. "You fucking owe her, you son of a bitch."

More silence, then finally when Pete was sure Slade wasn't going to answer, the man said, "She has to come in. I'll do whatever I can to make sure she gets a fair shake. If she cooperates, I'll make sure she doesn't get extradited back to Egypt. But there are going to be questions—even I can't get her around those."

"And what about you?" Pete asked. "You're just going to skate free like nothing happened?"

"No." For the first time, Pete heard regret in Slade's voice. "No. If she comes in, I'm going to have to fess up to what I did to help her. Christ, it'll probably make it worse, but I'll do whatever I can to make things easier on her. I swear it."

Pete realized in that moment that Slade was telling the truth. In his own way, he did care for Kat. Or felt guilty or maybe a little responsible. And in that same moment, Pete also realized the guy didn't know about the evidence Kat had stored in the pendant. If he did, he'd have convinced her to come out of hiding years ago.

He also sensed Slade didn't completely understand Minyawi's connection to Busir. Or know about Ramirez's involvement with the ELA. And those were two major bargaining chips Pete was willing to cultivate in any way he could.

Pete braced his hand on the desk and knew this was the jumping-off point for him. Once it was out, there was no turning back. "She'll come in. But on one condition."

"Are you trying to deal with me, Kauffman? You don't have a leg to stand o—"

"You bet your ass I'm dealing. And if you're smart you'll take what I give you because it's the best damn offer you're going to get. Kat will come in on one condition," he repeated. "She's cleared of all the charges against her. No questions about Ramirez's or Driscoll's deaths or any link back to her. You and I both know she didn't have a hand in either one."

"*Fuck*," Slade exclaimed. "I know she didn't, but she's got no proof. She never *had* any proof, which was one of the goddamn problems from the very beginning. The Egyptian government isn't as lenient on murder suspects as we are here in the States. And rogue Egyptologists who hook up with known felons linked to art theft and smuggling operations aren't people the U.S. is eager to get back in the country. The only thing she's got going for her right now is the fact she's on U.S. soil and she's willing to cooperate."

"That's not all she's got. She's got me."

"What the hell does that me—"

"Here's the deal, Slade. Kat comes in for safety reasons only and is cleared of all the charges. In exchange, I'll turn myself in. You wanna know how Minyawi's linked to the smuggling ring? I'm your guy."

Silence.

Well, that got the man's fucking attention, didn't it?

"You're serious?" Slade asked skeptically.

Yeah, he was serious. Deadly-frickin'-serious. More serious about this than he'd been about anything in his life. "I'll tell you everything I know. Names, locations, contacts in half a dozen countries that trade on the black market. I know who the weak link was at Kat's tomb, I know who the man dealt with, and I know how the pieces got out of the country. You keep Kat out of this, make sure she's safe, and I'll give you everything I know."

"And what about you?" Slade asked warily.

Pete leaned back in his chair. He was making a deal with the devil himself, and this time, there was no turning back. "I guess that's the sixty-four-thousand-dollar question now, isn't it?"

CHAPTER TWENTY-SIX

He was surprisingly steady for a man who'd just cashed in his own *go directly to jail, do not pass go, do not collect two hundred dollars* ticket. After signing all the papers his lawyer had faxed over and stuffing them back into the fax machine, Pete picked up the phone one more time and dialed the one person he knew was going to shit bricks when he heard the news.

The line rang three times before Rafe Sullivan answered in Puerto Rico, sounding groggy as hell and the slightest bit pissed at being pulled out of bed at—Pete glanced at the clock—1:30 a.m.

"*¿Qué?*" Rafe grumbled.

Despite everything else, Pete cracked a wan smile. "I hope that beat-to-shit voice of yours means you were asleep, not that you were about to get it on with your lady."

A soft chuckle came over the line, then a rasp of cloth, like Rafe was moving around in bed. "Already did the second. Was halfway into the first before you rudely interrupted me. Where are you, my man?"

Pete grinned. Damn, but he was seriously going to miss his best friend when all was said and done.

In the background he could just make out Lisa's voice ask, "Who the hell is that?"

"'S okay, *querida*," Rafe said in a muffled tone. "It's just Pete. Go back to sleep."

There was grunting, and more shifting around, then the sound of a door closing somewhere in the distance.

"I can talk now," Rafe said, his voice stronger. Footsteps echoed across the line, and Pete imagined Rafe walking through that big house he and Lisa had bought in Puerto Rico where they were getting the sister branch of Odyssey up and running in San Juan. He yawned as he said, "We've been at the hospital all day. Lisa's wiped."

Pete's chest tightened in a way that made his problems seem miniscule compared to what Rafe was going through. "How's Teresa?"

Rafe heaved out a heavy sigh, one that said the whole situation was pure shit. "Holding on. Every time I think that's it, you know, something happens and she perks up. She's been asking about you."

Pete leaned forward and ran a hand over his hair. "You know I'd be there if I could, don't you? Man, I just . . ." He hesitated, unsure what to say. Losing his parents or his grandparents had never been like this, mainly because he hadn't been particularly close to them. Teresa had a way of drawing everyone to her. You couldn't help loving Rafe's mother. Everyone did.

"It's okay, buddy. I know. Means a lot you called, though. But I gotta say, if it weren't for everything happening with *Mamá*, I'd be on the first plane up to New York. You know that, right?"

Touched, Pete smiled again. "Hailey blabbed, huh?"

"You bet your ass she did. She's worried about you. So's Lisa. We all are, for that matter. Pete, man, what the fuck's going on?"

Pete rubbed his free hand over his eyes. Eyes that were dog tired and scratchy from lack of sleep. "Hailey told you about Kat's necklace, right?"

"Yeah. Said you were both on your way up to get it. And can I just say, holy hell, is the woman really alive?"

That brought a reluctant chuckle from Pete. He'd told Rafe about Kat. Once. When he'd been drunk and pissed and feeling sorry enough about himself to open his big fat mouth. Obviously, Rafe hadn't forgotten. "Yeah, she is. I gave Maria the pendant just before the auction. Just our luck, though, Maria doesn't have it anymore." He told Rafe about the break-in at the warehouse and his suspicions as to who'd been behind it.

"Shit. You can't keep running from these guys," Rafe said in all seriousness. "We're talking about whacked-out jihad extremists here. The kind who shoot people on sight and don't give a flying fuck who lives and who dies, even themselves."

"I know. Believe me, I've been over and around this every way there is. She's got to turn herself in to the Feds. It's the only chance she's got."

"Which means what?" Rafe asked.

Now it was Pete's turn to blow out a breath. "Which means I need a favor."

"You know I'd do anything for you, Pete. What do you need?"

Pete pursed his lips, then decided, fuck it. "I just faxed you what I want done." He heard footsteps again, like Rafe was going into his office, then the crinkle of papers, like he'd pulled them from the fax machine. Before his friend could utter a word, Pete added, "Don't try to talk me out of it. Jerry and I have already been over it. I know exactly what I'm doing."

"*Fuck. Me.*" The springs in what had to be Rafe's desk chair squeaked over the line. "Tell me this is a joke."

"No joke, Rafe. All of it goes to her. Jerry's transferring all my assets into accounts in her name. I already signed over the deed to Odyssey and faxed both you and Jerry a copy. Jerry assures me the Puerto Rico branch won't be affected because of the nature of our partnership agreement. You and Lisa own the building outright. Any link to the Miami gallery is in name only."

"Pete, shit, listen—"

"Things are gonna get hot for me, but I don't want you

to worry. Anything I might admit to being involved with happened long before you and I partnered up. And everything since then has pretty much been on the up-and-up. Nothing you ever did can be traced back to me or Odyssey. The Feds'll probably come sniffing around. I just want you to be warned. I'm not gonna turn over anything even remotely related to you. I wouldn't do that."

"I know you wouldn't. Christ. This is . . . isn't there another way?"

Pete braced his elbow on the shiny desk. "I wish to hell there was, but I can't think of one. If Kat goes in alone, the Feds will rip her to shreds. She's already been through enough." Softer, he added, "I already made the deal with Slade, Rafe, so there's no sense trying to talk me out of it."

Silence. Then Rafe asked, "Is she worth it?"

"Yes."

"No hesitation."

"None."

"God, Pete. You could be looking at doing time."

Pete rubbed a hand over his mouth. "Yeah, I know."

"And shit, with all this, when you get out you'll have nothing."

Pete knew that, too. His future was a vast array of emptiness. Everything he'd worked for, gone. He had no idea how long he'd be sent up, but he knew one thing for sure: he owed her. This was his one chance to make up for all the shitty things he'd done before. If he hadn't screwed things up with her so bad, she wouldn't be in this mess to start with.

He shifted in his seat, hoping to help his friend understand. "Let me ask you something, Rafe. If it were Lisa on the line here? If she had to choose between running for the rest of her life or face being screwed by the government over something she didn't do, what would you do?"

Silence.

Finally Rafe sighed. "I'd do whatever it took to keep her safe. I'd give up everything I have to make sure of it. I'd even sacrifice my own freedom for her. No questions asked."

Pete closed his eyes and swallowed back the rush of emotions he felt. His life may have been for shit up until this point, but there were two people who'd changed it for the better. One was upstairs asleep. The other was on the opposite end of this line.

"I have one other favor to ask." Pete pinched the bridge of his nose and squeezed his eyes shut to keep from sounding like the pansy he was becoming. "I won't be around to make sure she doesn't get into trouble. And she tends to have a knack for it."

"I'll keep an eye on her. She could sell Odyssey," Rafe pointed out.

Pete dropped his hand. "It's hers to do with what she wants. If she wants to sell it, don't try to stop her. I don't care."

"Jesus, Pete. You've only been with her for two days."

Six years, six months and twenty-two days to be exact. Pete just wished he had the last two days to do over.

"You must really love her," Rafe said quietly when Pete didn't answer.

Pete looked toward the ceiling where he imagined Kat was sleeping. And his heart cinched tight. "You think that makes me a fool, don't you?"

"No. I think that makes you human."

To his credit, Rafe didn't try to talk Pete out of his decision again, and by the time they hung up a few minutes later, Pete knew his friend would do everything he'd asked. Even amid the turmoil of his own mother's illness, Rafe was the kind of friend a guy could count on. Even if he thought you were out of your frickin' mind.

It was well after two a.m. when Pete finally clicked off the light and headed for the stairs. With his decisions made, he had one last person he needed to talk to before morning hit and his deal with Slade became reality.

Hanif Busir looked up from where he was seated on the ratty couch and eyed Minyawi across the room. His nerves were shot to hell and back from lack of sleep the past few days, too many road and plane trips and trying to outwit one inconsequential Egyptologist.

They were holed up in a dive motel somewhere in Newark, waiting for news from Kalim. The walls of the room were a dingy yellow, and the stale stench of cigarette smoke felt like it was seeping into Busir's pores. But that wasn't what had him on edge. No, it was the look of pure malevolence in Minyawi's coal black eyes as he stared at Lauren Kauffman on the floor in the corner of the room, gagged with her hands and feet bound, her slacks riding low on her lean hips, her blouse pulled taut over perky breasts.

There was rank hunger in Minyawi's eyes, coupled with the kind of rage that fueled rapists and serial killers. Busir had heard stories of what Minyawi had done to women and children who'd gotten in his way over the years. Graphic, disgusting accounts of how Minyawi seemed to take pleasure in the torture. He also knew the man had something equally as horrendous planned for Katherine Meyer. But as they waited, he seemed to be contemplating practicing those moves on the blonde model in the corner of the room. And that didn't sit well with Busir.

She'd come to a few times after the drugs had worn off but was now asleep again, her head tipped to the side, resting on the grimy wall. Her breaths were even and slow, lifting her perfect breasts and dropping them in rhythmic succession. There were fresh bruises on her face from where she'd fought back and ultimately lost, but that hadn't slowed her. The woman was a fighter.

Of course, she was nothing to Busir. Frankly, he didn't care if she lived or died, but Kalim had very clear instructions she be left alone. And Busir didn't want to do anything to screw up this hit so they could finally end this fucking job. He certainly didn't want to watch as Minyawi used the girl for his own perverse deviances and then have to explain it all to Kalim later.

And he had a sinking suspicion if something didn't change soon, he'd have no other choice but to do both.

Minyawi stood from where he'd been seated on the opposite bed, staring at Lauren Kauffman, and moved forward. He crouched down close to her and ran his finger down her neck, across her collar bone, lower to the tip of her breast. Eyes closed and still half-drugged, the model moaned and tried to shift away from the hand that was groping her. Minyawi only chuckled.

Busir stood quickly. "*Kifaaya!* Don't touch her."

Minyawi turned those soulless eyes Busir's way and tightened his jaw. "What did you say to me?"

"She's not to be harmed."

"I'm not going to harm her," Minyawi said in an icy voice, shifting his attention back to the model. "I'm just going to have a little fun with her." His hand slid down to the model's slacks, and he used his finger to pull the cotton lower on her hip, revealing her creamy skin.

Minyawi's laugh deepened. And Busir saw their chance to finally end this shit assignment slide right down the drain because of Minyawi's volatility and unpredictability. He moved in a rage with barely a thought, kicked Minyawi in the kidneys and readied himself for a good knock-down, drag-out fight. He'd had it with this guy and every lost chance they'd had up until this point.

Minyawi rounded on him fast, but what Busir hadn't calculated was the knife Minyawi kept strapped to his thigh. Metal flashed, just before the blade sliced through

Busir's throat and a gush of liquid spilled from his body. He slumped to the mattress. Shocked. Immobilized. Eyes wide as he choked on his own blood.

Minyawi glared down at him and wiped the blade of the knife on his dirty camo pants. "No one tells me what to do."

Dimly, Busir heard a phone ring, and saw, though increasing darkness, Minyawi lift his cell to his ear.

"Yes," Minyawi said firmly, eyes still on Busir. "You're sure? They're alone in Dr. Gotsi's apartment?" A slow, victorious smile slid across his face as he nodded. "We will be there shortly. Busir? No. He's indisposed at the moment. Yes. It will be finished tonight. I guarantee it."

Busir opened his mouth to yell, just as his world went silent.

Okay, enough was enough.

Kat threw back the covers on the gigantic four-poster bed, clicked on the bedside lamp and scrambled out from between the sheets. The clock across the room read 2:10 a.m. as she dragged on her jeans and slid her feet into her shoes.

She'd been lying here for the past two hours, listening to the sounds of the rain pounding the city, waiting for God-only-knows-what. She was done waiting.

The dainty Victorian furnishings with their Queen Anne legs and that delicate rose wallpaper surrounding everything was making her head swim. And every time she looked up at the lace canopy above the monster bed she'd been laying in with its intricate carvings and wide posts, she wanted to puke because it made her think of Pete and what he was doing in another room in this enormous apartment right now.

She'd been stupid to think he would come to her. Obviously, what had happened between them in that motel room last night had been all about sexual tension, time and place and leftover hormones from being at that strip club. And his following her to North Carolina? Not about her, but about watching his back.

It didn't even bother him that she was up here and he was down there, with that . . . piranha.

She turned for the door, not caring that it was pouring outside, or that she had no idea where she'd go from here, or that Minyawi and his goons could be out there waiting for her right this very minute. If she spent another second in this penthouse, she was pretty sure she was going to lose it.

Her chest grew tight, and useless, pathetic tears she had no right to shed clawed up her throat until simply breathing was a major feat. She wasn't going to cry, dammit. The thought of melting into a puddle only ticked her off more. She didn't want anything to get in the way of the truckload of pissed-off that had dumped itself smack on top of her.

She grabbed her jacket, cursed the man who'd left her in this spot as she grabbed her backpack from the floor and yanked the bedroom door open. Then pulled up short when Pete's broad shoulders and handsome face filled her only means of escape.

Shock came first—that he was here instead of with that witch. Then anger that he would check up on her to make sure she sat tight while he had his fun.

"Get out of my way," she snapped.

He didn't move, just stood there with those insanely sexy, completely emotionless, smoky gray eyes as he stared at her. He kept one hand braced on each side of the door-jamb, preventing her exit.

"I'm leaving," she said sharply in case he'd missed the hint. "I'd appreciate it if you'd step aside."

"You're not going anywhere."

"The hell I'm not."

In response he dropped his hands and moved forward,

his body filling the space until all she saw was him. No more hall, no more door, nothing beyond the fresh, white dress shirt stretched across his strong chest.

With nowhere to go and her emotions almost at a breaking point, Kat stepped back. Then clenched her jaw to keep from lashing out at him. He closed the door at his back with one hand, never looking away from her face, and clicked the lock.

"You can't keep me here," she blurted. "I'm not your prisoner."

"You're not leaving, Kat." He took the backpack and jacket from her and tossed them onto a chair.

Who the hell did he think he was? She glared at him with all she had, and still his expression didn't change from calm and totally collected. She was quickly going from pissed off to irate, and he didn't even seem to care.

Those stupid-ass tears bubbled up again. Her nose tingled. She whipped away from him so she wouldn't embarrass herself more and blinked several time to keep from bawling like a baby. There were some things a woman shouldn't ever have to endure. Staying in this house, tonight, topped that list.

"Just go," she said in a voice that came out weak and stilted and not nearly as firm as she'd hoped. "I get it, okay? Just go back to your girlfriend and leave me alone."

"She's not my girlfriend." She didn't hear him move, but she felt him suddenly at her back, just a whisper of a touch as the air stirred near her. "If I wanted to be with her, I would be."

"So why aren't you?" she snapped.

"Because she's not you."

Those four little words were like a noose around Kat's heart.

"Something about your story's been bothering me," he said. "There's one part I can't wrap my mind around."

Her back went up. She pushed thoughts of their past

out of her mind and focused on the present. And why the hell he was bringing this up at two a.m. "I didn't lie about anything."

"No, but I think you purposely omitted something important."

She wanted to step away, but there was no place to go. In front of her was the bed, to her left the window. If she moved right, it would look like he was making her uncomfortable, and she didn't want to give him the satisfaction. She crossed her arms over her chest again instead. "I don't have a clue what you're talking about."

"Oh, I think you do. In fact, I think it's the whole reason you're here right now."

"You must be jet-lagged, Kauffman, or your brain's turned to mush from too much sex because you're not making a lick of sense."

"The only sex I've had was last night, and it wasn't nearly enough. Why were you at my auction, Kat?"

His revelation that he hadn't been screwing Maria downstairs was quickly overshadowed by a question that seemed to come out of left field. Puzzled, she turned her head slightly to the side and realized he was even closer than she'd originally thought. Mere millimeters from touching her. The warmth of his breath fanned across her cheek and sent electricity zinging along her nerve endings. Had he really not slept with that woman? "Wh—what do you mean?"

"Why now?" he asked. "Why was it so important you get that necklace back now?"

"I . . . you know why. I had to make sure you didn't sell it."

"Are you telling me you were never in Miami? That you never went to see for yourself that I still had it? Not once in six years?"

Her throat grew thick as she fished for an answer she didn't have. Of course she'd kept tabs on him and what he'd done with her pendant. She'd had to for security reasons. She'd even been in his gallery once when she'd known he was out of town. At the time, she'd been shocked by the sheer magnitude of what he'd built. But how did he know any of that?

He moved even closer, until she felt his chest brush her back and the warmth of his body pressing softly into hers. And that heart rate she'd tried so hard to contain shot straight through the roof. "You could have taken it whenever you wanted. You know I didn't have it locked up."

She swallowed. Thought about what she could say. He was right. She'd sneaked into his office that one time she'd gone to his gallery and seen the golden pharaoh sitting on a glass shelf across from his desk.

His fingertip brushed a stray hair at the nape of her neck. "You told me you stayed in hiding all this time to protect your family. If that's true, then why didn't you come for it after your mother died? Why did you wait so long?"

"It . . . it doesn't matter."

"It does to me. You could have cleared your name anytime. I think you stayed in hiding for a reason. In fact, I can only think of one reason why you wouldn't have come forward sooner."

Kat's heart thumped erratically against her ribs, and words lodged in her throat.

"No confession to make on that one?" he asked in an amused voice as he twirled his finger in a lazy circle against her arm.

She bit her lip.

"Then I think it's time you listened to mine."

He continued to swirl his finger in that languid way, keeping contact between them that did amazing things to her body but kept her head in a fog.

"You were right about why I went to your tomb that first time," he said. "About why I came back and why I asked you out. I asked you out because I knew you were an easy mark."

She stiffened, though she didn't pull away, because she sensed—okay, hoped—there was more to what he was trying to say. *Please let there be more.*

"You didn't know," he said as his finger brushed over her forearm, "couldn't know, what you did to me that night. For the first time in my life, I wasn't thinking about money or what kind of deal I was going to haggle next. That night, all I could think about was you."

Regret tinged his husky voice, and Kat found herself listening, praying what he was telling her would somehow change things and make them better.

"After that weekend at the Mena House, I didn't go back to the States like I'd told you. Instead, I stayed in Egypt a few days so I could back out of the deal I'd been brokering."

He hesitated, and a stillness descended between them, one that froze her pulse because she had a really bad feeling what he was about to say next was something she didn't want to hear.

"Ramirez was right about one thing. I did know Busir—I'd worked with him before."

Kat went cold all over, and a sick feeling bubbled up from her abdomen and shot into her veins. That hope she'd clung to burst in an explosion that rocketed through her soul. Everything she'd suspected about him but never truly believed was confirmed in that one instant.

And the heart she'd tried so hard to keep safe shattered at her feet.

She wheeled on Pete so fast, she nearly knocked him over. "How could you!"

CHAPTER TWENTY-SEVEN

"Hold on, now."

Pete grasped Kat at the wrists and jerked her against his chest before her fist made contact with his jaw. She barely heard his words or felt his strong grip. All she could focus on was a growing sickness at her naivety. After everything she'd done, how could he? How *could* he?

She wiggled to the side, then jabbed an elbow in his sternum hard. When he doubled over and loosened his grasp, she broke away and raced for the door.

Two powerful arms engulfed her from behind and lifted her off the floor before she reached the exit. She kicked out and tried to wrestle free. "Let go of me, you son of a bitch!"

"Not until you hear me out!" He muscled her arms around in front of her until he had them pinned in both of his hands. Groaning from the effort of controlling her flailing, he walked backward and dropped onto the bed in a seated position with her held firmly in his lap.

"Let me go," she growled again, struggling once, twice more to no avail.

"Not yet." He tightened his hold, flipped his leg over hers so she couldn't nail him with her heel. "Not until you listen to what I have to say."

"Go to hell!" She thrashed against him again, even though she knew it was useless.

"You'll probably get your wish." He shifted his head to the side so she couldn't crack him with the back of her skull. "Until then the least you can do is give me five minutes of your precious time. I've given you way more than that over the last two days."

She ground her teeth together, twisted in his arms, and knew she was stuck. But the minute he loosened his grasp . . .

In the silence between them, she heard his heavy breathing, mirroring hers, felt the beat of his heart at her back and wanted to scream for him to just get it over with so she could get as far away from him as possible.

But he didn't. He just sat there until she cooled down.

Which only pissed her off more.

Long minutes later, he finally said, "That's better."

"Fuck yo—"

"Kat." He dropped his forehead against her back, and there was such pain in his voice, she closed her mouth instantly. In that one word—her name—he sounded distraught and . . . sad. And though she didn't want it to, it softened her, just enough so she could listen to whatever it was he had to say without a brawl.

He heaved out a breath. "You don't have any idea what you did to me. What that weekend did to me. It changed everything. I cut off my deal with Busir. I went home to Miami and started cleaning up my business because I didn't want you to know what I'd been doing. I tried to stay away. God, I really did. But I couldn't. Do you have any idea how hard it was to stay away from you for two damn weeks?"

Yes, she did. Because at the time two weeks away from him had been like pure hell for her.

"It was worse than hell," he said, almost as if he'd read her mind. "I knew after we were together you were frustrated with me because I wouldn't talk to you about the gallery, because I was traveling so much, but I was brokering deals, working my ass off to get Odyssey on the level before your dig was up and you came back to the States.

I didn't want you to know the man I'd been. I wanted to be . . . better."

The fight rushed out of her at his words.

"I swear to you," he said, "I didn't have anything to do with the smuggling ring or Ramirez's death or what happened to your roommate. That day you came home from work early and I was packing—shit, I screwed up, Kat. Busir contacted me just after you left that morning and told me he had some new relics. I shouldn't have gone, but I went to see, and the next thing I knew, I had them. I didn't know they were from your tomb. I swear it. I fucked up. If I could go back and change that day, don't you think I would?

"I've spent the last six years paying for that one mistake. Knowing if I'd done things differently, you wouldn't have been in that car the day that bomb blew. You would have been with me. You've got no reason to believe me, but I swear to you, I cleaned up my act after that day. Even though I knew it wouldn't bring you back. I cleaned up because I owed you."

Kat's heart skipped a beat at what she heard. Then another. And another. And then it kicked in and started beating fast and erratic as the reality of what he was telling her took root.

He wasn't a saint. But he wasn't the sinner she'd pegged him as either. And she'd made her own fair share of mistakes, hadn't she? Could she really condemn him if there was a chance what he said was true? If he'd really been involved with the smuggling ring or Sawil's death, would he have been so upset with her accusations in Cairo? With her showing back up now? If he was being honest with her—and she sensed he was—then the only thing he was truly guilty of was poor judgment. Poor judgment and trying to clean up his life. For her.

"Oh, my God," she whispered as her eyes slid closed

and a thousand memories of the two of them together hit her from all sides.

He released his hold and gently turned her in his lap. Blood rushed to her arms, but she barely felt it, didn't struggle or try to move off him. Was too fixated on everything he'd just told her to consider going anywhere.

"All that stuff at the auction the other night," he said softly, "all of it was bought and paid for through legal means. You know I left everything I bought from Busir that day in your flat. The only thing I kept was the pendant you sent me. I swear it to you. Every time I've come across an Egyptian piece over the last few years I haven't been able to pass by without buying it and sticking it in storage because it reminded me of you."

That admission was so sweet, it touched her heart in a place she hadn't thought existed anymore. And when he brushed his thumb over her cheek in such an achingly tender move, tears threatened behind her eyes.

"Tell me why you didn't walk away after the auction," he said. "You thought you had the pendant. There was no reason to follow me. Why were you driving my limo? Why were you outside this building? Why did you bother to step in when Busir had me in the alley? Those aren't the actions of a woman who hates me."

"I . . . I never hated you."

"No?" A wan smile tugged at his mouth. "You sure didn't like me very much there at the end."

Six years of worry and regret, hope and heartbreak, betrayal and beliefs swirled inside her. And sitting there, so close to him, bombarded with questions she didn't know how to answer, it was too much. Hot tears filled her eyes. She covered her face with her hands to keep the dam from breaking.

She didn't fight it when his arms circled her, when his legs opened so she could sink lower onto the mattress between his thighs, when he pulled her close so her face was against his throat and she was surrounded by the familiar scent and feel of him.

"Just tell me," he whispered. "Why now? I need to hear it from you."

"Because I messed up," she managed. "Because after Busir and Minyawi saw me at the auction, I knew they were going to come after you. I . . . I couldn't let them do that. I spent too many years making sure they never—"

She closed her mouth tight when she realized what she'd been about to admit.

He tipped her face up. "You spent too many years making sure they never went after me," he finished for her. "You stayed away all this time because of me, didn't you?"

She couldn't deny it, not anymore. And part of her didn't even want to. She closed her eyes as the first tear slipped down her cheek.

"Kit-Kat," he whispered. "Look at me."

She opened her eyes to look up into his handsome face, a face that had haunted her dreams for so long. A face that was still sporting a shiner from Busir and cuts from their run-in in Raleigh.

"You sent that crouching pharaoh to me instead of giving it to Slade for security. So that in case someone did ever come after me to get to you, you'd have a bargaining chip. Even when you knew it could possibly clear your name." When she couldn't answer, he whispered, "Christ. Why the hell didn't you tell me this days ago?"

"Because I knew you wouldn't believe me. And I . . ." She drummed up her courage and glanced at the open collar of his shirt. "No matter what happened between us before, I was afraid if you knew, you'd walk away, and then you'd be in more danger than I'd put you in originally."

"You did all that, even though you thought I could have been involved in that smuggling ring?"

She hesitated but finally gave in and nodded.

When he didn't reply, she chanced a glance up. And saw eyes that went all soft and dreamy the way they had so many years ago in Cairo. In that one look her insides turned to Jell-O. Just liquefied, right there where she sat.

"I never got over you," he whispered. "You're the only woman I want. The only one I've ever wanted—"

She didn't let him finish. Through a rush of tears she kissed him hard, then nearly burst when his hands ran down her back to close around her. The kiss was so electric, her bones had no choice but to follow her insides and turn to butter. Had it not been for his arms wrapped tight around her, she was sure she'd have disintegrated into a puddle right there at his feet.

"You're not leaving this apartment tonight," he said against her mouth. "You're not getting out of my sight until I know you're safe. I can't go through what I did six years ago."

Her heart turned over at his words, at the vulnerability she heard in his voice. She lifted her hands to his face and kissed him long and deep, sliding her tongue into his mouth until she tasted his sweetness deep inside her.

"I want to stay with you tonight, Kat. No more running. Tell me you want that, too. Tell me—"

She nodded quickly. "Yes. Yes. I do. Oh, Pete. That's all I've ever wanted."

Whatever restraint he'd been exercising before broke with her words, and a low growl of victory erupted in his throat as his arms crushed her tight against him and his mouth closed over hers with stunning force. She felt the strong, steady beat of his heart against her own, the slightest tremble in his body when he kissed her. And when he shifted there was no mistaking the arousal stabbing into her hip that proved just how much he did want her.

He rolled her to her back, never once breaking their kiss or loosening his hold on her. Her hands raced to the buttons on his shirt, fumbled. When she couldn't get to him fast enough, she gave up trying and tore the shirttails from his slacks instead. As her fingers made quick work of his belt, she was oddly aware that tonight she'd gone from being in the throes of despair, to heartbroken and betrayed, to so damn happy she could barely breathe. But the how or why or when they'd gotten to this point wasn't important. Not anymore.

She found the button at his waistband and pulled him free of his slacks. He groaned into her mouth as her hands slipped over his back, ran lower to pull him into her.

"God, Kit-Kat. You have no idea what you do to me."

"Yes, I do," she whispered. "Because I ache inside from it."

He moved out of her grasp so fast she barely had time to react, leaned back on his knees and lifted her torso off the bed to tear the T-shirt from her body. She gasped at the rush of cool air, at the force with which he ripped her bra from her skin. Seconds later her jeans joined her shirt on the floor and his mouth was back on hers, kissing her hard as he lost his clothes and climbed back over her in all his naked glory.

This was so much better than the last time. Because now she knew how he felt. And it warmed the coldest spaces of her heart. She wrapped her arms around him as he moved up her body. Shuddered as his fingers delved between them and found her wetness. Groaning at the slightest touch, she let her head fall back against the mattress as he stirred and stroked and she held on for dear life.

He slid one finger deep inside, used his thumb to circle and swirl. Electricity shot through every neuron in her body until she felt like she'd come out of her skin.

"You're so tight," he said against her throat. His teeth found her ear, scraped across her lobe as he added a second finger and drove her to new heights. "That's it. Squeeze me. I love the way you feel."

"Pete." He was quickly pushing her toward the edge. She groaned again, lifted her hips to his incredibly talented fingers.

"That's it. Keep saying my name, Kit-Kat." He shifted, kissed his way south, slowly, inch by inch until she felt his tongue sliding over her most sensitive flesh.

Ooooh. She groaned. Arched as his fingers stroked deeper and flames ignited deep inside her.

But it wasn't enough. She loved what he was doing, but she wanted more. She wanted him. "Pete, please. I just want you."

Before she could open her eyes he was moving up her body. His mouth captured hers with an urgency she'd missed before. She tasted him, her, all the years they'd lost. When she heard the rasp of cellophane, she reached down to help him suit up only to discover she was too late. His hands raced to her hips as he pushed his way between her thighs. She gasped against his mouth as his pulsing erection brushed over her center, then groaned with pleasure when he sank into her in one mighty thrust.

Obviously, she'd said the right thing because he couldn't get at her fast enough. And oh, she loved it. She wrapped her legs around him, held him close as he pumped into her and she met him thrust for thrust. All the while he was kissing her, driving her crazy with his mouth, he made love to her with his body like it was the first time. The last time. Like every time they'd missed over the years.

The importance of the moment wasn't lost on her. Even as her orgasm built, and though she knew it was cliché and common and that there was a much better time, she wanted him to know how she felt.

She hooked her leg over his hip, used her hand to push against his shoulder to roll him to his back. He took the hint easily, rolled with her and gathered her tight as she settled on top of him and took control.

Those half-lidded, smoky eyes were lit with an erotic light that pulled at her. She kissed him, tightened her muscles and met his upward thrusts. "Kit-Kat. What you do to me."

Warmth gathered in her center. She was about to peak, but she didn't want to. Not until he did. With her hands braced on both sides of his head, she leaned down and rested her forehead against his. The medal around her neck fell over his heart, right where it was supposed to be. "I love you, Pete. I always have."

He exploded inside her on a long groan, and she held on tight as her own climax washed over her seconds later. In that moment, the past was finished and buried. Never to come between them again.

His mouth found hers, hot and wet and possessive. And she loved it. Loved those strong arms of his circling around to hold her close. Loved the way he couldn't seem to get enough of her. Loved the steady beat of his heart in time with her own.

Still joined together, she collapsed against his chest and pressed her face against his neck as she took long, slow deep breaths. The whole time, he whispered sweet words and trailed his hand up and down her spine.

She snuggled in and closed her eyes. For the first time in years, she was filled with a hope she was almost too afraid to believe in.

Every inch of her body ached.

Hailey lay still on her side and held her breath to keep from crying out. Not an easy thing to do considering it hurt like a son of a bitch even to breathe.

The vehicle she was in bounced and jerked her to the side, sending pain lancing through her torso where she'd been kicked. So much for all that self-defense training.

She'd let these creeps get the jump on her, and now she was in deep shit. And no doubt black and blue from scalp to toe.

Okay, think.

She had no idea where they were heading, but the rhythmic *whap, whap, whap* filtering through her mind told her they were most likely on a bridge.

Bridge . . . bridge . . . bridge. Hell, that could be anywhere.

Her memories were vague from the moment Minyawi had knocked her out cold in Lauren's house in Key Biscayne. She was pretty sure she'd been put on a plane, then stuffed into a car. She knew they'd called her by Lauren's name several times, so they hadn't yet figured out they'd fucked up. At one point she remembered being in some sort of dingy motel with Minyawi—yeah, he was a sick fuck—eyeing her like she was the last hooker in a brothel. But now even that, along with everything else, including the beating she'd obviously taken, was a fleeting blur. And thank God for that little side trip into amnesia-land. On top of the rest of the crap in her life, she seriously didn't need the trauma from this fucked-up nightmare.

With her hands tied behind her and a blindfold covering her eyes, she didn't know what kind of vehicle she was in now, or how long she'd been on the road. One thing she had paid attention to, though, were the voices of the two men who'd abducted her.

Heavily accented. Middle Eastern. Cold. Hard. Bordering on inhuman. One was definitely Minyawi. The other? She was almost sure he'd responded to the name Busir.

Oh, man. Pete owed her for this one. Owed her big-time. If she got out of this—*when* she got out of this—she'd make sure he paid up tenfold.

The only way to keep from freaking out was to use her brain and dial back in to her officer training. She counted the *whap, whap, whap* and the number of turns they took after leaving what had to be a bridge. When the vehicle came to a jolting stop, she clenched her teeth to keep from screaming as pain shot through her entire body.

A car door opened. Footsteps echoed around the back. A door near her feet was pulled open, and a blast of cold air rushed over her body.

They definitely weren't in Florida anymore. The air here was crisp and frigid and felt of snow. She went completely still.

"I'll be back for you. With a friend," the one she was sure was Minyawi said.

The door slammed shut, and a lock clicked, echoing through the interior of the car that had just become her prison cell.

One set of footsteps marched away from the vehicle, then faded altogether. She waited for the other door to open. For breathing to indicate she wasn't alone. Only there was nothing.

For some reason Busir wasn't with them anymore. Which meant she was truly alone. And this was her only chance for escape.

She bolted upright. Two things Minyawi didn't know. One, she wasn't as drugged as he'd thought. Yeah, she was fuzzy, but she'd been acting the past few hours so he wouldn't shoot her up again. And two, she wasn't the helpless female model he believed her to be.

Pulse pounding in her ears, she wriggled against the ropes at her back. When that proved useless, she rolled onto her stomach, eased back on her knees and tried to rub her face against her shoulder to free the blindfold.

It was like working underwater. Her arms and legs refused to work the way she wanted. Finally she realized she wasn't going to get anywhere until she remedied the situation with her arms. Rolling to her back, she lifted her hips off the floor and groaned as she scooted her lower body through the hoop her bound arms made and brought her hands to the front of her body.

Sweat covered every inch of her skin. A metal clanging from somewhere outside drew her up short. She waited. And prayed the entire time Minyawi hadn't come back.

When the sound stopped and it was clear it had been something unrelated to her situation, she went back to work, using her hands to push the blindfold free so she could go to work on the ropes at her feet.

It took a while for her eyes to adjust, but she quickly realized wherever she was, it was still night. City lights streamed in through the front windshield of the vehicle, casting shadows over the interior of what she guessed was a utility van. The walls were metal, the floor hard and cold, and along the back wall she saw two cargo doors. Behind her, a wire mesh net prevented her from accessing the front two seats.

The rope bit into her skin. Her fingers bled as she tried to free herself. But she didn't stop. Just when she was ready to scream with frustration, the ropes at her feet loosened.

Yes!

She kicked and wriggled free of the bonds and quickly jumped to her feet. No time to worry about her hands. She had to get the hell out of here.

The cargo doors were locked—no surprise—so that left the front. She ran her tied hands over the cage, trying to find a release. When that proved futile, she grabbed the metal between her fingers and cranked hard.

Still nothing.

"*Son of a bitch*! Come on!"

Her breaths grew labored and heavy. Sweating, she glanced along the edge of the cage at two tiny little clamps. Like the unit was snapped into place, not bolted.

Hope burst through her.

On her knees, she worked the latch at the bottom on

the right side until her fingers screamed in pain, then the one at the top. And nearly cried out in glee when the unit opened like a door hinging back.

She crawled through the space, dropped into the driver's seat and eyed the ignition. No keys.

Dammit. Well what did she expect? An engraved invitation to motor her way to freedom à la Greg Biffle?

She chewed on her lip. She needed to get to the authorities and get word to Pete about Minyawi. She could get out and run, or . . . she could hotwire the thing like Rafe had taught her to do when they'd been dating. Crap, she wasn't sure she remembered which wire went where.

Indecision brewing, she glanced up. Then realized in a flash where she was.

No goddamn way.

Forget NASCAR. She had a faster idea.

CHAPTER TWENTY-EIGHT

Pete was warm all over. Even his toes were toasty.

He smiled as he lay on his side watching Kat sleep, curled up facing him on the mattress in Maria's guest room. He'd turned the light off earlier, and now only the glow rising from the city outside the huge windows highlighted the angles and curves of her face, the soft skin of her shoulder, the way her hands were tucked in close to her body.

Man, he could just lay here for hours, staring at her.

The rain had turned to a light patter against the windows. The night sounds of the city were drowned out by her rhythmic breathing.

He couldn't bring himself to wake her, even though he

desperately wanted to make love to her one more time before dawn. So he contented himself with lying next to her, watching her sleep. He stroked her arm, marveled at the way her lashes fanned against her cheeks, how her lips parted as she breathed and that little mole near her mouth beckoned him to kiss her. He traced the line of her shoulder, drew his finger across her collar bone, followed the chain around her neck to the medal that fell between her breasts.

St. Jude. Patron saint of lost causes. She'd told him once she wore it because she was the biggest lost cause of all. But she was wrong. She was so much more than she realized.

A muffled thump cut through the night silence, and Pete's finger halted on Kat's medallion. He lifted his head and listened, only to have a second thump meet his ears.

Rolling to his back, he looked toward the tangle of clothing on the floor. He *seriously* didn't want to get out of bed, but some strange instinct was telling him to get up and check on that noise.

Maria slept like the dead and didn't get up for anything. And no matter how he tried, he couldn't come up with a logical reason for her housekeeper to be up and moving this early.

He hesitated until he heard it a third time, then rolled out of bed as quietly as he could so as not to wake Kat and pulled on his slacks. Most likely it was something simple like the wind lifting loose material on the roof of the building, but considering the situation, he didn't think it wise to ignore it.

He closed the door quietly at his back and moved barefoot through the upstairs. Every room he checked was empty. Nothing moving. Nothing out of the ordinary. He tiptoed down the stairs and hesitated when he reached the entryway.

The heating system hummed. Outside, wind howled,

and rain pattered against the panes of glass in the living room. He was just about to turn around and go upstairs when he heard it again.

A thump. Like something heavy being moved. Coming from Maria's room.

He eased down the hallway, staying in the shadows. Then wished like hell he'd grabbed his gun from upstairs. Glancing around the darkened passage, he spotted a tall, chunky candlestick on a side table.

Not a bat. But the best he could come up with. He grabbed it with a frown and turned it upside down to use like a weapon. Then he wrapped his hand around Maria's doorknob.

The room was dark, and it took his eyes a moment to adjust, but he didn't miss the muffled gasp.

Maria was on the floor between the bed and the window, hands and feet cinched tight, gag stuffed in her mouth and tied behind her head. Her flailing was the noise he'd heard from upstairs.

Oh, shit.

His blood ran cold, and he turned to race back upstairs. Maria's muffled scream echoed at his back.

He made it as far as the base of the stairs before he was coldcocked from behind and went sprawling to the hardwood floor. The candlestick sailed out of his hand, smacked against the far wall and broke into two. A set of familiar dark eyes and an ass-ugly mop of hair moved into his line of sight.

Minyawi.

No . . . not Minyawi. Someone he knew a whole lot better.

He flipped quickly to his back and managed one lethal blow before a hypodermic needle was thrust into his arm. He swatted at the sharp stab, flicked it away before the syringe was depressed all the way, then heard a chilling voice he remembered all too well echo in his already fuzzy head.

"Thank you, Pete, for bringing her right to me."

Kat woke with a start. She didn't know what had pulled her from sleep, but one glance around the dark room and a feeling of dread washed over her.

Pete was gone.

She dropped her feet over the side of the bed, pulled on her T-shirt and jeans and felt a moment of relief when she saw his shoes and shirt in a heap on the floor next to her things.

Okay, he wasn't gone for good. He'd just gotten up for something. She listened to see if she could hear him, and when she couldn't, that panic washed over her again.

She reached for the gun in her backpack. The house was too quiet.

She checked the magazine and clicked off the safety, then silently walked to the door. When she got to the top of the stairs, she listened again and hoped she could hear Pete clanging around in the kitchen, rummaging for a midnight snack.

Only there was nothing.

That dread ratcheted up a notch. She took the stairs one at a time, continuing to move like a silent shadow. She hesitated mere steps from the kitchen, surveying the area, holding her breath as she listened for sound from the other side of that closed door.

A loud shrill made her jump. She whipped around, gun held in both hands.

With her heart in her throat, Kat realized it was a cell phone chiming.

She blew out a long breath. Rubbed the back of her hand over her forehead and let out a pathetic laugh.

She was really losing it. That was probably what had

woken her. Just a damn cell phone going off somewhere in the house. For all she knew, Pete had probably been in the bathroom when she'd awoken and was now back in bed wondering where she'd gone.

A laugh bubbled through her as she turned for the stairs. The cell phone chimed again, but this time she expected it. She glanced around, curious as to where the thing had been left so she could turn it off.

She walked around the far side of the dining room table. And froze.

A silent scream tore from her throat when she saw Pete lying on his stomach, out cold. His cell phone was on the floor near his head.

"Pete." She set the gun on the ground and dropped to her knees by his side. Blood ran down his temple and dripped onto his bare shoulder.

She reached quickly for the phone, flipped it open to call 911, and went cold all over when she saw the picture message coming through. It had been sent hours ago by the time stamp, but Pete obviously hadn't looked at it yet. It read simply:

> Pete,
> *This is the most recent picture INTERPOL has on file for Minyawi.*
>
> H

"Oh, God." Sickness welled in Kat's stomach as she stared at the image of Sawil Ramirez.

She grabbed the gun and scrambled to her feet to get help. And made it two steps before she was grasped by the hair by a large hand that jerked backward until the air shot out of her lungs.

"It's about time you showed up, Kat. I've been waiting for you for six fucking years."

Spots shot into Kat's line of vision. Pain erupted in her

skull. She yelped and tried to swat at the hand that held her, but it pulled so hard the room spun. Sawil's shoulder plowed into the swinging kitchen door, and before she knew what was happening, she was thrown over the granite island and went skidding off the other side.

Pots and pans and utensils went sailing. The gun flew out of her hand and across the room. Kat hit the tile floor on the other side of the island with a *thwack* that cracked her skull and sent stars firing off behind her eyes. In a daze, she looked up to see Sawil standing over her, but this wasn't the quiet and friendly man she'd met in Cairo. This one was full of malevolence and a blinding hatred she could never understand.

"This is all your fault, you know. You couldn't leave well enough alone. And now look where we are." His accent didn't sound Brazilian anymore. It was very thickly Middle Eastern, and with his long hair and beard, he fit the terrorist profile better than she could have ever predicted.

She scrambled to her feet.

He threw a chair out of his way as he advanced toward her, eyes dark and evil. "Prove a point. Make my mark. I was doing that until you fucked it all up for me. No one was getting hurt." She darted behind the table. "Then they came at me. Said it was my problem. That you were my fuckup. That I needed to fix it. Fix you. You should have died that night in the tomb. Then Shannon would still be alive."

Her eyes flicked to the scar running down his cheek. The scar, she realized, she'd put there. He'd been the one to grab her from behind. He'd lured her, disappeared, then tried to kill her. He just hadn't expected her to fight back.

"It should have been you who was gutted, not Shannon," he growled as he threw another chair to the side. "Not her."

And, oh . . . shit. She realized then she was in serious

trouble here. What had Bertrand told her in the park? *Minyawi's been on a killing spree for five years. Rose in the ranks of his group like wildfire spreads across a dry valley.* The man Kat had known six years ago was definitely not the same one she was staring at now. If he hadn't killed Shannon, then it meant his organization had. To get to Kat. And he hadn't been able to stop it. Which meant he had double the reason to want to see Kat suffer.

Her adrenaline surged. She stumbled backward when he moved forward.

"No one's coming for you, woman. Before this is over you will beg me to kill you."

The hell she would.

When he came at her, she threw a chair from the kitchen table into him. He grunted as it hit him in the knee, then tossed it aside as if it were kindling. And still he kept coming.

"Run from me," he growled. "That's it. Run. It'll be that much better when I catch you and make you pay. I've been practicing. All these years, just waiting to make you pay like Shannon did."

The kitchen was big, but Kat was quickly running out of space. She couldn't beat him in a hand-to-hand fight. Her only option was to escape and regroup. She spotted the side door that led to the back stairs and turned to run. He dove for her, grasped her ankle, and pulled her down with him before she even got three steps away.

Her body hit the floor hard. She grunted in pain, kicking and struggling, but he flipped her to her back like she was a rag doll.

"Get off me!"

He wrestled her hands, grasped them at the wrists and pinned them beside her head. She continued to fight with everything she had, remembering what Pete had told her he'd done to Bertrand's wife. Knowing if she lost here, she was dead.

Don't let Pete be dead.

He growled close to her ear. "I like it when they fight back. Now beg. Beg me not to hurt you. Just like Shannon did before they cut her."

"No!" Sickness rose in Kat's stomach. She lifted her knee, nearly landed a jab in his groin, but he moved just before she made contact. The back of his hand sliced through the air and connected with her cheek with a loud crack.

"Do it!" he screamed. He shifted his legs so he had both of hers pinned beneath the weight of his body.

She lashed out. Her hand broke free. She dug her fingernails into his left eye. Blood spurted over her face and chest, making her gag. He screeched and jerked back, one hand flying to his face, the other still holding her tight. She turned her head slightly and saw her gun lying mere feet from her, just out of her grasp.

She was so close.

She kicked, tried to free herself, but he was too strong. Sweat and blood ran down her cheek.

He roared, and a menacing rage coated his features until she barely recognized him anymore. He wrapped his free hand around her throat and squeezed until she was sure her veins would burst.

Her vision dimmed. She gasped for breath, struggled harder. Met . . . nothing.

Oh, God. This was it. After all this time, after finally being so close to what she'd always wanted . . .

"Get your fucking hands off her." Pete's arm arced out, and the cast-iron frying pan in his hand cracked against the side of Sawil's head.

Sawil was thrown to the side and bounced off the kitchen wall.

Pete was on his knees in a flash, not a dream but reality, pulling her to him. "Talk to me, baby."

Her throat burned, but she held on tight, remembering

the way he'd looked in the dining room. Blood continued to run down the side of his face. "Pete—"

Sawil shot off the floor with a growl and plowed into Pete. Kat screamed as he was torn from her arms. The two sailed across the kitchen. Pete's head and back hit the cabinets with a deafening whack.

They wrestled across the floor, grunting and struggling. Kat scrambled for her gun and grasped it with two hands, but there was no shot. Their bodies slammed into another cabinet, and a pile of dishes above rocked and tipped and came crashing down around them.

Kat pushed to her feet. Sawil got the upper hand, rolled on top of Pete. He closed his hands around Pete's neck. "Should have. Killed you. Long ago."

"Why didn't you?" Pete spat as he fought back, nailing Sawil with a right hook that made the man reel, stop and shake his head, but still he didn't let go. Pete managed to push into a sitting position, his back Kat's way, blocking her shot.

"Because I knew you'd lead me right to her." Sawil tightened his grip. "You have her to thank for everything I am today. When you're gone, she's mine. And I will enjoy every moment of it."

Something snapped in Pete then. He cracked his skull against Sawil's. Hard. Dazed, Sawil loosened his grasp on Pete's neck as his head snapped back. Pete laid two right hooks into Sawil's face that echoed through the room, then scrambled out from underneath him.

Sawil stumbled, righted himself, shook his head and stood. Kat trained the gun on Sawil as Pete pushed himself up, swayed and caught himself. Both men were breathing heavily and looked like they could go down in a light breeze. Confusion colored Sawil's eyes. He stumbled back two steps and fell against the counter behind him.

Kat's pulse pounded. Sweat slicked her skin. The silence that fell over the room was more deafening than Sawil's enraged shouts had been. Could she kill him? Would she? She had the shot. She could end this right now.

She hesitated. Torn.

Sawil's eyes glazed over, and he swayed. And hope leapt in Kat's throat. He was going down on his own.

Then at the last second his hand snaked out. He grasped a knife from the knife block on the counter behind him and lunged.

Years of practice condensed into one split second. Kat pulled the trigger once, twice with hands steadier than she'd ever imagined.

The gunshots echoed through the massive kitchen and hit Sawil square in the chest. He fell inches from Pete's bare feet.

Dimly she heard a frantic voice at the kitchen door-way. In a blur, a rush of people swarmed the room, from where, Kat didn't know. All she saw was Sawil's lifeless body on the tile floor, facedown in a growing pool of blood.

She'd done that. She'd been able to take a life, after all. The life of someone who had once been her friend. And she knew the moment would haunt her for the rest of her days.

She dropped the gun and took a shaky step back.

Pete caught her with both arms before she fell. "I've got you," he said into her hair. "Hold on to me. Just hold me, Kit-Kat."

Her whole body started to shake, but she grabbed on with what little strength she had left. "Don't let go," she whispered.

"I won't, baby. God, I won't."

Pete looked up from where he was seated at Maria's din-ing room table. His head was still a little fuzzy from the drug Ramirez—or Minyawi, or whatever the fuck the guy's real name was—had stuck him with. But at least it cut the sting of the alcohol the med tech was rubbing on his temple.

Thankfully, the wound wasn't deep enough for stitches. He flinched when the tech slapped on a butterfly bandage, then pissed him off royally as she flashed a light in his eye to check for a concussion.

"Cut that out." He pushed the light away and went back to watching Kat.

She was sitting on the sofa across the room getting the same mend-and-bend from another paramedic. Police and what he suspected were FBI swarmed the room, conversing with one another, checking the scene. Maria was near the window, talking with a plainclothes officer as she gave her statement. Pete had a vague recollection of seeing Slade somewhere in the group and absently wondered who the hell had called him, then dismissed the thought. The only person he cared about right now was on that couch.

His heart pinched in his chest. Bruises were forming near her eyes and across her cheek. He knew if she hadn't killed Sawil, he would have. For what he'd done to her in that tomb. For the years of hiding he'd forced her into. For the few minutes she'd been alone with him in the kitchen when Pete had been out cold.

"There. You're done," the woman finally said.

Pete smothered a groan as he rose and began buttoning the shirt someone had brought down for him.

The sound of shoes skidding to a halt in the open penthouse doorway brought his head around. Shock, then disbelief, then confusion whipped through him as he saw Hailey standing there, looking not much different than Kat.

"Pete!"

Hailey threw herself into his arms. He winced and pushed her back as he studied her bruised face, which was laced with a lot of relief and a bunch of pissed off. "What the hell happened to—"

She smacked him in the shoulder. "You owe me, you son of a bitch. And I've got a laundry list of ways you're going to pay me back for this." She glanced around the room. "Man, I'm glad the police got here in time."

He was having trouble following Hailey's words, but two things got through. One, she'd known what was going down here, and two, somebody'd roughed her up good.

Oh, shit. Hailey.

He gripped her arms. "What happened?"

"Two creeps showed up at Lauren's place when I went to make sure she wasn't home." Her eyes darted to the side and the gurney being rolled out of the kitchen. "Which one is that? The dark-haired one or the bald guy?"

His stomach churned with the knowledge she'd been alone with either.

"Minyawi," Kat said at his side in a quiet voice. "The dark-haired one."

Pete looked Kat's direction. She was standing just out of his reach, her skin pale, eyes unsure. She gripped a blanket around her shoulders like it was her last lifeline.

"Good," Hailey muttered with ice in her words. "The prick deserved to die."

Pete's gaze snapped back to Rafe's ex-wife, and a terrible feeling rolled through him. "Hailey, did he—"

"No," she said quickly, reading his reaction. "He didn't do anything other than knock me around a little. I know how to take care of myself. I'm fine."

She was. Pete could see it in her eyes. Hailey Roarke was one of the toughest women he'd ever met.

She turned her attention to Kat. "I'm Hailey, by the way. An ex-friend."

"Good friend," Pete corrected.

A half smile curled Hailey lips. Kat glanced between the two with a whole lot of uncertainty.

"I had the bad sense to marry his partner at Odyssey," Hailey explained. "But I wised up." She grinned at Pete. Bruises and all. "Saved your ass, didn't I? See, Kauffman? There's hope for me yet."

Pete couldn't help it. He chuckled. He'd always liked Hailey, so it was no skin off his nose letting her think she'd saved the day. "You did. I stand corrected. You're the best damn cop I ever met."

Hailey rolled her eyes. Kat smiled slowly as she listened to the banter.

"So, Kat," Hailey said. "Is it wishful thinking to assume you're going to do something about Pete's mood swings? Because I have to tell you. I love him like a brother, but the man's got a serious attitude problem."

He was just about to defend those so-called mood swings when he noticed a shy expression skirting Kat's features. Then she shocked them both by stepping forward and walking right into his arms.

And oh, yeah, he was the biggest sap on the planet, and he didn't even care. His arms closed around her tight as he kissed her temple. Over Kat's shoulder he saw Hailey smile and wink his way.

"About damn time," she said.

Pete's smile faded. And glancing around, he was rudely reminded any happily ever after had probably come and gone. That feeling was confirmed when he saw Slade striding in their direction.

He tensed. Kat pulled back and turned to look.

"Kauffman," Slade said as he stopped next to Hailey. "Kat," Slade said softer, his dark eyes somber. "How are you doing?"

There was a second where Pete thought Kat would go to Slade, and he steeled himself for the moment. They were friends. He knew Slade had tried to help her once. Mentally, he'd already accepted that. Emotionally, though, right here and now, was a different story.

But when she didn't make a move out from under the arm Pete had looped over her shoulder, he had to admit a spurt of relief raced through him. Either she loved him enough to know her going to Slade wouldn't sit well with him, or she wasn't quite sure about Slade anymore.

Both, probably, he realized.

"A couple of my officers are going to need to get a complete statement from you, Kat," he said, "but after that, you're free to go."

Kat's brow drew together. "But what about—"

"There's been no sign of Busir," Slade said quickly, turning his attention to Pete. "We've got people monitoring the borders, but it's possible he's already left the country."

"He was at the motel with me for sure," Hailey interjected. "I'm not entirely sure what happened because I was blindfolded, but the two of them argued. Whatever they fought about, it was over fast. Minyawi was the only one with me in the van on the way here."

And that was how the police had shown up, Pete realized. Hailey had called in the cavalry.

Slade turned his attention Hailey's way. "I don't suppose you remember where that motel was, do you?"

"No, but if you get me a map, I can probably figure it out. Even though I was blindfolded, I paid attention to the route we took, and I'm familiar with New York. I can probably tell which bridges we crossed."

Slade shot a questioning look at Pete.

Hailey saw the expression and turned toward Slade. "Officer Hailey Roarke. Key West PD. I don't think we've officially met."

Slade reluctantly returned her handshake. "Marty Slade."

Hailey's eyes narrowed. "CIA."

"That's on a need-to-know basis." When Hailey tipped her blonde head, he added, "Trust me, Officer Roarke. You don't need to know." Slade motioned to a man in a suit near the door. "Officer Crowly will take the rest of your statement and get you anything you need."

Hailey obviously knew a dead end when she saw one. She pursed her lips and turned toward the dark-haired officer walking her way.

Slade's gaze followed her as she moved away. "Key West PD?"

"Ex," Pete said. "She's on leave right now, helping out with her family's business in Miami while her father's ill."

"What business is that?"

"Hotels."

Slade's eyes widened as obvious links fell into place. "Hailey Roarke? As in, daughter of hotelier Garrett Roarke, of Roarke Resorts?"

Pete nodded. Sometimes it was even hard for Pete to grasp. The Roarke name had become as well-known as Hilton over the last few years. And Hailey—as unreal as it was to believe—was an heiress.

"So what now?" Kat asked, pulling Slade's attention back to them. "We all know Minyawi and Busir weren't the ones behind all this. What happens next?"

"We monitor the borders and send out a notice to the Egyptian authorities about Busir's actions here," Slade said, refocusing. "But without proof of a higher-level involvement, the other person you say you heard in that tomb walks away."

"That's not right," Kat stated emphatically.

"Right and wrong don't matter much in international politics," a dark-haired, dark-skinned woman dressed in a black suit said with a Middle Eastern accent as she stepped up to the group. "Unless, of course, you can positively identify that third party."

They all looked at the newcomer.

She nodded to them as a whole. Her features were sharp and striking, and there was an air of authority about her everyone caught. "I'm Agent Tiya Hawass with

INTERPOL. The apprehension of Aten Minyawi has been one of our top priorities. We've lost several good agents because of him, including Dean Bertrand, whom I'm told you met in Philadelphia."

When Pete and Kat exchanged glances, she said, "Minyawi popped onto our radar about six years ago. He quickly rose in the ranks of the Egyptian Liberation Army, though we suspect he was with the organization a lot longer than that. He served in the Egyptian military for a short stint in his late teens, but his expertise was antiquities, which explains how he got involved with the artifact ring.

"Several years ago he switched focus, however. We're not entirely sure why, but he became one of their leading hit men. He often operated outside the ELA, like we think he did in this case because of a personal vendetta, but his association with their organization as a whole is well-known and well-documented. We know from surveillance that Hanif Busir has been smuggling archaeological treasures out of Egypt for years—they'd be sold for a hefty profit on the black market, and a portion of the proceeds were funneled back into the pockets of the ELA, thereby funding their cause. What we've never been able to prove is the link between the artifact black market that exists throughout Africa and Asia and Europe, the SCA that governs archaeological research in Egypt and the ELA."

"Until I came along," Kat said quietly.

"Until you came along," Agent Hawass repeated, nodding her way. "Which is why we took a backseat and monitored Minyawi's movements these past few days here in the States. When it came to my attention that you were in fact alive, we hesitated to become involved, hoping you could provide the evidence we needed. However, when we realized Bertrand was operating on his own, we were ready to step in. The incident in the park was unfortunate, and had you not rushed out of there so quickly, we could have ended this then and taken you into protective custody. Of course, that didn't happen." She glanced between them. "So now it all boils down to evidence. And from what I understand, there is none."

Kat looked at Pete with creased brow as Agent Hawass turned to Pete. "Because of the international implications of this case, Officer Slade has agreed to let me sit in on your questioning. Your cooperation will be noted when your case is prosecuted."

"It's about time, Kauffman," Slade said. "We need to go."

"Wait a minute," Kat interjected. "I'm not sure what's going on here, but I have proof—"

Pete's chest tightened. Yeah, their happily ever after had just crashed and burned.

"Can you give us a minute?" he said to Slade and Hawass.

The two exchanged glances, then nodded and stepped back to the door.

Kat turned wide, confused eyes up to his. "What's going on?" she asked with a hint of panic in her voice. "Pete, what questioning are they talking about?"

He took both of her hands in his and squeezed them, feeling the warmth of her skin against his own. "I want you to do me a favor."

"Anything."

"When you leave here, I want you to go see my friend Rafe Sullivan. Hailey knows how to get in touch with him. He's got something for you. In Florida. Trust him like you trust me, and don't give him a hard time about this."

"What do you mean by 'this,' Pete?" She tightened her grip on his hands and searched his face for answers to questions he guessed she was already figuring out. The blanket around her shoulders fell to the floor. "Tell me what's happening."

"Maria can't find your necklace, Kat."

"But—"

"I've done a lot of stupid things in my life. I stayed ahead of most of it, covered up my tracks, didn't care who was hurt as long as I got ahead. I was careful, and I was smart. And I made sure it wouldn't ever come back to bite me in the ass. There's never been anything in my life I've believed in enough to make me change my thinking. Not until you."

She darted a look at Slade near the door, then back at Pete's face. "What did you do?" she whispered.

He lifted his hand and rubbed his thumb over her soft cheek. "I did exactly what you would have done. What you did. And I don't regret it. Not even for a moment."

"No, no, no," she whispered. "Pete." She didn't try to hide the tears. They just spilled over her sooty lashes and slid down her cheeks. "Tell them you changed your mind. Tell them—"

"It's already done, Kat."

Her words fell silent at that revelation, but her tears continued to fall, and her hands tightened on his as if she didn't want to ever let him go.

In the silence between them he fingered the medal at her chest. "You were wrong, you know. About this. You're not a lost cause. You never were. And you were wrong about what happened. You didn't ruin my life, Kat. You saved it. In the best possible way."

He let go of her hands, cradled her face in his palms and kissed her ever so gently.

"Please don't do this," she whispered, grasping his forearms. "I can't live without you."

He rested his forehead against hers and drew in a long breath, her words warming the coldest corner of his heart. "Yes, you can. God, Kit-Kat, you can do so much better than me. I want that for you. I want you to have everything."

"Pete, please."

Letting go of her then was the hardest thing he'd ever done. Harder than hearing of her accident, harder than going to her memorial service, harder still than living with the belief she'd been dead. But he forced himself to do it. As he reached the door where Slade stood waiting to take him into custody and turned to look back at her, he knew her grief-stricken face was going to stay with him forever.

Just the way it should.

CHAPTER TWENTY-NINE

Florida
Three weeks later . . .

Kat sank down to the end of the bed and stared in stunned disbelief at the thank-you card in her hand. She'd picked it up when she'd been downstairs getting coffee this morning and had brought it and a few other pieces of mail back up with her while she got ready for the day.

She thought she'd cried herself dry weeks ago when Pete had made his deal with the government and been taken into custody. Obviously, she'd been wrong.

She reached up to rub fingers over her medal and read the last line of the letter one more time.

> . . . *We cannot begin to tell you what your dona-*
> *tion means to us here at St. Thomas's Orphanage. You*
> *truly are a gift from God. May the Lord watch over*
> *you always.*
>
> Sister Mary Francis Gilbert

Six million dollars. Every last proceed from Pete's auction in New York City had been donated to St. Thomas's Orphanage outside Seattle. *Her* orphanage. After reading the letter, Kat had called Pete's lawyer and discovered the arrangement had been made two weeks before the auction. Two *full* weeks before he'd even known she was still alive.

A tear slipped down her cheek and landed against the paper in her hands. In a blur she looked up and scanned the bedroom of the house she'd been staying in since coming to Miami.

Pete's bedroom in Pete's big house in Miami Beach, with its leather and mahogany headboard, dark woods, sleek lines and masculine colors. She hadn't heard from him since that morning at Maria's apartment, and no one was giving her answers. And she was dying inside not knowing what was happening.

She'd been heartbroken when she'd met his friend Rafe and he'd told her of the deal Pete had made with the government. Then shocked speechless when Rafe and Pete's lawyer had shown her the papers transferring his assets into accounts with her name on them. But the clincher, the one that had her picking her jaw off the floor and wiping the gush from her eyes whenever she thought of it, was when she'd realized he'd turned Odyssey over to her.

In that one act she knew he didn't think he was coming back. Not anytime soon. He'd made that deal and given up everything. For her.

That pressure returned, right beneath her breastbone. Every time she thought she was doing better, that breathing wasn't such a monumental feat after all, something happened—like getting this thank-you card—that brought her world spinning back down again.

She closed her eyes tight, unsure how she was ever going to be able to go into Odyssey today and pretend to run a gallery she had no clue how to operate. Even with his sister Lauren volunteering to help, it was more than she could handle. The thank-you card slipped from her grasp and floated to the ground.

Being here was tearing her up. Seeing everything he'd built and envisioning him in this house surrounded by all his things was slowly eating away at her insides. Imagining where he was now while she sat on the end of his bed, wearing one of his Turnbull & Asser designer dress shirts like she'd done every night since she'd been here, was slowly killing her.

"I can't do this much longer," she whispered into the stillness of the morning.

"Do what?" a voice asked from the bedroom doorway.

Pete dropped his duffel at his feet and tried to steady his racing heart as he watched Kat lift her head and turn his way. Those molten chocolate eyes of hers, damp as if she'd been crying, focused, then widened in shock.

"Pete!"

She launched herself at him and took him down to the floor before he even realized he was off his feet. He landed half in the hall, half in the bedroom. But that wasn't what got his attention. It was her mouth closing over his in a hot, greedy kiss that tore a groan from his chest and sent blood pounding right to his groin.

Her hands were everywhere, her mouth wet and demanding against his own. She took exactly what she wanted and didn't give him a chance to say yes or no or anything in between. And thank the stars above for that. In seconds she had his pants undone and pushed down to his thighs as she continued to kiss him, and then all rational thought slipped from his brain when she hiked up the dress shirt she wore, straddled his hips and took him deep inside her steaming wetness.

"Kit-Kat." He groaned and thrust up to meet her, as frantic as she was to get to him. And when they both reached the peak together moments later, he was gasping for breath like he'd just run the Chicago marathon.

She dropped her face against his neck. Pressed one hand to his shoulder. Her medal fell against his shirt, and her heart raced in time to his as he blinked up at the hall ceiling.

Now that was a homecoming.

She fisted his shirt into her hand and breathed deeply. "I'm so mad at you, Pete."

He drew in two slow breaths and tried to regulate his heart rate. "If this is you being pissed at me, then I'm thinking we definitely need to fight more often."

"That's not funny," she said against his neck.

"I don't hear anyone laughing."

She pushed up on the hand she had braced against the floor and looked down at him. "Oh, Pete. Please tell me this is real."

He smiled up at her and brushed a lock of hair back from her temple. "It's real."

She moved off him so he could sit up, but she didn't go far, easing back on her heels so he could pull up his slacks. "I don't understand. What happened? I called every day. No one would tell me anything."

"That's because they couldn't." He fixed his shirt. "Two days after I was taken into custody, Maria found your necklace."

Kat's eyes widened. "She did?"

"It had been sent back to Greece already. And you were right. The proof was all right there on the camera card. Minyawi and Busir in the tomb that night before Minyawi went back to get you. Busir and some other guy plotting what they were going to do to you and to Shannon if you didn't cooperate."

When her face paled, he added, "The other guy, the third one that you said you never saw? Dr. Omar Kamil. Director of the Cairo Museum."

Kat's eyes grew even wider. "He's with the SCA. No wonder my complaints never went anywhere."

"He's also a member of the Muslim Brotherhood, which has links to the ELA. Ramirez—Minyawi—whatever you want to call him was his inside man. Somehow they got Latham involved—blackmail, it looks like. But together they were making a butt-load of money skimming pieces coming out of there and selling them on the black market. Latham left notes in that journal we got from his wife. Notes, Kat," he said, still unable to believe it himself, "which prove how small time he really was. Busir was their go-to guy."

When her eyes slid closed, he knew what she was remembering—the horror in that tomb, what she'd done in Maria's kitchen. He closed his hand over hers in a tight grip. "It's over, Kat."

"Do they have Kamil?"

"They do now."

Her eyes popped open. "What do you mean *now*? Why do I get the feeling—"

"The evidence on the tape was inconclusive. There was never a clear shot of Kalim's face. But as soon as Maria saw it, she knew it was him. She had dinner with him the night we went to her apartment. He was the man we passed getting on the elevator in her building. That's how Minyawi knew we were in New York."

"So what happened?"

"My lawyer cut another deal."

She eyed him warily. "I'm starting to dread your deals, Pete."

He laughed and reached for her other hand. "It worked out, didn't it? I'm sitting here with you now."

"I'm still not sure how that happened. And why you couldn't call and tell me any of this was going on. I've been worried sick about you."

"I know. But I couldn't because I've been in Cairo the last few days, Kat."

"What?" Those almond-shaped eyes of hers widened again until he saw the whites all around her mocha irises.

He shrugged and tried to downplay the situation. "Turns out INTERPOL, in conjunction with the CIA and the Egyptian government, was more concerned with nabbing Kamil and closing down the ELA's link to the SCA than they were in holding me. In exchange for helping them set up a sting to get Kamil and his few remaining accomplices—one of which was the guy who was shooting at us in Raleigh—I got a get-out-of-jail-free card."

He grinned, but she continued to gape at him like he'd grown a second head. "You *what?*"

He tightened his grip on her hands, fearing her trust in him was once again teetering on the edge. "Don't freak out. I haven't dealt with any of those guys in a long time, but I still know some contacts running underground. It wasn't as difficult as one might think to set up a deal and lure Kamil in."

"And you did."

"Not all on my own. I just . . . helped."

She stared at him with big, unreadable brown eyes. "With a man known to be linked to a violent terrorist faction."

"Yeah," he said hesitantly, because she was looking at him now like she suddenly didn't know him anymore.

"Without telling me what you had planned," she added way too calmly.

"Yes."

Her jaw clenched.

Okay, she was mad. And she had every right to be. But he hadn't wanted her to know. Though it hadn't been as difficult as he'd thought to arrange it all, it had still been dangerous. And if it hadn't worked out, he could have wound up right back in jail. Or worse, dead.

"You could have been killed," she said with narrowed eyes.

"But I wasn't." He leaned forward and tried to kiss her. She eased back out of his reach.

"Come on, Kit-Kat. It's all good now. I'm safe. You're safe. Everything's back the way it should be. We've got this great big bed." He nodded into the bedroom and lifted his brows, hoping to lighten the mood. "Be a shame to waste it right now when I've been gone all this time. You know I didn't get any conjugal visits."

"If everything's back the way it should be," she said, cocking her head to the side and ignoring his joke, "I suppose that means you want your gallery back. And the house and everything else."

"No," he said, choosing his words carefully because he didn't want to risk screwing anything up at this point. "It means I love you, and I just want you back. None of the rest of it means anything to me if you're not a part of it."

That did it. Her eyes softened, just enough so he knew he had her. "If you want a job you're going to have to apply for it."

He barked out a laugh and pulled her tight against him before she could move out of his grasp.

"And if you plan on staying in this house, no more hiding the truth from me, Pete. Ever."

"Deal." He was smiling as he moved to kiss her, but she turned her head so all he got was her ear.

"And," she went on, hands braced against his shoulders, "while I appreciate the generous . . . gifts . . . you gave me, my new lawyer—"

"You mean my lawyer," he said, still grinning, deciding to go ahead and kiss her ear because it couldn't talk back at him.

"That's what I said. Though I appreciate what you did, my lawyer informed me I'm going to take a serious hit come tax season because of the nature of the transfer of assets. If you want to work for me at Odyssey and you expect to get back in this house, then you'd better do something about that situation."

He chuckled while she straddled his lap on her knees and pushed back with her hands on his shoulders. She was all business as she looked down at him, his beautiful Egyptologist turned suspect-on-the-lam turned suddenly confident negotiator.

"Are you trying to cut a deal with me, Kit-Kat?"

"Yes," she said without flinching.

"And what do you get in return?"

"Hopefully a joint tax return."

His heart skipped a beat. "Are we talking marriage here?"

"I am. I'm not having your baby without a marriage certificate."

"Baby?"

"I'm not pregnant," she said quickly at what he knew was his shocked expression. "But considering the way you tackled me when you got here, anything's possible."

"The way I tackled you!"

"Denial is a river in Egypt, Pete. I should know." She lifted a brow. "Wish you'd stayed in Cairo now?"

He flipped her to her back so fast she gasped. "Not on your life."

"Wait!" She smiled against his mouth. "I'm suddenly afraid you might be agreeing to marry me just to get at my money."

"Kat," he said in all seriousness as he looked down at her. "You're not getting out of this one. When I make a deal, I'm in it for the long haul, no matter where it takes me."

"Promise?"

The mischievous glint in her eye told him the future would never be easy where she was concerned. Lucky for him, that was just how he liked it.

"Absolutely. Now shut up and welcome me home all over again."

ELISABETH NAUGHTON

STOLEN
FURY

DANGEROUS LIAISONS

Oh, is he handsome. And charming. And sexy as all get out. Dr. Lisa Maxwell isn't the type to go home with a guy she barely knows. But, hey, this is Italy and the red-blooded Rafe Sullivan seems much more enticing than cataloging a bunch of dusty artifacts.

After being fully seduced, Lisa wakes to an empty bed and, worse yet, an empty safe. She's staked her career as an archaeologist on collecting the three Furies, a priceless set of ancient Greek reliefs. Now the one she had is gone. But Lisa won't just get mad. She'll get even.

She tracks Rafe to Florida, and finds the sparks between them blaze hotter than the Miami sun. He may still have her relic, but he'll never find all three without her. And they're not the only ones on the hunt. To beat the other treasure seekers, they'll have to partner up — because suddenly Lisa and Rafe are in a race just to stay alive.

ISBN 13: 978-0-505-52793-6

To order a book or to request a catalog call:
1-800-481-9191
This book is also available at your local bookstore, or you can check out our Web site **www.dorchesterpub.com** where you can look up your favorite authors, read excerpts, or glance at our discussion forum to see what people have to say about your favorite books.

Nationally Bestselling Author

Anna DeStefano

"Die!" scream her nightmares. The voice is her sister's, the compulsion stronger than any ordinary dream.

Maddie Temple can't go through this again. Her twin has been in a coma for the last ten years. Their psychic link was severed. At least, that's what she thought.

But there's a lot Maddie doesn't know—about the 200-year-old curse on her family, about the shadowy group that wants to exploit the Temple twins' powers for themselves, about the sexy psychiatrist offering to help her. The only way to find the answers and avoid being pulled into the abyss of madness is to trust her heart and confront her

Dark Legacy

"A SURE WINNER."
—*NEW YORK TIMES* BESTSELLING AUTHOR
LORI HANDELAND

ISBN 13: 978-0-505-52819-3

"Kate Angell is to baseball as Susan Elizabeth Phillips
is to football. Wonderful!"
— *USA Today* Bestselling Author Sandra Hill

KATE ANGELL

WHO'D BEEN SLEEPING IN KASON RHODES'S BED?

The left fielder for the Richmond Rogues had returned
from six weeks of spring training in Florida to find someone
had moved into his mobile home. That person was presently
in his shower. And no matter how sexy the squatter might be,
Kason wanted her out.

He had his trusty dobie, Cimarron; he didn't need anyone
else in his life. Not even a stubborn tomboy who roused all
kinds of wild reactions in him, then soothed his soul with
peace offerings of macaroni & cheese and rainbow Jell-O.
The bad boy of baseball was ready to play hardball if need be,
but with Dayne Sheridan firmly planted between his sheets,
he found himself . . .

SLIDING
HOME

ISBN 13: 978-0-505-52808-7

LEANNA RENEE HIEBER

What fortune awaited sweet, timid Percy Parker at Athens Academy? Hidden in the dark heart of Victorian London, the Romanesque school was dreadfully imposing, a veritable fortress, and little could Percy guess what lay inside. She had never met its powerful and mysterious Professor Alexi Rychman, knew nothing of the growing shadows, of the Ripper and other supernatural terrors against which his coterie stood guard. She saw simply that she was different, haunted, with her snow white hair, pearlescent skin and uncanny gift. This arched stone doorway was a portal to a new life, to an education far from what could be had at a convent—and it was an invitation to an intimate yet dangerous dance at the threshold of life and death . . . .

The Strangely Beautiful Tale of Miss Percy Parker

"TENDER, POIGNANT, EXQUISITELY WRITTEN."
—C. L. Wilson, *New York Times* Bestselling Author

ISBN 13: 978-0-8439-6296-3

✂ ☐ YES!

Sign me up for the Love Spell Book Club and send my
FREE BOOKS! If I choose to stay in the club, I will pay
only $8.50* each month, a savings of $6.48!

NAME: _____

ADDRESS: _____

TELEPHONE: _____

EMAIL: _____

☐ I want to pay by credit card.

☐ **VISA**   ☐ MasterCard.   ☐ DISCOVER

ACCOUNT #: _____

EXPIRATION DATE: _____

SIGNATURE: _____

Mail this page along with $2.00 shipping and handling to:
Love Spell Book Club
PO Box 6640
Wayne, PA 19087
Or fax (must include credit card information) to:
610-995-9274
You can also sign up online at **www.dorchesterpub.com**.
*Plus $2.00 for shipping. Offer open to residents of the U.S. and Canada only.
Canadian residents please call 1-800-481-9191 for pricing information.
If under 18, a parent or guardian must sign. Terms, prices and conditions subject to
change. Subscription subject to acceptance. Dorchester Publishing reserves the right
to reject any order or cancel any subscription.

DEC 1 9 2009